ONE MISTAKE IS ALL IT TAKES . . .

When the knock came at the door, she jumped like she'd been shot. He had come. It was all up to her. She walked slowly across the room and stood next to her bag.

"Yes? Who is it?" she called out in a controlled voice.

"Flowers," a voice answered.

Evelyn mustered all her courage and reached for the gun, the handle grasped firmly in her grip. The .38 felt light. Quickly she examined the cylinder . . . She had made one fatal mistake.

ANNE REED ROOTH

FATAL STRANGER

B

BERKLEY BOOKS, NEW YORK

FATAL STRANGER

A Berkley Book/published by arrangement with
the author

PRINTING HISTORY
Berkley edition/June 1988

ISBN: 0-425-10923-2

A BERKLEY BOOK® TM 757, 375
Berkley Books are published by The Berkley Publishing Group,
200 Madison Avenue, New York, N.Y. 10016.
The name ''BERKLEY'' and the ''B'' logo
are trademarks belonging to Berkley Publishing Corporation.

PRINTED IN THE UNITED STATES OF AMERICA

10 9 8 7 6 5 4 3 2 1

To my good friend, Quinn Martin, a champion whose standard of excellence in television and motion pictures brought entertainment to millions, but whose greatest joy came from championing others in their efforts. Though gone, he will always be looking over my shoulder.

FATAL
STRANGER

PROLOGUE

TIGHTENING THE BELT of her terry-cloth robe, Sara paced the hotel room, willing the call to come. Her aspirations, a commodity in short supply, hung in the balance. She stubbed out her cigarette in the overflowing ashtray and lit another. The bathroom door she had left open in case the phone rang while her bath water ran, was still ajar. She could see that the black dress she had unpacked and positioned carefully over the tub to steam hung limp. Her sister's sable fanned across the bed, her diamond ring sparkled on the dresser. Neither the ring nor the coat, borrowed to impress, had the anticipated magical power to transmit their owner's charm and self-assurance. Since childhood she had been a mere parody of Evelyn, at best.

Sara moved to the window and gazed at the skyline, at the dark ocean, which was a backdrop to the necklace of lights on the freeway. He was out there somewhere. Seeing her own reflection in the glass, Sara rubbed a finger down the bridge of her nose, feeling the imperfection. She drew in her stomach, wishing she had dieted more strenuously. Unlike Evelyn, her determination fierce once committed to something, Sara was defeated before she started. Food, like cigarettes, was company. She checked her watch again.

Turning from the window, Sara stared at the silent telephone. He had changed his mind. His overtures, so tantalizing, had temporarily revived long forgotten emotions. She should not have tuned out warning voices or expected more. Her spirits, soaring when she had registered, were losing altitude at a rapid rate.

She jumped when the phone rang, and bolted across the room. Clutching the receiver, she answered.

"Sara, things took longer than I expected. I'm sorry."

"We aren't going to have dinner," she blurted out, her dreams only quicksilver now. At least he called to explain, she rationalized.

"Sure we are. I'm just leaving. Meet me in the lobby in thirty minutes. I wanted to send flowers, but they won't give out your room number."

"Eight-two-four," she responded quickly, elated by the reprieve. "But you don't have to go to that trouble for me."

"I want to. See you in the lobby."

Downstairs, he replaced the receiver and folded back the telephone booth door. Glancing across the lobby toward the switchboard operator, he made his way to the elevator and punched the 8 button.

The hallway was dim and deserted. He knocked on 824 and said, "Flowers."

There was a click and the sound of a bolt being released. The door opened and Sara stood on the threshold. Her hand went to her hair. "I'm not ready. I had no idea it was you."

He stepped inside, closing the door. His eyes never left her. "Just a little joke about the flowers to get you alone."

It was Evelyn's smile she was borrowing now, hope taking root again. And to think, without Evelyn's nudge she might have canceled the trip. He moved closer, embracing her. The terry-cloth robe dropped to the floor. His arm moved across her bare shoulders, his hand caressing, gently at first, then more urgently before grasping her throat, the grip tightening.

Startled, she looked up, a feeling of unease deepening steadily toward fear. Something had happened to his face. It had darkened, his eyes ugly slits, the smile gone, the mouth a compassionless crescent. His breath, hot on her face, was a touch from Hell. She tried to wrench free, but there was no escape from his stranglehold. Sweating and shivering at the same time, she prayed the terror would stop her heart before he could. As a sharp pain ripped through her, a vision of Evelyn flashed in her mind. She struggled to cry out, but no sound escaped her constricted throat. The mordant smell of her own blood filled her nostrils, a world turned murky closing in.

Consciousness had already begun to fade when he released his hold, leaving her to slump to the floor within an ever-widening circle of blood. He twisted out the knife, wrapped it in a handkerchief, and replaced it in his inside pocket. His eyes strayed toward the diamond and thick wallet on the dresser. Turning his back, he opened the door, braced his foot against it and wiped the knob with the tail of his coat. Stepping out, he hooked the Do NOT DISTURB sign on the outer knob as he closed the door behind him and sauntered down the hall.

CHAPTER 1

THE SAN DIEGO HOMICIDE DIVISION buzzed with activity. Evelyn Casey assumed the ordinary-looking men in drab polyester suits were detectives, as they trudged by her carrying grease-stained paper bags and styrofoam containers. The place smelled more like a short-order greasy spoon than a police station. The surroundings—institutional-green walls, old, battered, styleless furniture—had immediately reminded her of the high school study hall back in Longview, Texas.

Evelyn wondered how long Captain Daniel Gordon would keep her waiting before condescending to see her about "Sara's case." She hated referring to it in such terms, but that was what her sister's sudden, violent death had become. A murder case. Evelyn could still visualize the bold type in the Dallas paper. SISTER OF OIL HEIRESS MURDERED IN SAN DIEGO HOTEL. As the widow of Andrew Casey, former president of Cypress Oil, Evelyn was focused on more than Sara in the story.

Uniformed policemen eyed her with minor curiosity as they hurried back and forth, files in hand. Even under this casual surveillance Evelyn felt uneasy. She could imagine the state of mind of a criminal under arrest.

A woman with kinky, carrot-colored hair and a buttermilk

complexion dotted with freckles caught Evelyn's eye. Pad in hand, the redhead repeatedly approached detective after detective only to be rebuffed. Finally, she shouldered through the crowd and flounced down in disgust two chairs away from Evelyn. Stretching her legs out, she flexed her feet. Orange freckles peppered her shins as well as her face.

"Shit," the woman said, confronting Evelyn's absorbed stare. "With the story I've been assigned to cover by my editor no wonder I get treatment about equal to a leper around here."

Evelyn looked away and ran her hands beneath the collar of her navy wool coat, flipping out her long blond hair over her shoulders. Cool as it was in the station, she felt a growing dampness under her arms. She longed for privacy and comfort, a hot bath, and a drink.

Two weeks ago when notified of Sara's death, Evelyn had flown immediately to San Diego to identify the body. Two homicide detectives had met her at the airport and questioned her there before taking her to the morgue. She had told them she dropped her sister, who was traveling alone, at the Dallas airport the previous day to catch a flight for San Diego, where she was to attend her tenth college reunion. That had been the last time she had seen Sara alive.

Numb with grief, Evelyn had thought the morgue seemed surreal, especially her sister's serene and composed face, which in death looked more content than it ever had in life. As if sleepwalking, Evelyn had made arrangements to bring the body home for burial, then she had returned to Dallas.

After the funeral, Evelyn had continued to brood about the circumstances of her sister's death. This was no ordinary case of dying and mourning. Someone had taken her sister's life. And that someone was at liberty to take other lives, unpunished for the terrible crime of taking Sara's, a life barely lived at all. Outrage and anger had surfaced in Evelyn. Too much time was passing. What was being done to apprehend the murderer?

From her home in Dallas she had called the San Diego Homicide Division and asked to speak with the person in charge. Quickly transferred to Captain Daniel Gordon's office, Evelyn was firmly informed by a Lieutenant Adams that

Captain Gordon was not available to talk but she could call back. The lieutenant attempted to assure her that the detectives on her sister's case were doing all they could. She was anything but reassured and doggedly tried to contact Captain Gordon, only to have the scenario replayed. "We'll call you if anything turns up or you can call back."

Call back! Evelyn had been enraged and informed the officer she would not call back. She would fly to San Diego to see Captain Gordon in person. He could expect to see her the next afternoon in his office.

Grief and shock were no strangers to Evelyn, but nothing she had experienced in the past prepared her for the emotions that now stirred within as she waited in the homicide division. She hurt savagely, and the only way to stop the pain was to find and punish the person responsible for Sara's death. Perhaps face-to-face Gordon would answer her questions. Perhaps he would tell her a full-scale investigation was in progress and detectives were pursuing hot leads. She knew they would notify her if they caught the killer, but would they keep her up-to-date on the case if she did not check regularly? Would they stay on the case if she didn't push? Had she been too impulsive, too aggressive, in coming to San Diego?

Preoccupied as she was with conflicting thoughts, Evelyn became aware of something out of sync in the room. She looked up and instantly recognized the man leaning against the wall to be one of the detectives who had questioned her. Staring directly at her, his chocolate-brown eyes were awash with sympathy. He had a solid muscular build, a nose with a suggestion it had been broken innumerable times and a wispy moustache. Evelyn stood, stiff from sitting so long, and crossed the room.

"Sergeant, I'm Evelyn Casey." She extended her hand, which he took hesitantly as though it were breakable. "Do you remember me? You met me at the airport when I came to . . ." Evelyn's voice faltered. A flash vision of Sara's placid face above the white sheet suddenly materialized. She swallowed hard and continued. "When I came to identify my sister's body two weeks ago. You and another detective met me. I'm sorry. I don't remember your name."

"Manuel Castro. Manny, for short. Of course, I remember

you.'' He spoke with a light trace of a Spanish accent. He motioned with his head toward where she had been sitting. ''You left your purse over there on the chair.''

''Oh,'' Evelyn said with a faint smile. ''Shouldn't it be safe in a police station?''

Castro grinned. ''I wouldn't be so sure.''

Castro walked a little behind Evelyn as she returned to pick up her handbag.

''Captain Gordon said you were coming in to see him. I know what you're going through. It's tough to lose family that way. It's a lot different than by natural causes. I've been through it myself.''

Evelyn looked down at her navy-and-white spectator pumps, suppressing an impulse to inquire about his loss. Then her eyes returned to his steady gaze. ''Yes, it is different. One day I'm so sad I can't do anything. And the next, I'm so furious I could kill.'' Evelyn relaxed the choking grip on her purse.

Castro folded his arms over his chest, shifting his weight from one foot to the other, waiting, it seemed to Evelyn, for the inevitable questions she had to ask.

''Are there any leads? Suspects? Any breaks at all?''

''None. Nothing at all.'' Castro shook his head.

''It's been almost two weeks.'' She hated the way her husky voice cracked when she became excited.

''The statistics on solving homicides of this kind are pretty low. Odds against finding the perpetrator increase rapidly forty-eight hours after the crime and keep increasing until the odds are that the crime won't be solved at all. That's no help to you, I know, but these are facts. The way it is.''

''But you keep on trying, don't you? I mean you don't just give up after forty-eight hours?'' Evelyn noticed out of the corner of her eye that the redhead's attention was riveted on them. She actually leaned toward them to hear what they said.

Castro jammed his hands into his pockets, staring over Evelyn's shoulder at the skyline filling the window. ''We're shorthanded. In almost every case I see loose ends that should be followed up. I try. A lot of us do. There's not enough time and not enough of us to go around. A lot of cases just solve themselves. The criminal makes a mistake." He shrugged. "Sometimes we get lucky and make an arrest, but only five percent of felony arrests eventually produce convictions."

Castro paused. "I know the question you're going to ask. Why? Right? Well, I'll tell you. Not enough evidence to stand up in court. And the way evidence has to be gathered is a tricky situation, too. You practically have to catch them in the act. The law works more for the criminal than against him."

Evelyn wanted to blurt out that she was aware of those facts, but Castro had no way of knowing her educational background. Even though what he said was true, the idea infuriated Evelyn. "Not this time. Sara's case is going to be different. It's going to be solved and her murderer convicted. I won't give up, not for one minute, not until Sara's murderer has been brought to justice."

Evelyn and Castro stared intensely at each other, barely registering the red-haired woman's muttered "Right on."

Evelyn dug in her purse, producing a clipping from the *Dallas Morning News* that she had almost missed because of its obscure placement.

At that moment, a voice bellowed, "Castro, come in here."

"Excuse me," Castro said and walked across the room to the open door bearing the name CAPTAIN DANIEL GORDON in bold black letters. Standing just inside, a thick-set man with a bulldog neck stood gripping the doorknob with pudgy fingers. Evelyn immediately noticed his almost colorless steel-gray eyes. His lips, though fleshy, did not alleviate the hard line of his mouth. He looks mean, Evelyn thought.

As Castro approached the door, Gordon emerged, blocking his way, standing nose-to-nose with him.

"Is that who I think it is out there next to that fucking reporter?" Captain Gordon snapped.

"That's Evelyn Casey, sir." Castro lowered his voice. He knew it was hard for a man to shout questions when replies were softly given.

"What I thought." An eye for detail, Gordon studied Evelyn for a moment. He pegged her to be in her mid-thirties. With such fine-chiseled features, silky blond mane flowing to her shoulders, and honey-complexion, she could pass for a cover girl. Just sitting there she projected a certain strength. He could see determination in those aquamarine eyes. He distrusted attractive women. "Fine-looking broad, that one, eh, Castro?"

Castro shrugged.

"Fucking pest, though. She's called here enough in the past two weeks, asking questions, trying to dig around in her sister's case. Now here she is in person."

"She's flown out here from Dallas to get an update on the case. It's her *dinero*. I guess she's entitled."

"*Dinero!*" Gordon's eyebrows met as he spat out the word. "Castro, cut out the Mexican shit and talk like an American. You're a police officer not some fucking wetback." Gordon peered intently into the face so close to his own and hissed, "Another thing I've been meaning to bring up. Shave off the Pancho Villa lip duster. In the old days when we had a code, you wouldn't have lasted two seconds around here with hair on your face."

Daniel Gordon knew his town, San Diego, where most Mexican-Americans could aspire to employment no higher than gardening, playing in a mariachi band, or mixing margaritas at the neighborhood bars in "flea town," and Gordon personally thought that was exactly as it should be. They all belonged back in Tijuana selling pottery and that included Manuel Castro, whose first mistake was being born Mexican-American and whose second was becoming a policeman. And now, he was about to make his third. Sergeant Manuel Castro was bucking to take the officers' examination. Next he'd be trying to make captain, the first of his breed in the city. The son of a bitch was breathing down his neck. But not for long, Gordon vowed. All he had to do was bide his time and wait for the right moment to kick his ass into the street where he belonged.

"Castro, tell the woman to come on in my office, so I can get it over with. Run to the lab and get the victim's personal effects. They've been dusted and analyzed. Don't need them anymore. Don't forget the release forms. On the double."

Gordon took a step back, wheeled around and disappeared into his office, leaving the door ajar.

Castro returned to Evelyn. "Captain Gordon's ready to see you. You go right on in."

Evelyn watched Castro hurry out of the room, his movements as fluid as if his joints had ball bearings. She rose and took a deep breath, wishing Castro was the captain she had to confront.

"Say, I couldn't help overhearing what you and that detective were talking about."

Evelyn regarded the redhead with annoyance. Couldn't help overhearing, she thought, what a line. She had been eavesdropping and quite obviously.

"I'm Carole Wheeler. I'm a reporter at the *Union*. At the moment, I'm reporting on how crimes against people considered unimportant are handled. That accounts for my low popularity rating. Anyhow, the angle *was* that the P.D. doesn't do as much about solving murders when the victim is, say, an itinerant farm worker, as opposed to some millionaire. The murder of somebody like your sister, for example, wouldn't be considered top priority around here without you involved. I mean she didn't have your last name, so the connection wasn't obvious until the press linked her to you."

Evelyn was startled that the woman knew who she was and about Sara's case. And what she said was more than likely true.

Carole Wheeler continued to observe Evelyn intently and resumed, "I read the story about your sister. And then I recognized you from the picture that ran with the story. Because it interested me, I couldn't help but eavesdrop on your conversation." She rolled her eyes. "It just blew the theory. It doesn't sound like your sister's case is top priority." She shook her head. "No, the slant was wrong. Maybe they don't do enough about *any* murder case."

Evelyn was struck by the reporter's intensity, her staccato delivery. "That's a pretty broad assumption." Evelyn turned to leave.

Carole Wheeler jumped to her feet, green eyes flashing, and moved in front of her. "I'm trying to sell my paper on a series of articles called 'The Woman in the Case,' whether she's the victim, the perpetrator, the judge, the police officer . . . where there's a woman in the case, it's going to be different. You know what Freud said, 'Biology will out.' So far they haven't bought it yet. But I'm not giving up. Worse comes to worse, I'll just write a book and screw the newspaper series. For that, I'd have to find just the right case to focus on. You know"—she held up her hands, making brackets with her fingers—"featuring one big story like Tommy Thompson with *Blood and Money* or Shana Alexander's *The Nutcracker*. The topic I want to examine is, if a woman is the central figure in a case, how the actual circumstances of a crime can be misconstrued so that innocent victims end up being viewed in the wrong light. Let's face it, women think and feel differently from men. Sounds chauvinistic, but it's true. I can show you several cases I've been studying. Really." She mugged. "Guess I do like to spew when I get started."

Spew! Evelyn smiled at the woman who didn't know the meaning of a period.

"Back to your sister's case. Maybe we should talk later. If you really mean to get this case going, maybe I can help you, if they won't."

Evelyn could not help responding to Wheeler's ingenuous offer. "Well, thanks for your interest. I really don't know what to say at this point. I'm going in now to see Captain Gordon. Have you got a card?"

"Sure do. Just hang on." She pulled a card from a pocket in the back flap of her notebook. "It's got my office number and my home number on it. Best thing to do is leave a message on my machine at home." Carole leaned closed to Evelyn. "That Captain Gordon is a first-rate son of a bitch. Him, you can have. You'll see."

Evelyn tucked the card into her bag with the newspaper clipping she was still holding and made her way to Gordon's office, where she rapped lightly on the glass.

The now-familiar strident voice commanded, "Come in."

Gordon motioned toward the scarred chair next to his desk. "Have a seat, Mrs. Casey."

Evelyn seated herself, observing the half-eaten hamburger and scatter of French fries spread over a white paper sack. A styrofoam cup held steaming coffee, tan from a heavy hand with the cream. Evelyn's stomach knotted tighter as she seated herself.

A shrill squeak broke the silence as Gordon stretched back in his swivel chair, hands clasped over his head. "What can I do for you, Mrs. Casey?"

"Catch my sister's murderer." Her tone was cool and laced with all the authority she could muster.

The captain swung forward in his chair, resting forearms that looked like fresh hams on the desk. His cold gray eyes searched hers. "I assure you we are doing everything we can to do just that. The case is not closed, but there simply are no leads at all."

Evelyn sat erect in the hard-seated chair. "I realize that, but I want to know what you've done to date. I'd like to see your reports. Maybe there's something I can do to help." Evelyn wondered if she should tell Gordon that she had a master's degree in psychology with special training in criminology. His frown was the deciding factor.

"Ongoing police investigations are confidential. If we let anyone unofficial go through them, this place would turn into a shambles."

Gordon tried for a smile, showing stumpy yellow teeth that reminded Evelyn of a row of old tombstones, and continued. "I'm sure you have no idea how many homicides we have a week in San Diego. Mexican population distorts the total figures, stabbing each other on Saturday night, so that this city looks like it's under a constant fucking . . . excuse me . . . constant crime wave. Pardon my language."

"I've heard the word before, captain." Evelyn thought his language wasn't half as bad as his racist attitude and would like to tell him so, but she hadn't come for that. "I'm sorry about all of those homicides, quite naturally, but I'm interested in only one of them. Can't you just summarize the police report findings?" She hadn't come fifteen hundred miles to be put off so easily. She kept her eyes trained on him.

Gordon pushed his chair back, the wheels scraping the floor, and lumbered away from his desk to the file cabinet, where he pulled open the second drawer. He returned with a thick file and sat heavily in his chair. Evelyn leaned forward, and Gordon shifted his body and the folder so she could not see the contents.

"To start at the top and briefly," he intoned with heavy emphasis. "One, Sara Marley, was found stabbed to death at approximately two o'clock P.M., May 20, at the Eastgate Hotel, room 824, by a Juanita Sanchez, employed there for five years as a maid. Previous record on Sanchez . . . two counts of shoplifting." Gordon lifted his eyebrows. "Not surprising." He continued. "The night-desk clerk, a George Peterson, stated that Sara Marley checked in at approximately 6:30 P.M. on May 19. She was alone. No record on Peterson. The bellboy who carried her bags up was interrogated. His 'make' showed a few minor traffic citations. No outgoing calls were made by your sister. The cab driver who took her to the hotel from the airport was located. She was alone in the cab. We questioned the guests on the eighth floor. Ran checks on them. All clean. No forced entry to the room." Gordon glanced up at Evelyn, with something in his eyes and an expression she couldn't pinpoint. "That did give me cause for some speculation. I could spin a dozen theories." Gordon pursed his lips, eyes shifting to one side as if reflecting on past suspicions. "The coroner's office places her death somewhere between 8:30 and 10:30 P.M. May 19."

Gordon rubbed his stubby fingers around the edge of the report. "I have your statements to the investigating officers that your sister was in San Diego to attend a college reunion. She hadn't informed anyone she was coming. We sent two detectives to that reunion that your sister never made it to, and we questioned everyone who attended, ran the names through our computers, and nothing unusual came up."

Gordon looked with satisfaction at the report in front of him and closed it with a snap of the wrist. He reached for his coffee and blew on it.

"You see, Mrs. Casey, most detective work is hard, grinding, routine labor. Clues and leads don't show up like on television, pointing to the murderer while rock-and-roll music in the background keeps the beat going for you. We have only percentages to go by. They tell us we probably won't nail anyone."

Evelyn gripped the edge of the desk, trying to think logically and without emotion. She didn't want to alienate Gordon. "But, Captain Gordon, someone got in her room without forced entry. I know my sister, and she would never have opened the door unless she thought she knew who was on the other side. A key? I've left hotels before and forgot to turn in the keys."

Gordon made a show of studying his watch before resuming eye contact. "Mrs. Casey, that hotel has been open twelve years. Can you imagine how many people have stayed in 824. Accurate accounts of keys are not available anyway. You dropped her off at the Dallas airport. We know she boarded the plane and arrived in San Diego, checked into the hotel alone. So we have to surmise the killer was a stranger. Your sister was a random choice. I could get into any room in this city. A knock on the door and a few simple words. Room service. A package. Fruit from the management. Boom!" He hit the palm of his hand with a fist. Evelyn jumped. "I'm in. People are gullible. That's what the criminal relies on most."

Evelyn focused on the styrofoam cup still half filled with coffee and wished he'd offered her some. "But the motive? She wasn't robbed or raped." Her back was ridged with gooseflesh.

"Could have gotten scared off for some reason before he could accomplish what he came for. There are several things we know from the P.M."

"Postmortem?" Evelyn snapped to attention. She hadn't thought about what clues that report might hold, because she hadn't wanted to envision an autopsy.

"Right." Gordon reached for the hamburger and chomped out a wider crescent. He swallowed and continued. "We know from the angle of thrust of the weapon—which was a knife blade, wider than two inches, no more than four—that the killer was a man or a very strong woman. Percentage probabilities point to a man. The location of the wound tells us the perpetrator was six feet or more. Entry was made from the back, severing the fourth . . . ." Gordon stopped. "There's no need for me to go on with this. It's not pleasant listening and doesn't help solve anything."

As much as she disliked Gordon, Evelyn appreciated this

small gesture of kindness. "Is there anything else I should know?"

Gordon picked up a paper napkin, and like an elegant lady finishing afternoon tea, blotted his lips. "The scrapings taken from under Sara Marley's fingernails showed no skin or hair, therefore, no apparent struggle. She was discovered nude, lying on top of a yellow bathrobe, close to the door."

Evelyn was shocked by these previously unknown facts. Gordon's sordid insinuation was clear now. The brutality of Sara's death was hard enough to contend with but the sexual overtones were impossible to confront. Nude? Not shy, modest Sara. The man before her, who had never seen Sara, except in death, was passing judgment on her morals. It stung her to picture Gordon voicing his speculations, bouncing sleazy scenarios off fellow officers. Evelyn was grateful the nudity had been excluded from the newspaper accounts of Sara's death.

Captain Gordon's intercom buzzed. He punched the button. "Yes?"

"Sir, they're ready with the lineup."

"Be right there." Pushing up from his chair, Gordon rounded the desk. "Mrs. Casey, I'll have to go down the hall for a few minutes. You can wait here for Castro to bring your sister's belongings."

Evelyn stood. "But . . . I haven't finished . . ." Gordon might be relieved by the interruption, but she wasn't.

Gordon jerked open the door and exhaled. "Okay. You can walk down to the lineup room with me, and we can talk on the way. Got an eyewitness on another case, supposedly. A woman says she can positively identify a murder suspect."

Dodging detectives in the hall, Evelyn hurried to keep pace with Captain Gordon. He looked over his shoulder at her. "You know, Mrs. Casey, the great majority of homicides are committed not by strangers but by relatives or acquaintances of the victim. Seventy-five percent of the victims murdered in the U.S. last year were related to their assailants. In other words, when I see a homicide, I look to home."

Evelyn's eyes widened at Gordon's lack of subtlety. "And have you checked me out?" She felt a flush rise to her cheeks. The man knew no bounds.

Pausing before a door, he turned to her. "You hinted maybe we hadn't been thorough. We checked you out, you being her only relative, her looking so rich with everything she had with her. The diamond ring. Sable coat. Money. You were in Dallas at the time of death. You're not six feet tall. You supported her. There was no insurance, no inheritance. No unusual withdrawals from your bank account."

Evelyn couldn't bring herself to reveal to a stranger like Gordon that the ring, the coat, the money, were hers, borrowed by Sara to impress old classmates. Let Gordon think the fine articles were Sara's. Finding the killer would not only ease her pain but also exonerate Sara's reputation as well. It was now even more important to uncover the circumstances surrounding Sara's death. "You mean by the last statement that I didn't hire anyone."

"It's my conclusion."

He pushed on the door and went in, Evelyn following. The small room had four metal chairs arranged before a wall of glass. Evelyn knew the suspects on the other side could not see into the room. A police officer stood next to an elderly woman, who clutched a battered purse close to her chest, twisting the straps with gnarled hands. Gordon nodded to the officer who turned to the woman.

"Okay, just take it slow and easy, Mrs. Strauss. Look at those five men, one at a time. Study the faces, their height and weight."

The woman leaned forward, nose almost touching the glass, her eyes narrowed in concentration. Her head bobbed as she looked from man to man. Evelyn watched her eyes shift, then hold on one man. She cocked her head to one side, then mumbled something to herself.

"Now, Mrs. Strauss, the men will turn to the side so you can see their profiles," the officer explained.

The room was quiet, almost claustrophobic. Evelyn could hear Gordon wheeze as he breathed.

Lifting her chin in triumph, the old woman turned to the policeman. "It's the first one on the left. That's him! He was the one who run out of my neighbor's apartment after I heard her scream. The one on the left killed her." She nodded, then looked at Gordon. "That's him all right."

Gordon and the police officer exchanged glances. "You're positive?" Gordon asked.

The woman eyed Evelyn suspiciously, then moved close to the police officer. "The one on the left. I'm positive. I'd remember that face anywhere."

Gordon stalked to the door, opened it and motioned to Evelyn.

Walking down the hall, Evelyn saw Gordon's jaw pulsing. "Was that the right suspect the woman picked out of the lineup?"

Gordon shook his head. "She picked out a police officer," he spat out.

Back in Gordon's office, Evelyn settled into the chair, Gordon behind his desk. Thinking of the newspaper article in her purse, Evelyn reached a decision not to show it to Gordon. He would think she was even more ridiculous than he already did. Maybe it wasn't even a lead. "I'll hire someone, a private detective to work full-time on the case. It's the one last thing I can do for my sister."

"Like people who buy the most expensive caskets for the deceased, thinking they're doing them one last favor? A private investigator will do nothing more than lighten your bank account."

There was a short rap on the door, and Sergeant Castro pushed in, carrying Sara's handbag and carryon, her garment bag slung over his shoulder. A sheaf of papers were stuffed in his jacket pocket.

"Your sister's belongings." Castro's voice was easy and sympathetic. "Regulations require that you look them over before signing the release papers."

He unzipped the bag and shook out the sable coat. Evelyn drew in a quick breath as she took it from him. From his pocket he produced a small box and opened it. Under the harsh lights the brilliance of the diamond came alive. Evelyn rubbed a finger over the stone and gazed at it hypnotically. Its inner depths had seen what happened. If only some image of the murderer were trapped there.

She rummaged through the bags and wallet. She signed the release papers quickly, anxious to leave the police station. Reaching for the bags, she faltered, suddenly feeling dizzy.

"Here, I'll help you with these," Castro offered. "Do you have transportation?"

Evelyn nodded, taking a deep breath. "I have a rental car." She turned her full attention to Captain Gordon. "I'm not leaving until the murderer is caught. He'll be caught. That's my gut feeling."

"Mrs. Casey?"

Evelyn glared back over her shoulder at Gordon as if she could strike him dead with a sudden bolt from her eyes.

Gordon rose, moved away from his desk and rubbed his forehead as if to wipe away the wrinkles. "You know, Mrs. Casey, a lot of people don't like policemen. In cases like this they transfer their fury to them. I try to tell it like I see it. My advice to you is to stop this obsessive behavior, go home to Dallas. I'll call you if a break comes."

It might be easier to do just what Gordon suggested, but the determination that had brought Evelyn through so much reasserted itself. "I can't do that. I just can't. To think that I urged Sara to make the trip."

Gordon followed them to his office door. "Mrs. Casey, I suppose you have a reservation for the night."

Evelyn nodded. "At the Palm Court."

"Castro see the lady back to her hotel."

Evelyn glanced at Castro. "You don't have to come with me."

"He can call a police cruiser to pick him up," Gordon said as he turned and walked back to his desk.

In the parking lot, Castro stowed the bags in the back of Evelyn's rental car and turned to her. "How about letting me drive? I know the way."

Evelyn handed over the key, grateful that she didn't have to fight traffic in a strange city. Her emotions had already been strained, then the fact that Sara was discovered nude hit her even harder. She slid into the passenger seat, and Castro started the motor.

As he eased the car into the late-afternoon traffic, Evelyn thought about her statement to Captain Gordon. She had really meant it. She glanced at Castro. He, too, knew Sara had been found nude, and no doubt, formed his own opinions. "You wouldn't know a private detective I could hire, would you?"

Castro stared fixedly out the window as though he hadn't heard her.

She remembered what Carole Wheeler mentioned. "Circumstances surrounding someone's murder may not be what they seem. I'm not giving up on Sara's case, but I need to have a plan. Somewhere to get started." She realized what desolate prospects she faced. "It's something I have to do. Isn't there anyone you know who could help me?"

"Only one name comes to mind, but I haven't seen the guy or talked to him in over two years. And I don't think this kind of case is his forte. Last I'd heard he'd gotten involved in corporate investigations, contract work. Big-money stuff."

"I'm willing to pay big money." Evelyn eyed Castro. She sensed he wanted to help. "What's his name?"

Castro shifted uncomfortably in his seat. "Hawk Sullivan, but he isn't the kind to accept assignments if results aren't possible. He's not exactly a detective . . . an investigator maybe, but he's more of a . . . ."

"He's what? What is he?" Hawk Sullivan. Here was something tangible to try and grasp.

"I guess I'd have to say that he's a handler of extreme or unusual situations. I guess you'd call him a contract agent. He's got a real talent, maybe even a genius, for seeing things most people don't and making connections where nobody would ever think to connect. Sullivan used to be with the FBI. Came from the Dallas office to be special agent in charge here in San Diego, but got eased out because he didn't go by the rules. Several of his cases had big notices in the papers. You may remember. Some South American-based employees of a U.S. company were kidnapped, and Hawk Sullivan was sent there to negotiate the ransom." Castro chuckled. "Instead, he chucked the whole idea of money, found out where they were being held, busted in under heavy security and rescued them. Walked them clear across the border into Bolivia." Castro accelerated, and the car surged forward.

Hawk Sullivan. Evelyn rolled the name over in her mind. He was real and taking shape, somebody out there who could help her. Already she was thinking of him as some daring renegade who could turn miracles.

"He sounds just like what I'm looking for. Do you know his telephone number?"

Castro nodded. "By heart. Hawk's a friend . . . or was. He and his wife used to come have dinner with my wife and me. We'd go over to his place, go out on his boat sometimes. Then . . ." Castro sighed, his face clouding as if something had come to mind he didn't care to dwell on. "Then, we just lost touch. I was just a cop. Maybe he kind of outgrew me. As I said, I haven't seen him in almost two years, but he was the best." Castro glanced out of the window. "The very best. Trouble is, it's unlikely that Sullivan would take on a murder case. From what I've told you, you can see how he operates. Big-time cases, broad scopes, investigations on an international scale. Don't get your hopes up about hiring him."

Castro swung into the parking lot of the Palm Court and pulled into a vacant space. Evelyn turned to him. "Now who is going to place that call to Hawk Sullivan? You or I?"

CHAPTER 2

A RIOT OF RED BOUGAINVILLEA spilled over the waist-high stucco wall surrounding Hawk Sullivan's property at 60 Becker Street. Clusters of palm trees on either side of the front lawn stretched toward the sky, swaying slightly in the breeze from the glistening ocean visible in the distance.

The Spanish-style bungalow's interior was cluttered, informal, revealing a history of Sullivan, furnished with memories, each piece a fine one, bargained for in some foreign bazaar. Hawk Sullivan sat deep in his favorite chair, one large hand wrapped around a crystal tumbler, the other pinching a smoldering cigarette. He crushed the butt in the overflowing ashtray next to the bottle on the table at his side and reached into the ice bucket. Dropping three cubes into his glass, he poured a generous measure of Jack Daniels over them. A dull headache had just begun to nag him, and he was sure his two visitors were directly responsible for its onset.

For over an hour they had talked in circles, stating meaningless generalities about politics and image, about political leaders and international crises. Hawk had done a black-bag job for them the year before as a contract agent, but this time they seemed to want him for something much bigger.

Hawk eyed the two men with distaste. He was tired of their forced diplomacy, their moth-and-flame routine.

"Positive no one wants a drink?" Sullivan gestured toward the walk-in bar. Although he felt otherwise, he was trying his best to sound cordial. "Gin? Scotch? A cold brew?"

The two of them, one short and wiry, the other short and stocky, murmured negatives. Sullivan wondered if being short was now an agency requirement.

"Can we get to the point, then?" Sullivan leaned forward in his chair, his muscular, tanned forearms resting on his knees, eyes, attentive and shrewd. "This guy you keep talking about, this unnamed, prominent politician, is no mystery man to me. I know who you're talking about, but what's the point? What do you want from me?" He lit a cigarette and rested it in the ashtray.

The stocky fellow leaned forward as if ready to spring, his attention close on Sullivan. "He's an embarrassment to our government."

Sullivan slumped back into the depths of his chair, ran his hands through his disheveled, sun-streaked hair and down his unshaven cheeks and chin. His kidneys felt close to bursting, but this was not exactly the right moment to make for the can. Or was it? Lighting a cigarette, he noticed he had one going.

The thinner man, whose crewcut bristled as though electrified, stood, hands rammed in his pockets and paced the room, his shiny black shoes squeaking. Sullivan studied him with casual interest, his judgment deferred. "You're in debt, Sullivan. Way over your head. We have an allocation that can fix that. This job is worth three hundred thousand. Half now, half on completion. You'll have all the technical backup and personnel you need to see it through."

"To see what through?" Sullivan enjoyed stopping the little guy in his tracks. "Just what is the assignment?"

"Interested?" The man looked at Hawk without emotion.

Sullivan drained his drink and wiped his mouth with the back of his hand. Plainly the agency didn't want to be directly associated with the matter. And if things went wrong, denials of involvement, as usual, would be forthcoming, putting Sullivan's neck in the noose. "Anybody is interested in three hundred thousand dollars."

The man smiled, handing Sullivan a check. "The job will be a piece of cake for you. Really simple, and when you're done, you're home-free. Everybody can breathe easier. More problems solved than just your financial ones. Now I want you to think of it is as a public service. Just think of it that way, Sullivan."

Sullivan took the check and stared at the figure. It was his for the taking. Had his name on it. The same amount to come upon completion of whatever the job was. A whole set of troubles put behind him with such numbers.

The man leaned forward slightly. "I know how it is to live with debt. A man can't think right, much less function. Money of that kind puts an end to misery. Believe me, it's worth it, especially when you're doing something really worthwhile."

Sullivan looked up. "What do you want me to do?" Placing the check on the table next to his chair, he noticed his hand shake. He glanced back at the numbers, hoping he could swallow the assignment without compunction. He desperately needed that money. "Just think of it as a public service," the agency man said.

The other man still seated on the sofa took his cue. "The man's sick. He's going to die anyway. We want that hastened in the interest of national security."

The words burned like hot grease thrown in his face. It has come to this, Sullivan thought, as he heaved himself from the chair, stalked to the double French doors and flung them open. The cool, lightly scented evening air rushed past him into the stuffy, smokey room. He studied the faintly ringed full moon, which suggested bad weather on the way. In his garden, buds had begun to pop, but unlike the old days, he took no joy in it. His angular face contorted with anger, he whipped around. "I don't kill people for money. Not for any amount." His jaws were clenched so tightly that his teeth ached.

"But this would be . . ."

Hawk Sullivan remained rooted in place, cooled by the breeze behind him. "Get out. Get out of my house and my life. Take your fucking dirty check with you."

The door slammed after the two men. Sullivan heard a car

start up and accelerate. He stood looking out into the darkness until the only sounds he could hear were the distant roar of the ocean, seagulls, and foghorns.

Hawk lumbered to the fireplace, poked the coals around, and flung on another log. Tiny orange flames crackled. He closed the screen and settled down in his chair.

Hawk looked around the room at the messy stacks of books and magazines covering the tables. He thumbed through a detective novel and tried to find his place. He couldn't recall what he'd read the previous evening and hurled the book across the room, aware that his anger came from the agency's assumption that he had fallen so low, that a lifetime of service had wound down to such a disgraceful conclusion. Worse was the fact that to wipe his troubled financial slate clean he had been vaguely tempted to accept.

His eyes held on his wife's picture. Karin had been so lovely that summer, a time when his life held nothing but promise. Sullivan was not moved by many things, but he'd allowed himself to be moved deeply by her. Now he sometimes felt as if he were a transient speck on a passing parade.

Lost in thought, Sullivan suddenly became aware of the phone ringing, probably had been for several seconds. He snatched the receiver from the cradle and gave the caller a gruff "Yes?"

"Sullivan, Castro here. How've you been making it?"

"Making it."

"Olga and I both tried to call. Time after time."

Sullivan remembered all the unanswered messages. He must have bruised the Castros' feelings, but there was no room in his life for company. Only work. Pay off bills. Then he'd see. "I sort of lost track of old friends. Been busy. What's up?"

Castro hesitated, then cleared his throat. "I hate to bother you at this time of night, but there's this woman here from Texas, the widow of Andrew Casey. She needs some help. I was wondering if you could talk to her?"

"Andrew Casey, big oil dough. What kind of help?"

"Ah . . . I, maybe it would be better if she explained herself."

Sullivan cradled the phone on his shoulder, reached for a

crumpled pack of cigarettes, then crushed it in his fist when it proved to be empty. His eyes searched the tabletop near his chair and sighted his last pack, which he remembered finishing off while his visitors from the agency had been there. "I'm really crashed out tonight."

"Couldn't you do it as a favor to me? I halfway promised her you would. Tonight, I mean."

With his free hand Sullivan massaged his temples. He felt a new prick of annoyance. Why did everybody want something from him? Tonight of all nights, for Christ sakes! He supposed for old times he should agree. Anyway, he'd have to go out for cigarettes. "Okay. Where?"

"Palm Court. I'll wait with her in the bar."

"Out near the airport?" The location couldn't be more inconvenient.

"Right. Thanks, amigo. I owe you."

"And you know I always collect." Sullivan hung up.

Sullivan hovered over the bar sink, slugging a drink for the road. His old habit of picturing a person just before he was about to meet them for the first time started working. Casey's widow—he couldn't remember if Castro had said her name— would be sixtyish, dressed fortyish, more than likely a golfer or a tennis player in the mornings, afternoons reserved for cards, charity meetings and martinis, a Texas matron with an abrasive twang and more diamonds and emeralds than brains. He'd known plenty like that. Question was, what did she want with him?

After checking in and quickly depositing the luggage in her room, Evelyn joined Castro in the hotel bar. Seated at a leather banquette facing the door, they ordered drinks, a vodka on the rocks with an onion and a twist for Evelyn, a beer for Castro. The dim room was dotted with large wooden planters holding palm trees. Small pinpoints of light from the ceiling bathed the foliage with a diffuse glow, giving the overall ambiance of a tropical forest setting in moonlight. Wide expanses of glass offered a view of the harbor. In the distance, an ocean liner, its carnival lights blazing and strung high, slid into the velvet of the night. Evelyn would have liked to be on board, carefree, sailing off to some unknown destination. But, here she was, weighted down with burdens that had to be faced and solved.

As they waited, Castro bombarded her with more tales of Sullivan's exploits. He was a legend, Castro said, filled with energy, determination, an incredible memory, and above all, total dedication whenever he committed himself. She was burning to meet this man who could move mountains. If he were only half of what Castro had described, she would be satisfied and said so. Castro, again, warned her not to get her hopes up about Sullivan taking on a murder case.

"There he is." Castro stood and motioned to Sullivan.

Evelyn turned to see Hawk Sullivan looming in the entry-way. The rangy man nodded at Castro and walked toward them. His face, one that only tough experience could have chiseled, was tan and craggy. Even in the dimness Evelyn noticed that his clothes were wrinkled, his sneakers dirty and full of holes. Still, there was a rumpled elegance about him, broad shoulders straining the fabric of his shirt, narrow hips and long legs below them. He looked like a cowboy to Evelyn.

Castro pumped Sullivan's hand. "Good to see you, old buddy."

Sullivan squeezed Castro's bicep. "Been a long time."

"I'm Evelyn Casey." She looked up and gave Sullivan her best smile.

And got in return, a cool look of assessment. He clearly wanted her to know that no one could push him in a direction he didn't care to go, and he didn't intend that she should be an exception. She felt momentarily defeated.

Castro checked his watch. "The cruiser should be out front now. I'll just be moving on and let you two talk." Picking up his beer, Castro swigged the last few drops. "Good to see you, man. Let's keep in touch."

Sullivan edged around the table and sat next to Evelyn. Even his old ability to picture someone fairly accurate before he met them was way off target, he thought. Evelyn Casey was an outstanding-looking woman, not the tacky Texas matron he expected.

They watched, in silence, as Castro made his way out.

Sullivan motioned toward the bartender. "Jack Daniels on the rocks."

Sullivan lit a cigarette and let it dangle at the corner of his mouth. As he watched the waitress set down his bourbon, he squinted. Smoke spiraled upward, bringing to prominence tiny lines around his eyes. "Thirsty?" he inquired, raising his glass and spilling a few drops.

"Yes, I could use another drink." Evelyn thought Sullivan's eyes were the deepest shade of green she'd ever seen, but they clearly held a trace of sadness.

"Another of what she had," Sullivan mumbled to the waitress and downed half of his drink in one gulp.

After the waitress rustled away, he turned to Evelyn. "What is it you want to talk to me about?" He looked past her as if what she had to say was of no interest to him.

Evelyn fixed her eyes on him. "I wanted to talk to you about my sister's murder. Hire you to investigate it."

"That's Homicide's bailiwick," Sullivan snapped, eyes still averted from hers.

"I know, but they've almost dropped the case. Captain Gordon looks at it with such a jaundiced eye."

Sullivan took a slug of his drink, then wiped his mouth with a fist. "Look, the police are hard-working. They don't forget a case. It's always on hold until it's closed."

Evelyn bit her lip. "That's just the problem. It's on hold while the murderer is getting away with it. I'm determined not to let him. I keep thinking how frightened my sister must have been." Tears welled in her eyes, but she was determined not to let them fall.

Sullivan eyed his empty glass, then directed his attention to her. "Tell me the facts about the case."

Much as it pained her, Evelyn reviewed the circumstances of her sister's murder, hoping to outline them without emotion. "My sister, Sara, flew to San Diego for her college reunion. She came alone. She didn't want to come, but I thought it would be good for her. You see, Sara was such a shy, almost reclusive, type of person . . . would have never done anything . . ." She groped for the right words, then continued. "Anything out of line. Place herself in some situation . . . ." Evelyn wished the waitress would hurry with her drink.

Sullivan exhaled. "Facts, I asked for. Don't get off on personality or speculation."

Evelyn swallowed hard. "She rode from the San Diego Airport alone in a cab to the Eastgate. Checked in, and according to the coroner's report, was murdered, stabbed to death, in her hotel room within the next two to three hours. She wasn't raped or robbed."

When the waitress arrived and served Evelyn's drink, Sullivan ordered another. "Make it a double, this time. The barkeep's got a weak hand."

Evelyn swigged her drink, feeling the rush of relief it brought. She ran her fingers around the square cardboard coaster, feeling Sullivan's eyes on her.

He picked up a swizzle stick and tapped it on the table. "Any sign of forced entry into her room?"

Evelyn shook her head, feeling a knot forming in her throat.

"Who found the body?"

She didn't like Sara called a "body." "A maid in the hotel . . . next day." Her voice cracked. It was coming. He had her hemmed in, and she wasn't sure she could admit it when asked.

When the waitress placed Sullivan's drink before him, it provided Evelyn with a moment to regroup. She watched Sullivan's Adam's apple bob up and down as he swallowed. Setting down his glass, he lit a cigarette and squinted. "You said she was stabbed. Was the body mutilated in any way?"

"No." Evelyn drew in a quick breath, deciding to face the subject and finish with it. "She was found nude . . . close to the door."

Sullivan raised his sun-bleached eyebrows. "Look, I don't think I'm the man for the job."

"But," Evelyn interrupted, "I'll pay your price. The price you would get for doing . . . well, for doing whatever it is you do. Contract work is it called?"

'Assassinations, maybe,' he wanted to say, but instead, held up his hand. "Hold it! Don't be goddamn anxious to part with your money. Money isn't the only issue here." His tone was brusque, and Evelyn regretted her hasty words. She had not meant to insult him but feared she had.

"I'm sorry. I don't mean to sound like I'm trying to buy you. I have to do all that I can to find my sister's murderer. I know money isn't the only issue with you, but just solving my sister's case isn't the only issue here with me either."

Sullivan stared at her, her lovely face filled with pain, eyes pleading for an audience. "Go on. I'm listening."

"Well, Sara and I were raised by our mother after our father drowned in a boating accident. We were very young. Mom worked all the time to support us and put us through school, so, because I was older, I took on the role of mother and looked out for Sara. When I married Andrew Casey, she came to live with us, and Andrew found her a job at Cypress Oil. That was his company. After Andrew died, we naturally grew even closer, but I worried about her not having any life of her own. So, when the announcement of the college re-union came, I urged her to go. To get out and see old friends . . ."

Evelyn stopped and looked out at the ocean. "He's out there somewhere. Sara's killer. He's looking at the same moon, breathing the same air. He gets up in the morning and goes about his day, just like you and me, only he's a killer." Her eyes filled again, and her throat tightened. She dared not look at Hawk Sullivan.

"Go on," he said gently.

"I made her go," Evelyn almost whispered. "I thought it would be good for her. Better than sitting home watching television and reading romance novels. Maybe she would meet somebody. And . . . when Sara left at my insistence, I looked forward to a break from her constant presence. Oh, God. I did. I actually did." Evelyn was sobbing. After all she'd been through, she had finally broken down. Finally gotten to the source of her pain.

Sullivan bowed his head and studied the table. Guilt, he thought, always guilt. Guilt was no stranger to him. He lived with it every day. His was the guilt of the survivor. So was Evelyn's.

Evelyn blew her nose, regaining her composure. She no

ticed the waitress looking at her. "If you'll get the check, I'll sign my room number."

Sullivan didn't like the way her statement made him feel. He pulled out his battered wallet and laid enough money on the table to cover the check. He was tired and wanted to go home. Just thinking about his condition in the morning made him wince.

"Won't you just consider taking the case. I've got to find someone to help."

"Let me think about it. I'll sleep on it. Call me in the morning." He didn't want his better judgment eclipsed by liquor or sympathy.

They walked to the lobby and said goodnight. Key in hand, Evelyn headed for the bank of elevators and rode to her floor.

Sitting on the side of her bed, Evelyn felt calmer and more in control than she had since Sara's death. Although she regretted her emotional outburst in front of an almost total stranger, she was relieved that what had caused her so much distress had finally surfaced. In that moment of desperation, when pleading her case to Hawk Sullivan, something had broken loose within her, and she understood why she felt so compelled to find her sister's murderer.

Unconsciously, she believed what happened to her sister was her fault. Just as she always assumed responsibility for what happened in her sister's life, she accepted responsibility for her death. She had made a terrible mistake . . . a fatal mistake . . . in forcing Sara to go to San Diego. Now, she had a twofold responsibility facing her—not only to find her sister's murderer and see that he was punished, but also to erase any hint of seamy circumstances surrounding her death. That would not bring her sister back nor would it ease the grief and remorse she felt, but it was the only thing she could do for her sister and herself. But it all depended on Hawk Sullivan.

Sullivan was certainly not what she expected from Castro's description. Her first impression was that he was too burned out to conduct any investigation, but the more she talked with him the more convinced she became he was the man for the job. Besides, he was all she had.

Anxiety gripped her again. What if he wouldn't take the

case? It was obvious he wouldn't simply for money. And the case was not nearly as challenging an assignment as freeing hostages in South America. Yet Evelyn had felt him wavering despite his negative response, sensed it in his silence as he walked her to the lobby. He just might do it, she decided. And, if he did, Evelyn knew instinctively, that his reasons would be as personal as hers, and, in time, she might learn why.

Undressing, Evelyn realized that in her effort to convince Sullivan to take the case, she had forgotten to show him the newspaper clipping she felt might be a lead. It could be the trump card to induce him to take the case, and she'd have to play the hand correctly. When the article caught her eye, she hadn't been aware that Sara had been discovered nude. It might just be the ticket that eliminated any easy "pickup" connotation to Sara's death. She pulled the cover up and slipped into a deep, untroubled sleep for the first time since the telephone call that had shattered her life.

CHAPTER 3

HAWK SULLIVAN ROLLED OVER and reached for the pillow on the other side of the bed, the sheet twisting tighter around his leg. Slowly he focused on the ceiling where shadows of palm fronds cast odd patterns. They looked to Hawk like hands trying to touch, but when close enough, they pulled back as if afraid of contact. How very human, he mused, thinking how much he had isolated himself since Karin's death. He was immediately annoyed at these first, unprogrammed thoughts of the day. He was careful to live one day at a time, looking neither back nor forward. Forget the big picture.

The phone rang. He knew who was calling. He picked up the receiver after the first shrill ring and listened.

"Good morning. It's Evelyn Casey. Awake?" Her voice was fresh and clear.

Sullivan cleared his throat. "For hours."

"If you haven't had breakfast, I thought we might meet for something. I'm at a coffee shop called Grounds, not far from your house according to my map. Afterwards we can talk about the case."

"Why don't you pick up something and come here? I'll

provide the coffee and juice. I'm not one for public places much before noon. Think you can find your way here?''

"Sure. What would you like?"

"Anything. Just give me time to take a shower and check my messages.''

He hung up and noticed that there was one call registered on his answering machine. Last night he forgot to check. Punching the button, he listened to the tape, which sounded like a strangling Donald Duck rewinding. He touched PLAY and stepped back as if standing too close to a person about to speak.

"Sullivan, thought you might just reconsider the proposition after mulling it over. The offer still stands. If you're interested, you know where to reach us, but don't take too long. Timing is urgent.''

Sullivan hit the STOP button. Fully awakened by a surge of anger, he muttered under his breath, "Sons of bitches didn't know how to take 'no' for an answer.'' Still took him for a hit man. Legalized crime for the country. What hypocrites. Simmering down, he decided not to take it personally, strictly business, strictly patriotic business, used to be. But maybe it was for just that reason that he had been lured into it in the first place. With the FBI out of his life, he had still wanted to contribute to the country. And then there had been the money.

Sullivan had always been a free-spender, and when he and Karin married, he had gone all out. They honeymooned all over Europe and South America on plastic and were then ironically sent back to some of the same places, courtesy of the FBI. Karin worried about his safety, but he'd done his utmost to play down his high-wired activities, separating career from the kind of marriage he wanted: an old-fashioned, even middle-class union.

When the agency called him home, he bought the house and mortgaged it to the hilt. Secure in his mind with the bureau, he borrowed more to buy a boat. Sullivan, a nonconformist in a team organization, set his own guidelines, consequences be damned. The agency had other plans for men who bent rules to achieve results. Then, after he was edged out and denied his full benefits, Karin's morning sickness, which they hoped was a prelude to a happy event was diagnosed instead as leukemia, a devastating blow they were forced to absorb.

He investigated what paths were available under the circumstances and found only millionaires could afford the finest clinics, doctors involved in research, interferon shots at fifteen thousand a whap. When the boys in the dark suits had looked him up, he was ready for anything. The ratio of time spent to money earned was the clincher, providing the opportunity between jobs to spend time with Karin.

As far as Sullivan was concerned, money was only as good as the use it was put to. Nothing the doctors tried was effective on Karin, and the expenses far exceeded his income. Selling the house and boat could help settle accounts, but they were so much a part of Karin that to dispense with them was to lose her again. He knew it was unhealthy to keep a hand on the past. Karin would be the first to blast him for it. What irony that she had feared for his safety and was first to go.

Hawk felt the dead weight descend, as it always did when he thought about that terrible year. At the end of it, he had felt as dead as Karin, except he continued to breathe and walk and talk. With enormous debts, it was easy to immerse himself in dangerous exploits for huge payoffs.

Now, here was Evelyn Casey and her routine murder case. He admitted the lady herself was far from routine and circling a situation possibly tawdry. Taking the case was a chance to do something for someone else and still make money. Not three hundred thousand, but it was clean. And instead of being a murderer himself, he might bring one to justice. Call it an exercise in humanity. A penance, even. Everyone was entitled to their own private lunacy, after all. It would be like the old days. Before everything had gone wrong. Maybe he'd do it. Maybe not. He'd see.

Sullivan leaned closer to the mirror and pulled at a hair in his temple. He had thought the ones framing his face were blond, but on examination he decided some were gray. At forty-five, he suddenly realized that more than half of his life was behind him.

Thirty minutes later, he was showered and dressed in clean khakis and a white cotton turtleneck pullover he was suprised to find neatly folded in the bottom of a dresser drawer. Hawk rummaged around the closet floor, looking for his loafers. No clean socks for his sneakers could be found.

At last, the shoes surfaced, and Hawk headed for the living room, where he made a quick roundup of glasses and ashtrays. In the kitchen, he ran a sink full of hot, soapy water and slipped the glasses in to soak. Then, he put water on for coffee and opened the refrigerator. He pulled out a pitcher of orange juice, pausing only for a moment before returning to the den bar, where he picked up an open bottle of vodka and splashed in a few fingers. A cure for his headache, he temporized, and Evelyn Casey would never be the wiser.

Back in the kitchen, he emptied the ashtrays and lit a cigarette, inhaling deeply. He choked and coughed and quickly swallowed the orange juice laced with vodka. Looking out the window, he saw faint forms of runners on the beach. For years, he and Karin had run every morning and every night, but now he couldn't remember the last time he'd run alone. The kettle whistled. Hawk ground the coffee and emptied it into the filter on the pot as the doorbell rang.

"Door's open," he bellowed.

Sacks under both arms, Evelyn pushed in. "You forgot to lock your door!" She glanced around.

Sullivan shrugged. "Locks don't keep anybody out. If they want in, they'll get in." He sipped his juice slowly, knowing that this would probably have to hold him until the sun was over the yardarm.

Evelyn quickly surveyed the surroundings. Comfortable, she thought, and in need of a good cleaning. The furnishings could only be described as eclectic, but all the pieces were good and somehow worked together. French and English antiques mixed with California Mission, and the pièce de résistance was a massive black lacquer chinoiserie breakfront. Two impressive ivory and jade figures sat on the mantelpiece and the Oriental rug was unusually patterned with vivid colors.

She walked into the kitchen and dumped the two shopping bags on the table. "Why don't you just sit down? Let me find my way around and get things together."

"Jesus! Look at how much you brought."

With his juice, Sullivan settled in the den, where he could see through the open serving area into the kitchen. He thought he could smell croissants. She swept around his domain, taking down plates from the cupboard, moving things around on his counter, ripping open sacks. Her blond mane was tied neatly back with a ribbon. She wore jeans, sandals, and a blue pullover. Hardly the image of a pampered woman. Some people preferred to dress in direct contrast to their status. Surprisingly, she seemed at home in the kitchen.

"Do you have any napkins?"

"Just paper towels. Haven't seen a real napkin around here in years."

"Everything's ready." She stood in the doorway. "Where do you want to eat?"

"Out on my patio." He pushed up. "I pay minimum wages and no carfare. I want that understood from the start," he barked, then cracked a smile.

"And I don't do windows." She laughed. "See, I didn't bring so much." She looked around as if expecting to see someone.

"Just me here. We can split what's left."

He helped her carry the plates to the patio. The glass table was spotted with bird droppings, the chairs damp with moisture. She hurried back to the kitchen for a rag. He put down the dishes and waited. She had croissants, brioches, too, and cantaloupes scooped into balls, marmalade, and crisp bacon. He glanced through the open door at his row of gourmet cookbooks. Could have whipped up eggs Benedict or a fresh herb omelette, had he been of the mind to do so. It'd been quite a while since he'd done his number in the kitchen. Too long, maybe.

Evelyn wiped off the table while he polished off his orange juice.

"It's going to take me a few days to sort out what I'm going to do next. You might as well go on back to Dallas. I'll call you when I've decided." He massaged his temples.

Evelyn doubled a stick of bacon and shoved it in her mouth. "You've decided not to take the case." Her voice cracked. More than likely his refusal was based on his idea that the job was a routine murder case. If he thought it was something more, he might reconsider. Now was the time for the clipping.

The pounding in his head grew harder. "I didn't say that. I've been offered a big job, and I'm expecting to be called in on something else soon. I'm considering my options, that's all. In the meantime, I guess I could do a little background work on your case. Get hold of the file from Castro and see what Homicide's done."

Evelyn realized that she was holding her breath. What did he mean? Was he taking the case or wasn't he? She got up from the table and retrieved her shoulder bag from the kitchen. She handed him a dog-eared piece of newsprint. "I want to show you something. I have a hunch there might be some connection between this and Sara's murder. It was in the Dallas paper, local news. I just happened to see it."

Sullivan looked at her and then at the clipping. "A hunch, you say?" He quickly skimmed the article.

MEMORIAL HELD FOR SLAIN SCHOOL TEACHER

Memorial services for Mary Kenworth were held today at the First Baptist Church of Fort Worth. A school teacher for ten years in the Fort Worth Public School system, Miss Kenworth was found stabbed on May 21, the day she arrived, in her room at the Larramore Hotel in Los Angeles, California, where she was to attend a three-day educational conference. According to a spokesman from the Los Angeles Homicide Division, there are no reported suspects. Mary Kenworth resided with her only survivor, an aunt, Miss Avery Kenworth of Fort Worth, Texas.

"My sister was murdered May 19th. This Kenworth woman was murdered two days later in a hotel in Los Angeles the day she arrived."

Sullivan shifted in his chair and reread the article. He put it on the table and stared at the sky, a deep crease furrowing his forehead. "Could be just a coincidence, but there are similarities."

"That's why I happened to spot it. It's so small, but I was

thinking of Sara as I read it. Do you think there could be a connection?''

Sullivan lit a cigarette and confronted Evelyn's intent stare. ''Million-to-one shot.'' Sullivan picked up the article again and squinted at it. ''But million-to-one odds turn me on. We can't afford to rule anything out this early in the game.''

Evelyn swallowed hard, her pulse racing. Had she heard him correctly? ''We,'' he had said, ''we.''

''So,'' she said, not missing a beat, ''what do we do next.''

''Theorize. Maybe your sister had some secret love you didn't know about. Maybe after you dropped her off at the airport, he was waiting for her in the terminal. Flew to San Diego with her. They argued over something. Maybe she was giving him the shaft. He lost control and killed her. That would account for her having not been raped or robbed. A crime of passion, as they say.''

Evelyn shook her head. He, like Gordon, hadn't ruled out the familiarity aspect. ''No, not Sara. Remember, I told you she rode alone in the cab? The police reports have that on file from the cab driver. If someone had traveled from Dallas with her, they would have ridden with her to the hotel.''

Sullivan nodded, agreeing with Evelyn's logic. ''Maybe she had someone meeting her at the hotel.''

''She was alone when she checked in, according to the reports. Sara didn't have anyone interested in her, or I would have known.'' Evelyn looked down. ''I would have known because Sara would have been so proud.''

''Could it be that you didn't know your sister as well as you thought? She could have picked up someone.''

''People just don't change that suddenly. Sara was too shy. I know why you keep pursuing this line of thought . . . because she was nude. But maybe someone slipped into her room someway while she was taking a bath or dressing . . . maybe some psycho going through hotels looking for women alone.''

Sullivan avoided her eyes as he talked. ''Well, let's just suppose the killer was a stranger, some psycho making a random choice. Case over, unsolvable.''

''You believe she was a random choice?''

"I don't believe anything. Let's suppose the killer was someone she knew. By someone she knew, I mean someone she'd just met."

"Just met? I told you how timid she was. I can't see Sara striking up with a stranger."

"Someone on the plane. Her seatmate, possibly. People tend to get chummy with fellow travelers, more so on planes than anywhere else. They feel safe talking to strangers, might tell them more under those circumstances than they would any other place. Did Captain Gordon mention checking that angle?"

"No, he didn't."

"I can see why they might have overlooked that and focused elsewhere. An airplane is a public place, so to speak. She arrives safely in San Diego, goes alone in a cab to the hotel and checks in. Please tell me she rode first-class."

Evelyn blinked. "She did. Why?"

"Good break. About sixteen people on first-class. Hundred or so in tourist. I'd hate to have to check them all out."

"You mean you believe it could be someone she met in first-class? Her seatmate? Told him where she was staying, then he came to the Eastgate . . . maybe the same thing happened to the Fort Worth woman."

"It's a theory. Works better than anything else if what you say about your sister is true. That's where we start. With the list of first-class passengers on your sister's flight. Castro can get the records. I'll call Mary Kenworth's aunt. I suppose there was a lot of publicity in the Dallas papers about your sister's murder."

"Yes, there was. Here in San Diego, too."

"Must have missed it. I was probably out on my boat fishing or I would have caught it. Any pictures in the paper?" He knew she could tell nothing from his face that he didn't want her to see.

Evelyn nodded. "Mine."

Sullivan lit a cigarette. The killer knew who Evelyn Casey was and what she looked like. "Do you have a picture of your sister?"

Evelyn took her wallet from her purse and showed Sullivan

Sara's picture. He stared at it, then glanced at Evelyn and handed it back.

Evelyn studied the small photograph for a moment before returning it to her wallet.

"There's no reason for me to go back to Dallas; maybe I can help you with this."

"Help? Just exactly what kind of help do you have in mind?" His tone was deliberately mocking.

Evelyn moved in the seat and crossed her legs. "My background. I went back to school after I was married, but I never had a chance to do anything with what I learned. I have a master's degree in psychology. I took extra courses in subjects that really interested me the most . . . deviant behavior, criminology . . . wrote my thesis on sociopathic and psychopathic personalities. I know I could be of some help to you."

"Oh?" He thought receiving her degree was admirable, but why would the wife of such a wealthy man subject herself to rigorous academics. Was she bored with life or just enterprising enough not to want to be her husband's satellite?

"Why those subjects? How'd you get interested in them?" He drained the last of his orange juice and vodka, wishing for a full glass.

Evelyn glanced out toward the ocean, then focused on Sullivan. "My father . . . before his accident. I told you I was young when he died. So was he . . . just getting started as the assistant district attorney. It was a small town, but he was fascinated by some of the cases his office handled . . . the criminal mind. He told me stories like other fathers would tell fairy tales. I never forgot, the subject so stimulated my interest."

Sullivan took a deep breath. "Look, I work solo. I've never been any good at collaborating or delegating. The FBI can attest to that."

Evelyn was not to be deterred. "I won't interfere or get in your way, but I want to be involved. I could do some of your leg work. Follow up."

Hawk stared at her. This woman did not quit. She was determined. And a potential nuisance.

"Nothing for you to do. I can't force you to go back to

Dallas, but you'll be wasting your time here if you think you've got some job to do with me."

"Okay, I understand you. But let's do this. I'll stay and I promise not to interfere or bother you, but if there is something I can do, you'll tell me and I'll do it. Is that fair?"

Sullivan scratched his head, humor replacing annoyance. She was so sincere and earnest that it was almost funny. What could he do but acquiesce? "Okay, fair enough. I'll call Castro."

Evelyn stood on the patio looking out at the distant surf. She had never known a man like Hawk Sullivan. He was mercurial. Impulsive. He said he had not made up his mind about taking the case, and here he was plunging right in as if he had. Maybe he himself did not know what he really wanted or meant.

"Castro's on his way over," Sullivan offered over his shoulder while he dialed again. "Fort Worth? I'd like the number of Avery Kenworth." He hung up and once again dialed. "Pick up the extension in the den."

Evelyn scuttled into the den and located the phone on Sullivan's desk. Turning so she could see him in the kitchen through the open serving area, she picked up the receiver. In a moment, a quavering voice came on the line. "Hello?"

"Hawkins Sullivan, ma'am. I'm investigating the murder of a woman from Dallas that occurred in similar circumstances to that of your niece. There's a remote possibility that there is some connection between the two crimes. I'd like to ask you a few questions." He looked straight at Evelyn. She hoped it meant an acknowledgment, even partial belief, in her theory.

"Well, sir, I'd be glad to talk to you. I'll be home all afternoon. You can come on over. Won't take you more than forty minutes from Dallas if you take the turnpike. About two or two-thirty would be convenient. After that, I take a nap. Be sure to bring plenty of identification."

"Miss Kenworth, I'm in San Diego, California."

"What are you doing there? You said the murdered woman came from Dallas. Why aren't you in Dallas?"

"I'm sorry, ma'am. Didn't make myself clear. The victim

whose death I'm investigating lived in Dallas. She was murdered in San Diego. Night she arrived.''

"Like what happened to Mary, only in Los Angeles. You San Diego policemen are a whole sight better than the Los Angeles ones. Haven't heard anything from them. Guess they're not even looking for the murderer anymore.''

Evelyn shook her head, knowing how the woman must feel.

"I'm not with the police. I'm a private investigator. I would appreciate your spending just a few more minutes on the phone if you would, Miss Kenworth, to answer a couple of questions. This might help solve your niece's case, too, if there's some connection between the two crimes.''

"Shoot, then.''

"Your niece, Mary . . . the papers said she was murdered in a Los Angeles hotel. Did she travel there alone?''

"She went everywhere alone when she went anywhere at all. Didn't mix much 'cept at teachers' conventions. Guess most teachers are like Mary, kind of quiet-like. She felt at home with her kind.''

"Was your niece expected by anyone in Los Angeles, someone attending the conference?''

"Not that I know of. People just turn up at those things unannounced.''

"Could you tell me what flight she took?''

"Not right off. I guess it must be on her ticket. The police returned all her stuff.''

"Could you go and look, Miss Kenworth?''

"Guess I could. It's in her room.''

"Miss Kenworth?''

Sullivan held his breath, hoping to beat the odds. "By any chance did your niece fly first-class?''

"That I can tell you right off, Mr. Solomon. Mary went without lunches just to have money to impress people with when she went out of town. Didn't make much sense to me.''

Evelyn heard Sullivan exhale.

"Would you mind getting the flight information for me, now, Miss Kenworth?''

"It'll take a minute or two. You hold on.''

Evelyn winced as the receiver was banged down.

"What do you think?" Evelyn whispered into the receiver, unable to control her mounting excitement.

"Take it easy. There's nothing to think."

Evelyn turned and looked at the jammed bookcase, running her fingers over the spines. Selections of an intelligent man: Dickens, Melville, Trollope, Willa Cather, Lewis Carroll. She smiled at the collections of Agatha Christie, John Le Carré, Lawrence Sanders and John D. MacDonald.

"Are you there, Mr. Solomon?"

"Sullivan, ma'am. I'm here."

"Mary flew on American Airlines flight 235 on May 21st."

"Thank you very much, Miss Kenworth. I'll be in touch if anything turns up."

Sullivan hung up, keeping his hand on the receiver. After he received the list of passengers from both flights, he might find one name that turned up twice. He walked into the living room where Evelyn was staring at the picture on his desk.

"My wife," Sullivan stated flatly.

Evelyn jumped. "A beautiful woman."

"Very. She died of cancer two years ago."

The doorbell chimed and Castro came in wearing a blue short-sleeved sport shirt and denims the same color. "Anybody got a cup of coffee for a tired public servant?" Castro hesitated in mid-smile as curiosity overtook him, his eyes shifting from Hawk to Evelyn and back. He glanced in the kitchen at the breakfast leftovers, a slightly amused expression on his face. Evelyn knew how easily the scene could be misinterpreted. He'd introduced her to Sullivan the night before and here she was at breakfast the next morning.

"I'll get it." Sullivan went to the kitchen, wondering how he would finesse pouring vodka into his orange juice in the den. Then he remembered the Stolichnaya in the freezer. He returned with Castro's coffee and his tumbler, looking amused, too.

The three settled in the den, Sullivan in his favorite chair, feet propped up on the matching ottoman, Evelyn and Castro side-by-side on the couch. Evelyn felt awkward, wishing she could explain.

"I need a favor, Manny." Sullivan explained about Mary Kenworth and his theory. "I can't get a list of passengers

from the airlines, but you can. I want both flight lists, Sara
Marley's and Mary Kenworth's. Where the flights originated.
Dallas, I hope, otherwise there's a lot more checking to do.
All the information's on computer. Names of all reservations
made, how each passenger paid, check or credit card. Then
we'll have all the addresses. Seat assignments, especially. I
also want the L.A.P.D. report on Mary Kenworth. Also want
a Xerox of the police reports on Sara Marley's case . . . just
to make sure nothing was overlooked.''

"You know that's against regulations,'' Castro interrupted,
reaching for his coffee.

"Screw regulations.'' Sullivan glanced at Evelyn, then
fixed his eyes on Castro. "One turn deserves another.''

"I'll have to sign the log to Xerox the file, you know.
That's a red flag to Gordon. He's just waiting for me to
fu—mess up.'' Castro flushed, looking away from Evelyn.

"So you're working on your own time on a case that
interests you.'' His tone held a trace of mockery. "You're a
conscientious cop. Happens all the time around the station
house. You guys get the bug.'' Sullivan's eyes held on
Castro.

Castro finished his coffee, exhaled deeply and headed for
the door. "And just when am I suppose to do all this? I go on
duty in an hour.''

"When you get off duty.''

"When do expect me to rest?''

"Tomorrow, next day.'' Sullivan was closing the door.

Castro grabbed the knob. "You know something, Sullivan?''

"What's that?''

Castro looked at Evelyn and lowered his voice: "You piss
ice water.''

Sullivan grinned. "Cubes.''

Castro stared at Sullivan. Sullivan stared at Castro. Like
two territorial dogs, Evelyn thought. Neither spoke for what
seemed a long time.

Castro moved through the doorway, then looked from Evelyn to Sullivan as if he still wondered what to make of the
scene. "I'll drop by on my way home with whatever I've
come up with. Figure about six or seven.''

"I owe you one, buddy." Sullivan popped Castro on the shoulder with his fist.

"One?" Castro smiled slowly. "Sullivan, for this, you owe me your life."

When he had gone, Sullivan turned and was startled by Evelyn's sudden distress. "You okay?"

"I was just thinking. I'd feel terrible if Castro got into trouble on my account."

Sullivan followed Evelyn back to the patio, where they sat at the table.

"Manny's shrewd. He's doing this because we go back a long way and because we've both stretched our necks out a few times." Sullivan lit a cigarette, blew a smoke ring and watched it dissipate. "When I first met Manny, he was nineteen. He lived with his grandparents and a cousin they'd taken in. The cousin was a real rotten egg, always in trouble, the old couple trying their best to discipline him, make him tow the line. Then he disappeared and the old couple filed a missing persons with the police. After forty-eight hours the FBI steps in. Another agent and I went down to the Mexican district to talk to them. We walked into a mess. The old couple had been robbed and bludgeoned to death. Cops all over the place. And there was this kid standing there in shock. He said he'd gone to a movie and come home to find his grandparents dead and the apartment ransacked."

Sullivan took a drag on his cigarette. "Some of the cops really got into doing the third degree on the kid because he was a Mexican. I knew right away there was no way he could have done it. There was something about him. I told the cops to lay off. I worked hard to get the kid off the hook and to track down the missing relative. Took me the better part of five months to locate this cousin and get a confession that he had gone berserk when the grandparents caught him stealing money and he had bludgeoned them to death. The kid I got off was Castro. We got to be friends. I think all of that was why he became a policeman."

"So that explains Castro's unusual empathy. It's happened to him."

"He's a good cop. My wife used to say that he was the only person she knew for sure was incorruptible." Sullivan paused, his eyes burdened with pain.

Evelyn glanced at her watch. It was clearly time to go. "I have to make some calls to Dallas, so I'll go back to my hotel. If it's all right with you, I'll come over about six so I can meet with Castro, too. You haven't agreed to take the case yet. Maybe after we hear what Castro has, we'll have some things to talk over. Could I take you to dinner?"

Sullivan looked at her as if she were a stranger, and then his face cleared as quickly as it had clouded. He didn't want to go out to dinner. Truth was, he could care less about eating another meal with her, but she needed to hear firsthand what Castro might find, so a concession was in order. "I'll cook."

"I don't want you to go to any trouble for me."

"No trouble, I assure you. I like to cook. I'm a pretty good one, too. I unwind in the kitchen. All that chopping, mincing, and mixing is good therapy."

Yet another paradox, Evelyn thought. The man was most unpredictable. "See you at six, then. Shall I bring red or white wine?"

Sullivan laughed. "You never miss a beat, do you? Red." He glanced around the patio, noticing the place looked a little overgrown. If he could find his shears, he might do some clipping later. Karin had liked gardening and kept the place immaculate. His domain had been the kitchen. He thought of his favorite recipe—beef stew in Burgundy with a Parmesan crust. Karin had even cultivated parsley and basil for his dishes.

Evelyn got her purse and started for the door. "Only a few more hours and we'll know something."

Sullivan didn't want to dampen her spirits; neither did he want to give her false hope. "Could find something, could not . . . long odds there. We'll see what we see. There could be no two names alike on those lists. If there's nothing suspicious about any of them and all are accounted for, we'll have reached the end of the line. Your sister was probably just the killer's random choice. I want you to realize that."

Back at the hotel, Evelyn dialed Carole Wheeler's number, expecting to get her answering machine but instead found a live voice on the line. Carole had been occupied at her desk since six with research on condors and their danger of extinction. She was ready to polish off her assignment with a visit to the San Diego Zoo, complete with photographer.

"Sorry I can't have lunch. You see, my editor has given me another zinger of a story. The condor is close to becoming extinct, and one was just born . . . excuse me . . . hatched . . . so guess who gets to cover this big event? I'd like to meet with you after I finish."

They agreed to rendezvous in front of the lion's cages at twelve. Evelyn felt the need to tell the reporter about Captain Gordon's attitude and how she'd been compelled to hire a private investigator. Plus, having another woman's opinion, especially one knowledgeable on the subject of crimes involving women, might prove beneficial.

Following her map, Evelyn arrived early, bought a hot dog and sat on a green wooden bench facing the lions. A cub, paws too large for his body, rolled over, then sprang forward, frisky in the bright morning sun. An older lion stood on a tall rock and stretched majestically, his wise eyes surveying the confined area. The animal smell was rank. Across the way tropical birds screeched in the aviary. Children giggled and threw peanuts at the monkeys.

Carole appeared on the hill and walked down the sloping sidewalk. A bright vision in a blue and orange full-skirted print dress, she scanned the area and waved to Evelyn as if they were old friends.

She sat down next to Evelyn, holding a large paper cup filled with a strawberry-colored drink. "Hi. Hope I'm not late. I'm a real nut about punctuality. And deadlines, too. It's my saving grace."

"I got here early. Would you like a hot dog?" Evelyn turned to the vendor's cart.

"No, thanks. You wouldn't believe the parts they use." She pulled out a Kleenex filled with sunflower seeds, spread them on the bench and popped a few in her mouth. "Want some?"

Smiling, Evelyn shook her head. "You eat enough health food and it'll kill you."

Munching away, Carole said: "I'm glad you called. You've been on my mind. Anything happening with the case?"

"I've got someone considering working on it, and I've decided to stay here to do what I can to get the investigation going. I have a feeling this man is going to take the case."

"Who is it? Most private dicks are schmucks or con artists."

"This one's not," Evelyn hedged. "He comes highly recommended. Knows about police work." Sullivan had been so reluctant, not actually saying he would take the case, that Evelyn didn't feel at liberty to reveal his name.

"Is Gordon doing anything useful?"

"I doubt he'll do any more than he has to under regulations." Evelyn watched a Japanese tour group, cameras around their necks, admire the lions.

"You're right about that. And biased! Thinks all women are whores just because he sees so many brought in. What an asshole! That's not to say he's not smart. He's one shrewd son of a bitch. Strictly out for number one and what makes him look good." She pointed to herself. "Me, I know. If I were a man, I'd get a little more respect around the old station house. Same at my office. My editor gives all the juicy stuff to the male reporters. Wants me to stick with fluff. Condors, for Christ sakes! Covers up his prejudice in assignments by saying he needs a woman's point of view on a certain subject . . . da de da . . . etcetera."

Carole downed half of her drink in one gulp. She had a roguish animation, like a leprechaun, that intrigued Evelyn. She was dressed like a funky fortune teller, even down to the scarf knotted to one side of her orange curls. Rings on every finger, bracelets on each arm clanging as she gestured.

"You mentioned when we met that you might be able to help me if I decided to get involved with the case. I don't know exactly what you had in mind . . ."

At that moment a clown selling balloons materialized. Both shook their heads, then he pulled out some postcards. He quickly moved on when he spotted better prospects. Evelyn resumed.

"Your project—'The Woman in the Case,' that you intend turning into a book if the newspaper series doesn't pan out— especially the part about how circumstances surrounding a

crime could be misconstrued and put the victim in a bad light—
How'd you get on that subject? Have you done any research
on it?''

Carole pursed her lips. ''Well, there was a big murder case
here a few years back. Prominent woman found strangled in
her car way out in the boonies, a secluded area in the hills
known as a lovers' parking place. Not raped, but semen all
over her. Looked like a classic case of picking up some
stranger for sex, then changing her mind. He got angry,
strangled her, then did his business all over her. That's the
way the papers played it. Ruined her reputation, disgraced her
husband and kids. Turned out she had an appointment at a
nursery up in that area to pick out some plants, got lost and
stopped to ask a guy on the road for directions. He jumped in
the car with her. The landscape man didn't know her and
didn't connect her to the name listed in his appointment book.
When the police caught the guy trying to do the same thing to
another woman, he admitted to the first crime. Then the
landscape man made the connection and came forward with
his information. It was a little late. The damage was done.''

Evelyn let out a rush of air. ''Such an injustice.'' Tracking
down Sara's killer would surely prove something just as
innocent had happened to her. Birds screeched in the
background.

''Nobody ever said life was fair.'' Carole clicked her tongue.

Turning to Carole, Evelyn leaned forward. ''There's another case similar to my sister's. There could be a connection
between the two.'' She told Carole about the Kenworth case.

Frowning, Carole rested her arms on her knees and leaned
toward Evelyn. ''The two cases do have the same earmarks.
If there's a connection—one man out there committing multiple murders—we have here a serial murderer.'' She leaned
back against the bench. ''Jesus!''

''A similarity in murders always points to that possibility.
Now and then that type of killer crops up, and they cut a
bloody swath before they're stopped.'' Evelyn finished the
last of her hot dog, wadded the paper napkin and dropped it
in a trash can. ''To me, it figures some psycho, certainly a
stranger to her, murdered my sister. Rape or robbery certainly
wasn't the motive in Sara's case, unless the murderer got

scared off for some reason. I think Captain Gordon attaches some sort of sexual note to Sara's murder, maybe holds the thought that she gave some stranger the 'come-on.' '' Since the fact that Sara was discovered nude wasn't in the paper, Carole would have no way of knowing it, and Evelyn wasn't about to mention it.

"Yeah, like they always do when some woman gets raped. Blame her for egging some joker on."

"Just like the case you told me about, Gordon might even think that after Sara picked up some stranger, she had second thoughts, turned him down and it so infuriated him that he stabbed her. But, if there's a connection to the Fort Worth woman's murder, what does that suggest to you?"

Carole rolled her eyes. "That your sister was an innocent victim, singled out by the murderer for some reason."

"Most psycho killers go for the same type of victim over and over again, victimize a certain type because of something in their own background." Evelyn sighed, the full impact of her statements hitting hard. A serial killer on the loose foreboded more murders to come. "All mass murderers or serial killers have a tattoo," she said idly. "Isn't that an interesting quirk?"

"Yeah . . . really odd, like they have to mark themselves with an identity." Carole flicked at a leaf that had fallen from a tree. "How do you know about these things?"

Evelyn told Carole about her master's degree.

"That's terrific." Carole interjected. "I like to see women do things, especially when they don't have to. Now . . . your sister arrived alone at the hotel, just like the Fort Worth woman. Does Gordon know about this other case?" Carole raised her pumpkin-colored eyebrows.

"No, he doesn't."

"What if there's no connection with the other case? Maybe the killer has some vendetta against your family. You don't think you could be in any danger?"

"I don't think so. Now, if he were a serial killer, as I said, he would go for the same type of woman. Sara and I weren't anything alike." From what the Fort Worth woman said about her niece, Evelyn couldn't help but make comparisons to her sister.

"You might be betting a lot on that theory."

Evelyn looked at Carole, considering what she said. It was a bet she had to make.

"This is really grist for my own mill." She gazed across the tree-shaded area, deep in thought.

"I'm going to stay here as long as it takes to get to the bottom of this. I have to admit staying in a hotel alone makes me a touch uneasy."

Carole snapped her fingers. "Just happens that I have a friend who is going to China for six weeks on an assignment for *Time*. He's frantic about leaving his apartment with nobody to look after his plants. I, like a sap, volunteered to water them for him. I'll have to drive from one end of San Diego to the other to take care of his jungle and whisper sweet nothings in their leaves. You'd be doing me a favor it you'd house-sit."

"I don't think I could accept such an offer. I would like to have a kitchen. It's handy. Maybe the hotel has a suite with one."

"Yeah, but you said staying in a hotel makes you uneasy. I can't blame you, either. You should see my friend's place."

"I don't want to impose. I could find my own apartment."

"Look, they're not easy to come by in San Diego, especially nice ones . . . especially ones on a short-term basis. This is perfect for you. Really you'd be doing *me* a great favor, too."

"Well . . ." Evelyn hesitated. She was still reluctant to accept.

"Come on," Carole smiled. "It's a 'fit' from both sides."

Evelyn shrugged. "Be sure it's okay with your friend first."

"I will, but I know him. It'll be fine."

"Okay. A deal. When could I move?"

"I'll check with him and let you know." Carole held up her hand, the bracelets rattling. "Well, I've got to be moving. Got a little more work to do."

The two parted company in the parking lot, and Evelyn drove back to her hotel. She picked up her messages at the front desk. Walking down the hall to her room after she got off the elevator, she shuffled through them, stopping when she came to one from Quinn Stewart. The call to him was going to be difficult.

Evelyn knew Quinn Stewart always had her best interests at heart when it came to running Cypress Oil and handling her personal financial affairs. He would not be pleased when she told him what she was going to do. He would urge her to return to Dallas. And it was going to be hard to resist his pressure.

For years, Quinn Stewart had been Andrew Casey's second in command, serving as president of Cypress while Andrew was chairman of the board. A brilliant negotiator and a shrewd tactician, Quinn contributed to the spectacular success of the company. After Andrew Casey's fatal heart attack, Quinn Stewart succeeded him as head of the company.

There had always been a strong but unacknowledged attraction between Evelyn and Quinn, but, out of loyalty to Andrew and Stewart's wife, of whom Evelyn was fond, nothing had come of it. When Quinn and his wife separated six months after Andrew's death, Evelyn had detected a subtle, but distinct change in Quinn's attitude. He had become almost proprietary and overly protective not only of her financial interests but also of her personally. More and more she had become dependent on his counsel and unwavering devotion, but she tried hard not to let it show.

In her room, Evelyn first decided to call her housekeeper, Mary, to send more clothes. Then, she called Quinn who, to her relief, was out of the office. Her life in Dallas seemed far away and Quinn Stewart a distant presence. Almost as distant as Andrew.

Evelyn checked her watch, then slipped her shoes off and stretched across the bed, thinking about Hawk Sullivan. The root of his problem was probably related to his wife's death, she decided. She suspected he was a man who once had a big appetite for life. Closing her eyes, she drifted off.

When she woke, she wasn't sure where she was. Someone was knocking on the door. Her eyes searched for the telephone. Heart pounding, she jumped off the bed and grabbed the telephone, clutching the receiver as through it were a weapon. The base of the phone slid off the table and clunked on the floor.

"Who is it?" Was this how it happened to Sara, she thought in frightened confusion? Had she fallen asleep and without thinking, opened the door?

"Housekeeping," a female voice responded. "Fresh towels."

She remembered Gordon's words. "Fruit from the management. A package. Boom! Open the door and someone's in."

Evelyn stood rooted to the spot. "I have enough towels, thank you." She looked at the receiver in her hand, a symbol of her loss of control. The anxiety attack she experienced pointed to her high-pitched state of mind.

She should take a shower, she told herself, and dress for dinner, but she couldn't move. She knew she was due at Hawk Sullivan's soon, but she didn't want to leave the safety of the room. To open the door. To walk down the deserted corridor. Someone with a knife might be waiting.

Sinking into a chair, she waited for the panic to subside. Gradually, her heartbeat returned to normal, and she began to chide herself for being so foolish. She replaced the phone on her night table.

When she was calm, Evelyn went to the bathroom, turned on the shower and slipped out of her clothes, leaving them in a heap on the floor. Something she never did at home. The hot, pulsing water soothed her.

Purposely keeping her eyes away from Sara's luggage, Evelyn pulled a simple, cream-colored silk dress from the closet. Dressed, she grabbed a matching sweater, draped it across her shoulders and hesitated in front of the door.

She opened it and looked out, first to the right and then to the left, where, at the far end of the hall, she saw a maid pushing a linen cart. A man waited near the elevator. She closed the door, checked the knob to make sure it had locked, then proceeded to the elevator.

As she approached the man, he turned away, providing only a glimpse of profile. He was impeccably groomed, his suit expensive and well tailored to his tall, lean frame. When the elevator doors opened, he stepped back, allowing Evelyn to enter. She turned to face him. Then, as if he'd forgotten something in his room, he whirled around and hurried down the hall. But in that split second, Evelyn had seen a strikingly handsome face with high cheekbones and dark almond-shaped eyes. The man's skin was tan, straight black hair gleaming in the faint hallway light. He looked foreign, Evelyn thought, as the elevator descended. The doors opened and Evelyn hurried through the brilliantly lit lobby to claim her car that had been brought from the garage.

Sliding behind the wheel, she envisioned the computers that had been clattering away that afternoon, spilling out information that would point the way to Sara's killer. She accelerated, anxious to get to Sullivan's to hear what Castro had found.

CHAPTER 4

EVELYN SAW that Hawk Sullivan's front door stood wide open. The house was ablaze with lights within and the dusk outside reverberated with the coloratura aria from Mozart's *The Magic Flute*. On the doorstep, she stopped as the Queen of the Night performed vocal gymnastics that made her shiver with pleasure. She made her way back to the kitchen, clutching a bottle of wine in a brown paper bag, knowing it made no sense to attempt to be heard over the bravura filling the air.

Dressed in gray flannel trousers, a crisp gray-and-blue striped, open neck shirt and a white ruffled apron that strained across his chest, Hawk was drying individual lettuce leaves on paper towels and humming tonelessly with the music, his foot tapping. For the first time, he looked well-groomed and carefully dressed. His feet in the freshly polished loafers were sockless.

He glanced up and waved a lettuce leaf at Evelyn. "Get yourself a drink at the bar. Te Kanawa's great, isn't she? Really belts it out." The aria ended and Hawk found himself shouting. He laughed sheepishly. "I guess when you go in to get your drink, you could turn the volume down a bit."

59

"It's okay. I love *The Magic Flute*." Evelyn sniffed the rich, spicy aroma. "Whatever you're cooking smells divine."

"Tastes pretty damn good, too, if I do say so myself. We can eat in half an hour. Manny said he'd be a little late getting by."

In the den, Evelyn walked to the bar. A crystal tumbler was set out next to the ice bucket and a saucer containing two twists and two onions. After she made her drink, she looked around. There was no mistaking it. The room had been put in order and tidied up. Tabletops shone, and magazines and books were neatly piled. It pleased her to think it might have been done for her benefit. When she returned to the kitchen, Hawk was just draining his glass.

"Can I get you another?"

"Nope. Thanks. I'll get it myself." Sullivan left the room.

Evelyn walked to the door that opened onto the patio where they'd had breakfast. The table was set for two; tall hurricane lamps held candles already lit. The tape stopped, and moments later, she heard the opening notes of a Mozart piano concerto.

"Time for a change of pace," Sullivan said, looming in the doorway. "Opera to cook by. Piano to eat by. But always Mozart. I'll open the wine and let it breathe."

Evelyn nodded and watched while he deftly extracted the cork. Suddenly she felt uncomfortable. The situation was intimate, having dinner at Sullivan's as if they were old friends or more. It was strictly business, she told herself. Nothing more. Two people mutually involved in a case, waiting for Castro's information.

"Listen, I've decided to take the case if something comes from the info Manny's bringing over, so we'd better talk business. Three hundred a day plus expenses."

"Three hundred? But that doesn't sound like enough. I know what kind of fees you've received in the past. I want to be fair."

"That's the figure."

"What made you decide to take the case."

Sullivan shrugged. "Nothing better to do right now."

"But you told me you had other posibilities."

"Hey, what is this? The third degree? You came here

begging me to take the case. Offered me any price. So, I'm accepting your offer. What's the problem?'' Sullivan finished his drink, turned on his heel, and walked to the bar in the den.

Evelyn stood still, her mind rapidly reviewing the exchange. She had come too close. He was right. It was none of her business what his reasons were for taking the case.

"I'm sorry. I didn't mean to intrude. I was just curious, that's all.''

Sullivan stood in the middle of the room, glass in hand, his irritation obvious. "No big deal. Forget it. Finish your drink and we'll eat. Why don't you go out on the patio and have a seat, enjoy the sunset.''

Dismissed, Evelyn slipped out the door and took her place at the table. Twenty minutes passed. Darkness closed in around her and the flickering candles on the table. Then, Sullivan opened the kitchen door with his foot and pushed through, carrying a steaming, earthenware casserole, his hands protected by a pair of dirty dishtowels.

"Ouch! Damn it!'' He placed the dish on the table with a thud and returned to the kitchen without another word. Evelyn eyed the bubbling contents with appreciation.

Sullivan brought out the wine, bread, butter, and salad in two trips. "Beef stew with a parmesan crust.'' Seating himself, he reached for Evelyn's plate. "Hungry?''

"Starved.'' She watched him serve her a generous portion.

After he served himself, he examined the label on the wine bottle. He held the bottle at arm's length toward the light, squinting. Evelyn wondered how he'd look wearing reading glasses.

"French. Saint-Emilion 1977. Very serious wine. The '78 is almost as good and half the price.'' He half filled Evelyn's glass, then his own, and raised his glass. "To law and order.''

Evelyn touched her glass to his and tasted the wine. It was perfect, like drinking velvet. She watched Sullivan dive into his meal, fork in one hand, and in the other, a generous chunk of French bread, which he periodically dipped into the sauce in his plate. As at breakfast, he didn't speak while he ate, so intense was his concentration on food. Evelyn wondered if this was the result of eating alone. She ate silently herself, eager for Castro's arrival.

His plate clean, Sullivan leaned back in his chair, savoring the wine.

"Ready for seconds?"

"It's delicious, but I don't think I could eat anymore."

"Are you one of those women always worrying about weight and picking at food?"

Evelyn had no response. She had just consumed a full plate of stew, a salad, and a large butter-soaked slice of garlic bread and had never been on a diet in her life. At five feet five, Evelyn carried her figure well and never worried about weight. A swimmer and runner since her early teens, she had always been fit with good muscle tone.

"You know," Sullivan continued, as though speaking to himself or no one in particular, "food is very important. Sharing a meal is an almost spiritual thing."

Evelyn blinked. Did he really think he was sharing a meal? She allowed him to proceed without interruption, wondering where this stream of consciousness would carry him.

"People who don't care about food, people who think food is just a filler, fuel for the engine, are, in my opinion, sensually deficient." He focused on her empty plate. "Sure you don't want more?"

What could she say under the circumstances? "Just a little." She noticed Sullivan's almost smug self-satisfaction as he ladled out her portion before he took his.

"Tell me about your sister. What was she really like?"

Evelyn started to say something, then hesitated.

"Describe your sister. I've seen what she looked like, but it's important to the case for me to know all about her personality."

"I've told you Sara was shy, almost timid. She lived with my husband and me. Worked at Cypress Oil. And she was a moral person." Evelyn twisted her napkin as she talked. "She didn't have any enemies . . . never hurt anyone, but herself . . ."

Sullivan saw a dull hurt in Evelyn's face. "I know it pains you to say something negative, but try to be impartial. Go on. It's necessary."

Evelyn looked directly into those eyes of Sullivan. They seemed different, not as burned out and dead as before, urging her to continue. "Sara was insecure, lived in a fantasy world. Constantly went to movies alone, sometimes seeing the same picture over and over. Made up things to compensate because she couldn't face reality. One time I asked one of the single men in the office to take Sara to the company Christmas party. She wouldn't go, faked the flu. She was overweight, not without potential, but too lazy to work at it. She smoked constantly to avoid eating, then she'd go on chocolate binges. She could never come to grips with anything, couldn't even decide what to wear. Changed two or three times before she went to work. She was assistant personnel director. Good at her job . . . could pick the right person and fit them in the proper job slot, but her judgment didn't spill over into the outside world." Voicing such views hurt Evelyn. Exploring such an assessment further suddenly implied to Evelyn that she had failed in helping Sara. Like some parents with good intentions, she might have robbed Sara of her independence. If Sara had been a different person, she might not be dead. And, if she hadn't insisted on the trip, for Sara's benefit coupled with her own selfish reasons, she certainly wouldn't have been murdered. Recoiling from the thought that haunted her, Evelyn continued.

"I tried to protect her, shield her from the hurts of this world, encourage her to develop herself. I guess we all do with someone we love."

Evelyn looked right at Sullivan, giving him the feeling she was also telling something important about herself. To him, it seemed this self-confident woman suddenly seemed vulnerable. The rise from a small-town girl without means to the world of wealth and status could not have been achieved as smoothly as it appeared.

Sullivan glanced out over his garden, then back. "I guess we all try to protect people we love, sometimes to a fault."

Sullivan knew Evelyn's observations about her sister weren't made easily and without a toll, recriminations even, from misplaced blame. What was good opportunity to one, devastated another. With what few resources she had in the beginning, Evelyn had succeeded, while her sister, given every opportunity, had failed to take advantage of what was so freely offered.

Sullivan picked up his fork. "You know, I think people are destined to be what they are. No one can make them into something they aren't. The old genes versus environment theory. People with the same heritage can be completely different no matter what the circumstances." He and Evelyn stared at each other for a long moment, then she blinked and looked away.

Silence reigned as they resumed eating. After they finished, Hawk went to make coffee. Evelyn lingered over the last of her wine, thinking over what she'd said about Sara. When Sullivan reappeared, Castro was with him.

"Good evening, Mrs. Casey."

"Evelyn, please."

Castro pulled up a chair from the darkened perimeter of the patio and sat next to her while Sullivan poured coffee from a glass expresso pot. Castro drained his cup in one gulp and Sullivan refilled it. Then Castro picked up the worn briefcase he had dropped next to his chair and pulled out a manila folder. "Here's the Marley file."

Sullivan reached for it, pushing his plate aside. He moved the hurricane lamp close to the folder, which he opened on the table. He flipped through the contents, his eyes scanning each page.

"After I gathered everything you wanted, Xeroxed the file, I ran into Gordon. He was leaving for the day. He commented on my working so late."

"Big deal. Like I said this morning, you're working on your own time," Sullivan commented without hesitation. "Wouldn't hurt to write up a 'Five,' just to cover all bases," he added.

Evelyn asked about a 'Five.' Without raising his eyes from the papers, Sullivan told her it was a supplementary investigation report, an obscure law enforcement procedure documenting evidence uncovered by an officer when working on his own time. He added that most detectives, especially those not sticklers for rules, neglected to file such reports, but in this case it seemed necessary.

"Have you looked at the reports from the airlines, Manny?"

"No, haven't had time. I just picked them up. The L.A.P.D. printout off the computer states that Mary Kenworth wasn't raped or robbed. No leads."

"Sara Marley did arrive safely at the San Diego airport and rode in a cab alone to the hotel. Both facts point away from the airline theory, so it didn't dawn on Gordon to check it out. Still, I'm interested in the airline's computer printout."

Unconsciously Sullivan groped for the wine glass, missed his mark, and caressed some invisible cylinder. He glanced away from his papers to make contact and sipped idly.

"Both flights originated in Dallas." Sullivan said to himself. "Sixteen people in first class on both flights," he continued, running his finger down the list.

"By the way, I added the Kenworth data to the Marley file, noting the possibility of a connection between the two crimes. It's only fair."

"I hope they appreciate you, Manny." Sullivan rambled on with his commentary. "Passengers and addresses. Stewardesses included. Methods of payment. Seat assignments . . ." he stopped. The gears of his mind seemed to have shifted and locked into some distant position.

"What is it?" Evelyn moved to the edge of her chair. "Sara's seatmate . . . who was it?"

Ignoring her question, Sullivan picked up the second flight list and laid the two side-by-side. The frown between his eyes deepened.

"What have you got, Sullivan?" Castro wanted to know.

Sullivan snapped back to reality. He looked directly at the anxious pair. "Sara Marley was assigned in the smoking section seat 5A. Seat 5B was occupied by a Mark Foster who lives in San Diego. Got his address and phone right here. But . . . Mary Kenworth's seatmate was a woman, Virginia Taubman from Los Angeles. That's not conclusive, but I'd say it shakes the theory about the connection of the two cases and there are no two names alike on the lists."

"Mark Foster," Evelyn repeated the name. "He and Sara must have struck up a conversation. She could have innocently mentioned where she was staying. That's how it all happened."

"How did he get in her room?" Sullivan stared at her a

moment, then picked up the two lists again and scrutinized them like a jeweler examining stones.

Numbed by Sullivan's statement, Evelyn stared at the flickering candles.

Reaching for his wine, he gulped half of it. Something about the lists didn't feel just right. Something was locked up there that he wasn't absorbing. He heaved himself up, moved to the edge of the patio and looked out at his garden. The probability that his instinct about the list amounted to anything was so remote that he hated to lend any verbal credence whatsoever to it. In past cases when he was on to something, he had experienced this little nagging sensation that he was feeling now. He turned and faced Evelyn Casey and Castro. Call it intuition, call it experience, call it nothing. Still . . . the feeling persisted. It had never failed him before.

"This Mark Foster . . . so, okay, he's not listed on Mary Kenworth's flight." Evelyn sucked in her breath. "I know it might point to no connection between the two cases, but I feel it so strongly. Have since I read that article. It was a feeling like being dealt a hand of cards and knowing you're going to win before you picked them up." She looked at Sullivan. "Maybe there's some explanation for him not being listed on the other flight, but Mark Foster was Sara's seatmate. He's got to be . . ."

Sullivan held up his hand. "Hold it. Just hold it. Don't go jumping to conclusions."

Looking at each other, they fell silent.

Finally, Castro broke the spell. "Looks like you've got your starting point anyway."

Without comment Sullivan turned his attention to Castro. To cover all bases, he asked Castro to run both lists through the NCIC in Washington. Evelyn wanted to know what the initials meant. "National Crime Information Center," Sullivan snapped. "There were five women in first class on Sara Marley's flight, three on Mary Kenworth's. The rest of the passengers were men. If anyone on board those two flights had records, especially Mark Foster, I want to know. Manny, check DMV for any driver's license and any car registered to Mark Foster. Vital Statistics for a birth certificate. I want to know everything there is to know about Mark Foster."

Castro looked at his watch. "Got to get moving. I'll be in touch with the info, Sullivan."

Sullivan and Evelyn walked Castro to the door. After he'd gone, Sullivan moved to the bar. "Want one?"

Evelyn shook her head. Now that they had a name, a pall, rather than an excitement, had settled over the evening.

Evelyn leaned against the bar counter. "I'm just certain the two cases are somehow connected."

"Why do you keep harping on that? It's like you want them connected. Looking at facts with a slant, trying to read something into them won't serve you in the long run." Sullivan broke a kitchen match trying to strike it and threw his unlit cigarette down on the counter. "What good is it for them to be connected? It doesn't make it any easier to catch your sister's murderer."

Evelyn turned sideways, not looking at Sullivan. "Because Sara was found nude, Gordon tacks a sexual scenario to her murder."

"What the hell do you care what Gordon thinks. Maybe you'd better examine your own motives."

"Sara was my sister. Don't you think I'd know how she'd behave?" Evelyn sighed. "It's clear you don't think the cases are connected."

Sullivan slugged down most of his drink and wiped his mouth with the back of his hand. "I don't know what I think right now."

"The connection of the two cases could have pointed to the possibility of a serial murderer starting a pattern. Sara and the Fort Worth woman would be innocent targets, picked because of some reason. That throws an entirely different light on the case."

Sullivan placed his hands on the counter, widening his fingers. "Maybe, maybe not. Look, I don't want to be rough, but to get to the bottom of things sometimes you have to be. Facts have to be faced no matter what the expense. If there is a connection between the two cases, there still could be sexual overtones. Those two women got hung up with the killer some way." Sullivan picked up his cigarette, rummaged in a drawer and found a book of matches.

Sullivan's suggestion struck Evelyn like a stab wound.

Sara's brutal murder was hard enough to accept without facing the possibility that it was committed under lurid circumstances. It had been a mistake to think she'd found a loophole to escape the sexual implications through a serial killer theory.

"I knew my sister . . . What are you thinking about Mark Foster? Are you going to question him?"

His face gave nothing away, eyes squinted against smoke from the cigarette dangling at the corner of his mouth. "Something like that. It's got to be the right approach. We've got his address, but who knows? Maybe he's left town."

"Even if he has left town, maybe you can track him down. Don't you agree?" Evelyn clasped her arms together, hugging her chest. "I think he's right here and you'll get him. He has no idea we're on to him."

"All this airplane business could be an exercise in futility, might not have anything to do with the actual killer. Your sister could still be just a random choice. I hope you'll keep that in mind." Sullivan didn't want to even consider how serious the situation could get if a serial killer was involved. They were the most vicious, cunning and elusive of all murderers.

"Have you got any ideas about how to approach Mark Foster?"

"I'm thinking about it. I can't just go barreling up to a possible murder suspect and start asking questions about your sister."

Evelyn picked up the telephone book and flipping to the F's, ran her finger down the list. She looked up at Sullivan, face clouding. "There's no Mark Foster listed. Oh, no. Maybe it's a fictitious name. Maybe there is no Mark Foster."

"Try Ellen Brooks. The airline printout shows his ticket was paid for with a credit card belonging to a Mrs. Ellen Brooks."

Evelyn turned to the front of the book. "Here's an E. Brooks. What was Mark Foster's address on the printout?"

The number was already imprinted on Sullivan's brain. "Sixty-four-five Kelvin."

"That's it! Right here. I wonder what's the connection between the two?" She was filled with renewed hope.

Evelyn tried to make eye contact, but Sullivan concentrated

on mixing another drink. He spilled ice cubes on the floor, then scooped them up and threw them in the sink. He splashed Jack Daniels on the counter as he missed his glass.

He ruminated on a swallow, rearranged bottles and glasses on the shelves and otherwise busied himself with actions he hoped concealed how industriously he was employing the time to absorb and think. He knew from experience that when things looked simple and easy, that's when they got hard and complicated.

"I'd still like to help you."

"You've said that and we made a deal. Remember?"

Evelyn made no response.

Sullivan looked at Evelyn Casey. There might be a lot of leg work to do. Routine checking and double checking. It seemed bullheaded of him, he reflected, to refuse her help. She was obviously an intelligent woman and had some background that might even prove complementary to his own. Her help might speed the investigation, and time was an important factor. The trail, already cold, could grow even colder. He stared into his glass. Reluctantly he acknowledged there was more to it than that. He liked Evelyn Casey. She was a fighter, persistent—qualities he admired.

Sullivan glanced at the picture on the desk. Karin would have liked Evelyn and her determination. She had been a determined lady herself. Right to the end. His eyes smarted, and he looked away from the face that had given him as much joy as it had sorrow.

"If you'll grab your purse, I'll drive you back to the hotel, then return your car to you tomorrow."

Evelyn smiled. "Really, I'm not afraid of going back alone." She wasn't going to admit how uneasy she felt.

"Maybe not, but it goes against my grain to let a lady drive around in a strange city when it's dark." He held out his hand for the car keys.

Back at the hotel, Evelyn found a message from Quinn Stewart: "Call tonight, regardless of the hour." It was just eleven in Dallas, but Evelyn debated making the call. It might appear she had not spent the night at the hotel if she didn't. Reluctantly, she examined that thought. Insecurity, rooted in her background, might have caused her to place too much emphasis on others' opinions, wanting acceptance and approval in the world into which she'd climbed, no inappropriate shadows cast, excelling far beyond the norm to show she could. Maybe Sullivan had been correct in suggesting she examine her own motives concerning the sexual implication Gordon attached to Sara's murder. She took Sara's picture from her wallet, looked at it, then tucked it away. Picking up the phone, she dialed.

"Quinn, I hope it's not too late."

"No, I've been waiting for your call." His relief was audible.

"Is there some emergency?"

"No, no, but I was concerned about you and wanted to know what your plans are."

"Well, I've hired a private investigator, and we're looking into a link between Sara's murder and a similar crime in Los Angeles just two days later. I'm planning on staying here as long as I can to assist the investigator." Evelyn felt good that Sullivan had said she might be of some help.

"Assist the investigator? Evelyn, what on earth are you doing? Who is this investigator? What financial arrangements have you made?"

Evelyn hesitated. Though she had expected opposition, she found it difficult to justify herself without sounding defensive. "Hawk Sullivan is his name, an ex-FBI agent. He was recommended highly by the detective handling the case here. I'm paying him three hundred a day plus expenses. More than reasonable. Anyway, Quinn, it's important to me in a personal way to find Sara's murderer."

"Evelyn, you're being irrational. Obsessive. It's not like you. You've got to try to put this thing behind you. The strain's too much. I want you to come home to be with me, your friends, where you belong."

"Quinn, please stop and listen to me. What may seem irrational to you is important to me. I feel responsible for what happened to Sara. Whether I should or not is irrelevant. I do. I have to find her murderer."

"And what if you don't? How long will you continue to pursue it?"

"I'm going to stay here for as long as I think I should."

Quinn was silent. Evelyn began counting slowly. She knew the ploy he used when opposed. He said nothing, counting to ten, waiting for his adversary to cave in. They generally did at seven or eight, he had told her. She counted to ten.

"I think I should fly out tomorrow, meet this investigator."

"No, Quinn. That's not necessary. I don't want you to do that. I'm going to move into an apartment right away. I'll call you and give you the telephone number."

"An apartment?" Quinn was incredulous. "I see."

Evelyn bit her lip, suppressing the urge to say, "No, you don't." "Quinn, you know how much I appreciate your concern, how much you've done for me since Andrew died . . . how you've held Cypress Oil together. I could never have managed without you."

"You don't ever have to, Evelyn."

Evelyn visualized Quinn Stewart, handsome and correctly attired in a dark, pin-striped suit, crisp white shirt, regimental-striped tie, a solid man, representing security, stability. A picture of Hawk Sullivan flashed through her mind.

"Thanks, Quinn. I'll keep you informed."

"I stand and wait."

So do I, she thought. Everything depended on Hawk Sullivan. Tomorrow might offer some answers.

CHAPTER 5

CAPTAIN DANIEL GORDON strode up the steps to the front door of the station house shortly before nine o'clock, carrying the morning paper tightly rolled to the thickness of a billy club. A pair of green globes flanked the wooden entrance doors. The doorknobs were the original brass ones that had been installed when the building was new, sometime in the twenties. Gritting his teeth, Gordon grabbed a knob, jerked open the door and stepped into the large muster room.

The high desk on the left side of the cavernous room looked like a judge's territory except for the waist-high railing before it and the uniformed man behind it. On one side it was framed by a sign that requested all visitors to stop and state their business, and on the other by an open ledger that held the booking records of the criminals who passed that way. The desk was manned by Sergeant Stires. He looked up as Captain Gordon passed the desk.

"Morning, sir."

Gordon nodded and kept going down the hall to his office, slapping his thigh with the rolled paper. He seated himself at his desk, unrolled the newspaper and opened it, carefully smoothing the curling pages. His stomach had contracted around his breakfast of syrup-soaked pancakes and sausages. Snatching open a drawer, he pulled out a tube of Rolaids and popped one in his mouth. He crunched down, breaking the sweet disc into bits. He then reread the article whose headline declared: SOCIALITE SISTER OF MURDER VICTIM TAKES LAW INTO HER OWN HANDS.

Gordon stared up at the ceiling. That fucking pair of women could roast in hell, as far as he was concerned. He knew Evelyn Casey was trouble from the minute he laid eyes on her. And the redheaded bitch . . . oh, but the third party . . . that's who he was going to get. Leaning forward, he punched his intercom.

"Have Lieutenant Adams come in here. Tell him to check the Xerox log to see who's signed it and bring the Sara Marley file."

Shortly, Lieutenant Adams poked his blond crew cut around the door. "Captain?"

"Come on in, Adams." Adams was what Captain Gordon thought of as a policeman's policeman. Steady, honest, dedicated, not always aspiring like that Mexican, but satisfied with his position and completely American. Those qualities fit Gordon's requirements precisely. Adams knew judo the way he knew the Penal Code and could lay a suspect on his back faster than any six men using fists.

"Have you read the fucking morning paper?"

"No, sir." Adams stood before Gordon's desk, shoulders squared, light from the above fluorescent bouncing off his freshly scrubbed, ruddy face. His hand grasped a manila folder.

"Sit down, Adams. I'll tell you what it says. It's that Carole Wheeler with a byline called 'The Wheel.' Real cute, huh? She's been talking to this woman, Evelyn Casey. She's the sister of the deceased in the Sara Marley case. You know, the one stabbed in the hotel."

Adams touched the manila folder without looking at it. "File 3-6-9-12-8."

Gordon smiled. Adams made him feel like a proud father. "First the article starts off with a bunch of shit about women in crime, how it affects them . . . blah, blah. Goes on to say that the P.D. doesn't do all it could about handling things,

then . . . then, cites the Sara Marley case and states that
Evelyn Casey has had to hire someone, unnamed, who is
familiar with police work to assist her in solving the case.
Assist her, get that. Says there's another case similar to the
Marley case. You know what the reporter is pointing to,
Adams. A serial murderer! I'll have City Hall, the mayor,
chief of police and every son of a bitch who holds public
office breathing down my neck if they think some maniac's
on the loose. The press will be calling any minute for a
statement. The fucking wire services will pick this up.''
Frowning, Gordon leaned across the desk, bracing his forearms on the edge. ''What case is similar to Sara Marley's and
just who has Evelyn Casey hired that knows about police
work?''

''Sir, I think I'd better tell you Castro put in a 'Five'
yesterday. It's in the Marley file.''

Gordon's eyes turned to flecks of glinting steel. ''I wasn't
aware that he was such a stickler for the rules. Covering his
ass is what he's doing.'' Gordon held out his hand for the
file. Leaning forward, Adams gave it to him.

''Sir, as you know, most guys don't even bother to write
up a 'Five,' and if they do, nobody pays much attention to it.
What difference does it make if a guy keeps working on a
case long as it doesn't interfere with his other duties?''

''In this case it just might, Adams. You checked the
Xerox log?''

Adams nodded. ''Yes, sir. Castro signed the Xerox log
yesterday.''

''And how many pages did he sign for? Wouldn't be 158,
would it?''

''Exactly.''

Gordon fingered the final page of the Marley report. ''What
do you think Castro's Xeroxing it for?''

''Working on his own time, like the 'Five' says. Maybe
Castro just doesn't want to give up on it.''

''Not very likely. You don't see Talbott, Castro's partner
on the case, turning in any 'Five.' ''

''Castro Xeroxing the case is not against regulations, sir.''

''It is if he showed it to anyone outside the force,'' Gordon
fired back. ''Or if he's using it for his own benefit.'' Gordon

relaxed in his swivel chair and made a sweeping gesture with his hand. "Say if someone's hired him to work on it privately . . . if Castro's taking money on the side. This Casey broad tells me she's hiring a private dick, then Castro escorts her back to the hotel. Next day he files a 'Five' on the case. What else is in the 'Five'?"

Adams gnawed on a cuticle. "All the requisitions he made are in the file. He made quite a few."

"Let's hear."

Adams face turned redder than usual. With the back of his hand, he brushed his forehead. "He put in a request to the airlines for a list of all first-class passengers on Sara Marley's flight. Included were addresses and phone numbers given by the passengers to the airlines. Methods of payments, seat assignments. Then he requested a flight list of all first-class passengers on American Airlines flight 235, May 21."

"That's strange." Gordon frowned. "Where did the flight originate and what was the destination?"

"Origination point, Dallas-Forth Worth. Destination, Los Angeles."

"May 21." Gordon bit the inside of his lip. "Two days after Sara Marley was murdered."

"Then he ran both lists through the NCIC. Next he requested the L.A.P.D. to wire a homicide report on a Mary Kenworth. He added it to the file."

Gordon nodded. "That's the similar case. Stake my life on it. But . . . how'd he get onto it? Anything else?"

"One last item, sir. Castro put a name through DMV and Vital Statistics. Mark Foster."

Gordon stared at the ceiling, jaw pulsing in and out. "Mark Foster. Just who in hell could that be?" He pulled a cigar from his pocket and chomped off the end. Lighting the stogie with a match, he then plowed through the file. "I want to see the airline lists."

Gordon huffed out a purple smoke ring, then coughed as he studied the lists. "The airplane angle. I can see what he's getting at. Sara Marley rode out here on a public conveyance and got to the hotel without incident. We were right to look in other directions."

Adams turned sideways in his chair and crossed his legs.

"I've seen guys get obsessed before, can't turn a case loose. Known some to even have a breakdown over a case they can't solve. So far, he hasn't done anything out of line."

Gordon glanced up at Adams. "I'll be the judge of that. If it isn't Castro, just who'd Evelyn Casey hire, then? Castro wanted those files for some reason. And if he's showed them to anyone else, I'll have his ass. I think he might have seen something we missed and is trying to make the most of it. Or, he's just stirring up a lot of dust making Evelyn Casey think he's doing some investigating and collecting money in the meantime."

Gordon returned to the files. "Mark Foster was Sara Marley's seatmate." He grinned. "Mary Kenworth's seatmate was a woman. No connection, there. Still, I'm curious about his idea of a connection with the Mary Kenworth case even though it doesn't seem logical after seeing the airline reports. I wonder how he got onto it? But I don't want to ask him. I don't want him suspicious of me being onto his little enterprise." If the airplane angle dawned on Castro, he should have thought of it also. "Adams, you call the newspaper and as my spokesman, deny any connection about the two cases. Tell 'em there's absolutely no evidence to link them, just pure speculation."

Gordon waved his hand at Adams, dismissing him. "Got to get back to my desk. Thanks, Adams."

After Adams left, Gordon picked up Castro's "Five" and tossed it in the wastebasket. As far as he was concerned, he never received one.

He thought for a minute before making a decision. He didn't want to make any rash moves or call attention to what information he had just yet. Then, Gordon pressed his intercom.

Low oppressive clouds hovered over the coast. The view from Sullivan's kitchen window offered sky, ocean and beach melding into a pewter glaze. Dressed in fresh khakis and old tennis shoes he sat at his breakfast table making marks with a fork on the tablecloth. He craved a cigarette but was attempting to push that first one later and later into the day. He dug a stroke into the material one way, overlapped the first with another, then paused to admire the design. He wondered what a psychiatrist might make of his doodlings. More important, he wondered what he actually made of his own observations of the Sara Marley case. He stared at the airline computer printout. Was he trying too hard to read something into the information? He gulped the remainder of his cold coffee.

The shrill ring of the phone jolted him. Leaning across the table, he grabbed the receiver from the wall set. "Sullivan, here."

"This is your free twenty-four-hour information service," Castro answered.

"And you've got?" Sullivan grabbed a cigarette and fumbled to strike a kitchen match under the tabletop.

"Nada."

Sullivan let out a plume of smoke. "Thought this was an information service."

"I've got plenty of information on what isn't. Ran both airline lists through NCIC. No records on any names popped up. Zero on Mark Foster. It's like he doesn't exist. No birth certificate registered in the state of California. Course, he could have been born in another state. No car registered to him. No voter registration. No driver's license issued to anyone by that name."

Sullivan massaged his chin. "Could be a fictitious name, then, but the woman who paid for his ticket exists. Ellen Brooks owns a credit card and is listed in the phone book. She ought to know who Mark Foster is or who he isn't. Castro, I appreciate your help. Hope I don't have to ask for more."

Sullivan stubbed out his cigarette and picked up the airline computer printout again. Mark Foster, Sara Marley's fictitious seatmate, suddenly loomed more suspicious than ever. Still, there was something else about the list that wasn't coming through. He slammed it down, got up and placed his coffee mug in the dishwasher.

Pulling on a green sweater, he glanced out of the window. Thick curtains of fog now hugged the surrounding mountains. He tried to decide if that was excuse enough not to go jogging. Already he felt defeated by the task he had laid out for himself. At least his usual headache had taken a temporary holiday. Consumed as he was with the case last night, he had drunk much less than his accustomed amount.

Evelyn Casey's rental car sat in his driveway because he hadn't wanted her out in the night alone. Now, he'd have to return it to her, which meant she'd have to drive him back, and there she'd be.

He opened the back door and strode away, erect in the early morning fog. Sticking the key in the ignition, Sullivan backed out and drove to Evelyn Casey's hotel.

Waiting in the lobby for her to come down, Sullivan sauntered over to the newsstand and bought a paper. Folding it under his arm, he stopped next to a telephone booth. Might as well give Ellen Brooks a call, he decided. His speech was ready. He dropped coins into the slot and dialed her number. A groggy female voice answered.

"Mrs. Ellen Brooks?"

She cleared her throat. "Yes. Who is it?"

"Donald Graves from the Master Charge Credit Bureau, Personal Service." He had no idea if there was such a thing and hoped she didn't either. Criminals, especially con artists, got as far as they did because people were basically gullible, would believe anything official sounding.

"I'm not over my limit, am I? I mailed in a check . . . two . . . three weeks ago."

"No, nothing like that. I just want to know if you're in possession of your card. It hasn't been stolen or anything?" He watched Evelyn Casey walk across the lobby. She couldn't possibly hear him, but he felt like an actor in a B movie. So far, Ellen Brooks was buying his spiel.

"Why?" Caution crept into her voice.

"Our service is entirely for your protection. If anything unusual pops up in our computers, we give the customer a call to make sure everything is okay."

"And what's unusual?"

"Well, let's see here . . ." He hesitated as if going over notes. "There's a charge to your card for an airline ticket in a different name from yours. A Mark Foster."

"That's my son, and it's perfectly legitimate."

So, the connection. "Your son, Mark Foster, he lives at your address?"

"Of course."

From her voice he tried to guess how old she was to determine the age of her son. Hoarse from sleep she could have been any age. He dared not press his luck with further questions that might arouse suspicions. He wanted to catch Ellen Brooks, and her son, Mark Foster, off guard.

"Hope I didn't bother you. We just want to protect you and your valuable credit."

"You're sweet . . . real sweet." The note of seduction was transparent. Ellen Brooks was going to be an easy mark.

Sullivan rang off and joined Evelyn in the lobby. Wearing a beige cable-knit sweater over matching slacks, blond hair flowing to straight shoulders, Evelyn Casey looked like a swirl of honey. Her freshly scrubbed face appeared less strained. He caught a whiff of subtle perfume that reminded him of Karin.

"Have you heard from Castro?"

Sullivan nodded. "Not encouraging." He told her about the reports.

The lobby was coming to life, people hurrying through with baggage, checking in, checking out for other destinations. Bellhops scurried about with loaded carts. A hostess pushed open wide double doors and stationed them to the wall, signaling the coffee shop was ready for business. The smell of coffee mixed with the aroma of fresh bread baking wafted through the lobby. He didn't intend to make a habit of it, but what was one more meal with her? Anyway, he was starved.

"How about some breakfast?" He started toward the door.

Evelyn hurried to keep up. "I can't operate without coffee, but I don't usually eat much breakfast."

He thought about her breakfast yesterday at his house and the meal she'd wolfed down last night. Women liked to deny they ate much. The hostess seated them at a table in the center of the room, dealt out menus and hurried to attend to other customers now crowding in. Laying the folded newspaper on the table, Sullivan told Evelyn about the phone call to Ellen Brooks.

"I do believe a lightning bolt is headed in your direction." She smiled.

He hadn't noticed what white teeth she had. Even, too. She sat erect, where some people seemed to collapse in a chair. He liked good posture. Came from his mother's training.

Evelyn picked up her menu, tracing the edges with her fingers. "What's your next step?"

"I'm going to watch Ellen Brooks's house a while, get a feel, see what's coming and going. If I get the opportunity, I'm going in and talk to Ellen Brooks and Mark Foster." Sullivan opened the menu.

"I wish I could go with you." Her eyes shone with anticipation. "A look . . . if only I could get a look at his face."

Sullivan closed his menu. "You can't go with me. This is not play. The killer knowing what you look like puts you at a big disadvantage. Damn newspaper reporters."

The waitress brought coffee and took their orders. Sullivan wanted two fried eggs and sausage, something he didn't cook at home because of the greasy mess it made. Evelyn chose dollar-size pancakes and bacon. And she had said she didn't eat much for breakfast, he noted.

He lit a cigarette, turned to the financial page of the newspaper spread out on the table, and looked up prices for stocks he had once owned. It was a senseless exercise he performed daily, but he remained curious about how much money he would have made had he been able to hold on to the securities.

Evelyn was staring out the window at the approaching clouds. "Looks like we're in for a storm. It's warm and the sun is shining in Dallas. I talked to the office this morning . . . to Quinn Stewart. He's a close personal friend and runs Cypress Oil now. When I talked to him last night, I told him about the case similar to Sara's but forgot to mention anything about Mark Foster, because we got off on another subject. This morning he called again, and I told him about Sara's seatmate. He's concerned and wants to fly out."

"And is he coming?" He certainly hoped not. Another meddler he could do without. In this case, two wasn't necessarily company, but three was definitely a crowd. Sullivan stubbed out his cigarette.

"No. Quinn's not coming. I asked him not to. I told him I

was okay." Evelyn removed her napkin from the table to allow the waitress to serve her plate.

Sullivan's eggs were fried too hard. He liked them runny, but he dug in, cutting a wedge and putting it on a toast point. As he chewed, he watched Evelyn eat. Was this Quinn Stewart someone important to her? Her expression had given nothing away. Somehow he had pictured her as a lone crusader, out there without backing trying to solve her sister's murder. He cut into a sausage. Evelyn Casey was a very attractive woman. How could he expect that she didn't have someone waiting back home? It had just never crossed his mind before now. He turned the newspaper over and continued to read.

Squinting, he laid down his fork and grabbed the paper. "Christ Almighty!" With both hands he held the paper in front of his face.

"What is it?"

Sullivan said nothing but continued to read.

When he finished, he pushed his half-eaten plate aside and lit a cigarette. Through a cloud of smoke he stared at Evelyn Casey. She was having trouble with a square of celluloid that held jelly. She tore at the corners. Looking up, she locked eyes with Sullivan. He looked as if he'd bitten into a wasp.

"What the hell were you doing talking to a reporter?" Sullivan was doing his best to keep control. He saw Evelyn's cheeks flush. They damn well ought to, he thought, and handed over the newspaper.

Evelyn raced over the article. Sullivan looked on, estimating the damage that had been done. When finished, Evelyn folded the paper and placed it next to her purse on the chair. She leaned back. He thought life must have taught her a good poker face.

"I can't believe it. Carole never said what we talked about would be in the paper. We talked about her book topic." Her voice cracked.

Sullivan took a long pull on his cigarette. "Now you're in a book? Who is this Carole? You owe me an explanation. I tried to help you, and you go louse it up by spilling everything you know. You've just compounded your problem is what you've done.'' He let all the anger he wanted spill into his voice.

Evelyn got through the explanation of how she met Carole Wheeler, then faltered, but went on to admit that she called the reporter and they made a date to meet at the zoo. She had no idea their talk would lead to the newspaper article. ''Actually the article doesn't reveal anything beyond the fact that I hired a private detective who is looking into Sara's case and a possible link to a similar murder that occurred in Los Angeles.'' Evelyn said that she was upset with Carole Wheeler, but perhaps the idea had later struck the reporter that the article might do some good.

''What good?'' Sullivan asked.

''Maybe it will keep him from killing again. The article states that there is another similar case. If there is a possible connection . . .''

''You back on that subject again?''

''I've been on it all night, and I've got some theories. If there is a connection . . .''

Sullivan cut in: ''And we don't think there is.''

''But if there is, the killer will be surprised that we've put them together . . .'' Evelyn's voice cracked again.

''And if there isn't, he'll laugh, knowing how far off we are.''

''Please let me finish.'' Evelyn leaned forward, arms resting on the edge of the table. ''If there is a connection between the two cases, it might shatter his psyche. He's thought he's had this secret all along. It might put him on the defensive, make him expose himself by making some kind of mistake. It could be a ripple effect, one isolated action setting others in motion.''

Sullivan slugged down the last of his coffee. If he was one thing at all, he was a pro. Here he sat with some tyro, listening to half-baked theories. ''You talk about a ripple effect like I haven't been in law enforcement for twenty years. Let me tell you one hard and fast rule and one you better believe in. Never open a door unless you're certain what's behind it.'' He lit a cigarette from the one he had going. ''Now let's go over the known points . . . the bad ones.'' His voice had a sharp edge. ''First, the killer already knew who you were and what you look like." He held up his hand and ticked off items on his fingers. "Now he knows you're looking for him. You've hired someone who knows about police work to help you. He thought he'd gotten away with your sister's murder, but, no, you've stirred up a hornet's nest. What's his next move?" Sullivan glared at her. "He might decide to come after you."

"I don't think so. If he's the type of killer that I'm thinking, his pattern usually doesn't change, sticks to the same type . . ."

"*Usually.* You bet your life on that word. Textbook stuff, for Christ sakes. This is real and you're dealing with a psycho who brutally stabbed your sister to death." He waved for the waitress to bring the check.

"If Mark Foster read that article this morning and if he is the killer, where do you think he is right now?" Sullivan fumbled in first one pocket, then another. He'd left his wallet on his dresser. "He's long gone. Slipped right out of my fingers because of this." He punched the article.

The waitress set down a plate with the bill on it. Sullivan stood. "You'll have to pay this. I've left my wallet at home." He turned to leave.

"Wait!" Evelyn went after him. "You're not going to drop the case? Please."

"There's probably not much case left. What there is, I'm hung with it. I can't just leave you in the lurch. You've made sure of that by making yourself a target."

He lumbered away. Again, Evelyn went after him. The waitress followed, waving the bill. People turned to stare.

"Where are you going now?" Evelyn glanced over the crowd, but then as though afraid he might disappear if she took her eyes off him, glanced back quickly.

Sullivan whipped around. "I'm going to watch that house."

"But you don't have your car." Evelyn scribbled her name and room number on the bill as the waitress glared at Sullivan. Diners had started to whisper, keeping their eyes on the trio.

"I'm going home to get it. I'll take a taxi." Sullivan stalked off.

"You don't have any money." Evelyn's tone was elevated.

People giggled.

Sullivan called out over his shoulders: "I do at home. The cab can wait 'til I get it. I'll get back to you if I learn anything."

Evelyn glanced around the crowded room. She wanted to run but turned casually, squared her shoulders and headed for the elevator.

Punching in her floor, she leaned back breathing hard. Emotions shattered, case blown sky-high, she couldn't think straight. Whatever progress she had made with Sullivan had been blown by the article.

Then, as she reached her floor, anger took control. Carole Wheeler was going to swallow the brunt of her frustrations. She marched down the hall, rammed her key in the lock, bolted the door from the inside and snatched the receiver from the cradle.

She dialed to reach outside, then punched in Carole Wheeler's number. Her answering machine informed Evelyn in a nasal twang that Carole Wheeler could be reached at *The San Diego Union*. No number was given. She slumped down on the bed, added up the situation and made change. The truth of the matter was that she was more upset by Sullivan's reaction than by the article itself. No promises of secrecy had been made at the zoo that day. Everything in the article was absolutely true. The stab at Captain Gordon secretly pleased her, but it couldn't erase the feeling that Carole Wheeler had betrayed her.

Evelyn looked up the number of the newspaper, dialed and asked for Carole Wheeler.

Carole came on the line with "Wheeler, here." Noise in the background almost drowned out her voice.

"Carole, this is Evelyn Casey." She tried to keep her tone moderate. "I read your article."

"I tried to call you earlier. How'd you like it? I turned it in as a filler, not even sure it would get printed. I try never to misquote."

"That you quoted at all surprised me. I just assumed we were speaking in confidence. I'm ticked off that you went public with our conversation. The last thing I wanted was to call attention to myself."

"More important, the killer is put on notice."

"That's exactly what the man I hired objected to . . . he's furious."

"I'll make a bet the article will end up serving a good purpose. The reason I called earlier was not only to discuss the article but also to tell you the apartment we talked about is available right away. My friend's leaving day after tomorrow."

"I may not need it now. The article may have blown the one lead we had." Evelyn wasn't about to mention Mark Foster to the reporter. She also figured at this point Carole wouldn't even ask.

"Just call me soon if you still want the apartment. I'd hate to see you lose it. Great place."

Evelyn hung up and walked to the window. She looked out at the threatening weather and thought of Sullivan, seething, alone in his car, watching the house where Mark Foster lived. She wondered when he'd call. He'd have to let her know something later today, but maybe not, not in his frame of mind. She might not hear from him for days. Mark Foster might have left town.

Depressed, she walked away from the window, thinking she might go somewhere. But where? She could shop or take in a movie, browse through an art gallery. If she left the room, she might miss Sullivan's call, if he called.

Opening the closet door, she pulled out Sara's bags and started going through the contents. There was her black dress she liked to wear for special occasions, only for Sara there hadn't been many special events. Cross-legged, she sat on the floor next to the open luggage. She clutched the dress close, the aroma of Sara's perfume faint, but still there. She felt tears coming to her eyes, warm and stinging, ready to river down her cheeks.

The rain streaked down, the sky all the colors of a prize-fighter's bruises. Sullivan's ashtray overflowed. When he cracked the window to let out smoke, he got drenched. He supposed he was lucky it wasn't cold. With the heater going he would have suffocated. About all he could say for the morning was that it had almost passed.

Thoughts of Evelyn Casey had ribboned through his mind.

No question he had intimidated her, but the newspaper article had fried him. Undoubtedly a breach had developed in whatever terms they had come to. He couldn't quite target their relationship . . . only professional, of course, he the hired help, she his employer, but still he was just beginning to like her. He lit a cigarette and hawked out a smoke ring, which quickly dissipated in the stale air.

Parked a ways down Kelvin Street, he kept his eyes burned on the small Taj Mahal that was Ellen Brooks's town house. The neighborhood was upper-middle-class, bordering on rich. Somehow it didn't seem fitting that a possible murderer lived there. He toyed with several ploys of gaining entrance, but settled on nothing specific. The credit card spiel had passed muster. Maybe it could be used again someway for an opening gambit. He concentrated on the idea of charging, of credit cards. Then, he bolted upright on the seat. He wanted to kick himself for not seeing something so obvious. Out of boredom, he was so accustomed to sedating himself with liquor that he wasn't thinking straight.

His heart gave an extra tick of excitement. The airline lists so far had been a soufflé that didn't rise. All the ingredients had been present, but the heat hadn't been turned high enough. Now he knew what had been bothering him about the lists. He turned on the ignition and gunned away. Seeing Mark Foster would have to wait.

CHAPTER 6

THE PHONE WAS RINGING as Sullivan dashed through the rain to his front door. Dripping, he duck-walked across the den rug and picked up the receiver. The airline lists lay side-by-side on his desk. He couldn't wait to get at them.

"Hello." He was almost positive the caller was Evelyn Casey.

"Sullivan, Manny. Wanted to fill you in on a piece of news. We picked up Mark Foster this morning for questioning. Talbott and I. He was my partner on the Sara Marley case. Captain Gordon called us in and told us he wanted him brought in for questioning."

Sullivan hitched in his breath and sat in the desk chair. "And?"

"Got an airtight alibi for the night of Sara Marley's murder. Was picked up at the airport by his mother, Ellen Brooks, and two men, friends and business partners of the mother. The four went to The Star of the Sea for dinner, then spent the rest of the night at the Ames Art Gallery, where Mrs. Brooks was sponsoring a show. Home around one thirty, when all the guests cleared out. He could produce a hundred witnesses if necessary."

"What did he say about Sara Marley?" Sullivan dug in his pocket for a cigarette, found a broken one and lit the largest half.

"Nothing of any value. Of course, he didn't know her name, but said he remembered the woman he sat by. She didn't say much to him, read most of the time. He didn't see her speak to anyone. Nothing out of the ordinary. Sullivan?"

"Yeah?"

"Mark Foster is a sixteen-year-old boy. A little skinny one."

"Well . . . ain't that a kick." Sullivan didn't count his day wasted. He glanced at the airline lists. "That's the reason for no driver's license, no voter registration . . ."

"And no birth certificate in the state of California. He was born in Texas. Back there visiting his father. Parents are divorced. He's a surly son of a bitch."

Sullivan fingered the lists. "Wonder how Gordon got on to this all of a sudden?"

"I asked myself more questions about that than I asked Mark Foster about himself. I turned in the 'Five.' Could have been from that, but I doubt it. Captains don't usually sit around reading those unless . . . they're suspicious about something." A note of unease laced his voice. "There was an article in the paper this morning . . ."

"Read it." Sullivan felt a flicker of irritation.

"Maybe it gave Gordon a push in another direction."

"Manny, I've got some other ideas. Something I hadn't thought about 'til a while ago. Maybe we could get together, Olga, too. For dinner or something." He was thinking of taking Evelyn Casey along.

"Give me a call. I got some free time coming."

They hung up and Sullivan placed the airline reports in front of him. Once again he felt that small stirring from within. The common denominator between the two lists stared back at him. With the exception of one name on Sara Marley's flight and one on Mary Kenworth's, all passengers paid by check or credit card. In a cashless society where people kept records for business expenses or whatever, those two names who paid with hard cash stood out. On Sara Marley's flight a man with a reservation under the name of Christopher Chalmers and on Mary Kenworth's flight a Charles Carter had paid cash for their tickets. Identical initials might be just too much to attribute to coincidence. At the time of making reservations Christopher Chalmers had given the airlines a number where he could be reached. A Dallas number. Charles Carter had done the same. Sullivan decided to call those numbers.

The number Christopher Chalmers had given, Sullivan was told by the operator, was not in service. After dialing the number Charles Carter gave, Sullivan reached a Thomas Davidson, who had never heard of Charles Carter.

Sullivan leaned back in the chair, staring at the ceiling. He burned to question Mark Foster in case the detectives had missed some fragment of information, just as they had overlooked checking out the flight list. Inconsequential things had trapped many a criminal. Maybe he'd get lucky. He'd check the stewardesses and all of the other passengers on Sara Marley's flight for a description of Christopher Chalmers. There had to be someone on the flight who remembered Christopher Chalmers, especially his seatmate, who according to the list was a Gloria Martin. Next, he'd tackle Mary Kenworth's flight to see if anyone remembered Charles Carter. If the two descriptions matched . . . a frightening thought struck him. Then another, far more disturbing than the first.

A big possibility that the two cases were connected had surfaced. Evelyn Casey deserved more credit than he'd given her. It was time for a report.

He was glad she was in and not sulking as women might. The tone of her voice suggested it was his move to set the pace. He rolled into the conversation easily, knowing she would anxiously sponge up the news.

Sullivan could tell she was disappointed that their prime suspect had been eliminated. Still, she didn't project a defeatist attitude. As she talked, Sullivan caught a note of excitement in her tone. Christopher Chalmers. Charles Carter. Fictitious names, but one in the same, she stated, conviction in her voice.

"If you're going to question Mark Foster, there's no reason I can't go with you now. He sat by Sara all the way out. I'd just like to talk to him."

Sullivan agreed, hoping she'd construe the gesture as a peace offering. She'd put the connection of the two cases together, no telling what she was capable of. He was willing to give it a limited whirl. He told her to wait for him on the sidewalk in front of the hotel and he'd pick her up in thirty minutes.

By the time they pulled up at Ellen Brooks's town house, the clouds had scattered and the late afternoon sun struggled to burn through the haze. Cars lined the driveway as if a celebration were in progress. Sullivan saw no need for deceptions this time. They walked up the aggregate concrete steps and rang the bell. Bronze urns holding poodle-cut plants flanked tall black-lacquered double doors.

The door opened. A black maid in a lace uniform said without inquiry, "Follow me." She tripped off on spike heels, bowed legs making an imaginary circle. "Brooksie's out by the pool. A few friends are over for cocktails."

Exchanging glances, Evelyn and Sullivan followed.

Brooksie, as the maid called her, was on the wrong side of forty for the scant outfit hugging her fleshy form. Expensive wrinkled leather came to mind as Sullivan inspected her skin with a quick sweep. Huge rhinestone glasses shielded her eyes from the glare. Several bikini-clad young men lounged around the pool. Sullivan wondered if Mark Foster was among them. One, hips swinging in an unmistakable gesture, sashayed to the umbrella bar for a refill.

"Thanks, sweetie." He chirped as Brooksie poured from a crystal pitcher.

Brooksie started as she spotted the new arrivals, then waved and rushed over. "You must be Elton's friends. Glad you could drop by."

"Afraid not. Mrs. Brooks?" He turned a cold appraising look to her crinkled protruding breasts. Old, they were, nothing to display.

"Brooksie," she answered and raked him over with seductive approval.

An ugly memory surfaced. Sullivan felt a small knot in his stomach. That same knot had tightened deep within when a woman much like Brooksie had tried to seduce him one rainy afternoon a million years ago. He was a rapidly ripening fourteen-year-old delivery boy, and the woman had practically trapped him inside her house. He had been frightened but excited at the prospect of experiencing something he'd only heard about. If you closed your eyes, a friend had told him, all women were alike. He did. It was pleasant. It was repulsive. It was his first. With that woman, his last. Guilt lingered a long time.

"We're here to talk to your son, Mark Foster," Evelyn said.

Sullivan realized he'd missed a beat and Evelyn had filled in.

"Who are you?" Brooksie was suddenly wary.

"I'm the sister of the murdered woman your son was questioned about this morning."

"And cleared of any suspicion," Brooksie snapped.

"Of course, I understand that." Evelyn gestured toward Sullivan. "This man is a private investigator trying to help me find out who did kill my sister. Your son sat by her on the plane. He was one of the last people to see her alive. He might be able to give us some scrap of information. It's so important that we talk to him. Even if he doesn't know anything, it would help me to at least talk with him. He was so close to her in her last few hours."

A little shift in Brooksie's posture indicated some sort of acceptance. She tore the sunglasses from her eyes. "Okay, but we've just about had enough of this for one day. We're trying to relax from the other ordeal. I closed my decorating shop for the day and asked all the boys over. Come on, I'll show you Mark's room."

With a crooked forefinger Brooksie tapped on the last door down the spacious hall. Skylights dotted the ceiling, letting in enough of the outside to keep the plants from wilting.

Shortly, the door jerked open. A red-haired teenager whose freckles and acne merged in a fiery blush glared at them. "What is it?"

Touching his slumping shoulder, Brooksie explained what they wanted. "Markie, tell them everything you know about the murdered woman you sat by on the plane just like you did

with the police. I'll just be out by the pool if you need me."
She flounced down the hall, heels striking hard on the parquet.

Sullivan and Evelyn stepped into the room and caught the
aroma of sweet smoke. The place was typical of a teenager
who had everything, from expensive stereo to an almost
life-size curved-screen television. Evelyn closed the door and
perched on an ottoman near the television, Sullivan and Mark
Foster on the edge of the bed. Sullivan nodded to Evelyn.
Obviously she knew more pointed questions to ask about her
sister. He'd take over if she faltered.

Evelyn cleared her throat. "You sat next to my sister on
that flight from Dallas. It's important for you to tell us
everything about her you can remember." Her voice was soft
but coercive.

Mark Foster shrugged impassively, his pale eyes distant.
"I already told the detectives everything."

Evelyn leaned forward. "She was my sister, Mark. It's
possible someone on that plane killed her, stabbed her after
she arrived at her hotel. He might have followed her there.
Did you see her talk to anyone?"

"I don't have to answer all the questions again."

He returned Evelyn's stare with sullen, hostile silence.

"No, you don't have to, but I was hoping you would.
Seems the least you could do in the face of a murder."
Evelyn drew in her breath and regrouped. "Did she say
anything to you? You must have talked some."

He picked a ripe pimple. "She commented about the weather
being bad that night. Said she hoped we'd have a good
flight."

Evelyn remembered that night well. Dallas had been under
a tornado alert. Sara was nervous about flying. "What did
you say back to her?"

The boy slouched against the fluffy pillows on his bed.
"Nothing."

Sullivan took an exaggerated sniff of air and caught Mark's
attention. Sullivan glared at him until he looked away. When
he glanced back, Sullivan's eyes were still on him, evaluating.

Mark squeaked out a little grunt and fidgeted with his shirt
collar.

Sullivan readjusted himself on the edge of the bed and

leaned toward Mark. He appeared relaxed, but his eyes had a cold determined set. "You think I was born yesterday, Foster?"

"What?" He sat up, staring at Sullivan.

"You think I don't know what that smell is?" Sullivan snapped, an edge of menace in his voice. "In five minutes I can have the narcs looking up your asshole. Where they'll put you, they don't have stereos and television."

Mark Foster's eyes narrowed. "That's what you think. They can't get me on possession."

Sullivan grinned. "That's what *you* think, greenhorn. They'll get you for anything they want to get you for. They'll plant so much grass on you, you'll think you're a lawn. I'll turn you in myself."

"I don't think so." A smirk plastered his features.

Sullivan locked eyes with the boy. "Want to try me? All we want is some information. Then you and I have no problems, but if you want to make it hard on yourself, fellow, go to it."

Sullivan allowed Mark time to evaluate the situation, then turned to Evelyn. "Now, this lady has some questions for you, and after she finishes, so do I. Let's get on with it."

Mark squirmed, rotating his shoulders. "The lady next to me didn't say anything much. She ordered a drink and just read."

Evelyn sat erect on the ottoman. "Read? Go on, Mark."

"She had a folder open, like a business pad. She worked some figures with one hand and held her drink sort of high in the air with the other hand. I remember because the plane was bumpy, and I kept thinking she might spill it." He looked proud of his recall.

"Are you positive?" Evelyn clasped her hands so tightly around her knees her knuckles whitened. Was Sara pretending to be an executive to impress a sixteen-year-old boy?

"I looked over at the pad once. She smiled at me but didn't say anything." Mark turned toward Sullivan as if trying to placate him by adding a footnote. "The lady I sat by reminds me of her." He tilted his head at Evelyn. "They look alike. At first I thought she was the same one."

Evelyn and Sullivan exchanged glances. Evelyn wondered if Mark might have seen some vague family resemblance she wasn't aware existed. Mark Foster was lying for some reason, perhaps making up a tale to satisfy Sullivan.

Offhandedly, she asked, "When did she find time to smoke, drinking and writing so much?"

"Smoke?" Mark's eyes widened. "We were in Non-smoking."

Not Sara. Evelyn batted her eyes quickly trying to assimilate the information. Something was wrong here. Maybe he was telling the truth. She scrounged in her purse, opened her wallet and pulled out a picture of Sara. Handing it to Mark she watched his reaction. He frowned as if puzzled and handed the picture back.

"This isn't the lady. The one I sat by was much better looking. Pretty. A blond, like you. Classy type."

Evelyn sat staring at the photograph of the plain, dark-haired woman who had never been described as pretty or classy.

Sullivan cut in: "The records show you sat in 5B. This lady," Sullivan leaned over and thumped the photograph, "sat in 5A, right next to you. Are you trying to pull something?"

Mark shook his head, his expression genunine. "No. I didn't sit next to that lady . . . oh . . . ." He rolled his eyes. "Maybe that was the first lady I sat by. I can't remember. I didn't sit in my original seat but just a few minutes. I exchanged seats with a man and went up to the very front row on the same side of the aisle to sit by the blond. I thought the blond was who you were talking about."

Sullivan pulled the airline list out of his pocket. The front row seats, 1A and 1B were assigned to Gloria Martin and the passenger who had paid with cash. He lit a cigarette and let the smoke out slowly. "The man you swapped seats with was Christopher Chalmers. The lady you went to sit next to was Gloria Martin. Tell me about the man. What can you remember?" Sullivan squinted. "This is important."

Evelyn whipped around to Sullivan. "The man . . . Christopher Chalmers, was already seated next to a woman . . . Gloria Martin. But, he wanted to change to sit next to Sara . . ."

Sullivan held up his hand. "Cool it a minute. You're getting off the subject. Now, Mark tell me about the man."

Mark Foster blinked. "The first lady looked out of the window at the bad weather. I couldn't see her face." He glanced at Evelyn as if trying to explain the mix-up. "As soon as we took off this man came down the aisle and whispered to me if I'd change seats with him."

"What excuse did he offer for wanting to change?" Sullivan's expression turned deadly serious. "Think. This man could be the killer."

"He said that he was supposed to be in the Smoking section . . . the airlines had screwed up and put him in Nonsmoking. Said he was dying for a cigarette and would I change with him?"

Sullivan moved closer to Mark. "About the man, can you describe him?"

Mark studied his hands, clasped and unclasped them. Sullivan suspected he was turning edgy, afraid he'd gotten in too deep.

"You've been a real help. If you can give me a description, that'll about do it. Think, now. He comes down the aisle. Is he short or tall? Dark-headed or blond? He came right up to you. Spoke to you. Think."

Mark bit his lip, apparently reaching a decision. "Tall, over six feet. Like an athlete sort of. You know . . . strong, good build. I can't tell about age."

Sullivan knew all young people thought anyone over thirty was ancient. "Forty . . . fifty years old. You said he looked like an athlete. He couldn't be too old."

"Forty!" He blurted out. "Something like that. Not real old. He had weird eyes."

"Weird?" Evelyn cut in. "What do you mean by that?"

"I don't know exactly. He had this kind of piercing stare. When he looked at you . . . well, you felt like he was looking through you almost, so you knew you had to do what he said. Real intense guy."

"What else can you remember about his looks?" Sullivan pressed.

"He was dark, not exactly a tan, but like it was natural, like a foreigner, but he didn't talk like one."

Sullivan turned over the description in his mind, trying to visualize the man. "When you got to the San Diego Airport, did you see him again?"

Mark shook his head.

Sullivan knew from Castro's conversation that Mark Foster hadn't told the police about changing seats, and obviously they hadn't shown him a photograph of Sara Marley to identify. Sullivan stubbed out his cigarette and stood. "You've been a big help, Mark. I appreciate it." He touched Mark's shoulder. "Everybody needs all their brain cells for the future. Quit burning them out with that junk. Get out and get some exercise and fresh air. Join a sports group. Chances are you'll make it if you stop wasting yourself getting stoned."

At the door, Evelyn looked back at Mark. "Thank you."

They hurried to the car, unnoticed by the crowd at the pool. Sullivan drew a deep breath. "Fresh air smells damn good. Screwed-up mother. Screwed-up kid. Same old story. About this morning . . ."

"Can we forget it?"

"I still don't like it one bit, but if you can, I can."

Sullivan started the engine and, letting it idle, glanced at Evelyn. Her eyes were set on the road. With a grind and a clunk the old Peugeot Sullivan called his "chug" agreed to go into gear.

Evelyn turned in the seat. "We've got to see Gloria Martin right away. You've got her address and phone number on the airline printout."

Sullivan nodded as he turned right on a downhill road leading toward the ocean. "As Christopher Chalmers's original seatmate, they might have talked. She could have noticed something about him, might be able to give us an even better description than Mark Foster did, tell us even more about him."

"Seeing her and talking to her might reveal more than that." Avoiding Sullivan's stare, Evelyn glanced out the window, feeling a growing excitement at exploring her theory.

Sullivan blinked, then returned his attention to the steep road. He knew Evelyn Casey's mental wheels were spinning. "I'll stop at the first service station and call Gloria Martin."

Three blocks down the way, Sullivan spotted a pay phone

outside a 7-Eleven. He pulled in the parking lot and got out, leaving the motor running. Evelyn watched him dial, hoping they could see Gloria Martin immediately. She felt as if she might burst with urgency if they had to wait another day. The woman could be out of town. Gone for weeks. Evelyn caught her breath in a silent prayer.

Walking back to the car after a brief conversation, Sullivan's expression telegraphed nothing. He opened the door and slid in. "We're in luck. Gloria Martin is a stock analyst, probably the luckiest one alive, only she doesn't know it, office located in the Wells Fargo Building downtown. People in sales are always ready to see somebody." He smiled, crinkles appearing around his eyes, and drove away.

They swooped into the underground parking lot, piled out and rode the elevator to the fifth floor of the Wells Fargo Building. They found Gloria Martin's office and were asked by the receptionist to be seated.

Sullivan surveyed the area. The appointments announced success: walls shiny black lacquer, contrasting with the almost blinding-white carpeting. Washed by overhead pinpoint lighting, free-form sculptures stood in all four corners. On the walls, blobs of wild colors passed for paintings. Sullivan commented that they looked as though they had been done by Rorschach.

"I hate this room," he said to Evelyn.

She liked what she saw, not because the decor was her taste, but it spoke of Gloria Martin. "Why don't you like it? Too old-fashioned for you?"

"Oh, no. You missed my point." Sullivan rolled his eyes. "It's just that it's so cheaply done. I bet she didn't spend more than fifty thousand on it. I hate shabby things." He grinned.

Evelyn turned sideways in the black lounge chair and faced Sullivan. "You don't seem to be wearing that end-of-the-month-sale, marked-down set of armor this afternoon."

Sullivan lit a cigarette and avoided her eyes. "Why do you say that?"

"Oh, I have the feeling that sometimes you stand in the wings and watch your own performance, and then wish you could rewrite your lines after you've said them.'' She stared at him, a hint of a smile on her lips.

Sullivan realized what an unusual creature Evelyn was. Complex, but with a personality that was intuitive and natural. And the eyes . . . not the color, a deep aqua, not the size, although they were undeniably large. There was more, an understanding shining from somewhere inside. He ground out his cigarette in an oval black glass ashtray. Set of armor indeed, he thought.

Evelyn picked up a copy of *Architectural Digest* and fanned through the pages, barely able to contain her mounting excitement. She knew it was important that the killer sat next to Gloria Martin first but chose her sister instead. There was a reason, and when they discovered it, more would be revealed about the murderer. From Mark Foster's description they knew Gloria Martin was a nice-looking woman, but personality, not appearance was what Evelyn was banking on.

In a tailored black suit, Gloria Martin appeared in the doorway, blond hair neatly fashioned into a bun. Her legs stationed apart as if staking claim to ground, she removed her horn-rimmed glasses.

"I'm Gloria Martin. Please come in." She had a longish nose, and right off Evelyn suspected she looked down it a lot.

Sauntering into the office, Evelyn looked around. Sullivan, following, introduced himself and Evelyn. Gloria Martin sat behind a Lucite desk, Evelyn and Sullivan occupying two white chairs facing her.

Gloria Martin opened a ledger, then cleared her throat. "What sort of investments are you looking for, tax-free income or . . ."

Sullivan leaned forward, forearms resting on the edge of Gloria Martin's desk. "Wish I had the problem, but we're here on an entirely different matter. I'm a private detective, investigating a murder." Sullivan motioned toward Evelyn with his head. "Her sister's."

"We'd like to talk to you about it." Evelyn sank back in the chair, catching a show of displeasure in Sullivan's expression. He intended for her to remain in the wings.

"Murder? I don't know anything about any murder," she snapped, her manner imperious. She looked from Evelyn to

Sullivan, eyes snapping like a set of whips. "What is this?"

As Sullivan explained the situation, Evelyn watched Gloria Martin, cataloguing the lady analyst's personality.

"I'd like you to describe that night to me, the flight, everything you can remember." Sullivan leaned back, crossed his long legs and prepared to listen.

"When you boarded, was your seatmate already there or did he come on later?" Evelyn asked.

"Hold it a minute . . ." Sullivan interrupted, his tone stern. "Let Ms. Martin tell it in her own words."

Gloria Martin glanced at her watch, then looked as if she had decided to cooperate, though obviously irritated. "Immediately after boarding, I took my papers from my briefcase and started to read." She picked up a cigarette and thumped it on the desk. Sullivan was quick with a light. "I didn't really give the man a second glance." She replaced her glasses and stared at Sullivan. "Do you pay much attention to someone next to you on an airplane?" she asked, on the defense.

"It's his business to be observant," Evelyn put in before thinking. Without looking she could feel Sullivan's eyes on her.

"Back on track." Sullivan shot a warning look at Evelyn. "Can't you remember anything about him at all? Did he say something to you or the stewardess, maybe? I'm sure you must travel a lot, but try to think back."

Gloria Martin pursed her lips. "I do remember the young boy who came to sit with me later."

"We've talked to him," Evelyn answered.

Exasperated, Sullivan let out a rush of air. "He was most cooperative." Sullivan decided a little jolt might help her remember something. "This lady here who's hired me to work on the case is offering a reward for any information that might help me track down her sister's murderer."

Evelyn sat very still, not looking at anything in particular.

Sullivan rubbed his chin, eyes trained on Gloria Martin. "Were you alone on the flight or traveling with anyone? Anyone see you to the gate?"

"I was alone. No one saw me to the gate." Gloria Martin

picked up a pencil and rolled it around in her hand. "Was the boy who sat next to me any help?"

Evelyn knew Gloria Martin had no further information, but she had helped more than she knew by confirming what type of woman the killer was not after. "He gave a good description of the man we're looking for."

"Oh, Gloria Martin stiffened, adjusted her glasses and lifted her chin slightly. "Will he be in for the reward, then?"

"Up to her," Sullivan barked, grinding out his cigarette in an ashtray on the desk.

Evelyn fixed Gloria Martin with a stare. "This man . . . he picked my sister over you. Even though he was in a perfect position with you, he made no attempt to even try to talk to you, went to the trouble to change seats, seeking out my sister. Instinctively the killer knew you weren't the victim he wanted." Evelyn turned to Sullivan. "He had a reason for his choice."

Gloria Martin looked offended. Under other circumstances Evelyn might have found some humor in her expression. It reminded Evelyn of a story about someone who bought flight insurance, then complained about wasting money when the plane arrive safely.

"We've taken enough of your time." Sullivan said, standing.

"Sorry you couldn't remember anything about the killer," Evelyn added. She'd bet Gloria Martin would notice her next seatmate.

Just as they reached the door and Sullivan jerked it open, Gloria Martin called out: "How much is the reward?"

Sullivan glanced back and said, "Five hundred thousand."

Evelyn hurried down the hall to keep pace with Sullivan. "Five hundred thousand. You sure are free with my money."

He glanced at her. "You sure are free with your interruptions. I wanted to tell you to butt out before you blew it in there. She didn't have any information to add anyway."

"Wrong," Evelyn said hurrying along by Sullivan's side. "I think the killer is after a certain type of woman. There's a deep chasm between Gloria Martin and my sister. I didn't much like Gloria Martin, but I have to admit she's an independent person, meets life head-on. Whatever the killer told Sara, however he enticed her, Gloria Martin wouldn't have fallen for it, and he knew it. Sara might have been naive, but for someone to . . ." She stopped. Proving a point to Gordon suddenly took a backseat to finding the man with the power to crack Sara's careful guard, which measured how dangerous he really was. Sullivan stabbed the elevator button and glanced up at the lighted sign ticking off floor numbers.

Evelyn moved so that she could see him, her eyes searching his face. "You thought the two cases weren't connected because the Kenworth woman's seatmate was a female. I'd be willing to bet she was asked to change seats just like Mark Foster. The two cases are connected . . . the two airlines lists, both having a passenger with the same initials, C.C., both paying cash, giving fake phone numbers. From what the Kenworth woman said about her niece, it sounded like she and Sara were alike. Their killer is a psycho picking a certain type of victim because of something in his background. He's a serial killer preying on weak women."

The elevator doors parted and they stepped in. As they rode down, quiet prevailed, each preoccupied with their own thoughts.

In the underground parking area, they got into Sullivan's car and he pulled out, stopping to pay the toll.

Evelyn braced herself on the dash as Sullivan screeched into the traffic. "Christopher Chalmers . . . whoever he is, murdered Sara and the Kenworth woman. We have his description. Now we've got to find out who he really is and catch him." Evelyn frowned. "It's not going to be easy."

Sullivan nodded. "We have some interesting facts assembled." He leaned forward, checking the sky through the windshield. Clear and purpling toward evening. "I'm starved. Haven't had anything since breakfast this morning. How about dinner? I know a good place. We can talk about what we have and what comes next." For the first time he felt enthusiastic about the case. There were roads to follow, tangible prospects to check.

Evelyn moved to face him. "I'd love it. I've got a few ideas. Came to me while we were talking to Mark Foster. I was thinking in terms of the killer . . . what kind of person would he be? A real charmer, but underneath a woman-hater, of course. And why would he hate women? He's someone who was abandoned by his mother, either emotionally or physically. See, once you establish the type of victim, you can psychologically profile the murderer. Bring him into focus, so to speak.''

Sullivan gave her a crooked grin. ''Textbook psych stuff.'' He held up one hand.

''Even if he wasn't so young, Mark Foster would have been an unlikely candidate anyway. His mother is overly protective. I think her behavior might make him feel superior to her . . . whereas a mother who is rejecting produces a seriously disturbed person who feels inferior and needy . . . your women-hater.'' She glanced at Sullivan's expression. ''Sorry about rattling on. I was trying to get a feel . . .''

She was looking for a psychological picture of the killer, while he was trying to put together a physical one. ''Well, you might say I'm a pragmatist, rely on provable facts and reality. I admit there's something to the other side, too.'' He grasped the wheel tighter and turned onto Interstate 5.

''I've taken an apartment. It's a good thing now that I did. Since we've got something to go on, I'll be staying. Carole Wheeler found it for me. I wanted to tell you that. Everything from here on out will be on top of the table.''

Looking at her he raised his eyebrows, then returned to the road. Traffic was heavy. Each year the tourists stayed longer, Sullivan thought. Each year too many came to stay. The whole area was becoming malls, high rises, fast-food joints, webs of freeways and littered beaches. Newcomers probably thought California had always looked that way. He resented the spoiling of such a beautiful land.

He turned off the freeway and headed toward the beach area. Brights from a car tailgating his Peugeot blurred his vision. Sullivan pressed the accelerator to escape the glare on his windshield. Pulling up to the Mon Ami restaurant, he felt lucky to find not one but two spaces near the front entrance. He swerved into one, making sure he'd left enough room for the car behind him. The car cruised by, then circled around the side of the building.

The restaurant's ceiling was adorned with wineglasses, the foot of each glass captured between wooden panels, the stem and bowl hanging upside down to create an overall impres-

sion of a vast chandelier glistening with reflected light from
the brick fireplace. Surrounding walls were paneled except
for the one facing the ocean, a wide expanse of glass through
which the water beyond could be seen. The bar was crowded
at that hour. Sullivan asked for a booth by the window.

Seated, Sullivan attempted to flag the waiter but couldn't
catch his eye. The candle in its holder cast flickering high-
lights into Evelyn's hair. She looked pensive and for a moment Sullivan debated intruding on whatever mood she was
sharing with the dark ocean waters. He watched as she removed an earring, stroked her lobe, then replaced the earring.
The gesture reminded him suddenly and painfully of Karin,
the tilt of her head, her hair cascading as Evelyn's was now.

Then she looked at him with embarrassment, as though
she'd been caught in an intimate act when she thought she'd
gone unobserved. "This is a lovely place. Did you . . . do
you come here often?"

"I used to come here with Karin. She liked it." He wondered if he were testing himself by bringing Evelyn Casey
here.

Evelyn excused herself, and Sullivan watched as she advanced through the restaurant to the powder room. Heads
turned for a second look, especially one whose face Sullivan
couldn't see. His broad back to Sullivan, he hovered over a
drink at the bar. Sullivan caught profiles of others. Thinking
of the description Mark Foster had given, Sullivan decided
more than half the men at the bar fit the specifications. How
many men in the United States were dark, athletic looking,
over six feet tall, around forty, with weird eyes, he asked
himself? He didn't like his answer.

The waiter arrived, took drink orders and hurried back with
their glasses. Service was still good, Sullivan mused and
started on his Jack Daniels. Thinking about Mark Foster,
Sullivan felt a little sorry for him. He'd have a tough time
becoming a man with Brooksie's influence. Like Evelyn's
sister, Foster, laden with all life's amenities, didn't understand how to cope and lacked the ambition to take advantage
of his privileged status. Sad commentary, he thought as he
suddenly saw himself as a boy, standing on the dock next to
the father he had adored. He could almost hear the water

slapping against the old wooden pier. Proudly he held a new rod and reel, which he somehow knew had gravely depleted his father's already thinning pocketbook. Gratitude overwhelmed him. In those Depression days luxuries were hard to come by, every possession a prized one, one to take care of and make last. It was a time when respect for elders was a foregone conclusion. He took nothing for granted and resented those who did. What did he know? Maybe if he'd had a son, he would have spoiled him. And, turning the tables on himself, hadn't he lost his drive and ambition when Karin died? Sullivan downed the rest of his drink as he spotted Evelyn making her way through the crowd.

The thought crossed his mind that she might have children, but he doubted it since she hadn't mentioned any. All he really knew about Evelyn Casey were her obvious traits. Now and then a sense of humor cracked through, showing it was waiting for the right time to make a permanent appearance.

She hooked into her chair, with her hair freshly combed, newly applied lipstick. "I feel better now." She picked up her vodka on the rocks that he'd known to order.

He lit a cigarette. "Think I'll make a run up to L.A. to question Mary Kenworth's seatmate. I want to see if she can give a description that matches the one Mark Foster gave, find out if she was asked to change seats, too."

Evelyn sipped her drink. "We're on the trail."

"You're one positive lady. We've got lots of unanswered questions. Besides Mary Kenworth's seatmate I'll question the stewardesses and every person on those flights if necessary."

Sullivan waved for the waiter. When the waiter took the drink order, Sullivan asked him to bring a phone to plug in by the booth. He'd conducted many business transactions in that very spot.

The waiter was back with his drink quickly and stooped to plug in the phone. Sullivan picked up the receiver, dialed Castro's number and waited, fingers tapping on the table. He was about to hang up when Olga answered.

"Is this who I think it is? It's good to hear your voice, Sullivan. We called so many times, came by the house, but you were never there."

"Guess I was out on my boat. I've missed you, Olga." He realized what he said was true.

"I was sorry about . . ."

"Me, too. Me, too . . ." he hesitated. "Is Manny there?"

"Just left a few minutes ago for the station. After tonight he's off for two days."

An idea struck Sullivan. "I wanted to fill him in on some things. Tomorrow I'm going up to L.A. for the day. Ought to know even more then. How about me taking you to the ball game tomorrow night when I get in? Been a while."

"I promised him we'd have a quiet evening at home, and I'd fix his favorite dinner, real Mexican food."

"That's my favorite, too." He grinned at Evelyn.

"It takes so long to prepare that we don't have it much anymore. I work, too, you know. I can easily make enough for three. You could talk to him before dinner. Just a few minutes, though. I know you two. I want it to be a social evening, not all business."

Sullivan smiled to himself, picturing little Olga, who thought of herself as tough. "Could you make it for four? I'd like to bring the lady I'm working for. She'll be interested in what we have to discuss."

"Easy. I'd like to invite her myself. How can I call her?" Olga was Old World, her manners and habits clinging to the past. He liked that. "She's right here. I'll hand over the phone. Her name is Evelyn Casey." He handed Evelyn the receiver. "Castro's wife, Olga."

Evelyn took the call and listened. "Thanks. You're very nice to ask. We'll be there." She returned the receiver to Sullivan, and he placed it in the cradle.

The piano player took his place, nodded to Sullivan and broke into a rendition of *New York, New York*. Sullivan smiled back, then looked around, deciding the surroundings didn't pain him as much as he had expected.

After menus were placed before them, Evelyn ordered a veal dish with noodles. Sullivan chose broiled swordfish and a cucumber, onion, and caper salad. As an afterthought, he added a chocolate soufflé.

Evelyn pressed her napkin across her lap. "This is an expensive place. You're keeping a running tab, aren't you?"

Sullivan downed his drink. The remark, although he knew it was unintentional, made him feel small. "Tonight's on me." He lit a cigarette. "Might as well have another splash while we wait for dinner."

Evelyn looked at her half-full glass. "I'll pass."

Over his drink, which he vowed would be the last of the night, Sullivan felt a sense of unrest. His life, his habits were a jumble he couldn't untangle. Now, on the brink of an investigation that required skill, he wondered if he had the touch he once had. To outwit a killer, he had to penetrate his mind, assume the criminal's thoughts and rationale. How did he expect to grasp the emotions of someone else when he didn't have a grip on his own? Advice so lavishly heaped on Mark Foster might well be heeded by himself. It seemed that his mind was a dark and seething hole, too many thoughts fighting for air. No suitable assignments were coming his way, as he'd told Evelyn Casey, only jobs no one else would tackle. This was his last chance. Suddenly he realized that in finding the killer he might find himself again.

"You're frowning. It'll make permanent lines."

"To go with all the others," he answered.

"Character lines, I believe they're called."

"Call them what you like. You want to drop me by the airport in the morning so I don't have to leave my car there? Then, you can pick me up and we'll go on to Castro's for dinner." He paused and looked directly into her eyes. "You can make good use of the day while I'm gone. I've got an assignment for you. A load shared is a load lightened." He grinned.

Evelyn's eye's widened in anticipation. "What do you have in mind?"

"Since you've got such good connections at the newspaper"—he made a face, then continued—"you can make use of their microfilm library. But for God sakes don't let that reporter know what you're looking for." Confirming aloud that a serial killer stalked out there somewhere made it all the more terrifying. "You said something about a serial killer just starting up. We already know of two similar murders . . . maybe he's been at it a while . . ." He raised his eyebrows. "How many more are there that we don't know about?"

CHAPTER 7

CASTRO AND TALBOTT caught the "squeal."

"We're rolling on a 10-29," Castro called out as he and Talbott bolted out of the squadroom to the parking lot. Castro slid behind the wheel of the car, turned on the ignition and gunned the engine. As Talbott slammed the door on the passenger side, Castro turned on the siren and flashing red light. He pushed the gas pedal almost to the floor, and the car squealed out of the parking lot on two wheels into traffic parting before them.

Nearing the homicide scene, radio blaring, Castro slowed the car. Stalled traffic and the curious onlookers prevented the car from approaching too closely. They got out and hustled through the jam other cops were trying to untangle. Department vehicles were parked on the sidewalks or double-parked in the street. Castro saw that the forensic van had arrived with the medical examiner. Nothing would be touched until the two homicide detectives were on the scene. Wooden barriers were up, spectators pressing against on all sides, not a gringo among them.

Castro and Talbott raced through a shabby foyer and up littered steps. An old condom full of someone's joy in a place where there wasn't much, lay in a corner. Below graffiti-covered crumbling walls, scrawls accused the neighborhood of sucking everything from dicks to fire plugs. Roach stubs browned the stairs. A boy with a stump for a leg and teeth that already looked like a rotting picket fence hobbled through the squalor to make way for the advancing officers. A cat, tail high, with an ass burned as red as the enchiladas it scrounged, scurried ahead. Human sweat and stench from overturned garbage cans permeated the still air. Castro remembered those scenes and smells from childhood, a time when a police uniform was something to fear.

On the third floor a crowd squeezed into the small apartment at the end of the hall. The police laboratory unit and photo unit had arrived. Bulbs flashed as Castro and Talbott pushed in.

The dead woman's body lay on its side, a knife protruding between her shoulder blades. Blood pouring from the fresh wound stained her faded robe a dark red. The medical examiner squatted by the body. Castro glanced around for the patrolman who had reported the homicide, found him and identified himself.

"What went down here?"

The young patrolman took off his cap and scratched his head. His face was so smooth and pink that Castro wondered if he shaved yet. "My partner and I got the 9-1-1 on the radio. We were in the area. A neighbor of the deceased called in saying she heard screaming in the next apartment, thought a fight was going on. Just as we pulled up, a Mexican hauled ass out of the apartment building." The officer's face flushed as he looked at Castro.

"Go on," Castro said, without change of expression.

"His clothes were bloody. He ran down the street. My partner got out and chased him. I called another backup unit before I went into the building. They struck out after him, too. They got him." Twirling his hat in his hand, he looked pleased.

"Have you identified the victim?" Castro asked.

"A Juanita Sanchez."

Castro and Talbott exchanged glances, both recognizing the name. Castro then stared at the crumpled heap on the floor, the face obscured by a mass of heavy, black hair. He remembered how the maid at the Eastgate who had discovered Sara Marley's body towered over him when he had questioned her. Arms muscled from hard work, she was unusually large for someone of Mexican descent. He felt his heart hit an extra beat. Was there any thread of connection to the Sara Marley case? Marley and Sanchez both stabbed to death. Castro eyed the knife, wondering if it could be the same one used on Sara Marley.

"I want to talk to the neighbor who reported this. Where is she?"

"Tina Gonzales, sir, she's in her apartment," the patrolman answered.

"Talbott you stay with the M.E. 'til he finishes. I'll talk to the neighbor."

Castro walked over to the medical examiner and told him to get started. He put the evidence bag down by the body. Careful not to touch anything, Castro leaned forward to look at her face. His mind raced with possibilities.

He straightened and walked with the patrolman to Tina Gonzales's apartment. Castro identified himself to the heavy woman with a lined face and graying hair. She made the sign of the cross and rubbed together hands as calloused from doing other people's work as his grandmother's had been.

"Tell me what you know about this, senora."

Tears welled in her eyes. "Juanita, she wasn't much good, but that Lopez. Carnie Lopez was a bug to squash under your foot. I heard them arguing as usual. He lived with her. Just mooched in. Juanita couldn't get rid of him. *Muy macho*, Carnie Lopez, always saying he was going to hit the big time. Always a scheme. Thought he was another John Travolta. Nothing but a punk. I called the police when it got to sounding bad. I cracked open my door and saw Carnie run down the hall. He did it."

Castro looked around the sparsely furnished apartment. Votive candles flickered before a large Virgin Mary statue.

"We may want to question you later down at the station. We'll be in touch."

Castro returned to the Sanchez apartment. The medical examiner was almost finished. He put the knife, which had been dusted, into the evidence bag. The fingerprint team had dust everywhere. The powder made Castro want to sneeze. The corpse was placed into a body bag and hauled away to the morgue.

Castro and Talbott pushed through the crowd to their car. Castro radioed to see if the arresting officers had brought in Carnie Lopez. With confirmation that the suspect was being held, Castro and Talbott headed back, ready for the interrogation. They were quiet on the way, Castro wondering if the Marley case was close to being solved.

Castro and Talbott pushed through the heavy double front doors and walked down the hall. The rotunda where prisoners were taken downtown to night court to be arraigned was full of cops and handcuffed prisoners. The two detectives walked down the stairs to the floor below where Carnie Lopez waited in an interrogation room.

The room was small, fluorescent-lit, with Celotex walls and ceiling. In the center stood a metal table surrounded by six folding chairs.

They relieved the two arresting officers, walked over to the table where Carnie Lopez sat and introduced themselves. They told the suspect anything he said could be used against him as evidence and that he was entitled to a lawyer. Lopez looked at them with cunning, streetwise eyes and said that he didn't need a lawyer. His cheekbones were high, his hair dark and glistening under the harsh lights. He was tall, just over six feet, Castro judged, with a body accustomed to regular workouts.

Talbott, who didn't smoke, lit a cigarette from the pack he always carried. If a prisoner was a smoker, seeing someone else puff away made him feel deprived. If offered one, a little bond of friendship between captor and prisoner formed.

Castro loosened his tie and perched on the edge of the table, facing Carnie Lopez. He caught a whiff of cologne mixed with sweat. Carnie Lopez eyed his shoulder holster but showed no fear. In his youth Castro had been acquainted with many macho punks like Carnie Lopez.

"Mr. Lopez. Let's hear what happened."

Carnie Lopez waved his hand as if to brush aside the

question as he would an insect that annoyed him. "Self-defense. Man, she was after me."

Talbott cackled. Carnie Lopez whipped his head around at him, his mouth turning into a defiant smirk. "What's the matter with you, man? You see Juanita mad, you wouldn't be laughing."

"You work out, Mr. Lopez?" Castro asked.

Carnie Lopez slicked his hair into place with smooth hands. He moved his head as if looking into an imaginary mirror. "I try to keep in shape."

"Weight?" Talbott pressed, blowing smoke at Lopez.

"Hundred and eighty." He looked back at Castro. "What's this got to do with anything?"

Castro ignored his question. "You look like you can take care of yourself."

"I see what you're trying to get at here. She was after me with that knife. Lucky I got it away from her or I'd be lying on that floor. Didn't you see her? See how big she is? It was self-defense, man."

Talbott put one foot on the edge of Lopez's chair and leaned into him. "So you couldn't stop her any way but stabbing her?" Talbott grinned. "Come on, who you think you're kidding?"

Carnie Lopez slid off his chair and strutted around the room, his hands fluttering and whipping like flags. "Man, a mad woman with a knife. Ever had one after you, you'd know how it was. Wild. She was crazy, lunging at me with that knife. I had me a time getting it away from her."

"Sit down," Castro said, his voice commanding.

Lopez narrowed his eyes but followed Castro's order. He slouched in the chair, crossing his arms over his chest. "Man, I'm telling you self-defense. You can't prove nothing else. You wasn't in that room. You didn't see it."

"No, I didn't see it," Castro snapped. "What I'm thinking is you say self-defense. She was stabbed in the back. How's that?"

"Me and Juanita was struggling, see. She's got the knife, stabbing out at me. I grab her wrist. We fall to the floor. She's on top of me. I get the knife from her just in time, reach around and stab her in the back. Like I say, self-defense."

"Mr. Lopez, if it was self-defense, why'd you run away?"

Throwing up his hands, Lopez shrugged. "Panicked, I guess. I couldn't look at her . . . the blood."

Castro eyeballed Lopez until he looked away. Until that moment he had been respectfully calling the suspect Mr. Lopez. Now he decided to switch to his first name, an old trick designed to place the suspect at a disadvantage. Calling a man by his first name instead of Mister was the same thing as calling him boy. It put him in his place at once, instantly making him feel inferior and defensive. "Carnie, I want to ask you a question."

Lopez looked up, recognizing the switch. He was a perceptive son of a bitch, Castro thought. "Carnie, who does the knife belong to?"

"Me," Lopez snapped, pointing to his chest with his thumb. "It's mine. I carry it for protection. You don't know what it's like living down there."

Castro tilted his head, remembering the cockroaches of his youth, many of them human. "Don't I?"

Lopez blinked. "Yeah, well, maybe you do." He looked at Talbott. "He don't."

Talbott shrugged. "Nah, I don't. Grew up in a palace. I just do this to keep in touch with the common man. Lopez, what do you do for a living?"

Lopez rotated one shoulder. "This and that. I make out."

Castro smiled at Lopez as if they were two Mex buddies, understanding each other. "Hard to get ahead down there, everybody against you."

Lopez nodded and cracked his knuckles.

"You run a few numbers, push a little, pimp?" Castro took off his jacket, realizing the session might be lengthy. He hadn't even started on the line he intended.

"Me?" Lopez looked offended. "Never. Nothing like that. That's for punks going nowhere."

Castro narrowed his eyes, no more the friendly cohort. He punched Lopez in the chest with his forefinger. "That's what you are, a punk. A fly, a zit. You're nothing." He unzipped the evidence bag and threw the knife on the table. "How many other people you stabbed with this, Lopez?"

Lopez's jaw pulsed. He looked like it was the first time he

realized he was in trouble. "Whoa, man. Don't be trying to pin nothing else on me. Nobody. I never stabbed nobody but Juanita, and it was self-defense." He stared at the knife, the blade gleaming under the lights.

Talbott picked up the knife, running his finger along the blade. "Punk. Scared of a woman. Maybe you didn't even stab Juanita Sanchez. Maybe it was somebody else who did."

"Yeah," Castro put in. "Maybe it was the neighbor, Tina Gonzales. She looks like she's got more balls."

"You motherfucker!" Lopez barred his teeth. "I got plenty balls. I don't have to go around being a cop to prove it. Everybody looks up to me." He lifted his chin.

Talbott's eyes widened as if he were suddenly impressed. He pulled out the pack of cigarettes and offered Lopez one. Lopez snatched one from the pack and held it to his lips, waiting for a light. Talbott obliged. Inhaling, Lopez blew out a cloud of smoke.

"Tell you something, boys," Lopez said, obviously harboring the illusion that he was back on familiar turf. "Everybody's afraid of me down there. Got a right to be. I'd cut 'em like I did Juanita they don't stay in line, but only in self-defense, understand. She had it coming, two-bit klept. Stole a bunch of crap all the time. I say to her, 'Juanita, you going to steal something, steal something big.' She was the punk. That's what I call her, and she gets mad, gets the knife and takes after me."

"Yeah, I can see it now," Castro said, leaning down at Lopez. "Should have known it. You're big-time." He put on his earnest face.

Lopez squinted at him, making sure he was serious, then leaned back in the chair and crossed his legs. He glanced around the room as if seeing it for the first time, a grin on his lips.

"Say, I'm kind of thirsty," Talbott said. "Like something to drink, Mr. Lopez?"

Lopez gave him a cocky look. "Yeah. Coffee."

"Cream or sugar? Their brew's not too good just black."

"Both," Lopez answered. "How about another cig?"

Talbott gave Lopez the pack and went for coffee. Lopez lit another cigarette and glanced around idly, his foot beating a fast tattoo on the floor. Castro picked at a hangnail, trying to decide if the time had come. He looked up.

"You ever been in the Eastgate Hotel?" Castro's question was almost casual.

Lopez looked insulted. "Where Juanita worked? Yeah, why not?"

"What were you doing there?"

"Same as anybody else."

"What's that?"

Lopez waved his hand. "Looking around, man. I can go there if I want to. Have a drink in the bar. Sit in the lobby."

"What about the night of May 19th?"

Surprise flashed in his eyes. "How do I know what I was doing then? What did you do that night or the 20th, the 22nd. Man, who can remember?"

Castro picked up the knife, turned it around in his hand, testing the weight. "Could be the one . . . about the right size."

Lopez whipped his head around. "Right size for what?"

Talbott came in with coffee and sat the cup before Lopez, casting his eyes at the knife in Castro's hand.

Castro laid the knife before Lopez and sat down beside him, leaning his elbows on the table. "A knife just this size was used on a woman in the Eastgate Hotel the night of May 19."

Lopez froze. "Hey, what are we talking about here?"

"Murder," Talbott said. "That's what we're talking about here, Lopez."

Lopez cried out, his voice shrill as broken glass. "You just wait one goddamn second. I didn't murder nobody. Ever. I told you I stabbed Juanita in self-defense, but that's all." His face clouded as he watched the detectives exchange glances.

Castro rose. He walked around to the rear of Lopez's chair, and placing his hands on the back of it, leaned down as though to whisper in Lopez's ear. "A woman was murdered in the Eastgate Hotel. She was found by Juanita Sanchez." Castro could hear his own breathing. Lopez could close the books on the Sara Marley case. All slates wiped clean. End of trouble.

Lopez shifted in his chair, wetting his lips with the tip of his tongue. "I know Juanita was questioned about finding the dead lady. She was the sister of a big oil woman from Texas the papers said."

"Maybe you did it, Lopez. You own this knife."

Lopez's eyes widened. Castro could see that fear in him had cranked up a notch. "Just cause that's my knife don't mean I killed anybody in that hotel. You can't prove it was the same knife. There's plenty knives like that in this town."

Castro nodded. "That's true, Lopez. Let me play you a little version of what might have gone down that night in the Eastgate. You were hanging around there, like you said you do . . ."

"I go there sometimes . . ."

"You went there," Castro corrected. "This rich-looking woman checks in alone. You see her. Maybe follow her to see what room she goes to. You go tell Juanita to give you the passkey. This is your big chance. Juanita's not above stealing, so she gives you the key. You go to the woman's room with the idea of robbing her. Maybe you were going to hide in the room until the woman goes out or takes a bath, then you'd rob her. The woman catches you. Maybe starts to scream. You have no choice, in your mind, but to stab her. You panic, like when you stabbed Juanita, before you can take anything and run away. The next day Juanita reports that she's found the woman. Go anything like that, Lopez?"

Castro could smell panic coming off Carnie Lopez in waves; it was like the smell of ripe, freshly-cut lemon.

"You're trying to pin this murder on me because you haven't got anybody else. I didn't do it. I never murdered anybody. You can believe it."

"This is too much coincidence for me to believe." Castro cleared his throat. "Juanita Sanchez worked in the Eastgate Hotel. A woman was murdered there. Sanchez was the person who found the murdered woman. You stab Sanchez. Was she going to rat on you, Lopez? You had to silence her."

Lopez shook his head. "That's not the way it was."

"How was it, Lopez?"

Castro and Talbott were still, neither looking at anything in particular or saying a word. Lopez followed suit, but he seemed to be weighing something in his mind, coming to a decision, Castro thought. Let him be the one, he halfway prayed.

The silence lasted. Castro was tempted to say something, anything to get Lopez off dead center, but he dared not. Talbott kept his eyes trained on the floor.

Lopez looked up at the ceiling, hooked his hands behind his neck, fingers twitching.

"You got me for Juanita. Self-defense, though. If I tell you what I know, would it make it lighter on me?"

"It could. I can't make any promises until I hear what you have to say. But I warn you, don't give me anything but the truth. You got that, Lopez. All I want is the truth."

"That's what I'm going to give you, the absolute truth."

Castro glanced at Talbott, his heart accelerating. "Let me buzz for a stenographer first," he heard himself say. His voice sounded like it was coming from a well.

He got up, went to the wall and pressed a button. Police stenographers were always on call to take down a confession. He buzzed three times, again, which meant the captain was to be notified of an impending confession. Standing there Castro watched Lopez sip his coffee. He could smell his own sweat, the sweat of anticipation he knew so well. He had been on the brink before with suspects and saw them change their minds at the last minute or feed him a bunch of lies to cover their own tracks. He didn't want Lopez to slip out of his grip.

In minutes a plump woman in her early fifties came in, took a seat without a word, and placed a shorthand machine on the table, fingers poised. Castro walked over to Lopez and sat by him.

"Mr. Lopez," he began, all business now. "Tell me about the night of May 19th at the Eastgate Hotel."

Lopez glanced at the stenographer, then cleared his throat. "I was just hanging around."

"Hanging around where?"

"At the Eastgate, waiting for Juanita to get off work. Around the back entrance. We was going out for a beer. She comes down with her old coat on she's left since winter in her locker. It's all buttoned up to her neck. It ain't cold. She says she don't want to go no place. Wants to go right home. She acts funny . . . nervous, kind of. She says she don't feel good." Lopez rolled his eyes. "I drive her home, and she goes straight to the bathroom without taking off the coat. I think that's strange. I hear water running."

"Okay, Mr. Lopez. What did you do next?"

Lopez looked at the police stenographer, her hand going at the shorthand machine like a jackhammer. "I go into the bathroom. Juanita's got off her uniform and is soaking it in the sink. It's got blood on it. A big splash and some little dots. I ask her what's happened, and she tells me she stabbed the rich woman in the hotel, was going to take her things, but got scared off cause she heard some people in the hall. See, I told you Juanita was two-bit."

"So, if Juanita Sanchez stabbed Sara Marley in her room, her uniform's got blood on it. How did Sanchez get through the hotel hall and down to the locker room with blood on her? Don't you think somebody would have seen her, especially in the locker room?"

Lopez shook his head. "Like I said, there was just a few spots, not too big except for this one splash. Juanita held some towels over it 'til she got to the locker to get her coat."

"What did Juanita Sanchez do with the soiled uniform?"

"She finally burned it. That's exactly what happened."

"Where'd Juanita get the knife she stabbed the woman with?"

Lopez pointed to his knife on the table. "She carried my knife lots of times . . . for protection, you know."

"So, the next day when Juanita Sanchez goes on duty, she reports the woman she says she's just found. Has to, because Sara Marley's room is in the section she works."

The door opened and Captain Gordon strode in, his eyes fixed on Lopez. He turned to Castro. "What's taken place here? Confession on the stabbing down in . . . the Mexican district?"

Castro knew Gordon wanted to refer to the barrio as "flea town." "Little more than that. It involves the Marley case." Castro filled him in. Gordon beamed as he whirled around to look at Lopez.

"You about got it wrapped up, Castro?"

"A few more questions, captain. Could I talk to you out in the hall?"

As they walked out, Gordon eyed Lopez like he'd just found a long-lost friend. Gordon turned to Castro, a grin growing wider. "Well, just like I said all along. A robber that got scared off. We can close the books. You want to call Evelyn Casey and tell her the news? I told her we'd let her know if we had a break. I'll call the press and give them the story."

Castro shifted his weight from one foot to the other. "Captain, I had to question Lopez along those lines because of the connection of Sanchez to the Sara Marley case. He could be lying to help save his own skin, to get him off a murder rap to self-defense."

Castro watched Gordon's eyes squeeze into slits, saw the muscles in his neck turn into cords. "Is there some reason you don't want the Sara Marley case closed, Castro?"

"No, sir, I just want to be sure it is closed."

"Juanita Sanchez was big and strong enough to stab Sara Marley. She's got two counts of shoplifting against her. She had a motive and had the opportunity. Carnie Lopez has told you Sanchez admitted it. What else do you want? If you intend on climbing up the officers' ladder, you better learn to accept facts, unless it's more beneficial not to." Gordon turned and lumbered away.

Coming in from dinner, Evelyn and Sullivan pushed through the revolving door to the hotel lobby. They spotted Castro in a chair near the elevator. Sullivan recognized that tired look of a detective just off duty. He wondered why Castro was there and not at home. Tie pulled loose from his collar, Castro stood, his face lined and somber.

"Sullivan, I called you at home, but no answer. Figured you two were out for dinner, and I'd catch you here when you came in. Got news." He glanced at Evelyn. "We know who killed your sister. We've closed the case." He let out a rush of air.

Evelyn's eyebrows shot up. "Who? How'd you find out?"

"The maid at the hotel who found your sister. Juanita Sanchez did it, intending to rob your sister. Sanchez was stabbed by her boyfriend tonight. Self-defense, he claims. He told us about Juanita killing your sister.'' Lines of fatigue webbed at the corners of Castro's eyes.

Evelyn and Sullivan looked at each other for a long moment, then broke eye contact and stared at Castro. They started to talk at once, asking for details. Castro explained what had happened. Sullivan felt as if the wind had been knocked out of him. The revelation was a complete letdown, not the expected triumph. He had wanted the case solved, expected to unravel it himself, but this was a fizzle, not fireworks. He should have been pleased that the murderer had been uncovered, but somehow he wasn't. Perhaps his reasons were personal, not professional, he thought. It was all over.

Evelyn looked at Castro, her face devoid of expression. ''You believe this Carnie Lopez is telling the truth?''

''He swears it. Juanita Sanchez was physically able to commit the crime, had a motive and the opportunity. Almost an eyewitness in Carnie Lopez. Case closed.'' Castro studied the floor.

Sullivan glanced toward the bar. ''Let's have a nightcap over this one. There are a few things I've come across today I want to discuss with you.''

Castro pulled back his cuff and looked at his watch. ''Okay, just one. I've got to get home.''

They crowded into the booth where Sullivan and Evelyn had first met and ordered drinks. Sullivan lit a cigarette and explained to Castro what he'd discovered that afternoon. He laid the airline list on the table.

Castro slugged his beer and ran his tongue over his teeth. ''Think what you've got, Sullivan.'' He held up his hand, ticking off points on his fingers. ''You question the sixteen-year-old, Mark Foster, after we do. He tells you he changed seats with a man so he could smoke. Big deal. The airlines screw up and place people in the Nonsmoking when they want to be in Smoking. That doesn't mean beans. There's no connection with the Fort Worth woman. Her seatmate was a lady. A man on each of those flights paid with cash. Cover up, I grant you. Maybe a weekend away from the little wife, so she wouldn't have any credit card stubs to catch him with. Then, you go question a Gloria Martin who originally sat next to the man who asked Mark Foster to exchange seats. Just because she and Sara Marley are opposites personality-wise, you start blowing up a serial killer theory. It's done. Over. You've got to let it go." Castro took a hard look at Sullivan, shifted his eyes to Evelyn, then stared at Sullivan, suspicion clear in his expression.

Castro was entertaining the idea that maybe he, Sullivan, had his hooks into Evelyn and didn't want to release his grip. He and Evelyn had been spending time together. Hawk hadn't missed Castro's doubletake the morning he arrived at his house and found Evelyn and breakfast dishes. She had money. Did Castro think he was hoping to cover his financial problems through a fling with a wealthy, vulnerable widow and for monetary reasons didn't want the case closed? It pained him to think Castro might have such an opinion of him. He knew it must have pained Castro equally to reach such a conclusion about a friend.

"Both of those men have the same initials," Evelyn cut in, breaking the awkward moment.

Castro grabbed the airline lists. "Let's see." He ran his finger down the page. Your initials are E.C. Here's an Edward Crawford . . . an Elaine Cramer, if you want a woman. Hawk Sullivan . . . here's a Henry Saunders, a Harmon Smith. Manuel Castro, well, let's see. That could be a tough one. But, no. A Marvin Caldwell was on one flight, a Madeline Covington on another." Irritation flashed through Castro's words. "So much for initials."

Sullivan picked up his drink. "Mark Foster gave us a pretty good identification of the man who asked to change seats with him. What if the lady seated next to Mary Kenworth was asked to change seats and could give the same description?"

"Sullivan, buddy, I think you're reaching. The Marley case is closed as far as we're concerned."

Evelyn leaned forward. "Not as far as we're concerned. It still doesn't fit right. I know it." She and Sullivan exchanged glances. "We have a few more things to check, and we're not giving up until we're satisfied."

Castro stood up and brushed at his trousers. "I still say you're reaching."

Evelyn slowly raised her eyes and focused on him. "Isn't that how you catch something? To reach for it?"

"See you folks at dinner tomorrow night. I think by that time the reality of what's happened tonight will have settled in on you both." He stared at Evelyn. "This is what you wanted in the beginning . . . to have the case solved. Remember at the police station, those were your very words. Now, you have it." He turned to leave, then hesitated. "Hawk, you've been around the old track before. Call it a day, man."

They watched him stride out. Hawk lit another cigarette and looked out at the ocean. Nothing was lonelier-looking than black sky meeting dark water. Maybe Castro had it all together, and he was an over-the-hill sot grasping for one last chance at someone else's expense. The obligation was his to convince Evelyn Casey to return to Dallas. She had accomplished what she had come for.

"Well, shall we have one last drink?"

Evelyn leaned forward, resting her arms on the table. "That sounds so final, one last drink."

Sullivan took a deep breath. "Guess it is." He bit his lower lip. "I think the time has come for you to make plans to go home. Your sister's murderer has been uncovered. Case closed. And, I'm ready to roll on another case. I gave them my word I'd be ready when they were. That project I'm committed to was about to cause a big conflict, and now that your sister's case is closed, I'll be free to give it all of my time. Things worked out right on schedule." He hoped his expression gave nothing away.

She clasped her hands together. "Please, not yet. Just a little longer. You know what you said at dinner. 'We know of two similar murders. How many more are there out there that we don't know about?' When I go to my room, I'll call Carole Wheeler and make arrangements to use the paper's microfilm library. See what I can uncover. You go to Los Angeles like we planned and talk to Mary Kenworth's seatmate, Virginia Taubman. See if she was asked to change seats like Mark Foster was. If she was and gives the same description as Mark did, we've got something. I still have the feeling there's lots more we don't know." She brightened. "Castro and the police are on the wrong avenue. I can't say I blame them. What can they do but accept what they're told and close their books? We have to keep trying . . . just a little longer.''

Sullivan couldn't help but smile. He had a growing respect for Evelyn's composure in a trying situation, an admiration for her tenacity. She would make a good detective if she went after every case like she did her sister's. She was willing to work to grind out her theories when she could be at home with no cares, living the life of luxury and Quinn Stewart waiting in the wings.

Sullivan glanced around the room. ''This is a little like déjà vu. Here we sit in the same spot with you trying to convince me to take on your sister's case.''

''Have I convinced you again?''

Sullivan made a face. ''You're good at that.''

''Not so good for the killer that we didn't give up.'' Evelyn stared at him. ''He's still out there, you know.''

CHAPTER 8

ON HIS WAY OUT, Castro glanced around the squadroom. It looked exactly the same every day of the week, weekends and holidays included. But on Monday mornings, sameness or not, the feel was somehow different, each man wondering what those next seven days held. Not one expressed concern, but it was there, fears left unsaid, hanging like humidity in the tropics after a rain. Would they still be around when the week closed? For the next forty-eight hours Castro didn't have to worry.

He pushed through the front door, thoughts of two days of free time cheering him after what he'd been through. As the Captain gloated to reporters over closing the Marley case at the early morning press conference, his eyes had never strayed from Castro, who kept waiting for him to refer to Carole Wheeler's article, which hinted at a connection with another case, thereby making the reporter appear ridiculous in light of the new developments. He should have known that Gordon, even at someone else's expense, dared not broach the subject of serial killings lest the press mention it in the interview. But reporters were a persistent lot, reluctant to let a hot issue drop and presented Castro with an opportunity to return Gordon's stare when one did bring up the article. Gordon, skirting a direct discussion, looked around theatrically, pointing out that the newspaper hadn't seen fit to send the overly-eager reporter who had made the wild speculations to cover the conference. He finished by stating the Marley case was an isolated incident and that it was also closed as the result of a near eyewitness who furnished complete details. Castro felt uneasy about the situation and his abruptness toward Sullivan. He'd smooth it over at dinner. For now he intended to put police work on hold.

Carole Wheeler pulled over to the curb, jumped out of her car and charged up the steps. "Sergeant Castro! Could I talk to you a minute? I just heard the news about the Marley case down at the *Union* office."

Castro dodged her without breaking stride and broke into a faster pace. "Case is closed."

Carole fell in with him, almost running to keep up. "But I just wanted to . . ."

"Bug off. It's over. I'm off duty." Castro kept moving, looking straight ahead at the parking lot.

Carole slowed, then stopped altogether, watching Castro put distance between them. She hurried back to her car.

Across the street from the station Castro noticed a man, standing next to a bus stop, who seemed more interested in the exchange than watching for the approaching bus. As Castro passed him, the man turned and focused on the parking lot.

Castro followed the man's line of vision. Lieutenant Adams was crouched next to Castro's blue police-issue car. He appeared to be inspecting the tires. Straightening up as Castro approached, Adams brushed imaginary dust from his trousers.

"Say, man, I thought for a minute your tire had been punctured. It looked low." Adams, reminding Castro of a used car salesman, kicked the tire. "Guess not. Been lots of slashing in the lot lately. They oughta put some guards on the unmarked cars. At least keep the gates locked, maybe add one of the dogs."

Castro leaned down to inspect the tire. "Looks okay to me. Maybe I just need a little air."

"Congratulations on closing the Marley case."

"Thanks." Castro turned back and saw that the man didn't board the bus. He wondered why his attention was so drawn to him, just a young fellow more than likely fascinated with policemen.

Adams eyes flickered over Castro briefly. "I saw on the postings you got two 'frees' coming. Mine's next week. Might get in a little fishing." Adams paused, as if waiting for Castro to offer his plans.

Castro opened the car door and slid in. "Hope the weather holds for you. This time a year you can't tell."

"Yeah." Adams turned and headed toward the gate.

Castro inserted the key and watched Adams mosey through the parking lot. A queer one, that Adams. His chilly demeanor had earned him the nickname "Ice Ass" from the detectives on the force. Being a protégé of Captain Gordon's further divorced him from the rest of the squad. Castro puzzled over their brief conversation. Other than the time of day, he couldn't recall Adams ever inquiring about anything from a fellow officer. His fingers performed a quick tap dance on the steering wheel. He started the engine and eased out of the parking lot, irritated that his mood had been spoiled by something he couldn't quite get a handle on.

Finished with packing, Evelyn picked up the phone to have the hotel garage send her car around. After taking Sullivan to the airport, she would return and, as previously arranged, meet Carole Wheeler and move to the new apartment. The night before, she tried reaching Carole but her answering machine, obviously on the fritz, cut on and off, making strange noises. Dialing the paper early that morning, she was told Carole was not in.

Now that her sister's case was officially closed, it was a must to furnish a logical explanation for staying. She liked Carole but from experience knew she couldn't trust her. Until their theory had more backup, she and Hawk weren't ready to go public. Proof, one way or the other, could come by the end of the day. There was also the matter of conning Carole into letting her use the newspaper's microfilm library without being privvy to the real purpose. She and Hawk could discuss a plan of attack on the way to the airport. They risked having their operation blown sky-high if they weren't careful.

A knock at the door startled her. Her heart bumped an extra beat. She replaced the receiver in its cradle.

"Who is it?"

"Me. Carole."

Evelyn winced, then checked her watch. Unsettled, with no way out but to wing it, Evelyn took a deep breath, unbolted the latch and grabbed the knob with such force that the door banged wide open.

"I didn't expect you until ten." She felt her cheeks flush.

"I just heard the news! Can't believe it was a woman who murdered your sister. Gordon can eat his insinuations about anything sexually lurid. Guess you're pleased the case is closed. I want to hear all about it. That Castro wouldn't give me the time of day. My paper didn't even let me know about the press conference." Carole eyed Evelyn's luggage, then looked at her. "You weren't going to leave for Dallas without calling me?"

Evelyn shook her head, mind churning with excuses. "Well, no, of course not. I mean . . . I'm not going back just yet."

Suddenly alert, Carole cocked her head to one side. "Oh? What's to keep you now?"

"I committed myself. I said I'd take care of the plants in the apartment for you. Anyway, I thought I might like to stay on a while."

"It's all over, or is it?" Carole had a quizzical look.

"Sure. Castro came by last night to tell us the news. I was just coming in from dinner with Hawk Sullivan. He's the man I hired to work on the case." Evelyn waved her hand, then reminded herself to watch the gestures. "A man they picked up for stabbing Juanita Sanchez confessed that she did it. She was the one who found Sara. Certainly had access to the room, which accounts for no forced entry. She had a record of stealing, so Sara's murder resulted from an interrupted burglary attempt, no doubt." Evelyn stopped and thought over her statement of facts. They *did* all fit. Maybe she *was* obsessed with the serial killer notion, off on some foolish odyssey.

"You feeling okay? Your color is sort of a weird shade of pink. Blotched."

Evelyn shrugged. "Guess the ordeal has taken its toll. I'm not ready to face going home yet. I've got lots of spare time now." Evelyn examined Carole's expression for any sign of suspicion.

Carole wore a denim prairie skirt brushing her ankles and a Hawaiian tourist shirt. On her feet were shoes that could pass for ballet slippers. Her purse was a bulging green tote bag.

Still standing in the doorway, Evelyn smiled, but it quickly faded when over Carole's shoulder she spotted a man by the elevator. He was turned so that she couldn't see his face, but he resembled the man she had seen by the elevator the day before. So what, she asked herself? He was staying on the same floor. Still, she was surprised at how much he had unnerved her. He was over six feet tall, dark . . . his looks, if she had a better view, might easily match the description given by Mark Foster.

"What's the matter?" Carole looked in the man's direction just as he stepped into the elevator.

"Nothing. For a minute he reminded me of someone." Catching a whiff of Carole's perfume, Evelyn moved aside so she could enter. She smelled as if she'd squirted on every sampler from a cosmetic counter.

Evelyn hurried to answer the insistently ringing phone and found another reporter on the line, wanting her reactions to the closed case. She realized how it must hurt Carole for her journalistic integrity to be dented, but she couldn't let her in on the serial killer developments just yet.

"I'm sorry, but no comments at this time. If and when I do there's someone at the *Union* I'll talk to." She and Carole exchanged glances. Evelyn hung up.

"Well, have you called for a bellboy? We could probably carry these." Carole grabbed a handle of the bag and tested the weight. "Even I don't travel this light."

Evelyn glanced toward the closet. "I've got my sister's things, too. Look, you were ahead of schedule. I promised Hawk Sullivan I'd take him to the airport. Something's wrong with his car. I'll do that, then meet you at the apartment."

Carole pursed her lips. "Waste of time and no reason to

make it so complicated. I'm already here and the apartment is hard to find. You couldn't by yourself. We'll drop your friend by the airport. It's on the way. After we see the apartment, I'll let you off back here to pick up your car. I pass right by your hotel on the way to the paper. Call and have someone sent up to help us.'' Carole hooked the tote bag's strap over her shoulder.

The position she was in filled Evelyn with unease. She had to hurry now or Sullivan would miss his plane. And Carole was so insistent. There seemed no choice but to go along. She didn't look forward to the two of them meeting.

Carole wanted to know everything about the case, how Evelyn felt now that she knew who the killer was. As Evelyn parried Carole's questions, she used last-minute packing chores to divert Carole's unwavering eyes. Faking enthusiasm that the case was closed, she thought continually of excuses to use the microfilm library. When the bellman came for the bags, Evelyn eyed him curiously. He, too, fit Mark Foster's description of Sara's seatmate. These comparisons had to stop. Everyone was becoming suspect.

Evelyn looked around, checking for something she might have forgotten. ''Well, time to go.''

Carole walked to the mirror and pushed her hair around, then leaned toward her reflection, eyes narrowed on Evelyn in the background. ''How far off base we were. Can't imagine it. Wonder how the Kenworth case in Los Angeles will end up getting solved, if it ever does?''

Evelyn shrugged. ''Probably some simple explanation like Sara's case. Hawk will miss his airplane if we don't hurry.''

Carole whirled around. ''Oh, that wouldn't do. So, let's make tracks.''

They pushed through the revolving door in the lobby. The air was crisp from the ocean's breeze, but the sun was out, the sky clear except for a few scattered clouds. If Evelyn stretched her imagination, one billowy puff looked like a fat lady drifting toward heaven. She took a deep breath. Such a nice day, she thought. It would be a relief if the murder were solved and put behind her.

''Here's my car.'' Carole pointed to an old yellow Honda, a plastic red flower attached to the aerial. ''We'll stack the bags on one side of the backseat. It's a great car for me. I like to take off and drive up and down the coast. I can pack my typewriter and books and sleep in the back if I position myself the right way.'' Evelyn winced as she imagined Sullivan's frame cramped in the small space.

As they chugged away, Evelyn thought she noticed the man from her hall get into a taxi. She looked back twice at the heavy traffic.

On the way to Sullivan's, Evelyn regaled Carole with tales of Sullivan, much the same as Castro had done with her. Their reverse roles amused Evelyn. She, once the skeptic, had now turned into his champion. Suddenly, without realizing it she had provided Carole with her logical reason for staying. She hoped Carole took the bait. Without pushing the subject, she'd let the innuendo sink in.

"I can't blame you for staying on. California's a great place. I come from your neighboring state, Oklahoma. What a dust pit! My mother was full-blooded Cherokee. Maybe that's why I go creeping around, sniffing out info to send out on my tom-tom.''

Evelyn looked at her with amazement. The explanation for Carole's looks came when she stated that her mother had married an Irishman, a freckled ginger-haired man. Evelyn supposed the Irish blood had routed every trace of Indian strain, stamping her father's looks on her. But where had she acquired her machine-gun-fire speech?

"I got a scholarship in journalism at New York University. I hated the weather there, the hustle and bustle of the city, so after graduation I took my first job offer as a cub reporter at the *Union*. Haven't come across anybody I wanted to marry or who wanted to marry me. Right now, when I'm not working, I'm remodeling my beach house myself.''

They pulled into the driveway, and Carole tooted her horn. Sullivan appeared in the doorway putting one hand over his eyes to shield the sun. His hair was plastered to his skull as if he'd just showered. He looked uncomfortable in a tie and a sport jacket, lapels slightly out of fashion. He reminded Evelyn of a tough little kid dressed for Sunday school in his brother's hand-me-downs.

Carole turned to Evelyn, features contorted. "That's him? He'd be perfect to play a tall Charles Bronson."

Sullivan lumbered down the walk, a hint of surprise and annoyance on his face. He leaned down to look in Evelyn's side of the window. "Is this a game of 'Sardines,' or are we going to the airport?" Evelyn caught the aroma of fresh soap, shampoo and Listerine.

Evelyn opened the door, got out and folding back the front seat, crawled into the back. "You'll be more comfortable in the front."

Sullivan slid in, adjusted his coat and glanced at Carole Wheeler. Before he could speak, Evelyn leaned forward.

"This is Carole Wheeler. Carole, Hawk Sullivan."

"Hi," Carole said, attempting to shift into reverse.

Sullivan nodded, sliding his eyes slightly to the left. A telltale tuck of displeasure played at the corner of his mouth.

The car bucked, started backward, and the engine died. Carole turned the key. The motor growled, then fizzled. She tried again with the same results. She stomped on the accelerator, at the same time flicking the key on and off.

"You'll flood it." Sullivan ran a finger around his collar as if it were too tight.

Carole threw open the door, marched to the fender and banged it with her hip. Back in the car, she turned the key and the engine purred. "Never fails." She nudged the gears into reverse, and they shot with a jerk into the street. A cruising taxi braked, tires screeching, the male occupant hurled against the backseat. As the cab sped away, the driver stuck his arm out of the window and gave Carole the finger. She returned the gesture as they lurched off down the street. Sullivan rotated his neck, then pulled a package of cigarettes from his breast pocket.

Carole glanced his way. "Sorry, but I don't allow smoking in my car." She pulled onto Interstate 5 and joined the traffic snaking south. The beach and ocean lay to their right.

Stuffing the pack into his pocket, Sullivan looked around at the car's interior, inspecting the torn upholstery, the cracked seats, the dusty dashboard. From a side view Evelyn could see his jaw pulsing, could almost feel him bristling. She tried to think of something to say.

"Going to Los Angeles on business?" Carole asked, eyes steady on the freeway.

"No, pleasure," Sullivan answered, an edge in his voice.

"I hear you didn't much like my article." Gripping the wheel Carole moved her thumbs up and down as she drove.

Sullivan lifted his eyebrows. "Much? That's not quite accurate," he paused. "I didn't like it at all. It was uncalled for, inappropriate, untimely and might have caused a great deal of damage."

Evelyn leaned back, admitting to herself there was little she could do to stop them from tearing into each other.

No one spoke. Tension in the confined space grew.

Carole slowly moved her eyes from the road and fastened them on Sullivan's. "One man's opinion. If you look on the other side of the ledger, it might have done some good. At any rate, we were all wrong." Her voice was steady, affirmative, not giving an inch.

His lips firmed a bit, as if he'd decided to take a stand. "Done some good for you maybe. Another byline notched in your belt. I agree that you had every right to print it at your own discretion. That's what I question . . . your discretion. Maybe you ought to explore it next time before you go to press. That's when a reporter turns into a fine journalist. Discretion over sensationalism."

"Still one man's opinion," Carole snapped.

Sullivan's hand relaxed its choking grip on the back seat, but his eyes remained on Carole, who ignored him by concentrating on the freeway.

Suddenly Evelyn felt relieved. Sullivan had given his opinion, not minced words, but kept himself in control.

"If you'll roll down the window, it's okay to smoke," Carole offered. Evelyn liked her for saying that.

Sullivan didn't make a move, finally saying, "I can wait."

Carole wheeled off the freeway onto Laurel, a street lined with old warehouses, junk furniture stores and refinishing shops. The street hooked right and headed into the airport boulevard, the ocean in view on the left. Glistening in the sunlight, huge Navy vessels, aircraft carriers, freighters, Coast Guard cutters were in port.

Sullivan looked back at Evelyn. "Guess you two are off to the newspaper's microfilm library next."

"What?" Carole jerked her head around.

Evelyn swallowed hard, realizing Hawk assumed that mission was settled because Carole was long. "I'll talk to you about that on the way to the apartment, Carole."

The three remained silent.

At Lindbergh Field's PSA terminal, Sullivan got out on the busy sidewalk and held the door while Evelyn crawled into the front. He pulled a cigarette from the pack, lit it, then leaned into the car. "Nice to meet you," he said to Carole, no real meaning in his voice.

"I'll be waiting here when you get back," Evelyn said as she watched Sullivan pivot and join the throng of travelers pushing through the double glass doors. He stood out in a crowd. Tall, erect, commanding, a special person. A flare of excitement grew in her stomach. In the space of hours they would have some answers. If what they discovered was a bust, there was no alternative. She'd be forced to go back to Dallas and try to resume her life. The thought saddened her.

Carole put the car in gear and pressed on the accelerator. "What was he talking about . . . the microfilm library at the newspaper?"

Evelyn looked directly at Carole. "I suppose I have to admit this to you. It's a way to hang around here without Hawk knowing the real reason. If I go back to Dallas, the distance will put an end to any chance of a relationship." Evelyn winced at the unaccustomed girl talk. "He knows my educational background, and Sara's case, even though it didn't turn out like we thought, made me highly sensitive to the problems that the 'other victims' in a murder suffer . . . friends, family, the survivors trying to get help from the police, looking for justice. See? I have lots of time on my hands now, so I thought I might use what I know, do some research for a project and write a book on the subject. I told Hawk I might be able to count on you for help with research. He agreed to help me, too. As an ex-FBI agent, he's full of ideas."

Carole shot her a skeptical look. "So are you. All of a sudden a book comes to mind, huh? You want me to arrange for you to use the newspaper's microfilm facilities?'' Her tone had a sharp edge.

"I'd sure appreciate it. Thought I'd start research here because I've already had run-ins with the San Diego police, so I'd like to get a feel for local cases, see if there are others out there who experienced my problems?''

Evelyn could sense Carole bristle. Did she think the request overstepped the bounds of courtesy? Maybe Carole thought the idea of a book infringed on her territory.

They rode in silence, other than the few comments Evelyn made about buildings, houses and the landscape in general.

The apartment building situated two blocks off the ocean front was a glass and rough concrete modern structure fifteen stories high. Carole swung into the half circle driveway, stopping in front of a yellow and white awning that stretched from the curb to the entrance, which was attended by a uniformed doorman. He called a handyman to help with the bags.

Evelyn took in the lobby with one sweeping glance. The floor was polished travertine topped by a large modern shag rug the colors of the rainbow. Overhead a large brass chandelier gave off muted light. Nubby upholstered couches and chairs made comfortable seating arrangements. Two potted plants flanked the elevator.

On the sixth floor, Carole opened the apartment door. The man put down the bags, and Evelyn wandered through as Carole conducted a tour in a monotone of disinterest. The small marble-floored foyer opened to a large living room with a wall of glass overlooking the ocean. Evelyn slid the door open. A cool breeze and the unmistakable smell of the sea filled the room. An entire wall served as the backdrop for a lush arrangement of exotic, green and flowering plants set among rocks and a small marble pool filled with fat goldfish.

Evelyn tried to concentrate on the decor, but tension between her and Carole tightened.

The living room furniture was leather-upholstered, typically masculine, in good taste with high-tech appointments. Glass and chrome coffee table. Chrome square chairs. From one side of the room a long-necked chrome lamp swung outward to hang above the chairs. There was a well-stocked walk-in bar. On the walls framed newspaper awards testified to the occupant's writing ability. He had a wonderful old rolltop desk that Evelyn guessed must have come with him from some other place. The pale salmon-colored walls and carpet softened the atmosphere, creating a warm glow.

In the small but efficient kitchen, Evelyn pulled out drawers and opened cabinets, peeked inside the stove. Everything was clean, almost sparkling, as if unused. Bachelors ate out often, she supposed.

The bedroom was large, airy, with the same view as the living room. The king-size bed looked comfortable. Evelyn and Carole couldn't help but giggle when they looked up at the mirror overhead. He might eat out, but he slept in.

"It's just right." Evelyn smiled, hoping to patch the sudden breach. She didn't want their budding friendship nipped, and she also wanted a shot at the microfilms.

She picked up the telephone and gave the operator her credit card number. "Want to make a couple of calls to Dallas to give them this number," she said to Carole, who flounced down on the bed, looking up at the mirror.

Evelyn reached her maid, gave her the number and a few instructions, then called Quinn Stewart's private line at Cypress Oil.

"Hello," he answered, dragging out vowels. His slight Texas accent reminded Evelyn of home and everyone back there.

"Quinn, I wanted to give you the news! Sara's case has been closed." She supplied the details in a tone the situation required.

"I'm happy that's it's all over. When are you coming home?"

"It won't be too long. This friend, a reporter, arranged for me to use an apartment. Remember I told you about it? I wanted to give you the number, Quinn."

"I don't understand why you're staying when the case is closed. What's going on out there?"

"Hawk Sullivan and I still have some business." She watched Carole rearrange herself on the bed, possibly playing out some fantasy. Momentarily forgetting the situation, Evelyn almost laughed.

"Evelyn, this fellow you've hired . . . Hawk Sullivan, you said was with the FBI here in Dallas at one time? Why did he leave?"

"Quinn, you don't have to check him out or anything, if that's what you're thinking. Trust my judgment." She wanted to tell Quinn that Sullivan was onto some good leads. She glanced at Carole, who now watched her intently, absorbing every word.

"What kind of business could you and he have?"

Quinn would be leaning back in his chair now as he did when he turned serious. Punctual almost to a fault, he always kept his eyes on the digital gold clock on his desk as he talked. To be late for an appointment or a squash game was, in his mind, unpardonable. "We'll talk about that later. Are you going to be home tonight?"

"I have the Wildcatter's dinner at the Petroleum Club, but it should break up early. I'll call you when I get home. Should be around eight your time. Will you be there?"

"Not then." She thought about dinner at the Castros'. What would Quinn think of her going to a policeman's house for dinner? She looked forward to it, but Quinn's opinion would be another matter. "I'm having dinner with some friends. Should be home by ten, I'd say. That's twelve your time. We'll talk tomorrow."

"Friends? Evelyn, where are all these people coming from? This person, Sullivan," he paused. "I don't want you mixed up with . . . well, hell, this person knows who you are . . . Cypress Oil and all. You're under stress. You understand my point of view. I don't want you taken in. It bothers me . . ."

"Quinn," Evelyn cut in. "It's okay. We'll talk tomorrow."

"Evelyn, is someone there with you? You can't talk right now?"

"You got it, Quinn. Tomorrow." She placed the receiver on the cradle.

Carole bounded up. "I'm going to the bathroom." She shifted the purse strap to her other shoulder and walked off.

Carole closed the door and looked in the mirror. "Something's wrong here," she whispered to herself as she always did when puzzled. Evelyn's phone conversation was cagey. What business could she and Hawk Sullivan still have? Romance? In the car he seemed casual to Evelyn. He acted, in his continued resentment about the article, as if he were still on the case.

She tapped her short nails on the counter. At first Evelyn's announcement about writing a book rattled her professional pride. *She* was the journalist interested in crime, not Evelyn who now wanted to rival her. Within hours after her sister's case was solved, Evelyn suddenly wanted to write a book? She didn't know Evelyn well, and it could be the natural channel of an obsessive-type personality to take now that her sister's case was closed.

Then, it dawned on her that this was just some cockamamie story, cooked up just to gain access to the microfilm library. Carole was alerted, but to what? Her journalistic credibility wasn't running high, but she had believed Evelyn was onto something once. Maybe she still was. Her article could have been on target all along. Immensely curious, she decided to go along with Evelyn's request. There might be a chance to exonerate herself and restore her credibility. Maybe the Sara Marley case wasn't solved. Evelyn wasn't talking. It was up to her to get to the bottom of things before anyone else.

She flushed the toilet and walked out.

"If you want to use the newspaper's microfilms, I'll have to put in a request for what you want and make up some excuse for you being there. Not just anyone is allowed in." Carole smiled.

Evelyn returned her smile, knowing Carole Wheeler hadn't suddenly turned magnanimous. She'd have to be doubly careful. Carole was playing her.

In real life most places do not look as they are portrayed on television or in the movies, but the newsroom of *The San Diego Union* was exactly what Evelyn had seen countless times on the screens. Row after row of desks were manned by frantic reporters, clattering away on typewriters and word processors as if their life depended on each word. Wire service teletypes spit out rolls of paper. Editors, sitting in glass cubicles partitioned off from the activity and noise but in full view of the action, labored over copy. Evelyn wondered how anyone could concentrate in such a chaotic environment.

People waved at Carole and gave odd signs with their

hands and fingers. Evelyn guessed they had a language all their own. One man yelled, "Hey, 'Carrots.' Out tracking serial killers?" Another called. "Top of the morning, 'Wheel.' If you got up earlier, you might not miss some interesting press conferences." Carole stuck out her tongue. It was clear that here she had found her place and what on the outside appeared eccentric was accepted as normal.

"I'll show you the library. My desk is over there." Carole pointed to an empty spot, papers piled high. "Wait here a sec while I tell the guy in charge of the microfilms you're doing some research for me. He'll come in the library and when he sees you, not me, he'll give you some grief, so this'll save you explaining. I'll get you a yellow pad and some pencils. Know you'll want to make notes."

Evelyn watched Carole flounce over to a man's desk for a rapid exchange. He glanced at Evelyn, then nodded to Carole. With her back to Evelyn, Carole rummaged her desk, shuffled papers, then whirled around and made her way through the desks to join Evelyn.

"I'll be working right through lunch and into the afternoon, but if you finish early, I can take some stuff home with me. Just come on back and get me and we'll go."

"I really appreciate the use of the microfilm," Evelyn managed over the din.

"Nothing," Carole said and led Evelyn down a long cavernous hall and kicked open a door. On a library table sat boxes that held what Evelyn had requested: microfilms of newspapers from San Diego, Los Angeles and San Francisco dating back through the beginning of the year. After she finished going through these, microfilms of the previous year's newspapers could be tackled.

Carole placed the yellow pad and pen on the table, pulled the projector to the edge of the table, plugged it in and explained to Evelyn how to operate the machine. After Carole left, Evelyn sat down, examining the equipment. Sullivan's idea had been a good one, and she felt excited at the possibility of ferreting out similar murders still unconnected to each other, gathering enough concrete information to substantiate a pattern.

She inserted the first spool of microfilm and started her

process. Clicking the lever, she moved from section to section of the paper. She blinked her eyes and strained into the projector, trying to adjust to the small print.

She quickly learned to eliminate useless sections and concentrate on parts where an account of a murder without sensationalism would be printed. This method was time-saving, but she realized she was in for a long session.

Checking her watch, Evelyn saw she had been at the task for over two hours now. It seemed more like five. Frame after frame had been scanned with no results. Beginning with the date of Sara's murder in May, she had worked her way back to March. She pushed back from the table, rubbed her eyes, then closed them. She rested her head on the back of the straight chair. Listening to her stomach rumble, she knew there was no time for a lunch break.

Pulling her chair closer to the table, Evelyn eyed the stacks of microfilm still to be scanned. So far, Sullivan's ideas weren't panning out. She wondered if it was a far-fetched exercise in futility. Castro could be right after all. She wondered if perhaps she should be grateful. If their theory were true, it spelled a gruesome fate for other innocent women. She plowed in again.

First a woman, then a man came in, interrupting Evelyn's concentration. Eyeing her, they went to the green metal cabinets and shuffled through files. Now and then the woman peered at Evelyn over half-glasses. Uncomfortable, Evelyn tried to settle down to business.

Well into the afternoon, a headache started to nag her. She felt tired and wanted to stop, but Sullivan's trust in her ability spurred her to continue. She took a deep breath and decided to take a small break.

Resting her head on the desk her thoughts centered on Sullivan. He was a man who couldn't deal with his own failure, so he had withdrawn from the game. She guessed his wife's death had played a part in his deterioration. In a way, the weaknesses she saw in him were curiously appealing. They made her even more aware of his strengths and made him seem more human. At dinner the night before, for a fleeting moment, she had thought he was going to say something special, even touch her hand, but she had been wrong.

But she wasn't wrong about one thing. Since yesterday she had sensed a struggle inside him, a critical point reached as if his very survival somehow depended on solving the case. She would like to think that she herself had prompted this new urgency for change, but judgment told her it had to do entirely with his own private battle.

She lifted her head, inserted another round of microfilm and continued the tedious job. Poring over the last week of March, she found the number of murders in San Diego staggering, but none similar to Sara's. Finished with that month, she replaced the microfilm in its proper container, closed the lid and started on the box marked February.

The door opened and Carole Wheeler popped in. "How're you doing?" Her eyes shifted to the blank yellow pad. "Getting anywhere?"

Evelyn let out a rush of air. "Not yet. Haven't found much of interest. Research is pretty boring. I might have picked too big a project. Maybe I'll just forget it."

Carole Wheeler looked at her for a moment before speaking. "Well, when you give up, I'll be at my desk." She turned around, looked back, then ducked out.

She checked her watch. A sinking feeling that she wasn't going to be able to produce anything to back up Sulllivan's theories settled over her. A discovery came clear in her mind. It was just as important to her to find something for Sullivan's sake as it was for her own reasons. But she had to face the fact that she and Hawk could have been off base all along and had now reached the end. Castro's version had smelled wrong, but maybe because she had wanted it to, had tried to make it so in her mind.

Discouraged by the passing hours, she flipped the lever, moving from frame to frame. Lead captions, mostly deceiving, slowed her work considerably. She felt as if she could wring the necks of some reporters. One story in particular irritated her. The words SLAYER SOUGHT caught her eye, giving rise to a wave of excitement. As she followed the article, it turned out that two deer had been found shot in the surrounding mountains. Revolving her shoulders, she plodded on.

She flicked the lever and suddenly, as if drawing a bead, squinted at the small article. The rush of triumph quickly faded. For a time she sat quietly absorbing the gravity of what she might have found.

Innately she knew she had just uncovered the beginning of a long chain of related bloody events. The impact of the discovery horrified her. With a quick intake of breath, Evelyn reached for the pen and pad to record the exact account.

Hours later, she looked at the long list of similar murder cases she had complied. She set things in order, folded her notes and put them in her purse. At the door, she turned back, hurried to the table and picked up the yellow pad. Her writing, as she had suspected, had imprinted through on the blank pages. On closer inspection, she found a piece of carbon paper taped on a page near the back. Smiling, she waltzed out with the whole yellow pad. Sullivan would have been proud.

CHAPTER 9

SULLIVAN'S PLANE touched down at 6:42 P.M. The twenty-minute flight from Los Angeles had seemed an eternity. Armed with more knowledge on which to build, Sullivan moved through the airport like a man with his back on fire.

Evelyn waited in the No Parking zone just outside. When he spotted her, he waved, approached the car and slipped into the driver's seat as Evelyn moved over.

"Glad to see the apparition's not along." He looked at Evelyn and grinned.

Evelyn's eyes widened. "I'm almost blind, but I've got what you wanted," she began, then snatched the note pad from her purse. "On March 10th, a woman identified as Margo Ames was found stabbed to death in the Hotel Coronado here in San Diego a few hours after she arrived. I've copied the exact newspaper account." Evelyn read word-for-word to him, then looked up. "There's more. On February 1st, in Los Angeles, a Bonnie Townes was stabbed hours after arriving at the Biltmore Hotel. January 3rd in San Francisco . . . a Judy Ellis . . . same thing. A Marianne Gray in Los Angeles . . . Hyatt Hotel. There are three more," she paused. "There's a common denominator. All of the women had arrived in the cities where they were murdered from the Dallas–Fort Worth airport.''

A policeman knocked on Sullivan's window, interrupting his concentration. He asked Sullivan to move out. Obliging, Sullivan pulled into the line of traffic. His worst thoughts were true and being proven right was little triumph. A serial murderer was on the prowl.

Evelyn moved sideways on the seat, facing him. ''Tell me what you found out this afternoon.''

Her hair fell softly around her shoulders. She still wore the skirt and blouse from the morning. He approved of her simplicity and understatment, a direct contrast to the role of the wealthy heiress she in fact was. Until now, the incongruity of taking her to a policeman's modest home for dinner had not struck him. He supposed it spoke well for her that it hadn't.

''Virginia Taubman, Mary Kenworth's seatmate, an elderly woman . . . a widow, had practically the same experience on the flight that Mark Foster did. A man came up to her and asked if she'd change seats. But this time, catch this, so he could sit in the Nonsmoking. She doesn't see well, but what she remembered of the man fairly well matches Foster's description.''

Both were silent.

After a few minutes, Evelyn broke the spell. ''What's our next step?'' She looked across the water at the small crafts bobbing up and down. A ferocious wind had stirred in from the west.

''Let's go over what we do have, Evelyn.'' He realized that he had called her by her given name for the first time. ''When Mrs. Taubman changed seats with the killer so he could sit next to Mary Kenworth, her new seatmate was a man. So that means the killer originally was assigned a seat next to a man. Proves what we thought . . . he's after women only.'' Sullivan fumbled a cigarette out of a package and punched in the car lighter. ''Before the killer changed seats with Mark Foster, he was already seated next to a woman, Gloria Martin. A blond who looks something like you.'' The cigarette dangled at the corner of Sullivan's mouth as he talked. "Proves, as we've talked about, he's after a certain type of woman. A woman like your sister and Mary Kenworth."

"And I've found that there have been a series of killings, not just two." The lighter popped out and Evelyn touched it to Sullivan's cigarette. "Now, I think we need a professional profile of the killer's personality type. We've talked about it . . . he's a woman hater . . . why? Rejection . . . I'll work on it."

Sullivan let out a cloud of smoke. "I'm about down to the grueling part. Just have to question every person in first-class on those two flights. Maybe someone will have some crumb of information . . . noticed something out of the ordinary. Then I'll have to check the flights of those victims you uncovered today." Sullivan sighed at the thought. Time wasn't on his side. "I can't think of where else to turn unless I sit at the Dallas–Fort Worth airport waiting for a tan man over six feet tall with weird eyes to turn up."

"When Castro hears what we have, maybe he can convince Captain Gordon to reopen the case."

Sullivan rolled his eyes. "We'll see." One thing he knew. When Castro heard what they had, it would reverse his opinion. Castro's suspicion that he had ulterior motives still bothered Sullivan.

Sullivan turned right onto Castro's street. It made him sad whenever he drove onto a residential street of "starter" homes inhabited by middle-age people who knew even when they were starting out that they would probably end up there.

Sullivan parked behind Castro's car in the circular concrete driveway Castro had poured himself. Round aggregate stepping stones led through a manicured lawn to the front door. The house was Spanish-style with a rust-colored tile roof. Ivy, like green fingers, clasped the sides of the stucco bungalow. The place wasn't as modest as Sullivan remembered. Castro had made some improvements. Sullivan wondered what his salary amounted to now and remembered that Olga said she worked, too.

Castro opened the door. "*Saludos, amigos. Entre mi casa.*"

Castro looked trim and fit in a blue-and-white-checked shirt and white twill slacks. Sullivan admired him with a touch of envy. Once he had been in such shape. He resolved to run a mile every day on the beach even if it killed him. Drinking heavily wasn't helping either. He was afraid he might be frozen into his present state, like in a warning of his grandmother's: "Don't cross your eyes, they might get stuck that way." The thought of resolving his inner conflicts cheered him. He simply had to do it.

"Olga's cooking my favorite dinner," Sullivan announced as if she were doing it solely for his benefit. Pulling off his tie, he stuffed it in his coat pocket, then unbuttoned his collar. He caught the aroma of tomatoes and onions and garlic. It reminded him of all the things he missed about a real home, including food cooking, anticipation of a good evening's companionship. The place was alive with warmth and love, the chintz-covered couch and chairs, small vases of daisies on tables refinished to a sheen by Castro. Even the television set looked good to Sullivan.

"Yes, I thought it was nice of her." Castro turned to Evelyn. "Glad you could come. Olga!" he called over his shoulder. "They're here."

Olga dashed from the kitchen, arms outstretched. "Sullivan! I'm so glad to see you."

Sullivan and Olga locked into an embrace. He towered over her. Finally, Sullivan pulled away and stepped back, holding Olga at arm's length. His eyes searched hers. "I've missed you." A flood of old memories pressed hard on his mind.

"I was so sorry . . ." She stopped mid-sentence and acknowledged Evelyn's presence. "Please forgive my rudeness. It's just that I love this old guy." She popped Sullivan on the arm with a fist, then extended her tiny hand to Evelyn.

Olga was small and dark with dancing eyes that hinted at mischief. She wore a crisp pink cotton dress, a matching ribbon holding an unruly ponytail.

Evelyn glanced at the walls filled with pen-and-ink drawings and commented on how good they were. On closer inspection, she recognized one as a protrait of Sullivan.

"They're mine," Castro said. "I wanted to be a police artist at one time, but there's not enough money in it. Can I get you two a drink?"

"Thought you'd never ask. The liquor flows like glue around here." Sullivan answered.

"Margarita? I make the best in town." Castro sauntered over to the bar cart. Evelyn and Olga accepted. Sullivan stuck to Jack Daniels on the rocks, calling mixed drinks, "Sissies."

Sullivan and Castro began discussing the case, with Sullivan explaining the new developments. Evelyn's discovery brought a clouded expression to Castro's face. To know that a serial killer's pattern was emerging frightened even the toughest professional.

Sullivan sipped his drink. "I'm convinced Juanita Sanchez didn't kill Sara Marley. A shame that she's dead and can't defend herself. Lopez was trying to make things light on himself."

Castro looked chagrined. "She might have not been the best of characters, but now her family will be dishonored because of what she's blamed for. I guess I wanted to believe Lopez. Maybe there's something I can do about it."

"There's no way to stop you two from talking." Olga gestured toward the kitchen with her glass. "Want to give me a hand, Evelyn?"

Evelyn followed her to the kitchen, where Olga began stirring a bubbly red sauce. "For the enchiladas. Nothing store-bought tonight."

Evelyn leaned against the counter, sipping her drink. "Tell me about Sullivan."

Olga raised her dark eyebrows into inverted V's. "Thought he worked for you."

"Personally, I mean."

"Well—" Olga hesitated as she pulled a chili casserole from the oven. "He's the greatest, most brilliant, kindest, toughest man in the world. Next to Manny, of course, but God! He looks terrible. He was so devoted to Karin." Olga closed her eyes for a moment, then shrugged. "She killed herself. Committed suicide with an overdose of sleeping pills."

Evelyn swallowed hard. Fumbling to set down her drink, she almost missed the counter. It was difficult to believe what she'd just heard. Why had Sullivan lied about his wife's death? Olga busied herself with the guacamole. "I'm a Catholic. Taking a life is a mortal sin. I hate to think of Karin not

being up there where she should be. I hope God understood."
She squeezed a lemon and whipped the green mixture.

"Why?" Her voice cracked. She wasn't sure she wanted to
know the answer.

Olga stopped stirring and holding a wooden spoon, turned
around. "She killed herself because of Sullivan."

There was a thud somewhere in her rib cage. She understood why people said hearts "sank." Evelyn picked up her
margarita, which now tasted watery and sweet. She swigged
the last of it, feeling slightly nauseated.

Olga put four plates into the oven to warm. "She was
going to die anyway. She had cancer. Poor thing . . . so sick
. . . turned into just a little bone . . . no hair. Sullivan was
spending every dime he had trying to get her well. Couldn't
afford to do what he did. He got so in debt. She did it to stop
him . . . to save him from completely breaking himself."

Evelyn stood still, almost holding her breath, letting the
information sink in. His wife's last act must have almost
killed him. He said his wife was dead and that she had
cancer. All true. He was too hurt to add that she had killed
herself for him.

"You feel okay? Manny makes drinks too strong sometimes."

Evelyn let out a rush of air. "As a matter of fact I think I'll
have another."

She walked into the living room, where Castro and Sullivan were deep in conversation. She stood for a moment
looking at Sullivan, then poured herself another drink from
the pitcher and returned to the kitchen.

Olga dabbed at her forehead with a white dishcloth. "Hot
in here. One of these days I'm going to put an air-conditioning
unit in the kitchen." She threw open the window over the
kitchen sink. "I sure hope Sullivan gets hold of himself.
You should have seen him in the old days." Olga smiled.
"He was something, he and Karin. What a pair! She almost
sparkled she had so much personality . . . and pretty—she
was a feast for the eyes. He always called her 'Dazzler.'
Karin was sometimes slow getting ready to go somewhere.
Sullivan would joke, 'Takes the Dazzler longer than most to
get presentable. She has so little to work with. We just gotta
wait.' "

Evelyn sipped her drink, imagining how she must pale in Sullivan's eyes compared to his wife. He hadn't really seen her in her best light. She had been under strain, depressed because of Sara, and intense. Why would she think he even compared the two, she asked herself?

Olga pulled tortillas from a steamer, almost burning her fingers. "I think everything is about ready. Would you call the sleuths into the dining room while I put the food on the buffet?"

Settled at the table with heaping plates, they began to eat. Castro poured beer for all but Sullivan, who nursed a Jack Daniels. Olga told Sullivan she had a job as a legal secretary now. She and Castro, having struggled for their educations, were putting her two younger brothers through college with ease.

"Tell me about you, Evelyn," Olga asked, drawing her into the conversation. "You're from Dallas. Ever seen J.R.?" She giggled.

"Only on television. About me . . . not much to tell, really." Evelyn glanced at Sullivan, who had quickly looked up. He rested his fork on the plate, ready to listen.

Under the table Evelyn refolded the napkin in her lap into a smaller square. "I was born in a small East Texas town, Longview. My father died young. There was only my mother, my sister, Sara, and myself. After I graduated from high school, I got a job in the local bank. I didn't go to college until after I married." With no hope of further education she had known her only ticket to freedom was to master typing, bookkeeping and shorthand. While Sara skimmed over movie magazines, Evelyn, because of her love for her father and the interest he'd sparked in his favorite subjects, bought as many books dealing with psychology and criminology as she could afford and devoured them in her spare time. "The oil boom hit our town. I met this man who worked for Cypress Oil. He had come from Dallas to buy up leases. We went out together, and I expressed my interest in going to the big city to find a job. He said he could get me a place at the oil company."

Cutting into a tamale, Evelyn remembered that hot summer day when the man who was to change the course of her life walked into the bank. Sitting there in a green dress and polished white shoes, she looked up at the smile on his boyish face. He wore a tie and smelled of cologne. Evelyn thought she could still conjure up the scent. He came from another world, one she was hoping to enter. He asked her for a date, and she agreed to meet him at a restaurant on the outskirts of town.

Olga propped her elbows on the table, cradling her chin. Her eyes widened as if she were a child listening to a fairy tale. "Was this your future husband, Andrew Casey?"

Evelyn glanced at Sullivan, then returned to Olga. She hoped her cheeks weren't flushing. Even thinking about the subject embarrassed her. "No, his name was Dave Thomas. Funny I only had one date with him, but I'll always remember his name." The vision of that scene floated up in her mind as clearly as a film projected on the screen. Outside the restaurant that night she slipped off the flat shoes she'd worn to walk the three-mile distance to the restaurant and retrieved the black pumps she treasured so from her purse.

"We drank martinis that night and got loaded." That much was true, but she wasn't about to admit the rest. At the time she had been unsophisticated enough not to know what a martini was or how to limit her intake. A tipsy Dave Thomas promised her a job at Cypress, then later in his car tried to collect the debt he thought was owed him. She winced as she recalled fending him off, then vomiting all over his seats.

"So, then you moved to Dallas, went to work for Cypress Oil and met the boss, Andrew Casey?" Olga pressed, obviously relishing the success story.

Evelyn nodded. "That's about it." Not quite, she thought. The threesome around that dinner table could never imagine how naive she had been at the time. Explaining to a tearful Sara that she'd send for her as soon as she could, Evelyn boarded the bus for Dallas. In her best pink print dress and new white shoes, she looked up at the towering Cypress Oil Building. Filled with enthusiasm, she squared her shoulders and marched in, thinking Dave Thomas's promise still held.

Pushing back his empty plate, Sullivan fired up a cigarette. "So exactly how did you meet Andrew Casey?" His green eyes twinkled with interest.

Evelyn cocked her head to one side. "Actually, I bumped into him in the elevator and we started talking. His secretary was leaving, so he hired me." That day in the Cypress building she had been directed to the lease department where Dave Thomas worked. Just outside the door she overheard him laughing about the bumpkin he'd met who wanted a job in the city. Said the hick who hadn't known what a martini was, had gotten skunked and puked in his car before he could get in her pants. In tears she rushed to the elevator and collided with a dark-suited man. Tan-faced under prematurely graying hair, body as trim as an athlete's, the man took her to his office. After she told him her story, Andrew Casey offered her a job.

Sullivan saw that Evelyn was smiling to herself, recollecting, he suspected, some lost incident. He wondered what it was. How little he knew about her. Suddenly, he found himself intrigued. He couldn't imagine Evelyn poor. The aura of wealth and gentility so hung upon her. He urged her to continue.

Evelyn blotted her lips with her napkin, positive she wore a greasy moustache from the enchiladas. "Andrew and I started having lunch. Lunches gradually led to dinners, and finally, I was his date at the office Christmas party, which meant our relationship was official." She smiled again. The peak came when she stood face-to-face with Dave Thomas. She enjoyed his expression, although she bore him no malice. After all, he was responsible for her good fortune. Then, Dave Thomas in his polyester suits looked very much out of place next to the sleek career girl and future wife of the president of the company he worked for. "Andrew and I had a small wedding and a large reception at his home. Went to Europe on our honeymoon. Afterward my sister Sara came to live with us. I went to college and got my degree." She looked down. "Andrew died from a heart attack two years ago . . . then Sara."

Sullivan wanted to know more about Andrew Casey. He'd seen pictures of the handsome man in magazines. He wondered about their relationship. Evelyn's lack of elaboration on that subject puzzled him. It had been his experience that women placed their dead husbands, whether or not they deserved it, on pedestals. He pushed away from the table.

"Great dinner, Olga. You outdid yourself." Sullivan rubbed his stomach, wishing he had been more circumspect.

Olga wouldn't hear of Evelyn helping with the dishes. She said she had her routine, then produced a platter of home-made pralines for dessert.

Castro offered brandies. Sullivan turned down the snifter and nursed a coffee. Tomorrow started the new regimen. He hoped. It made him feel good to think so. He glanced at Evelyn, then fixed his eyes on Castro. "Evelyn's going to work up a profile on serial killers. One of the best authorities on that subject is Dr. H. Menken Simms at the university here." He watched for Evelyn's reaction, not wanting her to think she wasn't capable. "Wouldn't hurt for us to go see him. He and Evelyn could compare notes. Know him, Manny?"

Holding the stem of the snifter, Castro whirled his brandy. "Only by reputation. He's a top criminologist and expert in psychopathic behavior patterns. The department has used him before."

Evelyn perked up. "I'd love to talk to him."

"From past experience I know something about their reasoning . . . the psychopath's . . . their compulsion to confess, let the world recognize what they've done." Sullivan said. "They are really screaming for help, asking to be stopped from something they can't help doing." He noted that Evelyn had been about to shake her head but had apparently thought better of it. He half expected her to interrupt, but she didn't. "They have their own private motives for killing. I've been thinking about the dates. The incidents are getting closer. What Evelyn found out . . . there was about one every month or six weeks when he first began. This month there are two within a space of a few days of each other. This tells me he's getting desperate." Sullivan frowned. "Know what I think you should do, Manny?"

Shaking his head, Castro picked up a pencil and pad and started scribbling.

"I think you should go to Gordon and have a talk about what we know. After all, you are the police. We need all the help we can get. With the 'Five,' that might just earn you some merits." Watching Evelyn, Sullivan lit a cigarette. "I'll keep on my end of it, but the department has got lots more resources to draw from. They've got to play it low-key. If this should get to the papers, it'll run the killer into a hole so deep we'll never find him. Gordon will handle it right. He may be a son of a bitch, but he ain't dumb." Sullivan pushed up from the table.

"Getting late. We'd better go."

Castro ripped a page from the pad and handed it to Evelyn. She eyed the drawing, then looked up at Castro, smiling. "It's me. What a good likeness! May I keep it?"

Castro nodded.

At the front door they said their goodnights to the Castros. Fleetingly, Sullivan glanced back around the room. Castro had come a long way. He wanted him to keep going.

The moaning wind seemed ominous as they dashed to the car, Sullivan holding Evelyn's elbow, she clasping her hair with both hands. Large rain drops splattered intermittently on the lawn. A saber of light slashed across the mountains.

In the car, Sullivan looked at Evelyn. She turned and held his gaze. Sullivan felt awkward. He nudged the gears in reverse and looking back, right arm braced across the seat, moved down the driveway. With the car on a steep incline, he turned his head forward. The position of his car offered a partial view of the underside of Castro's car. Suddenly, Sullivan's headlights showed a glint of something that caught his eye.

He slammed on the brakes, put the gears in park, got out and crouched by Castro's car. Rummaging underneath, his hand closed around a small metal object. With a quick jerk he pulled it free and turning it over, inspected the homing device, standard issue by all police departments.

Troubled, he looked toward Castro's house and made a tentative step forward. One by one, lights went off. He replaced the apparatus in exactly the same position and stomped back to his car, hair disheveled and hanging across his forehead.

Evelyn leaned across the seat to open the door. "What is it?"

Sullivan's eyebrows met in a frown. His stomach churned, offering up a taste of Mexican food. "As if I don't have enough on my mind. Castro's in trouble.'' He explained about the ''homer.''

Evelyn sank against the seat, small creases growing across her brow ''Oh, no!''

Sullivan slammed down on the gears, wrenched the wheel around and screeched off, gravel popping under the tires like grease in a hot skillet. He had caused Castro to overstep his bounds. He took his own chances, but when he influenced someone else in the wrong direction, the situation took on an entirely different light.

Evelyn braced her hands on the dashboard. ''Where are we going?''

''Back tò my house. It's not far from here.'' His voice, tight in his throat was too loud and laced with irritation.

Mentally cursing himself, Sullivan drove on silently. Evelyn sat with her back pushed into the seat, legs ramrod straight. For some reason Captain Gordon had it in for Castro. Legally the police had no right to employ the ''homer'' on Castro. That was one point in his favor and one against them.

Sullivan kept his eyes on the road, wincing as a driver failed to use his dimmers. Evelyn's voice seemed to slip by his brain without contact, Sullivan hearing only snippets of conversation.

At the front door, Evelyn at his side, he looked up at the sky. The moon lay well hidden behind dark, threatening clouds. Thunder rumbled in the distance like a battery of cannons. A hint of lightning flared in a zigzag over the mountains. The scene matched his mood. With a fierce kick and a rattle of the doorknob he opened the door.

''This whole thing is a royal mess.'' Sullivan headed for the bar, poured himself a large measure of brandy and downed it in one gulp. He refilled his glass, spilling as much as went in and lit a cigarette. Torn, Sullivan decided to let Castro have a good night's sleep. He could do nothing but agonize over the development. Sullivan could do enough of that for two. Flopping in his lounge chair, he settled in for a bout with brandy. He wasn't going to make his resolve. See, at first provocation he turned to liquor. He was finished. Should have known it all along.

Evelyn moved to the bar and fixed a vodka on the rocks,

then perched on the couch facing Sullivan. "You're thinking it's all my fault. You wished I'd never stepped into your life."

Sullivan looked at her, but remained silent.

"Tomorrow things will look different. We'll find a way out. Don't punish yourself."

Sullivan slugged down a swallow. "What way out? Want to try bribing the whole police department to leave Castro alone?" Involuntarily, he jerked back his hand, sending the snifter flying to the floor. He and Evelyn watched the brown stain widen in the carpet.

The phone jolted them. Both looked in its direction. Sullivan lumbered over to the desk. Late calls were never good ones. He picked up the receiver.

"Don't you ever check your answering machine?"

"Just got in."

"Sullivan, got something for you," a familiar voice said. "We want you to start first thing in the morning."

Sullivan listened, his grip tightening on the receiver. The agency wanted him to break into the Japanese Cultural Exchange in Santa Clara, a cover organization for a carefully financed industrial espionage operation. Involved in stealing, then modifying many American companies' secrets, the group had succeeded in undercutting domestic prices. The agency wanted to put the Japanese out of business by exposing them. For this they needed evidence, and the best way to gather evidence, as Sullivan had taught them, was to steal it.

Sullivan pivoted and looked at Evelyn. She sat sipping her drink, pretending not to eavesdrop. Here was the chance to back off gracefully from the Marley case. He could tell her this was the commitment he'd been expecting and let the police take over where he left off. But after the agency job, what was left? What about himself? What about their discoveries? He didn't want to give up, not on the case, not on himself. Not just yet.

Sullivan cleared his throat. "I've got a conflict. I'm not going to be able to take on the job."

Evelyn stiffened, turning her gaze on Sullivan.

Sullivan put his back to her as if that would blot out the

conversation. "You can get someone else. Plenty of contract agents around."

"We don't want just anyone," the voice urged. "You're best for this job."

Cradling the receiver on his shoulder, Sullivan lit a cigarette. "Sorry, got something I can't leave."

"We'll up the ante. How's a hundred thou sound?"

Sullivan blew out a cloud of smoke. "A lot of money. But after tomorrow I won't be in such a bind. I'm going to sell my boat." His words, the subconscious speaking, surprised him.

"Wait a minute!" Evelyn charged over. For a moment he thought she might snatch the phone from him.

Sullivan clasped his hand over the receiver, noting the urgency in her expression. "What?"

Her features looked pinched. "I'm complicating too many lives. The police can take over now that we've got something tangible. Take the job you're being offered." A tone of resignation rang in her voice. She walked back to the couch and picked up her purse. "Take the job. I'll leave you a check." Her voice had an edge to it as if any moment it might break.

Sullivan removed his hand from the receiver. "Give me a try again sometime. I can't make it now."

"Sullivan, you're a fool."

"You're not the first one to accuse me of that," he snapped and hung up.

He and Evelyn faced each other.

"Why did you do that?" Her eyes hinted at tears.

Sullivan shrugged, allowing a small smile on his lips. "Haven't the vaguest. Like the man said, I'm a fool. He's probably generous with his evaluation. Besides, we can't stop now. There's too much at stake."

Suddenly a clap of thunder startled them both. As if a light switch had flipped on, a crashing bolt of lightning turned night into day. Sullivan froze. He felt a stab of something very close to panic. Peering from outside into the room, a man stood perfectly framed by the window. As quickly as it had happened, the flash of light was gone and so was the figure in the window.

Sullivan raced to the bookcase where he kept his guns, threw open the doors, and grabbed his loaded .357 magnum.

"What are you doing?" Evelyn's voice thundered, her cheeks draining of color.

"I'm going after him," Sullivan yelled as he bolted through the front door into the blackness of night.

Thick clouds totally obscured any light from the moon. Sound was Sullivan's only ally. Breathing hard, he stopped and listened. Cocking his head, he heard sounds coming from the hill to the right away from the house. The man was moving at a fast clip. Sullivan struck out in pursuit, the darkness offering cover to both.

The hillside was overgrown with ice plant. Sullivan sprinted, slipped to one knee, rose, and slipped again. Down a second time, he could just barely make out that the man ahead had slipped, too. Lemon trees grew in abundance, their round symmetrical bodies sprinkled with fruit like balls on a Christmas tree. Up again, Sullivan hugged the tree trunks for balance, launching himself from one to the next. Ahead, he thought he could see the man on all fours, clawing his way down the steep embankment, but somehow the man was widening the distance between them. Sullivan cursed himself, then skidded, the plants slick, as if doused in grease. He saw the man disappear down the hill.

Chest heaving, Sullivan heard a distinct change in sounds. The man had left the grass and pounded down the sidewalk. The urge to fire a wild shot in that direction flared in Sullivan, but he dared not. He knew the chances of making a hit were next to zero. Besides, Sullivan wanted him alive. And not to be forgotten, his fire might be returned.

Running, Sullivan heard a car door open across the street. He was close. The engine roared to life. All chances evaporated except one. Sullivan prayed the man would be stupid enough to turn on his lights. From past experience he knew how many times that had happened from involuntary reactions.

No such luck.

In the darkness the car skidded wildly down the street, and as it did, a bolt of lightning filled the sky.

"MCM 4-5-9," Sullivan said aloud to imprint the license

number on his brain. He sank to the curb, gasping for air. His heart throbbed so irregularly he feared it might explode.

Another zigzag of lightning flashed in the sky. Sullivan looked up and grinned. "Thanks, Lord."

He heaved up from the curb and trudged toward his house, shoes making a squish as he walked, wet clothes stained and plastered to his body. The climb up the front walk seemed endless, the steps somehow multiplying before his eyes. He stopped halfway when he heard Evelyn's voice from the doorway.

"Are you all right?"

Sullivan closed the door and leaned back. "Nothing that getting into shape won't fix. I got his license number." He still labored for breath. His head felt as if it were floating on his neck. "Make some coffee, will you? I'm going to shower."

Hot water beads pelted Sullivan as he grew more relaxed, his equilibrium gaining momentum. He eased the faucets to cold and ran his fingers through his hair. Shaking his head, droplets of water flew through the air. He reached for a towel and scrubbed himself dry.

In the bedroom, he opened a drawer and, from the bottom of a stack of wrinkled pants, pulled out a crisp pair of khakis that had a small rip in the leg seam. Shopping had long been relegated to the back of his mind. There were so many things that needed remedying. He wondered where he'd find time. He slipped on a velour pullover and pushed his feet into a pair of topsiders.

Rounding the kitchen door, he smelled coffee brewing. Evelyn sat at the kitchen table, feet hooked around the chair legs, massaging her temples. She looked up.

"I was so afraid for you. I wanted you to catch him, but yet I didn't." She hugged her chest.

Sullivan stirred cream into his coffee and added a dash of sugar for the energy he'd heard it provided. If he ever needed it, now was the time. When he was twenty-five, stamina was just something that came with the body.

"I was afraid for myself." He took a sip. "Does that shock you?"

"No, it doesn't shock me. Means you're human." Her voice cracked.

Sullivan sat down at the table. "I learned a long time ago that being afraid keeps you alive. That's not 'Confucius say,' but Sullivan say."

Evelyn tried for a smile. He liked the tiny curving lines around her eyes. She was looking at his eyes. His creases were engraved, whereas hers were now only hints. Karin used to say they had stationed themselves there because he laughed so much. His heart accepted a small, prickling pain.

"First thing in the morning when I call Castro I'll ask him to buzz DMV in Sacramento. We've got a license number to go on. No telling where that'll lead." Here he was, wanting another favor from Castro. But this could be a big break. Sullivan grabbed a pencil and jotted down the number on a pad. "Just so I don't forget."

Evelyn's smile vanished. "Do you think that was the killer out there?" She shuddered. "So close."

Sullivan wanted to cradle her against him. "I don't know. Who would be looking in my window?" He tried to conjure up some image of the killer. The dawning of just how dangerous he really was struck Sullivan with full impact. Before, he had been just a shadowy figure, but now he had almost seen him. "Do you believe me now that you might be in danger?"

Evelyn's expression turned grim. "How could he have found me?"

"Maybe he's been tracking you since the newspaper article. Who knows? We're dealing with a clever person here. I'll do my best to offer you every protection, but you're going to need more." He picked up his coffee. "Come in the den, I want to show you something."

He opened the cabinet where he kept his .357 magnum and pulled out a small handgun. "This is a Smith and Wesson 38." He moved his hand up and down as if weighing the gun. "It's light . . . just about right for you. The magnum is way too heavy for you to handle."

"Me?" Evelyn sounded shocked. "I don't know anything about guns. They scare me."

"Tomorrow I'll take you to a firing range and give you a lesson. You probably won't learn to be accurate, but you can acquire enough skill to at least do some damage."

Evelyn bit her lip, weighing the suggestion like a child

considering accepting a ride from a stranger—dangerous, yet somehow appealing. "I'll give it a try."

Sullivan threw three big logs into the fireplace, crumpled an old newspaper, and set a roaring blaze. The fire provided an illusion of protection and safety with its warmth. They settled down, he in his lounge chair, she on the ottoman. Evelyn folded her arms around her legs. Patterns from the flames danced across her face.

"When will it all be over?" she asked.

Sullivan focused on the future. When the case was resolved— and it would be, one way or another—she'd go back to Dallas. Books closed. Strangely, the prospect brought a sort of sadness, a complete reversal of his thoughts when they first met. He wondered if Quinn Stewart was waiting to fill Andrew Casey's shoes.

"I have no way of knowing. We haven't gotten to first base yet. Maybe we're not even playing the right game."

"I wish you didn't have to sell your boat. Isn't there a way to hang on to it? I'd be glad to help in any way I can." She looked at him with genuine concern.

Sullivan reached for the poker and stabbed at the coals. "I am many things, but one thing I am not is a gigolo," he said without rancor. "I work for what I have, and if I can't pay . . ."

She broke in. "I didn't mean to offend you."

Sullivan held up his hand. "No offense taken." He thought about his financial situation, not half as bad as his personal status. Loneliness was the ultimate poverty. "It's high time I broke away from old habits. I never use the boat anymore. It doesn't really bother me to sell it." He couldn't tell if he was in earnest or lying to himself. "I guess the decision is sort of symbolic."

"Maybe like mine to throw down the gauntlet of finding Sara's murderer. Vengeance is not the point. We want to prevent it from happening to someone else."

Sullivan looked at Evelyn, the clinging blouse emphasizing the line of her slight frame. He realized he had been staring at her but seeing another. Now he focused his full attention on her, a woman who would stir interest in any man. It registered deep within that possibly his capacity for emotion had burned out. Since Karin there had been out of necessity a few

women to cross his path, but no one woman meant more than
the next. Again, he found himself wondering what kind of
man Andrew Casey had been and about their relationship.
Evelyn knew grief and loss yet didn't seem filled with the
same void he carried. She wasn't dead inside. He didn't want
to be. There was a life out there to be lived.

Sullivan lit a cigarette and decided that the best plan was to
have Evelyn stay in his guest room. He hated thinking of her
alone and frightened in a strange apartment. Surely this was
his professional judgment, not a personal thing to keep her
close. He'd sit by the fire and watch over the house until
morning.

She refused the offer. "As I said, when you're alone, there
are many things you have to make yourself do. What about
tomorrow night and the next? I can't sit up every night for the
rest of my life and neither can you."

Tough one, he thought, admiring her. Logical, too.

Evelyn stood. "It's best that we get a good night's sleep, if
we can. We've got lots to do tomorrow. Drive me back to the
apartment. I'll be fine."

Without thinking, he reached out and seized her hand. It
felt small in his. Quickly he released his grip. "Whatever you
say. I just don't want you to be afraid."

"I won't be." She picked up her purse.

They drove over slick streets, the car skidding once as
Sullivan turned a corner. Spikes of lights from motorists'
head beams looked to Sullivan like the Statue of Liberty's
crown. Streetlamps haloed by mist cast dim reflections into
puddles below. The city skyline, shrouded by low clouds,
was barely discernible. The whole area had a still, eerie
quality.

Out of the corner of her eyes, Evelyn watched Sullivan's
strong arms as he maneuvered the winding road, wishing they
were around her, imagining how she'd feel wrapped close to
him. Her attraction was too strong to deny and turning down
his offer to stay at his house had been difficult, but she had
been afraid she might make a fool of herself. There was only
one person in Sullivan's life, and he couldn't let her go.

The doorman at the apartment was gone. Evelyn wondered
aloud if he only worked days. Sullivan commented that San

Diego was not a sophisticated city like New York or Dallas. He was surprised that the apartment employed a doorman at all. The lobby was empty and quiet as they walked to the elevator, their heels clicking on the floor the only sounds. Evelyn noticed the door to the stairs was swinging slightly as if someone had just passed through. They watched the numbers over the elevator door flash in red. The doors parted on the sixth floor.

The hall seemed narrow at night, shadows bouncing off gray walls. Sullivan took the key from Evelyn and unlocked the apartment door. Switching on lights he looked around as if expecting to find someone.

"Want to look under the bed? How about under the rug?" Evelyn tried to laugh, but clearly a false note rang in her voice.

"Nice place here." Sullivan dropped the key in her hand. "I'll pick you up in the morning. You take care, now." He paused, standing so close she could almost feel his breath. She waited. He turned and went out.

Evelyn bolted the front door, then checked the slider to the balcony. She looked out at the dreary night, the harbor, the lights, a gauzy yellow smear on the darkness. It was strange how alive and sinister water could look at night, she thought. She drew the heavy drapes, closing out the scene. Leaving on two lamps in the living room, she opened the bar cooler and popped open a Tab. Walking through the kitchen, she flicked on a small light over the stove. She opened the refrigerator and looked in, the emptiness reminding her of how alone she was. Silence was as taut and alive as a scream. She could almost hear her own breathing. Passing back to the living room she flicked on the stereo. A Beethoven symphony filled the apartment. Drums rolled, cymbals clashed, sending Evelyn quickly back to the set. She found a station playing music from the forties and, walking into the bedroom, unbuttoned her blouse.

The phone rang, sending an arrow through her chest. Who could be calling so late? She picked up the receiver.

"Hello!"

Silence on the line.

"Hello," she persisted.

Quiet. She felt her heart accelerate. Someone was on the line, listening. There were no background noises from that end.

"Hello," she tried a third time, hoping the caller would hang up after realizing he had the wrong number. It crossed her mind that Quinn might be checking up on her, but he wasn't the type. Probably it was some crank or a girlfriend checking on the man who lived there.

"Matt Graham's not here. He's out of town . . . if that's who you want."

She had the overwhelming sensation that the caller was about to speak.

Suddenly, as if by a sixth sense, she knew the call was for her. Even over the phone she sensed an ominous presence, a vibration of horror.

She slammed down the receiver and and sank down on the bed, trying to reason with herself. The night had been filled with upheavals, and she was now blowing things out of proportion. Everyone had crank calls. It didn't mean anything. Under normal circumstances she wouldn't give it a second thought. But these weren't normal circumstances. Maybe the killer was tracking her, waiting for his opportunity.

CHAPTER 10

BY THE TIME MORNING DAWNED, Sullivan swore he hadn't slept at all, but knew he must have. He stretched and feeling a crick in his neck, rotated his head. He hoped Evelyn had gotten some rest, but doubted it. The night had been too emotionally explosive. He had hated leaving her alone, but the choice had been hers.

Checking his watch, he dreaded calling Castro. He yawned, grabbed his striped robe from the bathroom door hook, knotted the tie at his waist and padded down the hall.

After putting a pot of coffee on to perk, he sat hunched on the kitchen stool, mulling over what to say. He dialed Castro and waited. A sleepy Castro answered and Sullivan apologized for calling so early.

"Manny, unscrew the receiver and see if there's a bug in your phone."

"What?"

"Just do it."

Hawk listened to Castro fumble with the phone set.

"Nothing's there. What's going on?" His voice was suddenly alert.

"After I left your house last night, I spotted something

under your car. Standard-issue police homer. I left it there so whoever attached it wouldn't know you're onto them.''

"Jesus Christ!" Castro hesitated, then said, "Adams. It was Adams. Saw him by my car in the lot. He's Gordon's boy all the way.''

"You'd better go in and talk to Gordon about the 'Five' you turned in. Tell him about the new evidence we've come across. I really think that might counteract whatever they're up to. There's more . . .''

Castro broke in, "More? What else?"

"Last night after I got home, someone was looking in my window. I chased him and got the tag number. MCM 459. Call DMV and check it out for me. Tell Gordon about that, too.'' Sullivan repeated the number to Castro.

"Think it was the killer?"

"Don't know. The more I think about it, could be somebody who followed me home from your house. What a break if it was the killer.'' He jabbed out his cigarette. "I'll call you back later. Don't let Gordon get to you.''

Sullivan made an appointment with Dr. H. Menken Simms, then settled down with a cup of coffee to think. He smoked another cigarette. It tasted good. Actually, he didn't want to quit, just cut down. Surely ten or twelve a day wouldn't hurt. He decided to change into some jogging clothes and go to the beach. He always thought better there. After exercising, he'd take the Smith and Wesson, pick up Evelyn and go to the firing range.

An hour later Sullivan dropped off the title papers at the harbormaster's, took one last look at his boat, then picked up Evelyn. Her shining blond hair was swirled into a bun on the back of her head. In a white skirt and navy cotton sweater, she looked like a college girl. He wondered what people thought when they saw them together, she younger than her years, he older than his.

He explained that Dr. Simms, busy with classes all day, expected them at his home near the campus around six. In the interim she would practice target shooting, with him instructing her in the proper use of the weapon.

Evelyn asked about Castro. Sullivan told her about their

conversation. By noon Castro would have the information on the car tag.

Sullivan watched Evelyn toy with the radio, change stations, music to news, news to weather, then back to music. "I didn't like what happened last night, but with the license number, it'll be easy to track the owner." The car might be stolen, but he didn't mention it.

Clutching her purse close, Evelyn turned to Sullivan. "I had a strange phone call last night. Someone was on the line but wouldn't say anything. First I thought it might be for the man who owns the apartment or a prank. Then I got this weird feeling that it was for me . . . Maybe I was wrong, because I was upset about the man in the window." She glanced out the window. "I don't know."

Sullivan lit a cigarette, mulling over what she said. He didn't like what he heard. Had someone actually observed her relocation, checked the name on the mailbox, looked up the telephone number and called to make sure she was ensconced in that apartment? Too many unexplained incidents were cropping up. First the man at the window, now the phone call. They had to be getting close to something . . .

Castro pulled into the parking lot behind the police station. He eased into a space directly behind Lieutenant Adams's car. When he had looked under his car, the homer Sullivan talked about was gone. Apparently someone else had witnessed Sullivan's discovery. They knew that he, Castro, would be privy to the fact now. He hadn't mentioned the incident to Olga and wondered if he should to Captain Gordon. In all probability he was the one who ordered it. But why was he checking on him?

He looked straight ahead at Adams's car, wishing somehow through it he could put a hex on Adams. His grandmother had believed in such things. His eyes held on Adams's tag, the numbers jumping out at him. "MCM 459."

So Adams, not the killer, peered into Sullivan's window. He felt relieved and at the same time even more agitated. The back of his neck prickled. He opened the door and headed for Captain Gordon's office.

Still unsure of how he or Gordon would play the scene, he

settled down outside the captain's office to wait. He was correct in assuming that Gordon would let him sweat out an inordinate amount of time before admitting him. As the clock ticked away, an irrational part of himself tried to blame Sullivan for his troubles. He couldn't quite make himself buy it. He had acted entirely of his own volition. Rules many times were bypassed by members of the force. It was hard to believe that only yesterday he'd had no problem more pressing than whether to mow the lawn or paint the kitchen shelves.

Talbott came into the room and walked over. A flashy dresser when off duty, Talbott had a smile that rivaled his clothes. Part Italian, he gestured wildly with his hands, especially when excited. Castro thought about their interrogation of Carnie Lopez. Lopez and Talbott had the same moves. Castro liked Talbott and, more important, trusted him with his life, as any partner should. He'd seen Talbott blow away hoods without batting an eyelash.

"Man, what you doing back on your 'free'?"

"I wanted to talk to Captain Gordon about the Marley case." Castro told Talbott about the new developments.

Talbott looked apprehensive. "Gordon ain't gonna like what you have to say. He doesn't like to retract any decisions once they're made."

Castro winced. "Not looking forward to the conversation."

"You can add this item. Got a teletype from Chicago P.D. this morning requesting our files on the case. They picked up on it from the piece in the paper. Got on the wire service. First I didn't think much of the article." Talbott waved his hand. "Might've done some good after all."

Castro glared at Talbott. "The Chicago P.D. is a little out-of-date wanting to see a file on a closed case, don't you think?" If there was a serial killer surfacing, despite Gordon's reluctance to explore the possibility, and if that killer was responsible for Sara Marley's murder, not Juanita Sanchez, Gordon's reputation, to say nothing of his position as captain, would be put on the line. Now the Chicago P.D. must have a similar case. Castro felt a touch of pleasure at Gordon's possible predicament.

Captain Daniel Gordon opened the door to his office and stood framed there. "Castro, come on in."

"See you later, Mex." Talbott rolled his eyes and hurried off.

Castro walked into Gordon's office and settled uneasily into the straight-back wooden chair. Gordon strode over to his desk, giving Castro one of his mirthless smiles, a little more than baring his teeth. The air conditioning was on the blink again. Already Castro felt his shirt sticking to his back.

"You've read my 'Five'?"

"Pardon?" Gordon asked, as if he had no understanding of what a "Five" was. He rocked back on the swivel chair's rear legs. "What's it concern?" he asked, ignoring Castro's question. His voice was strident, his stare unyielding.

"The Marley case." Castro moved in the chair to cross his legs.

Gordon let out a rush of air. "The Marley case is yesterday's mashed potatoes. Why are you bringing it up again? Have you come across some new evidence? Something concrete?" It was a calm, patronizing inquiry.

"Nothing concrete, but some new connections to go on. I Xeroxed the case and took it home to study. I wanted to see if we'd overlooked anything."

Elbows on the desk, Gordon steepled his fingers. "And did you find anything?"

"Not about our investigation itself. But I believe the Marley Case is similar to others, up and down the coast . . . Los Angeles, San Francisco. Women who were stabbed in hotels the same night they arrived. None raped or robbed. Talbott just told me the Chicago P.D. wants a copy of the case. They picked up on it from the wire service story. I think Carnie Lopez lied to help himself. I think we should take another look at the Marley case."

Gordon's face flushed. A map of tiny blue veins appeared in his temples. "How come this case is so important to you? Wouldn't have anything to do with Evelyn Casey, would it? You know, Castro, there's a saying I like. 'Money doesn't talk, it screams.' How'd you get started on these cases up and down the coast?"

Castro inhaled. "Actually, the man who Evelyn Casey hired to work on the case came across the connections."

Gordon made a show of widening his eyes. "Oh? Who'd she hire?" His gaze turned judicial.

"Hawk Sullivan."

"That drunk? Run out of the FBI. He's capable of an investigation?" Gordon grunted. "He's an old friend of yours."

It became suddenly clear to Castro that Gordon suspected he was handling the investigation for money, using Sullivan as a cover. Castro cleared his throat. "I'm sure you're aware of some of the things he's capable of pulling off. Then, he had some personal problems . . . his wife . . . her death."

Gordon waved his hand to brush the subject of Sullivan aside. "Back to the other. The murders up and down the coast, Chicago, the Marley case . . . one killer, you mean. A serial murderer. That's the conclusion you've reached?"

"The conclusion Hawk Sullivan reached."

"I'm asking for *your* conclusions."

Castro cleared his throat, choosing his words carefully. He had to guard against any statement that might point to Sullivan's access to confidential material. "It's all in the 'Five' that I turned in to you. On Sara Marley's flight, according to the airline record, there was a man using a fictitious name, initials were C.C. Same as on Mary Kenworth's flight. She was a woman from Fort Worth, murdered in Los Angeles, circumstances similar to Marley's . . ."

Gordon broke in, "What a fucking can of worms."

"Sir, I haven't finished . . . about the seat changes . . ."

"What are you trying to do? Solve the L.A.P.D.'s cases for them? You work in San Diego, and the case you worked on is closed!"

"Well, if the cases are connected, we need to pool our information."

Castro watched Gordon heave himself up from the chair and walk to the water cooler in the corner. Pulling a paper cup from the plastic container, Gordon filled it, walked to the window ledge, and dumped the contents on an anemic-looking plant that had once sported a spray of violets. He raised the window. The air was hot from a Santa Ana wind whipping in from the desert, the noise from the freeway loud and unceasing.

"What you're implying is the biggest headache a department could have," Gordon said, without turning around. "A real ballbreaker.'' His tone was low, as if speaking to himself. ''The public and the guys from City Hall want to bust your heads in. They aren't mad at the killer, but with the police for not catching him. The media wants your ass.'' He shook his head. ''Build a reputation over a lifetime, and one psycho comes along and knocks it all down. I've seen it happen to the best.'' His voice gained momentum. He whirled around. ''Well, it's not going to happen to me. You single out a few incidents in your spare time and try to hang them all together in one tidy package. Try to make a name for yourself while others go under. Maybe you watch too much television. Sara Marley was not murdered by any serial killer. Maybe you're emotionally involved because one of your own is the guilty person. Ever consider that, Castro?''

Castro stared at Gordon, wanting to say that he felt any guilty person should be punished no matter what their nationality, but Gordon believed ethnics stuck together. Gordon was going to ignore the possibility that Sanchez was not Sara Marley's killer in hopes it might go away. He was trying hard not to make a connection between the cases up and down the coast and Sara Marley's because he was afraid there was one. ''I hope you'll consider my 'Five' and what I've told you.''

Gordon remained silent, but his expression transmitted a warning for Castro not to tread further into some territory Gordon considered his own.

''We practically have a fucking eyewitness in Carnie Lopez.'' He paused. ''Castro, experience teaches you how to separate things. You can't make assumptions. Facts are what you deal with. Maybe that pretty Mrs. Casey clouded your judgment. This situation has gotten into personalities, not issues. Go on home and enjoy the rest of your time off. When you come back you'll have a busy enough schedule studying for your officers' exams. Not good on your record to fail it.'' A veiled threat edged into his tone. ''That Mrs. Casey will go back to Dallas where all that money is. Hawk Sullivan will jump further into a bottle, and there you'll be left with what? Your bare ass hanging out. All for nothing.'' Gordon stared at Castro, one eyebrow slightly raised.

Deciding that mentioning the homer served no purpose, Castro stood. He felt defeated and perhaps a little foolish.

There was a chance that Gordon was right, hard as it was to admit. The only mistake he'd made so far was showing the police reports to Sullivan. That wasn't the most serious offense in the books. From now on, he'd look after his own best interests.

Across the city Sullivan and Evelyn walked out on the firing range. The facilities had an indoor range, but Sullivan preferred the outdoor one, finding it less intimidating for a novice, and he wanted every benefit for Evelyn. First, he loaded the .38, then unloaded it and handed the gun to Evelyn.

"Now you try."

Evelyn moved her hand up and down, testing the weight. About a pound, she judged, the ridged handle rough on her palm. She opened the cylinder and pushed the bullets into the slots, five in all.

"Okay, here's the safety." Sullivan put his hand over hers. "Always keep it on until you're ready to fire. One thing to remember. Never aim at anything you don't intend to fire at."

Evelyn looked at the stationary bull's-eye target fifty yards away. Next to it stood a target shaped like a man, points on his body to aim for circled. Flipping halfway, it moved as a man might. To the right, moving targets on a trolley rolled by in a straight line.

Sullivan showed her how to aim the pistol, one hand resting slightly on the other for balance. "Always squeeze the trigger. If you just pull it, the gun will jerk and the bullet will veer off course."

"Where do we start? Which target?" Evelyn stood with her legs slightly parted, eyes sparkling with excitement.

Sullivan chuckled. She'd seen that stance on television. "We'll start with the stationary target today. The moving ones are tough."

"Why are those points marked on the target that's shaped like a man?"

Sullivan looked over the open field, the wind lifting his hair. "That's a real pro's target. Those are points to aim for if you want to do a certain thing to a man." He pointed. "See the one on his shoulder. That's where you want to hit him if you want him to drop a gun he's holding. The one on his hip is where you aim if you only want to wound him. The one on the chest takes him out. Okay, let's shoot. Put on the ear-plugs. The noise is fierce.''

Evelyn aimed and hit the side of the bull's-eye target. She turned to Sullivan, making a face. He raised his fingers in a V sign.

''Victory! It wasn't a bull's-eye.'' She yelled.

He shook his head and pointed to his ears, communicating muffled hearing. Taking her hands again, he positioned them, then pointed to the target. She fired, hitting within the widest circle. Turning, she grinned at him.

''You know . . .''

Sullivan pointed to his ears again. Evelyn took the plugs out and motioned to Sullivan to follow suit.

''I feel better about last night. The call *was* probably just a crank. My theory. I'm not the killer's type.''

Sullivan pointed to the Smith and Wesson .38. ''Still we can't be lax where some psycho is concerned. We still have the question of who was looking in my window.''

Evelyn lifted the gun and aimed, wind whipping her hair across her face. Sullivan touched her shoulder. ''Plugs!'' He pointed to her ears.

As they continued practice, Evelyn surprised Sullivan with her performance. Her eye control and total concentration surpassed any beginner he'd ever seen. When she stepped up to shoot, she was all business. He suspected she could accomplish most anything once she set her mind to it.

''Okay!'' Sullivan held up his hands, then removed his earplugs. Evelyn followed suit, letting her arm relax.

''Hey! Get that pistol up. You want to shoot yourself in the foot.''

Sullivan fumbled in his pocket. ''Let's go back to the little house over there. You've got to be tired.'' Sullivan turned on his heels and walked off, stamping dust off his shoes as he went.

''Tired? You just want a cigarette.'' Evelyn smiled and rushed to catch him.

Settled on the porch of the frame house called a gun club,

Evelyn and Sullivan gazed at the targets. Sullivan checked his watch and stubbed out his cigarette. He went to a small table and fixed them some ice tea provided by the club.

"You did okay." He handed Evelyn a glass.

"Just okay?" She raised her eyebrows.

"Pretty good."

"Thanks." She looked down. "You know I didn't get much sleep last night, so I used the time to work on the killer's profile. I'm anxious to compare notes with Dr. Simms. I think he'll have some answers for us."

Sullivan squeezed lemon in his tea and picked out the seeds with a spoon. He glanced down at Evelyn's purse that now held the Smith and Wesson .38. "By now Manny may have some answers." He checked his watch again. "I'll wait five more minutes." He glanced at Evelyn as she dabbed a Kleenex on her forehead.

"Can I ask you a question?"

Evelyn shrugged. "I've never known you to hesitate before. What?"

"You ever go hunting or fishing . . . play golf or tennis . . . with your husband?"

"No. We didn't do things like that."

"You don't say much about Andrew Casey, what was he really like?" Evelyn ran her finger around the edge of the glass, her expression changing. Sullivan found it strange to think that she seemed to be preparing for a statement, like something for the press.

"A kind man. Good to Sara and me. He made me everything I am today." She finished the rest of her drink. He felt she considered the subject closed. Still, he had an inkling that things had not been perfect in what would seem to an outsider a kind of Camelot.

"I've said this before and I believe it. I think people are destined to be what they are. No one can make them into something they aren't." He and Evelyn stared at each other for a long moment, then she blinked and looked away.

Sullivan picked up the old-style black telephone off the floor and dialed Castro. He reached for a cigarette, then decided to put that next one off for a while.

After several rings he answered. "Yeah?"

"Thought for a minute you weren't home yet. How'd it go?"

"I was outside. Fair. It went fair."

"Tell me about it," Sullivan asked.

"Not much to tell," Castro said flatly. "Gordon wasn't impressed with what you've found out. No way is he getting off Juanita Sanchez."

"You're pissed about it, right?" Sullivan exchanged glances with Evelyn.

"Yeah. Don't like the part I've played in nailing Sanchez as a killer. Gordon danced around the subject of the 'Five.' The homer was gone this morning, so I didn't mention it."

"Gone?"

"Yeah, as in vanished, vamoosed."

Sullivan decided not to intrude further. "Okay. What about the number from DMV?" Sullivan felt a little catch of excitement in his chest. He reached for a cigarette. Evelyn struck a match and held it for him.

Castro hesitated, then said, "Didn't have to call. Saw the number on Adams's tag in the lot."

"Adams?"

"None other. Heard at the station that we got a request for a copy of the Marley case from the Chicago P.D. Similar case there. They got onto it from the wire service story. I told Gordon that, too. Listen, I've got to go. I left the hose running in the yard. See you."

Sullivan listened to the buzzing, looked at the receiver as if it could furnish an explanation, then replaced it. "This thing is eating Manny. I'd guess Gordon probably gave him a good working over. Gordon's not buying our discoveries. No help coming from that end. Last night outside the window . . . it was Lieutenant Adams. He's on the force. He may be a lot of things, but he's no killer." In a way, Sullivan was disappointed. A possible link to the killer had just evaporated. Still, he supposed he had to be grateful that the killer wasn't stalking them.

"What do you make of it all?" Evelyn asked.

"I'd have to guess they're putting the heat on Manny, maybe trying to run him off the force." His renewed friendship with Castro was valuable. He didn't want to lose it.

Evelyn took a swallow of tea, then set her glass on the floor. "Why would Gordon try to run him off the force?"

Sullivan stubbed out his cigarette. "Manny's a cut above Gordon. That stings someone of his caliber." He added the bit about the Chicago P.D. picking up on the wire service article written by Carole Wheeler. He supposed, after all, it had done some good, but he still didn't like putting the killer on notice that Evelyn Casey had hired someone to actively pursue him.

"He'd be a perfect partner for you. He's bright, intuitive. You'd make a perfect pair." She leaned forward, enthusiasm shining in her eyes.

"Just what are you talking about?"

"Castro and you. I was thinking . . ."

"Go on." Sullivan wrinkled his brow.

"I think you should go in business for yourself. A real business, with an office and regular hours. Imprinted cards, stationery, the whole bit."

He searched her face for some sign of humor. She was dead serious. "What kind of business are you referring to?"

"Where there's a real need, a service will succeed. I can attest to the fact that there's a definite need for this type of thing." She smiled. "A proper detective agency. All the ones around are seedy organizations, working mainly on divorce cases. Castro said so himself."

Sullivan held up his hand. "Wait a minute! Manny hasn't quit the force yet. It's his life. The force offers all kinds of benefits, retirement funds, medical insurance, all sorts of things. All that is beside the point. You know the kind of cases I usually work on."

Evelyn reached out and touched his arm. He looked down at her hand. "I know. I heard you talking to those men on the phone, remember? A job here, one there. With a steady business you wouldn't have to live hand-to-mouth. You'd whip yourself back into shape in no time, mentally, physically, and financially. You've got what it takes, or you had it. You can get it back."

He wasn't aware she was so tuned in to his situation but should have known she didn't miss much in summing up someone. He wasn't sure he liked all she said or thought about him, but he guessed she was right.

"Are you sure you're not the one who lives in a fantasy world?" He reached for his pack of cigarettes. "I don't have the money to go into business . . . office and all, like you said. You know my financial status. Besides I don't even have a license."

Evelyn pursed her lips. "Oh, the power of positive pessimism. I'd be willing to back you two."

"Like I said before, you're in such a hurry to get rid of your goddamn money. I'd advise you to hang on to it. The going's pretty tough without it."

"Tell me about it," she cut in.

Sullivan took a deep breath. "Jesus, I shudder to think what might happen if you ran into the wrong type of guy."

Evelyn met his stare. "Regardless of what you think, I'm not in a hurry to get rid of my money. I know a good investment when I see one. I'd certainly expect a more than fair return on my money."

Sullivan couldn't help laughing. "Lady, you are just too much to believe."

By five-thirty they were on the way to Dr. H. Menken Simms's. Sullivan drove east away from the beach toward the mountains. He noticed the abundance of pine trees as he negotiated the serpentine road. Indigenous to Northern California or the East Coast, they stood like refugees among the palms. He decided some industrious, or homesick, lumberman must have transplanted them to the area years ago. They reminded him of cool autumn days in the past. He missed a change of seasons.

In a new navy-blue jacket and light gray slacks, Sullivan felt good about himself for the first time in ages. After lunch they had passed his favorite men's store. On a whim, he had gone in to buy a few necessary items. Evelyn had suggested one article after the other, admiring him as he tried on new things. "What the hell," he had said to himself. He found the spree fun.

He glanced over at Evelyn. For a blond she was quite tan, the white blouse and matching pleated skirt emphasizing her

complexion. She had wanted to change for the evening. It
tickled him that she wanted to impress Dr. Simms. The
evening would be a big event for her, matching wits in her
field with an authority. She had doubled and tied a red-and-
white scarf around her head in a bandeau effect. Gold loops
hung from her ears. Around her neck a gold chain glowed in
the late afternoon sun.

"What do you think Dr. Simms will be like? I'm trying to
imagine him. A game I always play before meeting someone."

"Did you play it before you met me?" Evelyn turned in
the seat.

Sullivan thought back. "No."

"You're not telling the truth. I can tell. You said you
always played it."

He grinned. "Okay. I thought you'd be a fat rich lady."

Evelyn looked amused. "So I am. Hey, that must be Dr.
Simms's house."

"Can you read the sign?" Sullivan squinted at the small
print.

"Yes." Evelyn looked out the window. "Can't you?"

"Does it say Simms or doesn't it?"

"Just turn in."

The driveway was gravel and ambled through a clump of
pines to the house. The walls were stone, the architecture
English, an overall effect of welcome and charm. Sullivan
wondered if the occupant matched the Old World illusion.

An old Mexican woman wearing bedroom slides led them
to a comfortable paneled study that smelled slightly musty.
Evenings were much colder in the mountain sections and a
small fire crackling in the grate warmed the air. Leather-
bound books lay scattered everywhere, their open pages marked
by red satin ribbons. A Mozart waltz came from speakers in
the bookcases.

"Doctor will be back in a minute," explained the old
woman in broken English. "Be at home yourselves. Sherry to
drink on the table." She pointed to a crystal decanter filled
with amber liquid and three sparkling glasses, then shuffled
out.

They settled in dark red leather wingback chairs, Sullivan's
next to the polished wooden table holding the sherry.

"Like a sherry?" He glanced around, admiring the room. He could be comfortable in such an atmosphere.

"Sure. What a charming place. My study at home looks a little like this, only neater. Let's play your game. I'll bet our Dr. Simms fits the stereotype, a perfectly cast movie professor."

Sullivan poured them a glass of sherry. "I'm no detective," he said with a grin, "but, I'd say he's overweight, seventyish, has a great shock of white hair."

Evelyn took a sip and licked her lips. "Smokes a pipe. Wears a watch chain across his vest."

Sullivan cocked his head. "Has a Grover Cleveland moustache . . ."

The door opened and Dr. H. Menken Simms burst in. "Good! Good! Glad to see you're having some sherry. Mr. Sullivan," he said, extending his hand, then pivoting toward Evelyn. "You must be Mrs. Casey. Mr. Sullivan told me about your background.

"I'm Dr. H. Menken Simms, of course." He continued pumping Sullivan's arm.

As he settled back in his chair, Sullivan rotated his shoulder. Simms splashed sherry in a glass, rounded his desk and plopped in a chair.

Sullivan and Evelyn exchanged glances, then focused on Dr. Simms. A towel draped around his neck, he wore a navy-blue warmup suit and red running shoes. Sullivan guessed he was less than fifty and no doubt in perfect shape. His black hair brushed the tops of his ears. His face and arms were tanned a deep walnut. Eyes, large and shiny as black marbles, viewed the world through gold-rimmed half-glasses.

"Well, you told me enough on the phone about what you're interested in, so I looked up a few references in my textbooks." He waved his arms across the scattered volumes. "Now fill me in on everything."

Sullivan finished his sherry, refilled his glass, and furnished Simms with all his facts and theories. With his head cocked, Simms listened, eyes brimming with attentiveness.

"Uh-huh, uh-huh," Simms repeated after Sullivan finished. He moved his chair in front of them, straddled it and folded his arms over the back like a teacher ready for a bull session with students. He looked at Evelyn. "With your background you already know that the serial killer looks for one special quality in his victims. Identifying that tendency is a lot like going to a museum. If you know art, you can spot anything by Picasso. Something from their background triggers what type they target. Ted Bundy, for example . . . murdered forty young college women with black hair parted down the middle. The love of Bundy's life, or so he imagined, was a dark-haired girl who rebuffed him. In effect, he was killing her over and over again. John Wayne Gacy, Chicago serial killer, was convicted of thirty-three mutilation murders of young boys after he'd had sex with them. He was actually revolted by what he was, and by killing other homosexuals, thought he was ridding himself of the tendency. Now, what have you come up with on your man?''

Evelyn pulled a yellow pad from her purse. Sullivan was surprised at the copious notes. He'd be interested to see how she stacked up against Dr. Simms and if the expert thought her anywhere near accurate.

Evelyn scanned her notes, flipped to a second page, momentarily moving her lips. She looked up at Dr. Simms. "It's clear the type he's after. Weak, vulnerable women. Probably associates them with his mother, more than likely an uncaring person who spent most of her time away from him. He probably started out as a sociopath, feeling nothing for anyone but himself." Evelyn gestured with her hand. "Antisocial behavior. An inability to form attachments. In extreme the sociopath turns to violence." Evelyn crossed her legs, tugged her skirt down and smiled at Simms.

Sullivan watched Simms return Evelyn's smile, his eyes lingering on her. "Unlike mass murderers who vent their anger in one rampage, a killing spree, serial killers suffer from a dangerous form of personality disorder: paranoid schizophrenia. Sly, conniving, many times a genius-level I.Q., they do not go through the sort of dramatic breakdown that characterizes a mass murderer." Simms held out his glass for Sullivan to pour him more sherry.

Simms took a sip and continued: "Serial killers are generallly narcissistic individuals who can be creative and think they can get away with anything. They have perfected the mask of normalcy, the ability to fit in while planning their next move.

Serial killing is like a sex crime. There is a build up of tension and killing is like a release.''

Evelyn spoke up: ''That's why knives or strangulation rather than guns are used by the serial killer—to achieve intimacy with his victim.''

''And''—Simms raised a finger—''the serial killer receives lesser amounts of satisfaction from each killing, encouraging him to strike more frequently. You can see that from the pattern you've picked up.''

Sullivan looked from one to the other. It was a pleasure to watch the novice meeting the master in their chosen field. He'd been the same when he met J. Edgar Hoover.

Sullivan cleared his throat. ''So back to the profile of our killer we're trying to build.'' Evelyn and Simms glanced at him as if they'd forgotten he was there. ''One,'' Sullivan ticked off the first asumption on his finger, ''our boy had a bad childhood. Two, he had a weak mother. Three, from the description we have, he's most likely attractive, engaging.''

Simms swung his leg around, leaped up from the chair, and moved around the room switching on lamps. ''There is a common misconception that the serial killer wants to be caught and stopped. He does not. He wants to go on forever.''

The old Mexican woman pushed on the door, brought in a tray of food and placed it on the desk. She picked up one of the celery sticks, popped it in her mouth, and left.

''Have a bite to eat,'' Simms suggested.

Sullivan surveyed the tray. Nuts, raw vegetables, dried fruit and something that looked like birdseed didn't appeal to him. ''Thanks, but I don't want to spoil my dinner. Even though the serial killer often has a high I.Q., would you consider him insane?'' Sullivan decided against another cigarette. Simms was obviously a health nut and probably already offended.

Simms removed his spectacles and polished them on the tail of his shirt. ''Sane, insane, very little difference. Courts go by the M'Naghten Rule, a standard that a person is insane if he is unable to distinguish right from wrong. With the advent of Freud and his theories of unconscious motivation, attorneys began stretching the rule. The Durham Rule later outlined that a defendant must be judged not guilty if his act is the result of mental disease or defect. Then the middle ground was the American Law Institute's Model Penal Code, ruling a person is legally insane if at the time of the act he lacks substantial capacity to appreciate the criminality of the act."

Sullivan cleared his throat. "What I'm getting at is this: if the killer is caught, his chances of pleading insanity and staying out of prison are tremendous."

Dr. Simms pulled his mouth down into an inverted U. "I've testified in most of the famous cases around the country. Know what I think?" Behind the glasses, his eyes danced with excitement. "Serial killers or mass murderers should never be taken alive."

Sullivan kept his eyes on Simms. "A criminal has to succeed one hundred percent of the time. He fails once and its over. An investigator can fail ninety-nine percent of the time, succeed one percent, and he's still ahead of the game. This killer has been right so far, but by the law of averages, it can't continue. All I need is that first mistake." Sullivan paused and turned toward Evelyn. "He'll make one. All we have to do is wait."

Simms nodded, keeping his eyes on Sullivan. "There's one major point about a serial killer that we haven't discussed. A point very important to you. We said that he is narcissistic, but it goes deeper than that. He is almost fanatically interested in publicity about his case. Some have even gone so far as to taunt or provoke the police. He thinks of himself as a professional, his murders as accomplishments, and he wants recognition as such. As long as he's not caught, he's in his element, a force in this world. Now, what you have going for you is this." He focused his attention on Evelyn. "The newspaper article that appeared after Juanita Sanchez was stabbed credits her with Sara Marley's murder, case closed by the police. This will enrage the serial killer. It was his deed. Violence is his way of proving to society he exists. If you're on track about your man, he'll strike again soon."

Sullivan stared at Evelyn, hoping her theory that the killer preyed only on weak, vulnerable women was correct.

CHAPTER 11

THE MAN HOOKED the DO NOT DISTURB sign on the doorknob and sauntered down the hall. Inside the hotel room, the woman's hand shuddered, then moved, fingernails digging into the carpet. Struggling to pull herself up, she sprawled back on the floor, sapped of all strength. She clutched her chest and tried again, moving a few inches closer to the telephone. Leaving a bloody trail, she progressed several more feet, the robe tangled in her legs. She pushed on. Within arm's length of the night table, she collapsed, unable to continue. She grabbed for the phone cord but missed by inches. With all the effort she could muster, she used her toes to force her body those last few inches. She was within striking distance. Gasping the line in her hand, she wrenched the receiver from its base. It fell to the floor, the dial tone piercing the quiet of the room. She managed to punch the ''O'' button and waited.

Finally the line clicked and the operator said, ''May I help you?''

''This is Sally Bricker,'' she gasped. ''I've been stabbed. I need help . . .''

In khaki shirts and pants, Evelyn and Sullivan had just come in from the firing range. She was a natural with a handgun, not afraid of the weapon, but respectful of its potential, which in Sullivan's opinion was not only the correct attitude but also the only attitude.

Earlier in the day Sullivan had listened to Evelyn's call from Carole Wheeler. Bubbling with enthusiasm over meeting Dr. H. Menken Simms, she had explained to the reporter that from his pointers she was honing her ideas for her book project. Evelyn thanked Carole again for the use of the microfilm library and added that her research had proved helpful.

"I think you deserve a drink for your performance. I'll mix." Sullivan walked behind his bar.

"Thanks, kind sir. If you'll excuse me, I'm going to freshen up." She hurried down the hall to the bathroom.

When she returned, hair freshly combed, lipstick newly applied, Sullivan handed her a drink. "I'm going out to the patio to turn on the water. My flowers are wilting."

He took a sip of his drink and walked out. Evelyn could hear him humming.

Evelyn sauntered over to a chair, stopping as the telephone rang. She looked over her shoulder toward the patio. "I'll get it."

She picked up the receiver. "Hello."

"Evelyn, thank God you're there. I've called the apartment over and over." Carole Wheeler screeched.

"What's the matter, Carole?" An alert went up in Evelyn's mind. Something was headlines.

"Another woman was stabbed earlier this evening, in the Seawind Hotel. Got all the similarities to your sister's case. The woman had just arrived in town. Her name is Sally Bricker."

Evelyn gasped and truned toward the kitchen. Catching her expression, Sullivan hurried out. "What is it?"

"Another stabbing in a hotel here . . . just like Sara," Evelyn said to Sullivan, then returned to Carole. "Where had the woman come from?"

"Dallas, and Evelyn, she's not dead. Unconscious, but not dead. She's in UCSD Medical Center. I'm going there on the double. Big story blazing here. I thought you'd want to know. I'll be in touch."

Evelyn slammed down the receiver and faced Sullivan.

"He's struck again, and he's made the mistake you said he would. The woman's not dead. She's in UCSD Medical Center." She looked up. "Please, dear God, please don't let her die. She's the key to it all." Her voice cracked. "Think what she can tell if she lives."

Sullivan frowned. "Want to go down there so we can try and get a firsthand report? The place will be crawling with police and reporters."

Evelyn's eyes flashed with excitement. "Let's go. I'd never be able to sit here with that going on."

Uniformed policemen and detectives crowded together on the stairs leading to the front entry of UCSD Medical Center. Reporters milled about as television crews set up their equipment for on-the-spot interviews. Ambulance sirens wailed in the background. Carole Wheeler sat in her car in the dim parking lot, streetlamps casting arcs of light on the concrete. Gathering a big scoop required ultimate imagination. Her editor had, naturally, assigned the story to his two male aces. She had to best them by sheer moxie. Sally Bricker's room would be heavily guarded with no admittance except by authorized personnel.

Carole eased her door open and pushed out of the car. She tugged at her nurses' cap, hiding as much of her hair into it as she could. Putting on horn-rimmed glasses, she looked down at her feet and thought her shoes looked like two white boats. The rented white uniform made her look shapeless. Hall nurses were known to each other, but many patients had private-duty nurses. Adjusting her plastic Licensed Vocational Nurse's name tag, she set out across the parking lot to see how far she could get.

Going from floor to floor, Carole soon discovered where Sally Bricker was. Two police guards, their pistols shining, flanked her door. She was puzzled by the guarded room next to Sally Bricker's. She took up a position at the end of the hall to get her bearings and think. An overpowering antiseptic smell permeated the air. She wrinkled her nose and tried not to breathe deeply.

Doctors hurried in and out of Sally's Bricker's room, their expressions grim. A nurse pushed in a cart, vials of blood rattling as she went. Carole noticed that patient name cards were attached to each door with the exception of Sally Bricker's room. As if on the way to an emergency, Carole bustled down the hall. Passing the guarded room next to Sally Bricker's, she slowed long enough to catch a glimpse of the name posted on the door. She wondered who Crawford Evans was and why his room was also guarded.

Squishing past the nurses' station, she drew no attention. So far, so good, she thought stationing herself at the end of the hall away from Carole Bricker's room. For the time being she felt safer from that vantage point.

Standing next to the stairwell door, she pulled a piece of paper from her pocket, posing as a nurse reading a memo. She caught a movement out of the corner of her eye. The emergency door pushed open a fraction.

She grabbed the handle and jerked open the door, expecting to find a cohort anxious for a scoop. She froze, heart thumping in her throat. Transfixed, she involuntarily took a shaky step back. The tall, foreign-looking orderly glared at her, his face arrogant and his eyes . . . blazing, forbidding. For an instant the eyes reminded her of a childhood incident . . . of a bobcat caught in a trap she'd once seen back in Oklahoma. She had wanted to free the animal until she looked into its eyes. The eyes, like this man's, radiant with hatred, had drained her of all pity and filled her with terror.

She tried to speak, but nothing came out. He turned and hurried down the stairwell, leaving her with the uneasiest feeling she could ever remember experiencing. His footsteps diminished, and she leaned back against the wall to regain her composure.

After a few minutes she felt better, but not normal. She took a deep breath despite the antiseptic smell and returned to the business at hand.

Somehow she must get into Sally Bricker's room for an eyewitness account. The small camera tugged at her pocket. She hoped gaining entry wouldn't require any outside ledge climbing like in the movies. Story or not, at that she had to draw the line. Heights frightened her too much even for a scoop. Supposing the corner rooms at that end of the hall had the same configuration as the ones at the other end where

Sally Bricker was, Carole decided to go into the one that would correspond with Sally Bricker's.

She looked at the name card, put on a big smile and pushed in. "Hi there, Mrs. Moore. How are we feeling this evening?"

Eyes fixed on the ceiling, Mrs. Moore wasn't talking.

"Mrs. Moore," Carole whispered, approaching the hospital bed. She looked down at the withered figure and tried again to establish contact. Obviously the woman was awake, but unable to speak. Carole guessed the woman was paralyzed from a stroke and decided to make herself at home.

"Mrs. Moore, don't know if you can hear me or not, but don't be alarmed. I'm just here to make sure your room is comfortable." Carole grimaced to herself. Stranger things happened in hospitals to disturb patients' rest.

Carole glanced around the room, then bounced over to the window and tugged on it. "Ummph!" she grunted. "Good! Window's secure." She opened the small closet door. "Not much space, but, hey, who packs to come to a hospital."

"Gotta check the bathroom. Bathrooms are important, you know." She opened a door expecting a bathroom, but found a little hall that connected the adjoining hospital room. The hall had a door, which Carole opened. There was the bathroom serving both rooms.

So that was why the room next to Sally Bricker's was guarded. Corner rooms, although private, shared a bath with the adjoining room. That route into Bricker's room had to be protected along with the front door.

Back in Mrs. Moore's room, Carole picked up the phone, got an outside line, then dialed the hospital's number. She leaned down to Mrs. Moore. "Hope you don't mind. ATT wants us to reach out and touch someone."

"Good evening, UCSD Medical Center," a crisp voice said.

"Oh, good evening. Would you please ring Mr. Crawford Evans's room. Six twenty-four."

She listened to a buzz different from a regular ring and waited. She reached over and patted Mrs. Moore on the shoulder. Finally the receiver was lifted from its cradle, but she heard a clatter. Mr. Crawford Evans had dropped the phone. Pick it up, she willed him. Then, he did.

"Hello?"

"Hi there, Mr. Evans. This is . . ." She looked down at her plastic tag. "Nurse Meredith with the registry." Registry, she thought, whatever that is. "How's the stomach tonight?"

"Stomach? I've got a broken leg." His voice sounded elderly.

"I know about the leg, but sometimes it affects the stomach.'"

"Well, my stomach's fine if I had something decent to put into it. This slop you serve may kill me yet."

Carole smiled. He was a grouch, too. Good. "That's what I was calling about. Do you have a private nurse?"

"Can't afford these hospital room prices. How can I afford a private nurse?"

"You can now. I've been assigned to you by the registry for the evening. We pick out someone on each floor every evening to receive free service. Tonight you're it. Now since you don't have stomach trouble, that's why I asked, I'll bring some nice homemade brownies or chocolate cake. Which would you like?"

"Brownies," he huffed.

"I'll bring some magazines and read to you. After that I'll give you a nice shoulder and arm massage. Sound good?"

"Well, sure." His voice had turned receptive.

"If anyone asks, just say you're expecting me, your new private nurse, Miss Meredith. I'll be there shortly. Remember, Miss Meredith. You're expecting me."

As Carole replaced the phone, feeling triumphant, a voice called out. "What are you doing in here?"

Biting her lips, Carole turned slowly to face a large nurse standing in a slice of light. Her square peasant hand gripped the door.

She felt her face flush but knew it couldn't show under the heavy makeup as it usually did. "I was just checking on Mrs. Moore."

The fat nurse lumbered over and eyed Carole's name tag. "Where'd you come from? Mrs. Moore doesn't have an L.V.N. on duty."

Carole smiled and lifted her eyebrows. "I work at Scripps Memorial Hospital. Just got off duty. I was a friend of Mrs.

Moore's." Carole glanced back at the woman, hoping she wouldn't all of a sudden be struck with speech powers. "I was calling her second cousin to tell her Mrs. Moore seems about the same."

"Oh, okay." She turned and rumbled out.

Carole slipped out of the room and looked up and down the hall. The place was now jammed, police and reporters squeezing into the narrow area. She'd have to hurry or miss it all. She decided that even though she dreaded taking that route for fear of running into the weird orderly, she had to use the stairwell down to the next floor rather than pass the nurses' station on the way to Mr. Crawford Evan's room. A detour by the newsstand for magazines was necessary. What she'd do about the brownies was up in the air. She wished she wouldn't get so caught up in her own tales and make such elaborate promises.

With a *Playboy* and a *Penthouse* jammed inside a *Field and Stream*, Carole pushed open the stairwell door and peeked out. Taking a fortifying breath, she marched up to the two guards at Crawford Evans's door. With all the authority she could muster, she turned to the friendlier-looking of the two.

"Miss Meredith, Mr. Evans's private nurse." She glanced around, wearing her best puzzled look. "What's going on here? Mean old Evans murder somebody before somebody murdered him? Why all the police?"

The guard frowned and ignored her question. "I wasn't told a private nurse was coming on tonight."

"Tell that to old Evans. I'd as soon be off looking at TV instead of giving that old fart an enema. Look." She held up the magazines. "Just look what he asked me to bring." Carole shook her head. "Nasty old man. Listen, you'd better check with him. It's hell to pay if I'm a minute late. Tell him I'm here." Carole rolled her eyes.

The guard edged open the door and stuck his head in. "Mr. Evans, you have a private nurse coming tonight?"

"Of course," he growled. "Is she here?"

"She's here. What's her name?"

Cautious bastard, Carole thought. She hoped Evans remembered.

"What's her name? You think I'm senile? What's going on

out there? I hear all the commotion. It's disturbing me. What's it to you what her name is? Who are you?''

''Her name, Mr. Evans,'' the guard insisted.

''Miss Meredith and she's got magazines and brownies. Let her in before I complain. I'm a sick man.''

The guard nodded for Carole to enter. Just as she ducked in, she spotted Captain Gordon arrowing down the hall, Castro and Lieutenant Adams on his heels.

Carole smiled at Crawford Evans. Looking her over, his expression showed disappointment. She wondered how he'd react if he could see the real her. Bald with a puffy stomach, Evans's beady eyes danced as she handed him the magazines.

''Where's the brownies?''

''Coming. They're coming. Being baked fresh right now. I'll go for them in about fifteen minutes.''

''You can start the massage on my neck while I look at these.'' Evans leafed through one of the magazines, holding on a page featuring a nude woman.

''I've got to use your bathroom. Been on the bus for over an hour. Be right back. You just keep looking at the pictures.'' Carole hurried into the small connecting hall and pressed her ear to the closed door. Everything in the adjoining room could be heard. Carole recognized Gordon's voice. With one hand on the door for support, she gently grasped the knob and turned it as if any false move might trigger a bomb. The door was locked from the opposite side.

Hearing was acceptable, a decided advantage on other reporters, but Carole wanted a firsthand look and pictures. She glanced around. There seemed no way. She edged into the bathroom to explore possibilities.

A vent in the wall high over the bathtub caught her eye. Heaving herself from the tub's edge to the windowsill put her in eye range. She strained at the vent but saw only blackness. Climbing down, she knelt and looked under the sink. Probably backed to a sink in Bricker's room on the other side of the wall, she guessed. Plumbers kept their pipes close together. She had noticed that Evans's room had a lavatory on the opposite wall, so his was tied to the room beyond. Squinting, Carole thought being a reporter wasn't all it was cracked up to be. Here she was poking in roach holes when she could be on her typewriter banging away toward a Pulitzer.

She toyed with the round metal lip that circled the pipe heading into the wall. It slipped back easily, revealing a larger hole than necessary cut by some sloppy carpenter. Taking a bead on the peephole, she felt her heart expand with excitement. Obviously that same sloppy carpenter had been at work on the other side in Bricker's room. The round metal lip on the other side, which should be present to hide the pipe's entry into the wall was missing. It wasn't exactly a "bird's-eye view" but it was adequate.

"Miss Meredith?" Evans called out. "What are you doing in there so long?"

She hopped up and yelled around the corner. "Just getting freshened up. Be with you in a few minutes. Then, I'll start on the massage. Okay?"

Hurrying back into the bathroom, she crumpled down on the floor and took up her position under the sink. Feeling for her camera, she got it from her pocket and opened the shutter.

She watched Captain Gordon study the pale girl under the oxygen mask. Although she appeared to be dead, Carole assumed the machines surrounding her proved she was not. Carole snapped her first shot. A team of doctors and nurses stood by. One of the doctors said that her vital signs were diminishing by the minute.

Carole recognized Dr. Millard Coy, his bald pate reflecting the overhead lights. He removed horn-rimmed glasses and wiped his eyes with the back of his hand. Leaning toward Gordon, he whispered. "I don't like this. Ordinarily under no circumstances would I permit anyone to question someone in such critical condition. But when she temporarily regained consciousness, the woman seemed to put forth such a determined effort to have her say to the police. It seemed to her the most important act on this earth, maybe her last. I suppose it's the least I can do for her." He pulled back a portion of the oxygen tent. "Try to be as brief as possible."

Carole leaned forward, ready for another shot.

Gordon moved to the bed, Lieutenant Adams with pad and pencil in hand close behind. Carole pulled a small white piece of paper from her pocket and a stub of a pencil, all she could bring with her. She'd jot down as much as she could in her own shorthand and trust memory with the rest.

"Miss Bricker," Gordon said.

There was no response, only a flicker of eyelids.

"Miss Bricker," his voice rose slightly. "We're the police. We're here to help you. Can you hear me? Can you talk?"

Carole saw her eyes open, the mouth quiver. Carole held her breath. Come on, tell us. Talk, she prayed. Sally Bricker tried to raise an arm, a supreme effort. "Go," Carole mumbled. "Give it all you've got left. You're nailing a killer, babe."

Captain Gordon touched her shoulder carefully. "Don't waste any moves. Just lie still. Can you talk?"

She blinked her eyes. Again her mouth quivered in an effort to form words. Dr. Coy, obviously disturbed, moved to the window and looked out.

Sally Bricker raised inches off the mattress. "I want . . . want to . . ." her voice faltered.

Carol watched Gordon edge in closer. "Yes, you want to what? We're listening. You want to tell us about your . . ." He hesitated. Carole realized he'd almost said "killer." "Attacker," he continued. "Was it anyone you knew?"

She shook her head.

"Can you describe him, then? Tell us how he got into your room," he pressed.

As though some supernatural strength had surged through her body, Sally Bricker began to talk. Carole took notes. Sally Bricker told of a casual meeting on the plane and how the man who said his name was Carter Compton made a date with her. Later, coming to her hotel room to pick her up, he stabbed her after she let him in. Carole saw that Lieutenant Adams was also recording her words, his pencil moving like a tiny jackhammer.

With the detail of an artist's eye, Sally Bricker gave a minute description of the man. So far, Castro's pen had not moved, but now Carole watched as he began to make bold strokes on a page. It dawned on her that he was drawing a sketch from Sally Bricker's description.

Then, Sally Bricker's words trailed off. Dr. Coy hurried to

her bedside. "She's gone." Carole felt a wave of sadness strike her as she continued to watch the scene.

Gordon turned to Adams. "I'm going to tell the reporters outside that she died without regaining consciousness. I don't want any publicity on this. We'll circulate the description privately, not in the papers. Put the name Carter Compton on the wire and see what we get. Check the airlines for an address and so on. What we've heard here better never get out of this room. This is strictly confidential and police business only." He eyeballed Castro. Moving her camera directly at the hole, Carole snapped another picture.

Castro sauntered over to Gordon. "I don't think you'll get anything on a Carter Compton. More C.C. initials, exactly like the Sara Marley and Mary Kenworth cases."

Castro ripped the drawing from his sketch pad, ready to hand it to Gordon.

Gordon's face flashed with anger. He leaned close to Castro's ear, mumbled something Carole couldn't hear, turned his back and stomped out of the door, Lieutenant Adams following. Castro folded the drawing and stuffed it in his pocket.

Carole's knees popped like a gunshot as she straightened. She hurried out of the bathroom and darted for the hall. Passing Evans propped in bed, she called out: "I'm going for the brownies. They should be baked by now."

"About time," he answered.

In the hall Carole mingled with the crowd. Flashbulbs popped as Gordon announced that the woman died without regaining consciousness. There was nothing further to report. He answered a few trivial questions. Carole suspected Gordon thought the story would only merit a small write-up in the back section of the paper. No big item. Smiling, she knew she had news for Gordon.

Her smile faded when across the crowd she spotted the orderly who had frightened her. He hung back on the edge of the group but fixed her with a piercing stare. Unsettled, Carole pushed through to the elevator. On the way down she was assailed with a jumble of thoughts. As if hypnotized, she watched the floor numbers flash on and off. Her goals always clear, capable of snap decisions, Carole Wheeler was now vacillating. Hawk Sullivan's comments about solid journalism versus sensationalism pulled at her. With her potential headline information she could ruin Gordon but in the process jeopardize the chances of catching the killer by running him underground. Her initial article had boomeranged, damaged her credibility as a reporter and caused Evelyn Casey to distrust her to the point of withholding information. Here was a chance to clear her reputation at the paper if she went to her editor now, but an even bigger chance for an explosive story lay ahead if she joined forces with Evelyn and Hawk in a race with the police to catch a serial killer.

The doors parted and she stepped out into the marble-floored hospital lobby. Deep in conversation, Evelyn Casey and Hawk Sullivan sat on a vinyl couch in the corner. Carole approached them.

"It's me, Carole. Not Florence Nightingale."

Evelyn looked puzzled. "What in the world are you up to? What's happened?"

Sullivan straightened to full height. "Did the woman regain consciousness?"

Carole looked up at him and nodded. "I've got it all. Got everything down on paper. Pictures, too." She touched her pocket. "Castro even made a police sketch of the killer from the woman's description." Pursing her lips, she looked down at the floor.

"Well, I guess you're streaking off to the paper now." Sullivan brushed at his coat as if to wipe away some imaginary spot.

Carole screwed up her mouth. "Coming down in the elevator I was thinking of you. I'd like to talk to you both. Can we go somewhere for a drink?"

"Before you go to the paper or after?" Sullivan snapped.

The three turned as a crowd poured out of the elevator. Reporters and policemen scattered through the lobby and headed for the front doors. Carole saw the same orderly with the weird eyes. He glanced at them, then hurried down the hall toward the cafeteria. Carole turned back to Sullivan.

"I believe I recall someone saying to me that there was a boundary between good responsible journalism and sensationalism. I think I just crossed over that line. It's time for us to deal. You level with me and I'll tell you what I've got. How about your house for a drink and I can get out of these clothes?''

The dare-you-look he had disliked was back on her face. Now he found it somewhat appealing. Sullivan gave Carole a long appraising look, a crooked smile growing on his lips. ''You got it.''

Carole lifted her eyebrows. ''The man who stabbed this woman gave her the name Carter Compton, and then Castro said something to Gordon about more C.C. initials. You never thought Juanita Sanchez stabbed your sister. I want to hear the whole story. Maybe we can all help each other. After this is over, there'll be a big story. I want it to be mine.'' Her eyes beamed with excitement.

They watched her hurry away, white shoes slipping up and down on her heels. They turned to each other, the anticipation clear on both faces.

As they started for their cars in the parking lot, Castro streaked out of the elevator and hurried across the lobby. He spotted them, hesitated, then walked over to where they stood.

Sullivan reached out and shook Castro's shoulder. ''A big break, huh?''

Castro avoided Sullivan's eyes. ''No break at all. Zip.'' He shifted from one foot to the other. ''The woman died without regaining conciousness,'' he finished, but his words came out on crutches.

Evelyn looked at him. ''She didn't say anything? Never spoke?''

Castro shook his head, then checked his watch. ''Nada.''

Sullivan couldn't hide the hurt he felt. Carole Wheeler, practically a stranger, one who had been burned publicly, had leveled at great expense, whereas his old friend was lying, despite being confronted with more C.C. initials. Sullivan tried to understand. Gordon had the pressure on Castro. His job was on the line. Sullivan needed a look at that police sketch. He wondered if it was in Gordon's possession now or if Castro still had it.

''Okay, pal. Play it like you have to, I understand,'' Sullivan said, well aware of the flat tone in his voice.

Castro looked at Sullivan. "I'm just playing it like it is. That's all." He seemed to taste his words and not like the flavor.

"Sure. Sure." Sullivan snapped. "I feel like this killing is another connection . . . like we thought all along. Would have helped to have something more to go on . . . any scrap. What's Gordon think about it all? Does he admit the connections now?"

Castro didn't answer but looked as if he were weighing some decision. Sullivan kept his eyes on him.

Evelyn let out an abrupt rush of air. "Poor woman. Just like Sara. Too bad she couldn't have regained consciousness and been able to speak. She was his only victim so far that survived. If she had at least been able to give some information, her death would have counted for something. How long will it go on? C.C., whoever he is, has got to be stopped at any cost."

Sullivan touched Evelyn's elbow. "Let's get out of here. Everything stinks in here."

As they walked away, Sullivan felt Castro's eyes boring into his back. He jerked open the front door for Evelyn, and they stepped out into the crisp evening air.

Castro turned to leave just as Gordon stepped off the elevator, Adams following in a modified stalk. Castro caught up with them.

"Captain, I'd like to discuss that 'Five' with you."

Gordon whipped his head around at Castro. "What 'Five'?" He never broke stride.

Back at his house, Sullivan and Evelyn waited with drinks in hand for Carole to change. Sullivan listened to her banging around in his bathroom and smiled. The little reporter had, in his estimation, made giant strides tonight. She had rearranged his opinions. He tried not to dwell on his sentiments concerning Castro.

Without knocking, Castro pushed open the front door. His appearance startled Sullivan. It was as if Sullivan's thoughts had commanded him to materialize out of thin air.

Castro blinked, shifted his eyes from Sullivan to Evelyn and back. "I . . . I'm sorry about . . . the woman regained consciousness. I've just come from seeing Mark Foster. He identified the man who asked him to change seats from the sketch I made. I kept staring at that sketch. I knew I'd seen the face before. Then, it dawned on me. I spotted him outside the police station the other day, looking around, at me, Adams and the reporter. I guess that cinched it for me.''

Castro reached into his pocket. "Here.'' He handed Sullivan his drawing. "This is what he looks like. The woman gave a good description.''

Sullivan jerked the paper from his hand and frowned as he studied the sketch. "For Christ sakes! It can't be!''

"Do you know who he is?'' Evelyn's voice cracked with excitement.

Sullivan's eyes were riveted to the drawing. "What a resemblance.'' His shoulders slumped. "Looks like Charlie Christmas.'' He shook his head.

Castro's eyes widened. "The C.C. initials again. Who's Charlie Christmas?''

Sullivan looked up. "Charlie Christmas has been dead ten years.''

CHAPTER 12

EVELYN WAS TRANSFIXED by the drawing. The face was arrogant, tough, yet there was refinement, the lips and nose nicely formed, but the eyes . . .

"Think of those eyes coming toward you." She looked up at Sullivan, her complexion pale. "I see what Mark Foster meant about weird eyes. And, to think, Castro saw him hanging around outside the police station. He was *so* close. Charlie Christmas."

"Castro might have seen the man he sketched but he didn't see Charlie Christmas. He was stabbed to death at Huntsville Prison in Texas." Sullivan moved behind the bar and slammed three glasses on the counter almost hard enough to break them. He jammed in ice cubes and poured drinks, a Perrier for Carole at Evelyn's request.

"Charlie Christmas," Evelyn repeated. "The C.C. initials again. He went under fictitious names, but always used his real initials. You see, a serial killer cannot divorce himself from the past. It's where he lives, what he clings to because that's where it all started."

Sullivan fixed his eyes on Evelyn. The sketch haunted him, and the fact that Castro had seen the man disturbed him even more. Now Evelyn was off on a tangent. He wished he hadn't mentioned the sketch's similarity to Charlie Christmas.

Changed from the nurse's uniform, Carole Wheeler flounced into the room. She wore a bright green warmup suit and matching running shoes.

"I thought I heard somebody talking? Who was here?"

"Castro came with his drawing," Evelyn said. "Here."

Taking the drawing, Carole sank down in Hawk's favorite chair. Squinting as if to absorb every feature, she studied the sketch. She held it out in front of her, then drew it slowly toward her face, her eye twitching slightly. "Could be. The eyes. Yeah." She looked at Hawk, who rounded the bar and sat a Perrier on the side table for her. "I'm positive I saw this very man in the hospital tonight. He was an orderly, or more than likely dressed like one. He was on the stairway, peeping down the hall toward Sally Bricker's room. Then he was in the crowd of reporters. He stared at me. When the three of us were in the lobby talking, he came down on the elevator and looked at us." She glared at the drawing. "It's the same man all right."

Sullivan stopped in his tracks. "You sure? Castro thinks he's seen the man, too. This killer is moving in close, getting more brazen. He's watching." The idea sent a chill through Sullivan.

"Hawk says the sketch looks just like a man named Charlie Christmas."

"*Similar* to Charlie Christmas." His tone had an edge. "Christmas has been dead ten years." He turned to Carole. "The man you and Castro recognize is very much alive. I think that's what we came here to talk about. You tell us what went on in that hospital room tonight, and I'll tell you what information we've put together." Hawk took a seat next to Evelyn. He disliked sitting on couches, but Carole had his chair and he wasn't about to ask her to move.

Carole picked up her Perrier, took a sip and winced as bubbles tickled her nose. She repeated Sally Bricker's exact words, describing Gordon's reactions.

Evelyn sat quietly absorbing the news. "So that's how he did it. Hawk was right." Her eyes ranged over him. "Gained the women's confidence on the airplane, found out where they were staying, probably called them and found out their room number, then came on the pretext of picking them up for a date and stabbed them." She thought of Sara's naivete against such an engaging, charismatic personality.

Carole sat her drink down. "So, now to what you have."

Sullivan revealed their discoveries, then centered on the serial killer's profile Evelyn had compiled with Dr. Simms's help. When he finished, something flickered in Carole's eyes, excitement, but a sobering realization.

"We are really onto something."

Sullivan looked at her. "So's our killer, I'm afraid."

Evelyn flipped her hair out of her collar, a habit Sullivan had come to read as a sign of nervousness or frustration. "How do you know about Charlie Christmas? What did he do?"

Sullivan slugged his drink before answering. This hammering at a dead man irritated him. Their attention should be focused on the dangerous live one who was on the move now. "What difference does it make? Like I said, he's dead."

"But what did he do?" Evelyn persisted.

Sullivan clenched his teeth together, his jaw pulsing. "I was special agent in charge of the Dallas FBI office when it all happened. Guess you two were too young for the headlines to have made an impact. He stabbed fourteen pregnant girls in an unwed mothers' home. Christmas was sentenced to life at Huntsville Prison with no chance of parole. The death penalty had been abolished then."

Evelyn perked up. "That background fits . . . hatred of women."

Sullivan lit a cigarette, blew out smoke slowly and stared at Evelyn. "He was also a mass murderer, not a serial killer. Dr. Simms, remember, explained the difference. Anyway, all that's immaterial. He's dead. So let it drop."

Evelyn took a deep breath. "The man's not even human. Beyond belief. A person like that . . ." She hesitated, then looked at Carole. "He's capable of anything. Could you get the account of his death from the paper?"

Carole nodded, still appalled by the viciousness of the crimes Christmas committed.

"I want to read it." Evelyn toyed with her cocktail napkin.

Sullivan got up to mix another round. "Charlie Christmas is dead, and you're wasting time while a serial killer is on the loose. He's been spotted and now that we know what he looks like, we'd better start working toward some plan of trying to trap him. He may be on the run after what happened tonight. He knows he made his first mistake. He just doesn't know how bad it really was."

Evelyn avoided Sullivan's eyes. "Carole, I want to know everything there is to know about Charlie Christmas. Tomorrow, first thing." Evelyn stood and walked over to the bar, her eyes beaming with high excitement. She set her glass before Sullivan.

He looked at her, irritated that her good instincts were misdirected. "Evelyn"—his voice was stern—"good detectives don't get obsessed with an idea that is completely irrational. You can't have tunnel vision on a theory that has no basis. Charlie Christmas is about as suspect in this case as George Washington. They're both in the same place . . . the ground."

Carole Wheeler picked up the drawing and stared at it. Still holding the drawing, she dropped her hand to her side. "This man in the hospital tonight . . . the way he looked at me, then at all of us when we were together. I think he knows who all three of us are and what we're after. *Him*. We'd better find out who he is before he can do something about it."

Sullivan's eyes strayed back to Carole and fixed on her. A smile pulled up the left corner of his mouth. It was more bitter than amused. "I'm glad someone finally got the point. We're dealing with a clever, cunning son of a bitch here, and we can't afford not to come out on top."

The following morning, Evelyn coerced Sullivan into meeting Carole Wheeler at the *Union*. Evelyn had spent an almost sleepless night, drifting in and out of unsettling dreams. Despite her fatigue, she was anxious to see what Carole had dug up. Carole was pleased with herself as she led them down the hall to the same room where Evelyn had used the microfilm library. His personal interest in Evelyn growing strong, Sullivan went along with the idea only to appease her, hoping the exercise in futility might clear her thinking when she saw accounts of Christmas's death in print.

In the cold light of day Evelyn had to admit to herself that her theory was a long shot. If the sketch wasn't Charlie Christmas, only bore a strong resemblance, who was it? she kept asking herself. And not to be taken lightly was Carole's testimony that the man had seen the threesome together and observed them carefully.

Carole pointed to the stack of printouts. "Here is everything in print on Charlie Christmas. I've arranged it in an order . . . starting with his death in prison, the articles work their way back."

They sat down and began with the first page.

A-1 THE DALLAS MORNING NEWS

Saturday September 20, 1977

Christmas Killer Slain

by George Hodges
Staff Writer of The News

HUNTSVILLE, TEXAS—Charlie Christmas, convicted of crimes that revolted a nation, was fatally stabbed in the shower rooms at Huntsville Prison by an unknown assailant early Monday morning. Warden Underwood stated that an investigation into Christmas's death was under way, but he expected few results. "It's just not the same, here inside the walls," Underwood was quoted in an interview. "Charlie was probably the most hated and troublesome inmate we had here. His killer could have been any number of prisoners." Christmas's unclaimed remains were buried in the prison cemetery.

In December of last year Christmas was the

central figure in the sensational "Christmas Killings" trial. He was sentenced to life plus two hundred years in Huntsville State Prison for the brutal stabbing of fourteen pregnant women residing in the Edna Goodney Home for Unwed Mothers. Presiding at the trial, Judge Oliver Ute called it the most heinous crime he'd come across in his long career as a jurist.

"Look at this!" Carole pointed to the printout of the actual crime. "What headlines! Mass Killer Slays Fourteen Pregnant Women at Home for Unwed!"

Evelyn shook her head. "Counting the unborn babies, that's twenty-eight people he murdered." She shivered at the thought. "Slipped in the home for unwed mothers from a rear window and methodically stabbed every resident." Her eyes shifted from the printout to Sullivan. "According to the article, the Dallas police chief said he was baffled by the lack of motive. A neighbor who spotted a car parked outside the home wrote down the tag number because of the late hour. Then, when a man covered in blood returned to the car, she called the police, who arrived to discover the massacre."

Carole clicked her tongue. "If that neighbor hadn't seen him, had been asleep or watching television at that very time, Christmas might have gotten away."

Sullivan looked at the two women. "I've always said coincidentals usually trap a criminal."

"This next printout from the Dallas paper is where they identify Charlie Christmas." Evelyn held up the paper. "Christmas was a computer expert. Remember what Simms and I talked about . . . the high I.Q.?"

"This all happened around Christmas time, so the press dubbed him the 'Christmas Killer.' Reporters like to hang a tag on murderers," Carole said.

Carole handed Evelyn a stack of printouts. "A staff writer with the Dallas *Morning News* interviewed people who had known Christmas and wrote a series of articles titled, 'Who Is the Christmas Killer?' The first interviewed were his fellow workers. They expressed shock, but most said Christmas was strange and a loner, but considered very able. One of them said he lived far below his status, small apartment, always trying to save, sometimes went without eating. Took the bus to work. They all figured he was socking away his salary for the future.''

"Who'd the writer interview next?" Evelyn asked, anxious to reach back into Christmas's life.

"His former college roommate at Texas Tech University, where Christmas was on scholarship. The roommate said Christmas held down a series of jobs and always pushed himself beyond regular limits. Here's a direct quote. 'What it took for others to accomplish full-time, Christmas could handle in half.' Said Christmas went through school like a programmed robot, never forming any lasting relationships, but he could captivate anyone when he wanted to. When he graduated, job offers rolled in.''

Carole took a deep breath and continued: "Christmas grew up in the Texas State Orphanage.''

Evelyn gasped. "Abandoned! The profile fits exactly.''

Carole lifted her eyebrows. "The director of the orphanage said Christmas threw tantrums and one time he cut up all the childrens' Sunday clothes that were kept in lockers. He was small for his age, but his abilities in the classroom were extraordinary. The housekeeper at the orphanage said Christmas went to great lengths to curry favors but underneath was calculating and vicious. According to her, he was fascinated with the subject of death and cut pictures from magazines and newspapers of horrible accidents, especially to women.'' Carole handed Evelyn the last of the writer's series. "This one you should read. You, too, Hawk. It tells a lot.''

A-5 THE DALLAS MORNING NEWS

Sunday December 15, 1976

Who Is The Christmas Killer?

Fifth in a series of articles
by Terry Cook
Staff Writer

PECOS, TEXAS—Brother Ralph Cramer, now re- tired chaplain of the Texas State Orphanage, was the man who found accused slayer, Charlie Christ- mas, presumably abandoned by his mother in the winter of 1938. Held without bail in the Dallas City Jail, Christmas is awaiting trial for the mul- tiple slayings termed 'The Christmas Killings.' Living in an isolated community on the West Texas plains, Brother Cramer said he was deeply distressed to learn of the bloody massacre in the Edna Goodney Home for Unwed Mothers attrib- uted to Christmas.

Cramer recounted his discovery of Charlie Christmas: "The day before Christmas I was walking in the snow to town to gather candy for the children at the Home. Taking a back street, I stopped when I heard a noise in a garbage can. I opened it and found a newborn baby. His skin was nicked from the trash and turning blue, but by a miracle, I thought at the time, he was alive. Wrapping him in my coat, I took him back to the orphanage. I decided if he survived, I'd name him Charlie Christmas."

"Until he was four, Charlie spoke in a whin- ing, strange, animal-like tone that no one could understand. The children shunned him. Towns- people gossiped about various women with shady reputations. Some speculated Charlie had been dumped by passing gypsies. Many of the children paraded before prospective parents on Sundays were chosen for adoption, but Charlie was always passed over. On those Sundays he worked himself into a peak of excitement and anticipation, only to be let down."

"When he was six, Charlie was enrolled in the local school. At recess the first day, he found his origin had preceded him. Charlie was greeted by the town children with a chant to the tune of 'Jingle Bells':

Charlie Christmas
Charlie Christmas
Dumped in a can
Charlie Christmas
Charlie Christmas
Don't know his old man.

"Children can be mean sometimes," Brother Cramer concluded. "It was sad. I tried my best to help Charlie."

Evelyn handed the article to Sullivan and rubbed her forehead. "My God! I know this sounds terrible, but if only that man hadn't found Christmas, none of this would have happened."

Carole shuffled through more papers. "Christmas underwent a battery of tests from psychiatrists to determine if he was capable of standing trial. They concluded he was rational and understood his charges. Christmas was appointed an attorney by the court who entered an insanity plea on his client's behalf."

"How long did his trial last?" Evelyn asked.

"Three weeks. After the trial all the jurors commented to the press on how uncomfortable they were within range of Christmas's sinister glare. I can just imagine it!"

Evelyn exhaled. "Me, too."

"There's plenty more here," Carole said. "Editorials denouncing the abolishment of the death penalty." Carole rummaged through the papers. "This case sparked a campaign to reinstate the death penalty. I've never before seen such letters to the editor."

Evelyn looked up from the last clipping. "Hawk, think how close my profile of the killer comes to Charlie Christmas's life story."

Hawk twitched his mouth to one side. "Two differences." He held up his finger. "Charlie Christmas was a mass murderer. Fourteen at once. Our man is a serial killer, one after the other."

"And the other?" Evelyn asked.

"Christmas is dead."

Evelyn picked up a pencil and tapped it on the table. "For the sake of argument . . . just for a minute . . . say he's not dead. Could he have changed? Mass murderer to serial killer? I don't believe I've ever heard of it. We never talked about that point with Dr. Simms." She looked at Carole. "Is the phone over there a direct line?"

Carole nodded. "Who are you going to call?"

Evelyn took out her address book from her purse and flipped it open. "Dr. Simms. He said if we needed any more help to feel free." She checked her watch, then dialed. "I hope he's in."

"Dr. Simms!" Her relief was evident. She explained the situation and asked what he thought. As Simms talked, Evelyn nodded, keeping her eyes on Sullivan.

"Well?" Sullivan asked after she'd hung up.

"Dr. Simms said that, while the behavior is uncommon, it is not impossible to turn from mass murderer to serial killer. He examined Charles Manson before he was tried and believes Manson was turning. After those first mass slayings, he then had plans to single out individuals for execution. Simms also said that when Christmas exploded and killed those pregnant women, he was in effect killing his mother, obviously a weak woman not able to face reality or she wouldn't have abandoned him. If that wild urge to punish her was perhaps not satisfied as he expected it to be, then he might turn to serial killing, which in Simms's opinion, could be much more fulfilling to a clever mind due to the careful planning involved. Besides, he said, almost all mass murderers have been arrested immediately after the slayings, as Christmas was, preventing them from showing future patterns. How about that!''

"Jesus Christ! What a story! Unique." Carole Wheeler let out a rush of air.

"Have you lost your mind or something? You're forgetting the first printout we looked at." Hawk spoke with high irritation. "Talk about not facing reality."

Carole handed Evelyn a photograph. "Wait! The finale. In every newspaper picture Charlie Christmas always turned his head so the photographers couldn't get a good full shot. This one's pretty clear of him."

Evelyn grabbed the glossy, Sullivan looking over her shoulder. "It's just like Castro's drawing," she commented.

"It's exactly like the man I saw in the hospital. I would swear Charlie Christmas was in that hospital."

Evelyn searched Hawk's face before speaking, her eyes moving over his features, pleading. "Hawk, let's go to Texas where this all started. Let's go to Huntsville Prison."

Exasperated, Sullivan lit a cigarette.

Carole shook her head. "There's no smoking in here."

Sullivan looked at her as if to say, "Who's going to stop me?" and continued. "Let's talk this through slowly. Evelyn, a real killer is on the loose and we're back chasing ghosts. I admit the C.C. initials fit, but that's all."

Carole Wheeler popped her hand on her hip. "I think you should go. Get out of town for a while. Me? I'm going to start staying at a friend's. I didn't sleep last night. That orderly in the hospital . . . I'm afraid, I tell you. He knows who we are. He could have been following us to see what we're up to. When did he get onto us?"

"My picture was in the paper when Sara died, remember? You saw it and recognized me at the police station. Let's go over what the killer could know about us and what he couldn't." Evelyn glanced at the ceiling, deep in concentration. "He knows my identity." She focused on Carole. "He read the article, knows I've hired someone to investigate the case. Finds the hotel where I'm registered. Follows me to see what I'm about. He knows I've made friends with you. That phone call. I had the weirdest feeling it was someone checking on me. I moved from the hotel, but it looks as if we've found some line worth investigating because I didn't return to Dallas when Sara's case was officially closed.''

''He can't know what information we have about him, though,'' Carole interjected. ''How far we've come. The C.C. initials he travels under. The airline connections to other cases. The profile of his personality. And above all, he doesn't know his last victim lived long enough to give a description.''

''He can't know we think he might be Charlie Christmas.'' Evelyn glanced self-consciously in Sullivan's direction. ''About my profile . . . about him always going for the same type. If he thought he was going to be stopped by us, in desperation he'd have to act. We're not the type he's after, but to be able to continue his attacks, his main goal in life, he'd have to do away with us. We could be in jeopardy. Let's face it. He's got to be edgy. He made a mistake. Sally Bricker is his first victim who didn't die immediately.'' She turned to face Hawk. ''We don't really have anywhere else to look but Texas. Please, let's just give it a try.''

Hawk squinted at Evelyn, raising one eyebrow slightly. Maybe Texas wasn't such a bad idea. Evelyn could back off and take a fresh look. She had been under a strain. However, if the man Carole Wheeler saw was the killer, he was in San Diego, and they'd be fifteen hundred miles away. Unless, of course, he followed them to Texas. He'd keep a keen eye out.

He shrugged. ''Okay. We'll go.'' Turning to Carole Wheeler he looked at her for a long moment. Never would he have thought he'd reach the point of enlisting the aid of the press, but he couldn't afford to lose time despite the futile trip to Texas. ''Dr. Simms told us that the killer is fascinated by his publicity, even enraged if credit is given to someone else, as it was with Sara Marley's case. He said that the article that appeared after Juanita Sanchez's death might serve to flush him out. Well, it did. Maybe it's time for you to write an article, a red herring, so to speak.''

Panic in her wide eyes, Carole stared at him. ''Thought you didn't want me to go to press.''

''Hear me out. We want him to get even more edgy. That's when he's apt to make another mistake. Write an article, supposition on the reporter's part''—he held up his hand, making brackets with his fingers—''titled, 'What the victim could have told had she lived?' Let's give the killer a tag . . . How about 'The Sky Slayer'? Then, you go on to say that Sally Bricker had just arrived in town and assume she probably met her attacker on the airplane. She described him, remembering small details that will enable the police to track him. This is all fictional, remember. Maybe initials on a sleeve cuff or a briefcase, but for God's sake don't mention C.C. You give a description that she might have given. Yours will be vague, but enough on target . . . six feet tall, dark, handsome. You could have made that up for the readers. Tell how he approached her. Being a vulnerable woman, she swallows his story, makes a date with him. He comes to her hotel and stabs her.'' Sullivan dropped his hands to his sides. ''See what I mean? Something on that order, enough to scare him into action.''

''I'm in enough deep shit at the paper; my editor will never go for it,'' Carole barked, but her tone was a cover for the trepidation she felt.

''Make him,'' Sullivan countered. ''Tell him everything we know in strict confidence, not about the Charlie Christmas part though.'' Sullivan winced. ''But about the linkages, what the police are keeping quiet. You'll have to stake your reputation and career on it. If you're wrong, my guess is you'll be asked to resign. Are you willing to go that far?''

Carole took a deep breath and nodded. ''Yep. I'm convinced there's a serial killer on the prowl and this could *make* my reputation with a story that should go national. But, signing my byline to that. The killer would come after me then for sure.''

''Sign a fictitious byline,'' Evelyn suggested.

''And let somebody else get the credit?''

All three had to laugh at Carole's statement.

Sullivan's expression turned serious. ''We're toying with trouble, but it just might work. We just might stop him, rattle him into making a big mistake, but from now on, we've got to be cautious. We'll have waved the proverbial red flag at the bull.''

CHAPTER 13

AS THE PLANE DIPPED LOWER, Sullivan leaned toward the window and looked out at the lakes dotting the flat green landscape. He thought of Texas as a patchwork quilt. Large cultivated squares of color. He didn't think Texas was a beautiful state. There was no true sweep or grandeur about it like the awesome landscape of California. Still, there was an undeniable magic about Texas.

In the distance he could see the skyline of Dallas. The silver, copper, and glass buildings, glittering in the late sun, rose from the earth like giant fingers straining to touch the sky. Things had changed from the old days when he knew Dallas as an energetic, but still country-oriented city. Now, the sprawling giant had come of age, challenging the banking, oil, movie and garment centers of the world.

"It's so spread out, looks like Los Angeles," he commented. "Wish I'd brought some property back in the old days when land was cheap. Course I didn't have the extra money." He pictured the disappointment in his father's face after his graduation from law school and the announcement that he was planing to join the FBI. His father thought he would bc all set with fat legal fees coming his way, but he had been idealistic and full of enthusiasm. Now, he supposed his father had been right. "The FBI has good government pensions and perks, but you can't get rich in the service."

"You did what you wanted. That's the important thing." Handing her glass to the stewardess, Evelyn buckled her seat belt, then folded the morning edition of the paper they had bought at the airport in San Diego and read on the plane. She stuffed it in her purse.

"Carole really delivered the goods with her article."

Sullivan nodded. In his mind he recapped the article Carole Wheeler had persuaded her editor to let her write by dangling the promise of forthcoming headlines. More important, the story was a blatant invitation prompting the killer to make a move. Congratulations to Carole Wheeler were in order for such efforts, but he hoped they hadn't gone too far.

He wrestled with the possibility that the killer could be Charlie Christmas as Evelyn now firmly believed. The face in the sketch could be identified as Christmas's. The initials C.C. cropping up. The psychological profile fit perfectly, but Sullivan built on logic. Dead is dead. He was in Texas at Evelyn's request, not to hunt Charlie Christmas's ghost. Still, an Arthur Conan Doyle quote nagged him. "When you have eliminated the impossible, whatever remains, however improbable, must be the truth."

He looked at Evelyn in short snatches, shoplifting an image of her. Her hair pulled back neatly, the beige suit and blouse enhancing her honey-blond coloring. She had taken on a much more sophisticated appearance now that she was returning home. He wondered how he might fit in her surroundings. Maybe like some wines, he didn't travel well.

She pulled a mirror out of her purse and applied lipstick. Her cheekbones caught light and shadows in extraordinary ways. There was an alertness, an intelligence within the depths of those aqua eyes. He had become so accustomed to having her around that thinking of her stepping out of his life brought a jab to his heart.

"I have a car waiting," Evelyn said, snapping shut her compact.

That old uneasy feeling seized him again. He wasn't used

to a woman making arrangements. She was still his employer, he reminded himself.

On boarding he had checked out the passengers on their flight, even walking down the aisle from first-class to the back of the aircraft on the pretense of stretching his legs. Now as they disembarked and moved through the throng to the baggage area, he kept alert for anyone resembling Castro's drawing. At the revolving conveyor belt he watched passengers grab their luggage. He eyed people who met new arrivals, stragglers that milled around, and passengers arriving from other flights. When their bags popped up, Sullivan heaved them off the ramp and they headed for the sidewalk.

The chauffeur, a shining black man, who looked as if cellophane had just been torn off him, opened the car door and took charge of the luggage. After Evelyn settled in the backseat, Sullivan hauled himself in and leaned back against the plush gray velour seats.

Evelyn leaned back. Going home and taking Hawk Sullivan with her. She wondered what Quinn Stewart and her friends would think of this man she'd come to care for, admire, and respect, and realized their opinions didn't matter. Who you are when you're with a certain someone was what counted. With Sullivan she was complete.

Sullivan heard a solid click as the chauffeur pressed the doorlocks. They were passing through a section where poor black people sat on slanted front porches of dilapidated wooden shacks they called home. A maze of modest homes flashed by, then gave way to a section where yards spanned into acres. Sprawling mansions hidden behind gigantic oaks overlooked Turtle Creek, the small body of water centered in the fanciest residential area. Sullivan pulled the slack knot of his tie tight to his collar. He was in Evelyn's neighborhood.

A brick wall surrounded the property. The driver pulled up to high wrought-iron gates and waited for them to part. The gates groaned open, and they moved down a winding driveway lined with trees so thick they met at the top and formed a tunnel of greenery.

Evelyn's home, a columned two-story Southern mansion of beige brick, loomed before them. The oversize double front doors were flanked by bronze urns holding pyramid-shaped plants. Carriage lights beamed a welcome.

The chauffeur turned from the front seat. "Mr. Stewart is here, he's waiting for you," he said in a deep Texas drawl.

In the entry hall, Sullivan looked around. Floors of black-and-white marble square checks gave over to walls covered in hand-painted linen. Impressionist paintings of vibrant flower bouquets were lit by overhead pinpoints. Despite the grandeur, the statement of big money spent, the place spoke of personal warmth and taste. A thick Oriental runner held by brass rods at the base of each step covered the length of the stairway winding to the rooms above. A large crystal and brass chandelier cast a muted glow. Giant porcelain pots held lush green plants. The furniture, pieces he might have chosen, was French, wiped with a subtle beige hand finish.

The chauffeur came in with the bags, and Evelyn directed him to place Sullivan's in the guest room at the top of the stairs.

"I feel like I'm imposing. I should have stayed at a hotel. I remember the Baker."

"Nonsense." Evelyn laughed. "The Baker has been torn down." She waved her hand to the left. "The dining room and kitchen are over there. The living room's to the right. Come on back to the study, my favorite room. It's down at the end of the hall. Quinn will be in there."

Just then, a man emerged from the study and stood in the doorway. Evelyn walked toward him. Quinn Stewart, Sullivan presumed.

"Hello, Quinn," Evelyn said as he walked over and kissed her on the cheek. She turned to Sullivan. "I'd like you to meet Hawk Sullivan, Quinn. I've told you about him."

"Yes," Quinn Stewart said, raking Sullivan with appraising eyes. Stewart was a good-looking man, maybe halfway through his forties, tanned a deep cordovan shade and physically fit. "Good to meet you." He extended his hand.

Sullivan took it. "Same here." Stewart's grip was overly strong.

"Let's go in and have a drink. I've already mixed one for myself." Stewart pushed open the double doors to make a wider entry. "Evelyn, I've got some papers for you to sign on that new acquisition Cypress plans to make—Cougar Energy and Development. They're on your desk. I wouldn't bother you tonight, but we've got a deadline to meet. The closing is in two days. It's absolutely necessary for you to be there."

The brick-floored study was paneled in light wood with thick moldings. Ceiling-to-floor bookcases covered one wall, a marble fireplace occupied another. The room was dominated by a large leather-topped desk with brass fittings, a matching chair, a small, green-print upholstered couch and two side chairs. A green shag rug covered the floor. A bar with a brass sink was built into one of the bookcases. Glass shelves held rows of crystal, all shapes and sizes. Decanters were filled with liquor.

"Evelyn, I want us to sit down soon and go over your portfolio. With such a surge in the market, I think some of your stocks are fully priced and need selling. That will create some tax consequences, but I don't want to let that cloud my better judgment."

"Fine, Quinn. Whatever you say."

Quinn Stewart walked to the bar and took charge. Evelyn went to her desk and sat down. Sullivan sank into one of the lounge chairs and tried to feel comfortable in Quinn Stewart's presence. "Vodka, Evelyn? With a lemon wedge?" He sliced the lemon before she answered. "You?" He turned around to Sullivan

"Jack Daniels on the rocks, if you have it." Sullivan lit a cigarette, his first since leaving the plane.

"We have anything you might want," Stewart answered. He leaned back slightly and used his right hand to brush a flake from his pin-striped suit. Very cool. Self-satisfied, thought Sullivan as he loosened his tie. Stewart glanced at him. For some reason Stewart's piercing blue eyes offended him. He made him think of private schools, of rich kids in blue blazers and gray flannels, of trust funds.

Finished with his mixings, Quinn Stewart turned around, a glass in each hand. He smiled, a condescending twist to his lips that hinted Sullivan was clearly out of his element, but he'd bear him temporarily. "Here you go." He handed Sullivan his drink after placing Evelyn's before her on the desk, where she studied papers, occasionally scribbling her signature. Sitting, he crossed his legs and began rubbing the glass in little circles on his knees. "So you were with the FBI?"

Sullivan had the feeling Quinn Stewart had already worked out precisely what he was going to say. "For a lot of years, five of them right here as special agent in charge of the Dallas office, then they had some trouble in the San Diego office, and I was transferred there. Dallas has certainly changed." Sullivan thought his last statement sounded like a bore's comment.

Stewart fondled a Phi Beta Kappa key, which was attached to his belt loop. "All FBI men are lawyers or accountants, aren't they?"

"In the old days." Sullivan took a swallow of his drink.

"Which were you?"

"Lawyer."

Stewart raised one eyebrow slightly. "Where'd you go to law school?"

Stewart's accent was not entirely Texan but some hijacked mixture. Sullivan pegged him for a local boy who had gone to Harvard and come home to hit the jackpot. Now that Andrew Casey was out of the picture, the pot had sweetened.

"San Diego State." He kept searching for something of interest to say, something that Quinn Stewart would remember. He couldn't think of a thing and furthermore didn't know why he would want him to remember him at all.

Evelyn looked up from her paperwork. "Everything seems in order, Quinn." She got up, rounded the desk and came to sit on the couch.

Sullivan didn't like what he saw in Stewart's eyes for Evelyn. He decided the reason he'd disliked Stewart on sight was jealousy. Irrational emotion, but jealous all the same.

Evelyn moved her glass around, tinkling the ice cubes. "Quinn, guess what? I've learned to shoot a pistol, a thirty-eight. I brought it with me in case I have some time to practice. Couldn't pass security with it in my purse, of course, but I packed it in my luggage."

"She's a natural shot," Sullivan added, proud of his pupil.

"A pistol? Why on earth are you learning to shoot a pistol? A rifle or a shotgun for hunting trips I can see, but a pistol?"

Evelyn squared her shoulders and lifted her chin slightly. "Protection. We're into a situation that could be tricky . . ."

"I want to hear exactly what's going on with all this business. Sara's case was officially closed by the police. You're keeping it active for some reason. I'd like to know why?" Quinn Stewart eyed Sullivan. His expression suggested that he thought Sullivan might be the type to hang around school playgrounds.

Evelyn launched into their theories and plan to go to Huntsville Prison. She spoke of her friendship with Carole Wheeler and the article that might flush out the killer. Hearing it all in that form, not experiencing the step-by-step investigation that had led to their conclusions, did bring to Sullivan's mind Don Quixote, a man tilting at windmills. Who in their right mind could think a man dead for ten years could be a murder suspect? But he wasn't about to vent his own doubts in front of this man and put Evelyn even more on the defensive.

Stewart steadied his eyes on Evelyn. "This is madness, in my opinion. You've been in a state of depression over Sara and not thinking clearly. What's all this costing?"

Sullivan looked hard at Quinn Stewart. The man thought he was a cheap con artist, prolonging the investigation for monetary reasons, his tentacles firmly wrapped around Evelyn. Though he had no intention of taking her up on it, Sullivan could imagine Stewart's reaction to Evelyn's offer to back him and a Mexican cop in a detective agency.

"I can afford it, Quinn. What is money except what it can do for you? I want to get to the bottom of all this. If nothing else, it will bring me peace of mind. That's what I want."

Sullivan liked her for saying that, liked her more than he wanted to admit, and now he wanted to examine that liking growing in him at such a rapid rate, because he was feeling something he hadn't felt in years. He lit a cigarette and blew a smoke ring, savoring the moment.

Making leaving moves, Quinn Stewart stood and checked his watch, his mouth parenthesized by two crescent-shaped lines. "Evelyn, we'll get together alone and discuss some things as soon as you get back from Huntsville." He pronounced the word as if it were something dirty. "Our closing on that property is most important." Reluctantly, he turned to

Sullivan. "Can I drop you off somewhere . . . a hotel? Where are you staying?"

"Here," Evelyn said. "We're all uneasy. I feel better not being alone. The reporter, Carole Wheeler, is staying with friends, too. As I said, we have the feeling this killer knows about the three of us."

Stewart's eyes lost their sheen. They were studs in his face. "I don't like this one bit."

"We'll do the best we can," Sullivan added.

Sullivan mixed another drink while Evelyn saw Stewart to the door. When she returned, she walked to the bar, refilled her glass and sat on the ottoman next to his chair. "I should call Carole and tell her how much we liked the article." She frowned as thoughts of the killer crept back.

"I'll have to call the warden at Huntsville and make an appointment." Sullivan rolled his eyes toward the ceiling. "You're a reporter from California, in collaboration with me, an ex-FBI agent. We're writing a book on Charlie Christmas. I think it sails."

"I want to tell you how much I appreciate everything . . ." She touched his hand. It was like being slapped with an electrode.

Suddenly Sullivan thought the air was charged with electricity. They each became uncomfortably conscious of the other's presence. He thought Evelyn could hardly be aware of the emotions she aroused in him, but perhaps he had telegraphed his feelings.

"Evelyn . . ." he hesitated. He thought he might be drunk, but he'd had only three drinks. He set down his glass. The noise seemed exceptionally loud. "You're so . . . so damn beautiful." He looked down at his huge hands, not graceful or manicured like those of Quinn Stewart's. "You need someone who really cares about you. You'll find him or he'll find you." He burned to ask her about her feelings for Quinn Stewart but decided against it. He was certain society had decreed them the perfect couple.

From the ottoman, Evelyn leaned closer to his chair. He could smell her perfume. He reached out and drew her near.

Even as he was holding her, he was shocked, embarrassed to the core by the depth of his feelings. Not since Karin had he experienced such sensations toward a woman. Torn by conflicting loyalties, his heart seemed as though it were being squeezed by some invisible hand. He released his grip. Could I start something here? he asked himself. Do I want to start anything? he continued to question.

He looked at the floor. "I'm sorry. I must have had too much to drink. I've been slacking off, and I guess it all hit me tonight. Travel and all." He winced as he imagined her surprise if he had blurted out some sort of statement of his feeling for her, something that meant he wanted to push their relationship into deeper realms. Widowed only two years, her mind was still undoubtedly filled with memories of Andrew Casey. And here he sat in that man's home making moves on her.

Evelyn reached for his hand. "My fault. Being back home . . ." Her eyes watered. "Oh, I don't know. My emotions have been mixed up lately."

The phone jolted them both. Evelyn stood, walked to the desk and picked up the receiver. Carole Wheeler's excited voice rushed at her.

"Christ! I had a tug of war with my editor. He finally caved in when I said I'd deliver what I promised or resign. When the article was in print, he really liked it. Hope you did. It ought to break something loose. I told him I couldn't divulge everything I know just now, but I hinted at something *big* to come. Hope it won't mean obituaries for the three of us. You keep me informed on what you find out at Huntsville. I'm plenty nervous now that the paper has hit the street."

Evelyn looked at Sullivan. "We thought your story was great. We read it on the plane. You used a fake byline."

"Yeah, but I got a feeling our boy will know where it came from. I started to use the initials C.C., but I knew Sullivan would kill me. He told me not to mention that one. Anyway, I'm staying with two photographers from the paper. Both of them look like refugees from the San Diego Chargers' line. You be careful, too. Tell old Hawkeye to watch out."

Evelyn replaced the receiver and told Sullivan about the conversation.

He lit a cigarette, then ground it out. "I wish we had more to go on besides this Charlie Christmas tangent."

Evelyn looked at him. "It could be the right line to follow."

Sullivan sighed. He expected the visit to Huntsville would lay Charlie Christmas to rest a second time. In the meantime, maybe the newspaper article would pop something loose in San Diego. "I'm bushed. Think I'll pack it in for the night. Which room?"

"Upstairs. First one on your right."

He touched Evelyn's shoulder as he walked out. He went to his room and felt relieved to be alone. He wanted to unpack and get a good night's sleep, if possible. He never rested well in strange beds.

He stripped, showered, lay across the bed, trying to put everything out of his mind. He heard a soft knock at his door and thought he might have been dreaming.

"Yes?" he called out.

The door opened and Evelyn stood on the threshold. Through the dim light he could just make out the trim lines of her body under a pale blue gown. Without a word, she walked slowly toward his bed and sat on the edge.

He pulled her gently to him and buried his head in her neck. Arms tight around him, she responded and slipped in beside him.

Gliding his hands over her, he kissed her. He ran his fingers through her hair, feeling the silky texture. There were so many things he wanted to do, but he tried to restrain himself. It had been so long that he thought he might lose control, old forgotten pleasures so overwhelming. He could hardly enjoy how good it felt for worrying when it might stop.

Hammering through his brain was the idea that he was a surrogate for Andrew Casey. A man of his stature cast a giant shadow. Finally, he was able to lay the thought aside. Theirs was an urgent kind of lovemaking as only two people long deprived could know. He felt a quick jab of pain, a final twitch from that ancient wound and recognized the past for what it was. The past, a break that would splint well and leave no trace of a limp.

They lay there too spent to move, stuck with perspiration

of enjoyment, in a cocoon of their own. He was sure his face had contorted into an ecstasy so great that his features were in danger of shattering and falling into a million grinning pieces. As the thundering pleasure spread through him, he wanted to shout, "Hey! Look at me, I'm beginning to feel again."

He turned on his side, brushed a strand of hair from her face and looked at her. Her body was firm, yet feminine, skin soft and unblemished. He wondered how he made her feel and wished she'd speak without his asking.

As if on cue, she said, "Hawk . . . thank you." She reached out and touched his chest, letting her hand linger. "I've never been loved like that . . . intense and gentle at the same time. I suspected, but I never knew it existed." Sometimes in the despair of rejection, during those years of neglect, Evelyn wondered what sort of sex life she might have had if she'd been initiated in the car that night by Dave Thomas instead of by the genteel, lukewarm Andrew.

Sullivan reached to the bedside table for a cigarette, found a match and lit it. "What about Andrew Casey? I thought . . ."

Evelyn propped a pillow behind her. Sullivan's body was muscled and lean, a scar tracing his kneecap and a small one marred his shoulder. "We had a good life, Andrew and I, but not completely fulfilling, not what it could have been." Leaning back, she thought over their relationship. How many times was she hurt by rebuffs Andrew hadn't known he'd made? How many times had she put up a good front? She had married a man whose real kick in life came from making money, conducting business, spending money, showing off an elegant wife and home. Sex was a small side order for Andrew Casey, not a main course. She summoned the social vitality her husband's pyramiding activities required, but she became bored in the process. Along paths bordered by understanding, by total fidelity out of respect for each other, they began to go their separate ways. Andrew launched into business conquests, while her path led through the academic corridors, filling her time with subjects that had interested her from childhood.

As she put her thoughts into words, the revelation hit Sullivan that for all her wealth Evelyn had been a pauper personally. "Don't go on. I get the message. If only you had known some of the thoughts I had about measuring up to Andrew Casey.''

She laid her head on Sullivan's chest, blond hair fanning across his skin. "I had some thoughts, too. About your wife. I know you loved her, but that was a different segment of your life. She's gone and you have to enter a new stage. She'd want you to. I want you to.''

Sullivan stubbed out his cigarette and put both arms around Evelyn. "You're right, of course. I think I just entered that new stage, thanks to you.'' He felt her body close to his, thighs touching, a joining of unspoken thoughts, and beneath it all, a compelling sexual magnetism. He was starting to feel like the luckiest man in the world.

When the day dawned, it was bright and clear, without a cloud in the sky. It promised to be one of those dry, Texas summer days, mercury pushing the hundred mark. Sullivan released the drapes as he smelled freshly brewed coffee. He smiled to himself. Evelyn was up, assaulting the kitchen. He wasn't sure the emotion he felt for her was love; it was too soon to tell, but something definite was there, a familiarity, an understanding, a bond. The chemistry worked. And sex? Hell, it was great. He was young and strong and ready to tackle any problem.

He dressed with care and staring into the mirror, wondered where the tough-minded, no-nonsense fellow had gone. He shrugged, thinking every coin should have two sides.

He hurried down the stairs and walked into the kitchen. Evelyn turned from the counter, her smile betraying a trace of shyness. He kissed her on her forehead and ran his hands down her her neck and shoulders. A boundary had been crossed, and things between them would never be the same again.

They settled at the kitchen table and over coffee discussed their plans. As time for the trip to Huntsville drew near, the specter of Charlie Christmas returned to sabotage their newfound happiness.

The drive to Huntsville State Prison took just under three hours. For most of the ride, Evelyn sat with her hands folded tightly over her purse, those eyes fixed with fierce intensity straight ahead on the road. Her mind, Sullivan knew, was back on Charlie Christmas. Looking frequently in the rearview mirror, Sullivan had kept an eye out for anyone following. For a while a black car that Sullivan thought was a new model Ford, a rental-type, stayed behind them. On the pretense of stopping for a Coke and to use the restroom, Sullivan pulled into a service station as they neared the outskirts of Huntsville. The car zoomed past, the glare in the windshield obliterating any view of the driver. Feeling as uneasy as Evelyn after the phone call, Sullivan got back in the car, handed Evelyn a can of Tab and drove away.

Sullivan pulled into the Huntsville parking lot. Acres of cement covered what were once cotton fields. He switched off the engine, sat staring at the gray stone walls and thought about the mass of humanity contained there. The dregs of the earth, the scum, the vicious, the conniving, all living, breathing and scheming toward a common goal: to get out and get back at society. Virtually all who left would return one way or another to Huntsville to live out the remainder of their lives. In the distance Sullivan heard a bell ring, and then a whistle blew. Turning to Evelyn he said, "The inmates, like Pavlov's dog, are trained to live their lives by sounds."

He opened the door and started toward Evelyn's side, but she had already bounded from the car. Hair blowing in the dry, hot wind, she shielded her eyes from the glaring sun and squinted toward the awesome walls.

"It's a frightening place. I can't imagine being locked up in there." A dark shadow crossed her face. "To think Charlie Christmas was actually here . . ." Her voice trailed off.

Sullivan watched far above the horizon at the great flock of birds. They moved in unison, a giant black whip through the clear blue void. Unlike the humans below, they were free. Sullivan stared at the vast series of lone concrete buildings with narrow barred windows. The structures stretched over two miles, enclosed by forty-foot-high fences topped with barbed wire and multiple strands of electrical wires, punctuated at quarter-mile points by tall guard towers standing as warning sentinels.

Sullivan and Evelyn entered the administration building, pausing briefly while the guard on duty verified their appointment. Footsteps were loud against the silence of the cavernous hall as they were escorted to the warden's reception room. A black man, his back to them, busied himself at the file cabinet. His hair was so closely cropped his scalp looked like thousands of black dots. Evelyn stared at the numbers stenciled across his faded blue shirt, her face expressionless. As the convict turned, his eyes, flinty and warm as two black marbles, flashed recognition.

"Well, never thought I'd see you again." His voice was clipped, educated.

Sullivan stared at the strapping mocha-colored man, then offered him his hand. "Mike. Been a long time."

The convict ignored Sullivan's gesture. "Not Mike, now. It's Rashad."

Sullivan knew people who called men like him "Alabama Arabs." In his opinion everyone was entitled to their own beliefs. "I remember now. Read about you in the papers when the riots took place. Not the Mike I caught holding up small-town banks. Rashad Abdul Ali, a changed man, law degree by correspondence course, challenging the Board of Corrections for better facilities. You helped mediate with the prisoners."

Rashad looked around. "It helped me get this job as trusty in the warden's office. Made the Board of Corrections live up to their promises, too. I'm working on some prison reforms now. You still with the FBI?"

Sullivan shook his head. "Working on a book with this lady here. She's a reporter." He nodded toward Evelyn.

Rashad glanced at Evelyn, then addressed Sullivan. "What sort of book?"

"Ever know Charlie Christmas?"

Sullivan watched Rashad's expression change. For an instant he thought the man was going to shiver at some dark recollection. Evelyn moved in closer, her face intent on Rashad's. Before her stood a man who actually had known Charlie Christmas.

"What was he like?" she asked.

Rashad's thin lips drew away from perfect white teeth. "No words to describe him. The most vicious devil I ever saw, and believe me, I've seen some. So mean on the inside that it beamed right through to the outside. Smart and clever. Could fool anyone when he wanted to. Almost as if he could cast a spell over someone. He'd turn on the charm when it was to his own good. I knew he'd end up like he did. His kind don't live long here.''

Sullivan leaned against the file cabinet. "Tell us about Christmas's death.''

Rashad rolled his eyes until the whites showed. "I suppose he tricked somebody once too often and got himself cut to ribbons in the shower. Matter of fact, I helped carry his body or what was left of it out of the shower rooms and to the morgue.''

Sullivan's compelling stare forced Evelyn to meet his eyes. When his theories about a case hadn't worked, he experienced the same disappointment she felt, the weight of defeat, the anguish at being proven wrong, but those emotions would pass, replaced with positive ones. Enough vicious devils populated the world without Charlie Christmas's existence.

Rashad continued: "Everybody was gunning for Christmas to the point of the warden having to isolate him. They never found out who did it. Nobody much cared; even the warden didn't look too hard into the situation. I figured it could be any one of a thousand. Nobody liked Christmas except this one guard Charlie always sucked up to. The warden had to assign Christmas a special guard, see.'' With a thumb, Rashad pointed to his chest. "Myself, I always thought they might have something going on. Things like that happen in here. Charlie was a good-looker 'til somebody got hold of him. He had no face. All cut off and his fingers had been slashed and chopped to bloody stubs.''

Sullivan stood still, a sudden prickling sensation growing somewhere inside his chest. He hadn't known all the facts, only that Christmas had been hacked up in the showers. No face. No fingerprints. No identification. "And you're sure it was Charlie Christmas?'' Sullivan looked Rashad in the eye.

Rashad frowned, then seemed a little puzzled, as Sullivan's question sank in. "Why'd you ask that?''

"The body was all cut up you said.''

Rashad shook his head. "Never forget it. All the blood. Used to vomit everytime I thought about it. He was buried

out back in the prison cemetery where they put prisoners who
don't have folks to claim the body. I looked out the window
that day and saw the chaplain saying a few words over him.
Nobody else was there. Not a soul. I watched a detail throw
dirt over him, and I knew for sure one person who was in
hell.''

Sullivan lit a cigarette. Rashad's account of Christmas's
mutilation, no fingerprints, jolted him more than he wanted to
admit. Castro's sketch flashed in his mind. He was dumb-
founded. The impossible notion that Christmas might not be
dead was gaining some credence. The thought both enraged
and frightened him. If the serial killer they were after *was*
Charlie Christmas, they were up against formidable odds, to
say nothing of their personal risk.

''Mr. Sullivan?'' the warden called as he opened his office
and extended his hand. ''Please come in.''

With Evelyn at his heels, Sullivan entered the warden's
office. They settled in two hard-backed chairs before the
warden's desk. Evelyn's cheeks flushed with high color.

Sullivan knew Warden James Loftus's reputation. He was a
respected man, not only in the state of Texas but also nation-
wide. With degrees in criminology and penology he had
become renowned for innovation and the implementation of
new rehabilitation methods at Huntsville. His prison system
was considered a model, riots a rarity. He was a strict but fair
man. Prisoners were well-treated and given incentives to
better themselves through the educational system Warden
Loftus had established. Even the toughest of inmates admitted
to admiring the warden.

Loftus leaned back in his chair. ''To what do I owe this
pleasure, Mr. Sullivan?''

Sullivan introduced Evelyn by an alias. ''We are planning
a book on mass murderers. As I told you over the phone, I'm
no longer with the FBI. Decided to try my hand at writing.
Charlie Christmas, of course, will be included; and, since he
was an inmate here, we were hoping you could help us.''

The warden nodded, his bald crown shining under the
bright neons. ''What would you like for me to do? Tell you
about him?''

"That and let us look at his records, if possible," Sullivan answered.

"I can't think of anything wrong with that. Sure! I'll have Rashad make you a Xerox of them." He punched the intercom and gave instructions to Rashad.

The warden leaned back and arched his hands over his abundant stomach. "We have so many prisoners that it's impossible to become personally involved with them. However, I suppose because of Charlie's fame, if you could call it that, I do vividly remember the anticipation of his arrival. I was assistant warden then. I knew what would happen. Prisoners have their own codes. Those who murder women and children, rapists, child molesters are treated with the deepest contempt, which usually leads to violence. Murderers who have killed in the heat of passion, such as a husband who shoots his wife's lover, thieves, embezzlers, counterfeiters, and the like are our accepted members of prison society. Because Christmas's crime was so heinous, the warden tried to gear up for this by assigning a special guard to him and keeping Christmas isolated. He was a real loner anyway."

"Did he and the guard become friendly?" Sullivan asked, remembering what Rashad said.

"I'd have to say they were friends of sorts but nothing much in common. Charlie was brilliant, magnetic when he wanted to be. Sometimes he could almost make you forget his background when he was in one of his moods. Charlie confided in Henry Dobbs. They talked a lot since they were together constantly. Dobbs stuck by Charlie, especially at recreation period or shower times when prison fights are most likely to break out." Loftus sighed. "Of course in the end, the plan failed. You can't cover all contingencies all of the time. Dobbs felt badly about it."

Sullivan lit a cigarette and exhaled a large plume of smoke. "Maybe we should talk to this Henry Dobbs." Evelyn nodded in agreement.

The warden's eyebrows raised slightly. "Afraid that's impossible. Henry Dobbs is dead. Happened a few days after Charlie's death. Coming out of a roadhouse late one night he was attacked. The police figured the perpetrator was lying in wait in the backseat of Dobbs's car. Never caught him.

Unsolved case on the books. Happens a lot at the joints we have on the edge of town. Robbery is always involved, as it was with Dobbs.''

Sullivan moved to the edge of the chair. "How was Dobbs killed?''

"Stabbed,'' the warden answered evenly.

If someone wanted to make a motive for a murder look like robbery, it was easy to stage. Christmas was smart enough to figure that out. Sullivan looked at Evelyn, terrified of what lay ahead. It would be a long time before he could draw an easy breath. All points were converging on the reality that Charlie Christmas was alive. If he was, and knew about them as Carole Wheeler suspected, no way could he allow any of the three to live.

Evelyn and Sullivan stood and thanked the warden for his help.

In the outer office, Sullivan glanced toward Evelyn, then leaned close to Rashad. "What if Christmas is not dead?''

Rashad blinked, then narrowed his eyes. "What are you getting at?''

Sullivan shrugged and laid his hand on Evelyn's arm. "Here's a quote from Thomas Hardy. 'Though a good deal is too strange to be believed, nothing is too strange to have happened.' '' He turned to Rashad. "Would you be willing to help me if I need to prove Christmas is still alive?'' Evelyn's attention was riveted on Sullivan.

Rashad's eyes flashed, recalling old grievances. "You're sniffing up the wrong trail. Christmas is dead. Anyway, why should I help you?''

Sullivan smiled and slapped Rashad on the back. "Let's put it this way. You were on the street, going nowhere but down. I helped put you here, and look what happened. A reformed man . . . law degree. That bastard Christmas is inhuman. Not fit for outside or inside society. You know what he did to those women. If he didn't die here, he's out there somewhere, maybe doing the same thing again, only he's been too clever to get caught. You believe in prison justice, don't you? Maybe Charlie stuck it to everyone by escaping. Wouldn't you like to have that mother pay his dues like you and every other inmate had to?''

Rashad's lips hooked into a small grin. "Try me."

Sullivan fixed his eyes on Rashad and stared for a long minute. "If Christmas isn't in that grave, who is?"

CHAPTER 14

THE FILES WERE THICK and unwieldly, scattered about the cheap motel suite Sullivan and Evelyn had rented. Sullivan rubbed his tired eyes and yawned. He had started in chronological order with Charlie's first admittance papers, the prison psychiatrist's profiles, the state's counselor's progress reports, work and behavior records. He picked up the final folder, which contained, complete with pictures, the full account of Charlie Christmas's death. Sullivan held the death certificate in his hand, then laid it aside and began to read the last words ever written about Charlie Christmas. Massaging her temples, Evelyn pored over the volumes already finished and discarded by Sullivan.

Finally, Sullivan slapped the file closed, stood, and stretched. "Let's order something to drink and eat from room service. I'm starving. And I could use a drink."

Evelyn leaned back and rested her head against the vinyl-upholstered chair. "Have you found anything in the reports that really jumps out at you?"

Sullivan lit a cigarette and inhaled deeply. Such a pleasure from such a small thing, he thought idly. "Nothing that I didn't suspect after talking to the warden. Look at the menu and see what you want. I'll call down.''

Sullivan ordered a bottle of Jack Daniels, a bottle of vodka, ice and two club sandwiches. He looked around the plastic room as he replaced the receiver. Lamps were attached to tables, imitation paintings nailed to the walls. He wondered who would steal such trash. "Best Huntsville has to offer. Christ! What a sleazy place. Reminds me of the dumps I stayed in when I was on stakeouts. It's only seventy-two miles to Houston. We could have gone there for the night, but you brighten up any place." Quinn Stewart, he was sure, would never provide such accommodations.

Evelyn's smile showed her appreciation of his concern, but Sullivan noticed how tired she looked. "Thanks, but don't worry about me. It's clean. We're only here for a night. I could hug a bear that long."

Sullivan cracked a smile. "I'll just bet you could and tame him in the interim."

Evelyn picked up the picture of Charlie Christmas. "When the warden said Henry Dobbs had been stabbed, you admitted to yourself for the first time the possibility that Charlie Christmas is still alive."

"Nope." Hawk interrupted. "It was earlier."

"Henry Dobbs helped Christmas get out, and then he killed Dobbs. Look at this picture here of Charlie all slashed up and unrecognizable. The prison shirt has his number on it all right, but that's not Charlie in it." She looked up at Sullivan. "Who could it be?"

Sullivan wanted to reach out and plant a kiss on her cheek. "You're one hell of a detective."

"Don't forget it. Come on now, back to work. What does the report state, I mean the basics?"

Although he knew it by heart, Sullivan picked up the report as if he needed a reminder. " 'On March 25th, 1976, at 10:30 A.M., after recreation period, Charlie Christmas, prisoner number 2640, entered the shower area by the east door of building nine at Huntsville State Prison. After a period of approximately ten minutes, Henry Dobbs, employed by the state of Texas as a guard, thinking he heard a slight commotion, entered the shower rooms, where he stumbled on a slashed body identified as that of Charlie Christmas. Dobbs stated he saw no one other than Christmas enter the shower rooms. Assumption: the assailant lay in wait and exited by the west door. A note stuffed in Christmas's pocket read: "Now he won't get his hands on anyone else." ' " Sullivan threw the file aside and paced back and forth.

"The rest deals with the medical report. That note is what intrigues me." He stopped and faced Evelyn.

"Why is that?" Evelyn asked, locking eyes with him.

Thinking, Sullivan started to pace again. "Because, maybe, just maybe, it is an explanation to why Charlie's fingers were cut to ribbons, but actually the note could be a clever cover-up. No fingerprints. Positive identification erased. Christmas was shrewd, ready for any skeptics, so he covered himself. If that note had not been written, the slashed fingers would have pointed out that someone was trying to erase all identification and that might have led to further investigation. Charlie's face was cut beyond recognition, and he never had any dental work, therefore no dental record." Sullivan stopped and grabbed a package of cigarettes from the end table, examined a match folder advertising the motel, struck one, then lit his cigarette. "Yep, I believe Charlie Christmas is alive. He figured it all out. Now, I've got to be a little smarter and figure out a few things. Why did Henry Dobbs help him? Dobbs and Christmas were in constant contact. We know how persuasive Christmas was. The promise of money? How did they pull it off exactly? And . . . who is in that grave? Whoever it is has gone unaccounted for? How?" He took a long drag.

"Henry Dobbs has a widow. Are you going to call her? She might know something?"

Sullivan raked his hand across his face as if to wipe away the tension "She might. Jesus! I wish they'd come on with the drinks." The threat of Charlie Christmas on the loose bothered him more than he wanted to admit.

At the sound of the knock, Sullivan jumped. Evelyn walked across the room and admitted the room service waiter. "Just in time." She smiled. "The lion was about to escape."

The waiter looked puzzled.

Evelyn glanced over the cart. "Just leave the covers on the sandwiches. I'll serve them later."

Sullivan signed the check and stuffed some bills into the waiter's hand.

He limited his drinks to two, then devoured the club sandwich, while Evelyn only picked at hers. Usually she had an appetite that matched his. He thought the food fairly good considering the circumstances. To ruin a club sandwich took some effort.

He dabbed at the corner of his mouth with a napkin that had a hole in it, opened the phone book, and ran his finger down the D's. "In a town of twelve thousand people or so, there shouldn't be many Dobbs. She could have remarried. Been ten years." He stopped and tapped the book. "No, by God! Here it is. Mrs. H. Dobbs. That has to be it." He reached over and picked up the last wedge of Evelyn's sandwich.

Evelyn pursed her lips. "Well, are you going to call or just eat?"

"No, as a matter of fact, I'm not going to call," he answered between chews. "She might not see us. What's she got to gain? We'll drive to her house and pop in unannounced. Can't be far. We'll get directions downstairs."

Evelyn rotated her shoulders, moving her head to the side. "Mind if I stay here and take a long, hot bath? I have the makings of a headache. Been a long day at Huntsville and all." She poured herself another drink.

Sullivan looked at her, his eyes absorbing every part of her face and body. He didn't like leaving her. It had been an emotionally charged twenty-four hours: the night before in bed with him and then seeing Huntsville. He wondered about tonight.

"Sure, you rest, and I'll be back as soon as I can."

Evelyn touched his shoulder. She looked toward her bedroom. "Hurry back. I'm sure the bath will fix everything."

A smile crept across Sullivan's lips. He didn't have to wonder anymore. The suite, if it could be called that, had two bedrooms. He knew only one would be occupied. "I'll hurry." Just thinking about the night ahead filled him with intense desire. He turned to leave while he still could.

The business section of town stretched five blocks. Sullivan drove slowly down the main street. At seven o'clock, the stores were dark, the proprietors home for their evening meal and television, he guessed. He wondered if anyone in that quiet town held as high an anticipation of the night as he.

Huntsville looked like a place where nothing much ever happened, still the people lived in the shadow of that ominous institution dominating their community. Huntsville's walls were supposedly impregnable, a prison break a rarity. If one did occur, Huntsville was the last spot an escapee would want to linger.

As instructed, Sullivan turned right off First Street onto Elm and drove three blocks. Original with their street names, he thought. In front of a modest, white frame house, he slowed and squinted in the fading light to read the numbers.

He walked up the cracked sidewalk leading to the front porch. Suspended from the ceiling, a swing moved in the early evening breeze. The small-town and old-fashioned setting brought back boyhood memories, a time when summers were endless—his biggest problem: in which pond to fish.

He knocked on the screen door and called out, "Mrs. Dobbs?"

He leaned forward, peering through the screen door at the approaching figure. Thin and angular, Mrs. Dobbs wore a loose-fitting, flowered outfit Southern ladies called "house-dresses." Seeing his outline framed in the door, she stopped momentarily, then proceeded with caution.

Standing several feet way, as if in imagined safety, Mrs. Dobbs flicked on the porch light and craned her neck forward.

"Yes? What is it?"

Sullivan tried to smile reassuringly, "Mrs. Dobbs, wonder if I could talk to you. My name is Hawkins Sullivan. I'm writing a book about a man who was once at Huntsville . . . came down here to do some research. I understand your husband knew him."

Her eyes narrowed as she inspected Sullivan. "What man?"

"Charlie Christmas."

"Oh, that one. Yeah, Henry knew him all right. A book you say? You going to put Henry in it?" Her twang was sharp.

Sullivan shrugged. "Possibly. I have to know more about him. Things he told you about Christmas, how important he was in Charlie's life at Huntsville. You know, those kind of things.''

Mrs. Dobbs unlatched the screen. "Henry would have liked that. Come on in. I'll try to recollect what I can. Been a long time, you know."

Sullivan surveyed the room. Obviously Mrs. Dobbs was a homemaker, doing the best she could with what she had. Crocheted squares rested on the arms and backs of chairs. A knitted afghan draped across the couch camouflaged the faded fabric. On the walls hand-stitched pictures hung in neat rows. Sullivan focused on her. She was plain but not unattractive, skin tanned and wrinkled from the sun.

"I've just made some fresh coffee. Let me get us a cup."

"Fine," Sullivan said and settled on the couch. "Just black." He looked around. Evelyn had grown up in a small Texas town. He wondered if it had been in a similar home. It was hard to picture her in such a setting.

Mrs. Dobbs served the coffee in white mugs and sat on the overstuffed chair next to the couch. "Poor Henry, I guess you know about how he died. It was real terrible. Bad enough to die, but that way."

Sullivan sipped his coffee. "The warden told me. Shame they never caught him."

"Probably he was a drifter. Have lots passing through here. They work the fields, then pass on to some other crops that need harvesting when they finish here. Guess who done it thought Henry had money. Course, Henry didn't have much." She looked down and twisted the gold wedding band. "Guards don't make much, but Henry never gave up. Always full of ideas. Said his job was only temporary. Something would turn up. He worked there ten long, hard years. All I've got to show for it is his pension. It's real small. Can't hardly get by."

Sullivan imagined that Mrs. Dobbs was once a bright-eyed, simple, country girl, a woman deprived of education and doomed to a small-town life, ambitions dashed by Henry Dobbs.

"What did your husband tell you about Christmas? Did he mention him much?"

Mrs. Dobbs twisted her mouth, showing a fan of wrinkles

over her upper lip. "He sort of liked him. Maybe fascinated by him is a better way to put it. I thought Henry must be crazy . . . a man like that. I think that maniac halfway convinced Henry he was innocent. Henry kept on saying Charlie told him he was framed. They all say that, you know, them people out to the prison. 'Beefers,' that's what they's called. Henry said Charlie wasn't like the rest, though. He kind of got obsessed with him. Talked about him all the time, about how smart he was. I said if he was so smart, how come he was in Huntsville? Finally, I wouldn't listen no more being as what that man done . . . killing all those pregnant women." She nodded. "He done it all right. I told Henry I never wanted to hear his name again."

While Mrs. Dobbs answered his questions with simple rural candor, Sullivan lapsed deeper into a Texas drawl. Soon they were like two old southern neighbors exchanging stories.

"Anything more you can tell me about Henry's death? Anything he talked about in particular? His mood? How was he behaving the week after Charlie's death, just before his own?"

Mrs. Dobbs rolled her eyes toward the ceiling. "About two weeks before he was stabbed, Henry was really in a good mood, like when he thought he had one of his get-rich schemes going. He started buying things, a television, clothes, putting them on layaway. If it hadn't been for the insurance money, I'd a lost this house trying to pay off those bills. Anyway, Henry said he finally had it all figured out. Going to come into a lot of money. I didn't even ask about it, because he wouldn't have told me anyway. He used to, but after I'd tell him how idiotic some of his ideas was, he'd get real mad at me. Finally, he quit telling me about them, but I knew his mind was working on them all the same. This last time, right before he died, he'd just smile and say I'd see."

Sullivan sat quietly, hiding his excitement. Finally, he broke the silence. "Your husband was killed a week after Charlie's death. What did he say about Charlie getting killed?"

"He just came home and announced that Charlie had been stabbed to death at the prison. Never said nothing more about it. Didn't act like he cared, which I thought was funny, because he did like him. Me, I said it was good riddance. A person like that got no business living.''

"Mrs. Dobbs, I appreciate your help." Sullivan got up.

She touched his sleeve. "Put Henry in the book so's he can make the big time after all."

Sullivan winked. "I'll put you in the book, too."

Her expression was worth the lie. Something to tell her friends about.

In the car, Hawk sat looking at Mrs. Dobbs's house before turning on the ignition. Alone in the darkness, he tried to sort out what he faced, the danger to himself and others that Christmas's existence presented. As long as Charlie Christmas was a threat, no normal relationship with Evelyn was possible. His mind had to be clear, pointed toward one goal, not muddled with personal emotions. He was getting in deep with Evelyn and maybe had to pull back or lose it all. He couldn't afford to lose it again or even come close to letting his feelings rule his detective instincts.

He was grateful to Evelyn for helping him return to life, but he wasn't sure what he felt was love. Could he love someone else so quickly? Was he being fair to her? With Quinn Stewart, who obviously loved her, she could have an extraordinary life without him. He and Evelyn had been together constantly. He needed to be alone to think about Charlie Christmas and what he was up against, putting his personal quandary aside.

Sullivan turned the key and started the engine. Pulling away, he decided to stop at a bar he'd seen in town. Alone for a time, he might reach some worthwhile, life-saving conclusions.

Back at the motel, Evelyn luxuriated in a hot tub, the tension in her body evaporating. At least knowing who her sister's murderer was gave her tremendous satisfaction. And she had found something she hadn't been looking for. She had found in Sullivan what she always wanted and hoped for in a man. Strange that Sara's death brought them together. She suspected that Sullivan wasn't ready to commit himself to anyone, but he had emerged from his shell. She'd let things take a natural course, not push.

She leaned forward, ran more hot water, then lounged with her head resting on the back of the tub. In the quiet, she thought she heard a noise and sprang to attention. Sitting motionless, she strained to make out the noise. It sounded as if someone had tested the doorknob to see if it was open. Her heart pumped faster as she glanced around. Again, she heard the noise. The pistol was in the living room in her purse.

Suddenly, a soft knock came again at the door. Her first thought that Hawk was back relieved her, but why would he knock? Remembering that she had bolted the door, she sprang from the tub, wrapped a towel around her and raced dripping to the door.

As she reached for the chain, a signal in her subconscious flashed a warning.

"Hawk?' she called out.

"No, ma'am, room service," a voice on the other side of the door drawled. "Need to pick up the cart."

"I'm not dressed. Can you come back later?" Water ran down her legs.

"Well . . . we're short of carts in the kitchen. We do need it. I'll be in deep trouble if I don't come back with it. I'm new here and don't want to get off on the wrong foot."

Evelyn glanced at the messy cart, the dirty dishes. A cigarette Sullivan had stubbed out stood like a crooked birthday candle on a bread crust. A place like that probably didn't have enough kitchen equipment.

"All right. Just let me grab a robe."

She hurried to her overnight bag and rummaged through the few things she'd brought. Slipping on a blue silk robe, her eyes settled and held on her purse. Captain Gordon's words flashed through her mind. "Fruit from the management. Room service. Open the door. He's in." She stood a moment feeling paranoid. There was the cart before her. The waiter on the other side of the door was more than likely the same one who'd brought their food. He simply wanted to take away the cart: normal procedure. Still, precautions never hurt. Slipping the revolver in her pocket, she tightened the belt at her waist and moved to the door.

As he rounded the stairwell, Sullivan missed a step and almost stumbled as he focused on a tall man in a white waiter's jacket waiting outside his room, his hand on the knob, the other pushed deep into his pocket. His posture suggested he was trying to enter the room rather than leave. The waiter lowered his head and looked to his right. He wasn't the waiter who had served their dinner. Sullivan thought he looked familiar.

"Hey! What are you doing?" Sullivan called out and hurried down the hall. The man casually turned his back and sauntered in the opposite direction, disappearing down the service ramp.

Evelyn unbolted the latch, opened the door and found herself facing Sullivan.

"It's you!"

"You were expecting someone else?"

"The room service waiter knocked. He wanted the cart." Evelyn peeked down the empty hall. "That's strange. He was so impatient for it." She and Sullivan looked at each other, his face registering concern.

Sullivan walked in and grabbed one end of the cart. "Here, help me roll it out, so he won't come back." He noticed the bulge in Evelyn's pocket. At least she was cautious.

They pushed the cart into the hall and stationed it next to the wall. Hesitating briefly, Sullivan looked up and down the hall, a sense of foreboding settling over him.

"What are you thinking?" Evelyn asked, her voice cracking.

Sullivan took her elbow and guided her to the door. "Let's get back inside."

Sullivan picked up the phone and dialed room service. He asked if they had sent a waiter for the cart. No, they had not, he was told. He replaced the receiver.

After a restless night, Sullivan pulled back the sitting room drapes and glanced absently at the gathering clouds. The weatherman's forecast of rain looked promising, farmers' prayers answered. He wished his would be.

While Evelyn dozed in the bedroom, he lit a cigarette. He and Evelyn had spent the night in separate rooms, fighting for what sleep they could get. He tried not to dwell on the certainty that Charlie Christmas, posing as a waiter, almost found his opportunity with Evelyn, but there it was.

Before going to bed, he explained what he'd learned from Mrs. Dobbs. Henry Dobbs was a scheming, get-rich-quick type; Christmas, a trained spellbinder. A combination of the two made for an explosive connection. Christmas, a computer executive, had money. How much, Sullivan wasn't sure, but as little as ten or twenty thousand to Henry Dobbs would be a fortune. The scheme was as clear in Sullivan's mind as it probably had been in Charlie's. And if it failed, what did a "lifer" like Christmas have to lose?

Sullivan speculated that Christmas had exchanged numbered shirts in the shower with one of the other inmates, stabbed him to death, whittled his face beyond recognition and slashed off his fingertips, leaving a victim the approximate weight and height of Charlie. Freed, Charlie had completed his plan by murdering the only human who knew he was alive.

Evelyn had raised some baffling questions of which Sullivan was already aware. Who was the inmate that Charlie killed, and how did he go unaccounted for in a maximum security prison? Sullivan thought he had the answers or knew how to get them.

He checked his watch. Stubbing out his cigarette, he dialed Huntsville Prison and asked the switchboard operator to connect him with the warden's office.

"Warden's," Rashad barked.

"Sullivan here. I need a favor."

"Obviously my range is limited, but let's hear."

"Tell me what's the procedure for releasing an inmate?"

"One of the guards takes him to the out station. The guard fingerprints him and matches it to his chart. The prisoner signs some release forms, which the attending guard turns in, and then he's issued the belongings he checked in with, a new suit compliments of the state, and three hundred dollars. The guard escorts him to the front gates, where we have bus service into town if nobody meets them. That's it. Really pretty simple. Coming in, the process is much more complicated. Seems backwards, doesn't it?"

Sullivan caught a touch of resentment for the system in Rashad's voice. Good, he thought. "Rashad, Christmas was supposedly murdered in Huntsville on March 25th, 1976 at approximately 10:30 in the morning . . .''

"That's no news flash," Rashad interjected.

Sullivan ignored him and continued. "I want you to look in the files and see if any prisoner was released that day. Can you do that? Crossfiles or something like that to connect the dates?"

"Easy. You still thinking Christmas got out someway, aren't you?"

"I know he did. I saw him last night.".

"No shit, man! You sure?"

"Sure. Also, if a prisoner was released that day, I want his background, physical description, and name of attending guard. Okay?"

"You think Christmas killed some inmate and went out of here that day in his place?" Rashad hesitated, obviously considering the gravity of what might be possible. "You got it. I can't make outgoing calls. This isn't a hotel. You call me back in one hour, and I'll have what you want."

Rashad looked around the office as if seeing it for the first time, weighing what he was about to do. He treasured his job in the warden's office. A plum, it was. More important was his upcoming parole. Still, fair was fair. Charlie Christmas didn't deserve a break while others served out their terms. If Christmas was alive, Rashad wanted him behind bars. Rashad smiled. Somebody would finish Christmas next time.

A prison guard sat reading a paper by the door covered with a heavy wire screen. Rashad picked up a small note pad and went through a glass door into a long, narrow fluorescent lit room. The walls were lined with steel files, by the door a section of three-by-five files drawers. He went to the small-drawer files first and, after fumbling briefly, took out a card.

Copying the information, he proceeded down the aisle. He stopped and pulled out one of the larger file drawers, then a manila folder. On the flap was the name James Conners, Number 3696039. Glancing over his shoulder, Rashad opened the folder and read the record. He replaced the file and sauntered back to his desk.

An hour later, he picked up the receiver on the first ring. "Warden's."

"Got what I asked for?"

Rashad lowered his voice as he read from his pad. "One prisoner, a James Conners, was released the very day Christmas was killed. His time of release was stamped at eleven o'clock, about an hour after the thing with Charlie. Conners was born September 20, 1940."

"Puts him around the age of Charlie."

"Conners was in for armed robbery. First offense. Had trouble in here, so he was not paroled. Served the full term. His address was listed as 210 Cedar Street, Hillsboro, Texas. Course that was ten years ago. If your theory is correct, he won't be there now."

"He won't be. Who was the attending guard when Conners was released? Henry Dobbs?"

"Exactly."

"Dobbs had a busy morning that day. He okayed Christmas's fingerprints as being a match to Conners. Tell me about Conners's physical description."

Rashad read the description. "Struck me funny when I looked at Conner's picture. I didn't know him here, but he and Charlie looked something alike."

"Rashad, thanks. You've been a big help. If you need anything when you get out, look me up."

Sullivan looked for the turnoff from the highway to Hillsboro, a small town not far from Dallas. The countryside was parched a tobacco brown. Rain had not fallen in months, the sun had baked the cotton crops to ruin. Weathermen had said earlier that help was on the way. Sullivan wondered where it was.

Evelyn glanced out the window, her purse resting between them. She reached into her collar, lifted out the few strands of hair lodged there and shook her head. "No question that was Charlie Christmas at the door last night. Carole was right. He knows who we are. He's going to try and stop us from exposing him." She picked up her purse, twisting the straps. "If you hadn't come back when you did . . ."

If he had come back even seconds sooner, he might have cornered Christmas. Sullivan silently cursed himself.

"Hawk, he's following us."

Sullivan returned her glance. "Maybe to a degree. Maybe he's so smart he predicts our next move without following every step of the way. Just turns up where he thinks we're going, with the exception of our trip to Huntsville. He had to follow us there. That stop had to puzzle him. First of all, he can't know that we actually are onto his real identity . . . have a physical description that led us to find out who he really is." His tone was all business.

Evelyn turned sideways in the seat, facing Sullivan. "He's enough of an egomaniac to think his plan was the supreme maneuver, beyond the capabilities of others to detect. But, as you said, the trip to Huntsville has to puzzle him." She twisted around and looked out the back window. "If he should follow us to Hillsboro . . . James Conners, the man whose identity he used, lived there. Christmas may or may not know that."

"I've been watching all the way." Detecting surveillance of others and covering your own was one of the first points drilled into FBI recruits. Still, now and then he had an irrational thought that Charlie Christmas possessed near supernatural powers. If Charlie Christmas had any idea they'd put his plan together, he'd show up in Hillsboro.

A sign ahead announced that Hillsboro had a population of 7,400. Sullivan wheeled from the main highway to the farm road leading to the town and stopped at the first restaurant. A neon sign winked. Trucks aligned the gravel parking lot. Sullivan took it as a good indication. They knew where to eat.

"I'm starved. Let's get a bite to eat."

Evelyn checked her watch. "It's not even lunchtime." She was aware of Sullivan's strange behavior, his attitude change, and wondered if all personal bets were off until Christmas was captured.

"My stomach doesn't know that." If Christmas was following, Sullivan wanted him to think they had stopped in Hillsboro only to eat.

Inside, they sat in a back booth. Country music wailed from a red and yellow jukebox. They ordered the house speciality: chicken-fried steak, mashed potatoes and gravy, beans and cornbread. Sullivan liked the smell of the restau-

rant; it was like an old-fashioned kitchen, a forgotten pleas-
antry in the brassy world of fast-food services. And who ever
saw a jukebox anymore? He wadded his napkin and threw it
on the table.

"I'm going to look at a phone book," he said, edging his
bulk around the booth.

In moments he returned, glanced around the restaurant,
then slid back beside Evelyn. "There was only one Conners
listed. A Dan, but no James. Dan Conners Service Station."

"They're bound to be related to each other," Evelyn said.
"Remember, I came from a small town. People with the
same last name are usually kin."

Sullivan looked at the fat waitress waddling toward them
bringing dishes of food. She obviously ate as much as she
served. "After lunch we'll get gas at the Conners station and
ask him about James Conners. If he can be accounted for, I'm
back to square one. I'll lay you a hundred to one he can't
be." He was pleased that the puzzle was falling into place but
terrified of the picture the pieces made. His main objective
now was to formulate some plan to trap Christmas. At every
attempt his mind went blank, bringing a pang to his chest.
He didn't know if he had what it took anymore.

Following directions from the restaurant's cashier, Sullivan
drove to the station owned by Dan Conners. The place, off
the main stream of traffic, had seen better days. Nonworking
rusty equipment littered the garage. A ruddy-faced man dressed
in stained overalls approached them, wiping his head with a
yellowed handkerchief. Sullivan guessed the man was about
sixty.

"Help you?" he drawled.

Sullivan leaned out of the window and smiled. "Fill it
up."

The man stuck the gas hose into the car's tank, then came
to wipe the windshield. Sullivan cracked the door open but
didn't get out.

"I'm looking for a James Conners. With your name being
the same, I thought you might be a relative."

The old man stopped smudging the windshield and looked
at Sullivan. "Might be. What you looking for him for?"

Sullivan took a deep breath. "He's got a little money coming to him from the state."

"Much?" The man remained expressionless.

"Not much, but I have to see that he gets it. We haven't been able to locate him."

Dan Conners showed two gold front teeth when he smiled. "Neither has anybody else. I'm his only relative. The rest is all dead. Do I get the money if you can't find him?"

"Possibly," Sullivan said to the man who had now moved around to the door. "What can you tell me about him?"

Dan Conners rubbed his hand across a scruffy scalp. "We called him Jimmy. He was a rotten apple since he was a little boy."

When he finished rambling, he wiped his mouth with the back of his hand, leaving a greasy trace across his face. "That's about it."

"And Jimmy Conners never returned here after being released form prison?" Sullivan asked. "Did you think it was strange that he didn't come back to his hometown?"

"I thought the reason was he didn't want to face the people here and moved on somewhere else. Jimmy had a girl here. Name's Mary Baxter. Maybe that's why he never came back. Just didn't want to marry her. She still works at the telephone company just down the road. Finally married when he didn't come back. Last name's Moore now."

Sullivan paid Conners for the gas. As he rolled up the window, Conners reminded him about the money.

"I'll see if you're eligible for it."

Keeping an eye out for anyone following, Sullivan drove away.

"If you hadn't gone into the FBI, you could have been a great con artist." Evelyn kept her eyes on him, but he never looked her way.

The telephone company supervisor told Sullivan and Evelyn that Mary Baxter Moore would be right out and asked them to have a seat. In moments, a tall, pretty girl came in and introduced herself.

Sullivan stood. "Maybe you could help me. I'm looking for James Conners. Jim, I believed he's called here."

The girl stiffened and bit her lower lip. "I have no idea where he is."

"I wonder if you could remember when you last heard from him? Was it after he was released from prison?"

The girl shook her head. "Before. We planned to get married as soon as he was released from Huntsville. I never heard from him. I called Huntsville, and they said he was released the day that he was supposed to. Only the week before he wrote me that he'd be here that very afternoon he was let out and we'd to go Dallas and get married. He never showed up. It wasn't like Jimmy. I figured something happened to him, but there were no accident reports." Her eyes filled with tears. "I waited for him so many years. I don't know why he never came back. He promised. I wore my wedding dress that day . . ." She turned and hurried through the door.

So there it was, Sullivan thought. Everything fit. He wished he could have told Mary Baxter the truth.

Two hours later, Sullivan drove through the gates at Evelyn's house. He had agonized all the way to Dallas over a plan to trap Christmas. Making its regular rounds, a private security patrol car cruised past, the driver waving to Evelyn. Sullivan stopped the car, and they dashed to the front door as the expected rain started to fall.

Evelyn turned to Sullivan. "Would you like a drink?"

Sullivan shrugged. "If you would. Fine."

Settling in the study with drinks, Sullivan watched the rain pelt the windows and run down the panes like worms of water. His mind was clouded. Charlie Christmas was on the move. But where? The phone jolted his concentration. He watched Evelyn go to the desk and answer.

She held out the receiver. "Long distance for you."

Sullivan heaved himself up and took the phone. "This is Hawk Sullivan." He frowned as he listened.

In answer to Evelyn's inquisitive look, he clasped his hand over the receiver and said, "It's Castro," then returned his attention to the conversation.

Pinching the bridge of his noise, he kept his eyes averted from Evelyn and let out a rush of air. "Christ! They haven't got a leg to stand on.'' He listened some more, then groaned. ''You know I'll come testify for you. I'll be there.''

He hung up and lumbered to the bar.

''What is it?''

Sullivan jammed fresh cubes in his glass, spilling several on the floor. He bent to scoop them up, straightened and turned to face Evelyn. The thought of having to leave her tore at him. He'd like to keep her in his sight at all times now that Christmas had surfaced in Texas, but Castro deserved his help, and he was obligated to testify. He'd have to take her to San Diego with him.

''Captain Gordon took Castro off the Sally Bricker case because he kept connecting it with your sister's and the rest of those up and down the coast.'' He picked up his drink and downed most of it in one gulp. ''He reported Gordon to the Department of Internal Affairs for a review, pointing to the link in the murders. In turn, Castro was cited for insubordination and suspended without pay pending an investigation by the Disciplinary Commission. Gordon's accused him of taking money on the side.''

Evelyn raised her eyebrows. ''From me?''

''Yep.'' Sullivan grabbed a pack of cigarettes, snatched one out and lit it. He noticed that his hand shook slightly and turned so that Evelyn couldn't see it.

Evelyn got up and went to stand beside him. She could almost feel him bristle. ''You have to go to San Diego right away?''

Sullivan exhaled and picked up his glass, draining the last drop. ''Yep. I'm the one to refute the charge. You hired me, not Castro, and I'll testify to that. I've got to leave tonight. First plane I can get out. He needs me there in the morning.'' He could almost feel the wrinkles on his face. ''I can't leave you here with Christmas so close.''

''I can't go. I have to be at the Cypress meeting. You know what Quinn said. The closing of that deal depends on my presence.''

Sullivan shook his head. ''You're not safe here.''

''I've got my responsibilities here. Besides, in San Diego you'll be testifying in a committee, and I'd be alone. Here,

I'll be with someone all the time. Quinn . . . business people. With the burglar alarm I have here and the security patrol . . ."

An idea struck Sullivan. "Most big companies have security people. What about Cypress Oil?"

Evelyn busied herself at the bar, not looking at him. The specter of Charlie Christmas had temporarily ruptured their relationship. And they each had their own obligations to perform. "They do. I could get some extra help. Besides, the chauffeur lives over the garage. I can get my housekeeper, Mary, to stay with me, too. I'd be safer here than anywhere. Christmas wouldn't make a move on this place. Not with all of that."

Sullivan sighed. "Guess you're right."

Evelyn whipped around. "And what about you? He wants you, too." Her voice was filled with alarm, her expression more worried than Sullivan had ever seen.

Sullivan wanted to reach out and take her in his arms. "I'll be watching out for myself. You do the same. Everything depends on it." Everything depended on his coming up with a plan to stop Christmas, too, he thought.

"Everything," Evelyn repeated.

CHAPTER 15

THE TWO DAYS that Sullivan had been gone seemed like two weeks to Evelyn. He had called once to give her a report, his voice tired and full of concern. The committee was rough on Castro, the sessions long, sometimes lasting past regular office hours. Sullivan had been thrashing through ways of trapping Christmas, but nothing significant had surfaced.

At the desk in her study, Evelyn picked up a pen to finish signing documents Quinn Stewart had sent over by courier. He was due at five to pick them up. Closing the deal with Cougar Energy had gone without a hitch, and she was glad to have it behind her.

Scribbling her signature, she barely glanced at the papers that usually captured her undivided attention. She doodled on a blank sheet. Noticing that her desk drawers needed straightening, she rummaged through the contents, trying to decide what to discard. She pushed up, went to the bar and poured herself a vodka over the rocks. Slicing a lemon wedge, she squeezed it in her glass, sauntered over to the couch, and sank down.

It seemed that she'd spent the majority of her life looking forward to some future point in time, ticking off the present.

With Sullivan, she relished the existing moment, future be damned. Now she'd reverted to her old habits, anticipating when she'd again be with Sullivan.

When the door bell rang, she let her housekeeper answer. She listened to Quinn's chatter with Mary as his footsteps echoed down the marble hall. She wished it were Sullivan coming and realized how much he had changed her. Once, she would have been excited at seeing Quinn. She wore a beige warm-up suit and matching walking shoes. Once, she would have dressed for Quinn.

She rose to greet Quinn as he entered the room and walked over. Pecking her on the cheek like a husband home from the office, his hand lingered too long on her shoulder. He glanced at the desk, then looked back, keeping his eyes on her.

"I was pleased at how smoothly the closing went. Finished with the stack?" He smoothed back the parted side of his hair with the heel of his hand, then gently squeezed the soft silk knot of his tie. Those were all premeditated actions, Evelyn knew, to set apart the business from the personal.

Evelyn nodded, shifting her eyes from his intense gaze. "Would you like a drink?"

"I'll mix." Quinn walked to the bar, a spring in his gait. He was handsome in his usual attire, a dark pin-striped suit, Guicci shoes shined to a mirror finish. He looked equally as good in casual clothes, vibrant and young just off the golf course. She pictured him, comfortable in a tuxedo, gliding easily across the club dance floor. She couldn't imagine Sullivan in black tie. More than likely he didn't like to dance.

"I've been waiting to talk to you alone." He turned, facing her, eyes sparkling with enthusiasm. "Why don't we have dinner tonight? You could change, and we'd go to the club, celebrate the closing." He smiled the sort of smile that asked for one in return.

Evelyn moved to her place on the couch, Quinn settling in a lounge chair next to her. Suddenly she felt uncomfortable, as if she were doing something wrong. "Not tonight, Quinn. I planned to stay in." She wanted to be near the phone in case Sullivan called.

Quinn cleared his throat and took a sip of Scotch. "Evelyn . . . about this Sullivan. I can understand that you want

Sara's killer caught, but it bothers me that Sullivan might have put you in jeopardy. That, I don't like one bit." He leaned forward, hand clasped around the glass, manicured nails shiny. "Has it crossed your mind that this person could be an opportunist . . . even a con artist? What kind of future could he have without you?"

Or me without him, Evelyn thought as she felt herself stiffen. Someone who'd only met Sullivan once couldn't know the real man or have the license to degrade him. In charge of her affairs and Cypress Oil, Quinn Stewart would be an integral part of her life forever, and she wanted to set him straight without antagonizing him. "Quinn, I've gotten to know Sullivan well. He's as fine as they come. I think I'm a pretty good judge of character."

Quinn moved his glass, tinkling the ice cubes impatiently, a habit Evelyn never liked but overlooked. Now she found it irritating.

Setting the glass on the coffee table, Quinn reached out and took her arm, his grip firm. "I want to talk about the future . . ."

Evelyn got up for another drink, forcing Quinn to release his hold on her. "Quinn, I've been through too much recently. It's not over yet." She kept her back to him while she mixed. She didn't want the discussion continued.

"I've got a feeling this Sullivan has more to do with your feelings than anything that's happened to you lately. Am I right?"

Finished with mixing, she had to face him. Turning around she saw disappointment, even hurt in his eyes and was sorry. "I need time to sort things out. That's all." Her smile was intended as a suture to close his wound.

Quinn blinked his eyes, then looked at her for a long moment, as if he had something to say but couldn't find the words. He got to his feet and moved close to her. Taking her chin in his hand, he searched her face as if examining something he wanted most in life.

"You're right. Time will take care of everything, Evelyn." His face took on the set, stubborn look that she knew so well: he wore it when he had made a decision and someone tried to deflect him from his path. He kissed her gently.

After he had gone, Evelyn felt unsettled, emotions bobbing

like a boat cut loose from its mooring. She placed a call to Sullivan, but there was no answer. She had finished her obligations to Cypress Oil. Now, nothing was holding her in Dallas. Tossing around the idea of flying to San Diego to join Sullivan, Evelyn went to the bar and mixed another drink. Glass in hand, she paced back and forth, trying to reach a decision. Would Sullivan be pleased to see her or irritated that she had taken such initiative? She wanted only to be with him and lend support. He had wanted her to go in the first place. So, why not go now? She could fly out in the Cypress Oil jet.

Thinking of precautions as Sullivan had warned her to do, she decided that her chauffeur and the Cypress security man could drop her at the airport, and upon arrival in San Diego she would find Carole Wheeler and the two photographers she was saying with, if Sullivan wasn't home. She would never be alone.

She called Cypress operations and found out that their jet had flown to Houston to pick up two of their vice-presidents after a dinner meeting and would return in approximately four hours. She would go commercial.

After alerting the chauffeur and the security man, and calling the airlines, she hurried to her room to pack. Checking the chamber of her .38 to make sure it was loaded, she stuffed it in her large suitcase and closed the lid. She dialed Carole and, getting no answer, left a message on the answering machine. By the time she arrived, Carole would be home. She rarely went out after dark anymore.

On the way to the airport, the chauffeur slowed and glanced in the rearview mirror. Nervous, the security man looked around. "A car pulled away from a house down the street after we drove out of your driveway. It's still behind us. I don't like it."

Evelyn turned in her seat and stared at the car, a black new-model rental-type. She faced forward, thinking that kind of car wasn't seen often in a neighborhood of Rollses, Jags and Cadillacs. A sense of unease settled over her. "Try to lose him."

The chauffeur accelerated, made an unexpected turn right

to avoid the east airport entrance, then circled around and drove through the west gate.

Evelyn looked back at the stream of cars. The black one was nowhere to be seen. The security man seemed relieved.

Safely deposited at the airport, she walked to the gate, the security escort at her side. She eyed the gathering passengers. Charlie Christmas was not among them. When the flight was called, she thanked the Cypress security man. Preoccupied with thoughts of Sullivan and his reactions to the problems she had caused Castro, she boarded the plane. The first-class section was almost empty: Two women and an elderly man continuing their flight. She took a window seat and looked out.

The vacant seat next to her was soon occupied by a late arrival. Out of the corner of her eye she inspected the man as best she could. Holding a *Wall Street Journal* in front of him, his face could not be seen. Suddenly, he dropped the paper to his lap and locked eyes with her.

She sat immobile. Surely she was trapped in some wild nightmare. This was not, could not, be happening.

The man's face relaxed into a friendly expression. "By mistake they put me in the Smoking section. Glad the plane is almost empty so I could sit up here. I take this flight often on business and invariably, it's late. Looks like we're in luck tonight." He continued staring at her, his intense eyes urging a reply. Evelyn had the sensation of being hypnotized. It took great effort to break eye contact with him.

As the door closed, a constriction deep in Evelyn's chest widened. The object of their long hard search was within arm's length—Sara's murderer. For an instant panic struck. She wanted to run and call for help. She tried to think rationally. Here was an opportunity, a chance to trap Charlie Christmas and solve their problems. She tried to conjure up a vision of Sullivan and draw strength from it. He would expect her to handle the situation. Charlie Christmas knew who she was, but she had a leg up. He didn't know that she knew who he was.

Borrowing from Sara, she smiled timidly. "Yes, it irritates me to have to wait, but I'm not in any hurry tonight. No one is meeting me." She looked down and toyed with the straps of her handbag. "I just had to get away by myself for a while."

"Maybe a drink once we're up will do us both good."

She could see what power his engaging smile had. "Sounds good."

He introduced himself as Colton Carpenter, reaching over to shake her hand.

Evelyn cringed as his hand lingered too long, holding her fingertips. "Nice to meet you." She thought about a fictitious name, but that would arouse suspicion. "I'm Evelyn Casey." She withdrew her hand on the pretext of straightening her skirt.

"That's a beautiful suit you have on. The color suits your complexion." His eyes ranged over her, registering approval.

Her blush was not fake. She was surprised by her reaction to this man. She could imagine Sara up against such a force of charm.

He pulled out a book. "I was going to read this best-seller, been dying to have a chance to get at it." He shoved it back in his briefcase. "It takes a backseat to companionship like yours."

Evelyn had seen the title. "You like mysteries?"

He chuckled. "Sometimes I think I should have been a detective instead of a financial analyst. I can always figure out the ending."

A small sound escaped her throat.

He chatted about world affairs, the stock market, politics, terrorists and the latest books, making astute comments, mixed with humor. She watched his manner with the stewardess as he ordered drinks. He was a man who took charge, possessing a magnetic power she had never before seen in anyone. Had he chosen another course, Charlie Christmas would have been an unequaled success.

Evelyn watched him lift the glass to his mouth. After a small sip, he turned to her. "Do you like champagne? That's what we should be having instead of vodka. More of a celebration." He took her glass from her and waved to the stewardess. "Miss, I know you don't have Dom Pérignon, but on my last flight you had some pretty decent bubbles. Could we have some?"

Evelyn watched the stewardess melt from his smile. "Moët & Chandon White Star it is. I'll be right back."

He turned to Evelyn, his face lit with satisfaction.

Evelyn was afraid he might hear her heart pound. She tried to slow her pulse by holding her breath without him knowing. It was clear how Sara and the others had fallen into his trap, desperately lonely women whose self-esteem would be insidiously bolstered by attention from such a charmer.

Sipping champagne, she found it difficult to resist his appeal. It was a weird feeling . . . talking and drinking with a cold-blooded murderer. For a brief second she even doubted he could have done all that had been attributed to him; but an image of Sara flashed in her mind, giving her the ability to think clearly and the courage to make plans. The idea was frightening, yet she had no choice but to forge ahead. She reminded herself of his cunning and brilliant criminal mind and realized there was no room for mistakes. It was his way to lure, to entrap; his thrill to seduce and penetrate the exterior of his shy victims. She knew he felt confident of his power over her, as he had with the others. Sara hadn't been entirely innocent, but had been undeniably human.

As his conversation continued, turning personal, lies about his background, she tried to evaluate her situation and appear interested at the same time. She discarded the idea of talking to the pilot and convincing him to radio Sullivan or the San Diego police. The cockpit was clearly in Charlie's line of sight.

"Shall we skip the atrocious airplane meal and have dinner in San Diego? I know a wonderful Italian place on the ocean. After you've checked into your hotel, I could pick you up. Of course, if you'd rather not, I'd understand. I am a stranger." He grinned.

Her lips cracked into a smile. The bait was taken. "Sounds great." She turned to face him, hoping her performance wasn't wooden. She could discern no evidence of suspicion in his expression.

"Where are you staying?" His eyes looked as if they wanted to pierce right through and look into her core.

On an impulse, she answered, "The Eastgate." He should know Sara's hotel well.

"Fine! We could ride in together. I'm at the Hyatt. They are close." He seemed so sure of himself, as though everything was due him.

He sipped his drink. She found it hard not to stare at his hands. They were long and graceful, like those of a surgeon, but Charlie's hands had held knives that stabbed and killed. She tried to make a plan. She could call Sullivan from the Eastgate. When Charlie came for her, Sullivan would be waiting. But what if she couldn't get in touch with Sullivan in time? Help from Carole Wheeler was a possibility. Another idea struck Evelyn.

"Excuse me, I'm going to the ladies' room to freshen up."

Down the aisle she felt his eyes boring into her back. Locking the door, she dug into her purse, hand shaking, for a pencil and paper. On the pretext of ordering more champagne, she would stop by the stewardess' station and hand them the note. She scribbled emergency instructions, requesting that upon landing, Hawk Sullivan was to be notified at his number that she was registered at the Eastgate. She had made contact with C.C.

Folding the note, she opened the door and moved toward the small kitchen area. Turning the corner, she saw Charlie talking with the stewardess. He looked around. "Oh. I came up to tell her we won't have dinner. I ordered more champagne." He took Evelyn's elbow and guided her into the aisle. As she walked back to her seat, Evelyn felt the thrust of the jet engines propelling her nearer to San Diego. Crumpling the note, she stuffed it in her pocket.

Charlie checked his watch. "There's not much time left." Picking up his champagne, he downed half of it.

His words hung in Evelyn's mind. Her eyes returned to his hands. As the plane descended, she blinked and stared out at the blackness of the night, wishing she could turn back the time to the afternoon when she was safe at home. Tackling this alone could be a mistake. The mistake Charlie had been waiting for.

Leaving the cabin, she accompanied Charlie through the throngs of people. The airport was jammed. The entire Navy seemed to be present. The urge to cry out for help was almost overpowering, but this was the chance to catch Charlie Christmas and end their nightmare.

As they passed a restroom, she slowed. "Guess the drinks got to me. I'll have to go in here for a minute." She smiled.

"I'll get the bags to save time. It's crowded. Give me your stubs, and I'll meet you by the baggage claim." Charlie held out his hand.

Evelyn pushed through the swinging door and rushed to the pay phone. Fumbling for change, she spilled coins on the floor. She dialed Sullivan's number and let it ring ten times. A trickle of perspiration rolled down her spine. She banged down the receiver, waited for the return of change and dialed Carole Wheeler. The answering machine came on and took her message. She thought about calling Captain Gordon or Castro, but they were obviously still in the hearing with Sullivan.

She dialed the police, wrangled with the operator, and finally persisted in getting through to the desk sergeant.

"My name is Evelyn Casey. My sister Sara Marley was murdered here in San Diego a few weeks ago. Captain Gordon and Sergeant Castro are familiar with the case. I hired a private investigator to work on the case. I just flew here from Dallas, and the man who killed my sister and others . . . a serial killer . . . his name is Charlie Christmas . . . was on the flight with me. Please, can you send some officers to the airport . . ."

"Hold it a minute. Let's run through this again."

"Sir, please, there's not much time. I want you to send some officers to arrest this man."

"On what charge, lady?"

"Murder. I told you . . ."

"You sound alive to me, lady."

Evelyn slammed down the receiver. He thought she was a crank. She walked out of the restroom and headed for the baggage. She was on her own.

Gathering the bags, Charlie escorted Evelyn to a waiting taxi. On the ride into town she read the cabbie's registration over and over, memorizing his name and number. Why, she had no idea. Charlie pointed out the sights and she feigned interest. The ride seemed eternal.

At the Eastgate, Charlie helped her from the cab while the doorman took charge of her bags. She felt the strength of Charlie's grip and inwardly shivered. The gun in her bag was the only defense against such strength. She took solace in the idea that the .38 was a great equalizer.

"I'll call you after I'm settled, and we'll make our plans." He held her arm a bit longer than necessary. Again, she winced.

Relieved to be away from Charlie, she asked the clerk at the desk for a room.

"Reservation?" he questioned.

"Yes," she lied.

"One moment, please." He snapped through the cards.

She surveyed the lobby, wondering what ploy Charlie would use to gain access to her room number. It took some trick for hotels to give out such information, but she knew Charlie had a plan and events would accelerate quickly.

"What was that name again?" the clerk asked.

"Casey. Evelyn Casey."

"I don't seem to find it. I'm sorry," he announced as if glad about the situation.

The insignificant man behind the desk held the power to wreck her plans. "But I have to have a room. I have nowhere to stay. It's only for one night." She reached into her purse, pulled out a $50 bill and surreptitiously handed it to him.

His expression melted. "Well, let me see what I can do." He returned to the log.

Evelyn's heart pumped faster. Precious moments were wasting. She watched the clerk frown as he flipped through the pages. Picking up a registration card, he handed it to her and smiled. "Here's the key. A bellman will bring your bag."

Surveying the lobby once again, Evelyn stepped into the elevator and watched the floor numbers flash above the doors. She trembled when the number eight lit up. Sara's floor. What anticipation Sara must have experienced that night, waiting for Charlie Christmas to arrive. The numbers continued to flash and stopped on ten.

Evelyn walked down the dim corridor that seemed a mile long. She glanced at each room as she passed. Charlie Christmas was coming for her, too. Now that she'd met him face-to-face, he was more frightening than she could have imagined, much more cunning and devious.

The noise seemed exaggerated as she stuck the key in the lock and turned it. She jumped when she heard the elevator doors part. She whirled around and saw the bellman with her bag.

After tipping the bellman, Evelyn raced to the telephone and asked the operator to connect her with Sullivan's number. There was still no answer. Reaching Carole's number, she was again greeted by the answering service. Calling anyone else would prompt no response. What could she tell them, that she expected a killer to come to her hotel room?

She sank down on the bed. Maybe she should try to get away while there was still an opportunity, but that meant losing Charlie. Maybe, forever. Until he was caught, a normal life for her and Sullivan was impossible. Christmas stood between them, and she had to do all in her power to trap him so they could pick up the pieces of their lives.

Her eyes settled on her bag. She pictured a confrontation with Charlie and wondered if she could shoot another human. She looked down at the floor, her hands moist, wrestling with the question. She thought of Sara and the other helpless women. A steely resolve braced her. She looked up, keeping her eyes on the door. When he knocked, she would open it and fire at his middle section. She would leave nothing to chance. Charlie wouldn't.

She went to the window and glanced out. There was no balcony. The door was the only way in. Walking over to open her bag, an idea struck her. There was one more person in San Diego who was aware of the situation and could help.

On the second ring Olga picked up the phone. Evelyn explained her predicament. Catching the import of the situation, Olga responded with a minimum of words. Sullivan and Castro were still at the hearing with no way to be contacted. She would go to the commissioner's office to summon them. Evelyn hoped it would be in time.

Evelyn paced back and forth, checking her watch. Seconds melded into minutes. There might still be time to get away. She could simply pick up the phone and call for a bellman, who would accompany her to the safety of the lobby. But then Charlie would get away.

When the knock came at the door, she jumped like she'd been shot. He had come. It was all up to her. She walked slowly across the room and stood next to her bag.

"Yes? Who is it?" she called out in a controlled voice.

"Flowers," a voice answered.

Evelyn mustered all her courage and reached for the gun, the handle clasped firmly in her grip. The .38 felt light. Quickly she examined the cylinder. It was empty.

Charlie Christmas was always one step ahead. She had made one fatal mistake. She should have never given him her claim check. Left alone with her bag at the airport, he must have quickly opened it, found the gun and removed the bullets. She felt like a boxer who had been hit by a knockout punch but was still standing. She had to think what to do next, but her mind no longer worked. She tried to focus on choices that were left.

Heavy traffic delayed Olga as she made her way toward City Hall, her knuckles white on the wheel. She barrelled through a red light just as it changed from green, then weathered a battery of obscenities from a carload of teenagers as brakes screeched.

There was no parking places in front of the old brick structure housing the city offices. Without hesitation, Olga left the car in a No Parking zone and raced up the stairs, taking them two and three at a time.

Clattering down the dim empty hallways, she spotted a policeman standing in front of large double oak doors.

"Is this where the Internal Affairs hearing is?" she shouted.

"Yes," he answered, eyeing her. He placed his hand on the revolver. "No admittance."

"Please, I've got to get in there."

"I said, 'No admittance.' The room is barred to outsiders."

"I have to get a message to Hawk Sullivan. He's in there testifying for my husband, Manuel Castro." She grabbed his sleeve. "Please, you've got to help me."

"Lady, I can't go in there. It's a closed session. You'll have to wait until they're finished."

"It will be too late. This is police business!"

"I'm sorry, but the session cannot be interrupted. If you need the police, there's a pay phone down the hall."

As Olga burst into tears, the doors swung open and a group of mumbling men filed out. Olga saw Castro and Sullivan. Running to them, she collapsed in Castro's arms and between sobs, explained about Evelyn.

The three dashed out to the car. Taking the wheel, Sullivan gunned away. His eyes never left the road. With increasing desperation he pushed through streets at high speed, tires screeching as he turned corners. He could not accept the image his mind flashed on of Evelyn alone with Charlie Christmas. He thought of the .38. He prayed that she'd brought it and was capable of turning it on Christmas. Target practice was one thing, firing at a human another. He'd seen the best of marksmen wilt under pressure. Besides, Charlie was strong, one wrong move on Evelyn's part and he could overpower her. He felt a dampness, cold and clammy, forming on his forehead. After Karin's death he had lived with an unbearable feeling that all happiness had passed him by permanently, and now he was terrified that the same thing was happening all over again.

Olga leaned her head against Castro's chest. "What happened in the hearing?"

Sullivan shifted his eyes toward Castro. Looking straight ahead, reflections from street lights dancing off his face, Castro said, "I've been suspended from the force for a month without pay. Gordon was asked for his resignation. No pension. Adams got off with a reprimand."

Sullivan knew Olga and Castro were talking, but their words were a jumble, like sounds coming from a cave. "What's the room number again?" he shouted.

"Ten-seventy," Olga answered, bracing herself against the dashboard as they neared the hotel's entry.

Sullivan slammed on the brakes, leaped from the car, motor still running, and ran past the doorman, Olga and Castro on his tail. Sprinting through the lobby and into the elevator, Sullivan stabbed the ten button. The ride seemed interminable, Sullivan mumbling obscenities to himself. He caught his breath and held it for a moment.

The doors parted with a whish. Sullivan bolted out like a racehorse from the gate and propelled himself down the hall. Drawing his gun, Castro followed, Olga trailing behind. Pounding on the door, Sullivan yelled, "Evelyn!" He placed his large hands on the door as if caressing the wood.

From the other side, they heard her cry out. "Hawk!" Her voice cracked.

The door opened and Sullivan rushed in. He threw his arms around her. Castro and Olga crowded in.

"Thank God, you're safe," he said, closing his eyes. When he opened them, Evelyn was looking at him. They stood for a moment, looking at each other. Evelyn pulled him closer and hugged him.

"What happened?" Sullivan asked.

Shaking in his arms, Evelyn pointed to the two flower arrangements on the desk. One was roses, the other a small bunch of violets.

"Read the card," she said.

Sullivan released her, lumbered to the desk and picked up the card. "Roses are yellow, violets are blue. You didn't fool me and I didn't fool you. Changed my mind in midair, but want you to know I still care. When your guard is down, I'll be around." Still holding the card, Sullivan dropped his arm to his side. "Goddamn him!"

Evelyn touched Sullivan's shoulder. "I had to come. I . . . the way everything was left . . ." She glanced at Castro and Olga. She explained her encounter with Charlie Christmas and told how he had removed the bullets from her gun.

"And you opened that door?" Sullivan demanded, a frown growing on his face. He glanced over at the flowers.

"Not until I knew it was only a delivery boy. When he said, 'Flowers,' I asked who they were from. It was a logical question, and I was stalling, trying to think what to do. Then he read the card. Christmas wasn't about to come here and get cornered. I should have known. I had to try to trap him no matter how dangerous it was. I thought it might be our only hope of ever catching him. I bungled it. He was playing me all the time, wanting to show me how close he could get. We can't live with the threat of him hanging over us." Her eyes filled with tears, but they never fell.

Sullivan draped his arm around her shoulders. "No, we can't. I've got to nail him before he disappears." He thought about Christmas and how he moved so quickly and silently, like a deer in a forest, suddenly emerging from the undergrowth and then disappearing again just as abruptly. For now, Charlie was going underground to wait for his shot. Sullivan lit a cigarette, looking at the flowers.

The phone rang and startled them all. Evelyn walked to the night table between the beds and picked up the receiver. After listening a moment, she turned to Sullivan. "It's Carole. She wants to know what's new." They all laughed a little too hysterically. Evelyn returned to Carole and explained what had happened.

As the two talked, an idea struck Sullivan. He stubbed out his cigarette and fixed his eyes on Castro. "You don't turn in your badge until tomorrow, right?"

Castro nodded. "What's on your mind?"

Sullivan blinked his eyes, deep in thought, then snapped to reality. "That poem Christmas wrote. I knew something didn't ring just right. Roses are yellow? It goes, 'Roses are red, violets are blue.' Maybe I'm reaching, but I think he subconsciously gave himself away. Yellow rose of Texas! The son of a bitch is getting away, going to familiar territory. I've got a hunch he's going back where he came from . . . Dallas." He motioned for Evelyn to hang up.

Evelyn did as she was told and turned to Sullivan. "I think you're right about him going back to Dallas. Hasn't that always been his M.O.?"

Sullivan picked up the receiver and asked the operator to connect him with American Airlines. When the reservations agent came on, he inquired if they had a flight that evening for Dallas. No, he was told, they did not. The last one for Dallas left at six. Christmas couldn't have caught that one. Sullivan wanted to know if any other airline had a flight to Dallas. The agent went off the line to check. Sullivan tapped the receiver with his thumbnail, waiting.

"Are you going to Dallas?" Evelyn asked.

"If Christmas is on his way there, I will be, too."

Evelyn edged closer to Sullivan. "I want to go with you."

"No way. It's too dangerous. I think Christmas and I are

heading for a confrontation. You'll be safer here with Castro around to protect you. I want Christmas in Dallas, you in San Diego, fifteen hundred miles between you two.''

Back on the line the agent informed him that Delta had one leaving in thirty minutes. Sullivan slammed down the telephone and turned to Castro. ''Let's get to the airport. I'll lay odds that Christmas is on that flight.''

CHAPTER 16

SULLIVAN DROVE to Lindbergh Field in record time. He stopped in front of the Delta terminal and turned to Evelyn. "You and Olga wait here. Castro and I are going in. If I don't come back with him, the three of you go on to his house. Call Carole and her buddies to come over."

"What about you?" Evelyn leaned toward the door Sullivan had opened.

"I'll just have to see. If Christmas is on that flight to Dallas, I will be, too." Giving her a smile that said everything, he got out, Castro following close behind.

Before approaching the counter, Sullivan and Castro stood behind a marble column, Sullivan's eyes flicking over the line of passengers waiting to check in. No Christmas in sight. Sullivan wondered if he was even on the right track. Christmas's moves were hard to chart.

At the busy counter, they pushed ahead of irate travelers. The agent glared at them. "Hey, you'll have to get in back of the line and wait your turn."

Sullivan nudged Castro. Castro whipped out the badge he'd be forced to surrender the next day. "Official police business. I want some information."

The agent raised his eyebrows. "How can I help you?"

"We want to know if there's anyone on this flight with the initials C.C.," Sullivan snapped.

A passenger behind them craned forward to catch the conversation. Sullivan turned to give him a look.

After checking the computer, the agent reported that there was no one on the flight with the initials C.C. Sullivan frowned. He might not use those initials. Still, Sullivan felt he would. The psycho had his patterns. Sullivan thought of other airports within range. John Wayne Airport in Orange County was a little more than an hour away.

He leaned on the counter. "Any planes leaving from John Wayne for Dallas tonight?"

"Should be one sometime tonight," the agent answered.

"Check to see if there's a C.C. on that flight?" Sullivan entertained the thought that Charlie might not be flying at all. He might be driving or taking the bus. Still, flight was the fastest way out and home, if home was Dallas or the vicinity.

The agent pursed his lips. "There's a Craig Cramer."

Sullivan took a deep breath, his mind racing with possibilities. "Will the computer tell you when this Craig Cramer made his reservation?"

"Sure. Just a second."

Castro looked around the crowd, running a finger in his collar as if it were too tight. Sullivan knew he was nervous, but what did he have to lose?

The agent cleared his throat. "The reservation was just made tonight."

Bingo, Sullivan thought. He felt himself smile. All he had to do was to get to John Wayne and, without Christmas seeing him, board the plane. He could wear some type of disguise. "What time does that flight leave?"

"It should just be loading passengers now."

He would have to beat that flight to Dallas. He glanced at Castro, then looked at the flight information board behind the desk. The plane was scheduled to depart in ten minutes. "I want a seat on this plane," he said to the agent.

People behind them were becoming vocal, complaining loudly about the delay in line. Sullivan looked over his shoulder and ignored their insults.

The agent shook his head. "The plane is full. We've got a list of standbys, too. I'm sorry."

Sullivan eyed Castro. For an instant he thought Castro might groan, but he tapped his badge on the counter. "I'll have to requisition a seat on this flight . . . police business."

With a boarding pass in hand, Sullivan moved swiftly through the crowd. He gave Castro instructions to show his badge passing through security, escort him on the plane, then leave his gun with him.

Castro shook his head. "Jesus, man. What balls! And how the shit do you think you're going to beat the other plane to Dallas? It's just leaving and you're not off the ground."

Sullivan stepped through the door of the plane and smiled at the stewardess, then leaned close to Castro's ear. "You're going to stop that other plane from leaving for a while."

Castro's forehead wrinkled. "How?"

Sullivan settled into his assigned aisle seat in tourist, Castro hovering beside him. Sullivan looked at Castro as he slipped him the gun. "What holds a plane from leaving and keeps the passengers on board while a baggage search is carried out?"

Castro's eyes rolled toward the ceiling. "You don't expect me . . ."

"Exactly. As soon as you get off. Make a call from the pay phone. That'll hold them at least an hour while they look through all the bags. Then go keep the girls company until you hear from me." Sullivan buckled his seat belt as he watched Castro stalk down the aisle.

He leaned back, resting his head on the seat. The evening's tension had taken its toll, and it wasn't over. His neck felt stiff. He moved his head from side to side and heard a cracking noise.

He watched as droves of passengers pushed down the aisle and found their seats, some grumbling about their locations. The stewardesses were busy hanging up coats and preparing for takeoff. He felt a little guilty about the inconvenience Castro's call would cause the passengers on the other flight to Dallas, but the move had been absolutely necessary. And when something was necessary, Sullivan never worried much about the consequences. Means to an end, he always figured.

As the aisle cleared, Sullivan leaned sideways in his seat and saw the attendants ready to close the aircraft's door. One last passenger stepped through the opening and stood at the head of the plane, looking down the aisle as if presiding over the situation.

"Holy Jesus!" Sullivan mumbled to himself. He resisted the impulse to jerk himself out of sight and eased slowly back into his chair, keeping his moves easy, nothing to attract attention. Leaning on his armrest, he eased his body up so that he could just barely see over the seat in front of him.

There he was. Charlie Christmas. Once more he surveyed the plane, his eyes sweeping over the crowd, then settled into a first-class aisle seat. Sullivan had a perfect view of the back of his head. As if hypnotized, Sullivan stared at the killer's skull and thought about the confetti of evil that made up his brain. He knew how Evelyn had felt, what she had experienced. Reading about Christmas was one thing, seeing the real man in person, quite another. If possible, he felt an even stronger respect for her nerve.

Sullivan looked down at his hands and blinked, trying to appraise the situation. Charlie was not traveling under his accustomed initials. Had Christmas figured he'd check for a C.C. on this flight and, when he found none listed, would try the nearest airport and find a C.C.? Was Charlie confident Sullivan would now be wasting his time at the John Wayne Airport trying to locate him while he was safely on his way to Dallas? Or maybe the C.C. initials at John Wayne Airport were a coincidence Charlie had nothing to do with. Possibly he was crediting Christmas with too many amazing powers. Christmas was simply running, never figuring Sullivan would think he'd be on a flight so soon after arrival.

Sullivan eased up to catch another glimpse of Charlie. Sullivan was in the exact position into which he'd wanted to jockey himself: on the same plane with Christmas. He'd like to think he'd outmaneuvered Christmas, but he was on the same plane with him for more than likely all the wrong reasons. Still, his opportunity was at hand, and he intended to make the most of it. He had almost two and a half hours to make plans. He leaned back to concentrate. For the time being, Charlie was trapped.

The stewardess toyed with the oxygen mask, explaining emergency procedures. Sullivan leaned toward the window but could see nothing but darkness. A man occupied the window seat. A woman sat between him and Sullivan. From snatches of conversation Sullivan surmised they were traveling together. Being a nervous flyer, Sullivan preferred the window seat, but he was thankful for the aisle, which provided a perfect view of Christmas.

As they lifted off the runway, Sullivan again tried to catch a glimpse out of the plane's window. The aircraft strained to gain altitude, the lights below long lost beneath the cloud cover. Lightning ripped the horizon in a wide zigzag pattern. Bucking strong winds, the plane dropped like an express elevator. The wings shook violently, and Sullivan felt his palms dampen. How incongruous, he thought, if he and Charlie Christmas were trapped together in a tomb. Sullivan closed his eyes for a moment, and when he opened them, the moon was bright above the stars, the air calm and smooth. He took a deep breath and focused his attention on Charlie Christmas.

Christmas, obviously so sure of himself, so satisfied that he had escaped, chatted with the enchanted stewardess. She threw back her head and laughed at something he said. Sullivan could barely contain his anger. The urge to rush forward and attack Christmas was almost overpowering, but uncontrolled emotions had no place at this crucial point. Sullivan was well aware that this was his last chance to catch Christmas and there was no room for error.

Sullivan looked at the drink cart when the stewardess arrived, his eyes holding on the small bottles of Jack Daniels. He wanted a drink but was afraid to dull his senses. Declining, he pulled a pack of cigarettes from his pocket and realized he was in the Nonsmoking section. He sat, tapping his fingers on the armrest. He needed to use the bathroom, but the aisle was blocked by the cart, and, had it not been, he couldn't afford to show himself. He checked his watch often only to find a few minutes had crept by. His legs and arms tensed, drawn up as though their tendons were thongs of leather going dry.

The dinner service seemed interminable, people chatting,

ordering more drinks, diving into trays of half-warmed food, then sipping coffee. Every sound seemed magnified as he thought about what might take place when they landed. He felt his heart pumping. He was edgy, his nerves ragged.

He watched Christmas, drink in hand, saunter toward the front of the plane. Handing the glass to a stewardess, he glanced around, then ducked into the restroom. Sullivan kept his eyes on the door. Minutes passed and Charlie did not appear. He was taking an inordinate amount of time. Alerted, Sullivan sat forward, keeping his face out of view. What was Christmas doing, he asked himself? A jag of apprehension struck him. For a wild moment the thought crossed his mind that Christmas had somehow disappeared. They were thirty thousand feet in the air. Charlie was clever, but not supernatural. The door swung open and a smiling Charlie, his piercing eyes flickering over the crowd, walked back to his seat.

Sullivan felt the plane slowing and saw the seatbelt light flash on. They were starting their descent into Dallas. He had no idea of a plan. He'd have to follow Charlie's lead. React according to his actions. He wondered where the night would lead . . . where it would end. He gave himself a fifty-fifty chance, if all went right. One point in his favor was the fact that Charlie held the illusion that he had traveled undetected. Sullivan cautioned himself not to underestimate Charlie. First-class passengers would disembark quickly. Sullivan would have to fight the crowd to tail him.

The plane landed without a jolt, pulled up to the terminal and came to a stop. Eager passengers got to their feet, pushing toward the front door, some rummaging in overhead compartments for carry-on packages. Sullivan weaved back and forth, dodging the crowd, trying not to lose sight of Christmas in the maze. Standing on his toes, he could see that most of first class had emptied. He bulldozed through, commanding the crowd to step aside, police business his excuse.

Reaching the aircraft's door, he nodded to the pilot and hurried down the corridor, his eyes straight ahead. Turning right, he followed the flow heading toward baggage claim. Moving swiftly, but not fast enough to attract undue attention, he spotted Christmas near the baggage carousel. Surprised that Charlie had checked anything, Sullivan edged behind a large stone column and waited. Of course, he thought, Charlie would never be far from his knife. For security reasons it would be packed.

Charlie picked up a small leather satchel and headed toward sliding glass doors leading to the street. Sullivan hung back until Charlie reached the sidewalk, then moved along the wall until he had a clear view of Christmas. A cab pulled curbside. Christmas glanced around, then slid in.

Sullivan's eyes searched the line of cars for another taxi. Seeing one slowing, he bolted through the doors and hailed it. Keeping his eyes on the cab that had picked up Christmas, he instructed his driver to follow at a discreet distance. The driver called his dispatcher and reported that he had picked up a fare leaving the airport, destination not yet determined. Sullivan lit a cigarette and inhaled deeply, some measure of confidence returning. Christmas was heading to his roost. Once Sullivan knew the location, the game was half won.

"I always wanted somebody to say 'Follow that cab' like in the movies, but in all my years of driving nobody ever did, but you. Course you didn't say it quite like that, but it meant the same." The black driver, who looked like a tackle on a pro team, laughed. "What's happening here?"

From the backseat Sullivan leaned forward, resting his forearms on the back of the front seat. From experience he knew being a confidant in official business intrigued most civilians. Sullivan remembered his FBI card he still carried as a souvenir. In the darkness the cabbie might not see how dog-eared it was. He pulled it from his wallet and, holding it between his fingers, flashed it at the black man.

"FBI. Wish I could tell you exactly what I'm on, but it's top secret." He winked at the driver, who had turned to eye the card.

"Yes sir, I won't lose him."

Sullivan felt the driver accelerate. "Slow down a touch. We don't want to be obvious. Okay?"

The tollgate loomed before them. Christmas's cab slowed and stopped at the pay station. Sullivan's driver pulled into a parallel station, paid his ticket and pulled ahead of Christmas's cab as it joined the line of traffic on the highway into Dallas. Slouching deeper into his seat, Sullivan thought the move clever and said so but didn't want the driver to get too fancy with maneuvers.

The black driver slowed, allowing Christmas's cab to pass. Lights from the street lamps reflected off the passing taxi. Sullivan saw the numbers 6290 painted in black on the yellow vehicle as they sped by. Sullivan's driver let a few cars get between them and Christmas's cab. The terrain was flat, and Sullivan thought it was a textbook tail job.

Considering a confrontation with Christmas, Sullivan felt his heart pump faster. He was in the home stretch. He could almost taste the satisfaction capturing Christmas would bring, then cautioned himself not to be overconfident. Yards of tricky grounds were still to be covered.

On the outskirts of Dallas, just as he glimpsed the skyline, Sullivan saw Christmas's cab slowing to a crawl and bolted upright in his seat.

"Shit . . ." The black driver looked around at Sullivan and rolled his eyes. "Looks like something's wrong with that cab."

Sullivan grabbed the back of the seat, his fingers digging into the cracked leather. "Keep following, but don't get too close."

The driver nodded. "There's a service station up ahead. Looks like the fucker's trying to limp in."

The cab ahead bucked, choked, then started to miss as it coasted down the highway. Sullivan watched as it cruised under the glaring lights of the service station and come to a halt. Seeing no silhouette in the rear window, Sullivan figured at this unexpected mishap Charlie had slumped down in the backseat. He instructed his driver to stop, while darkness still offered cover.

The other driver got out, pulled a handkerchief from his pocket and wiped his forehead as he approached the attendant. After exchanging a few words, the attendant opened the hood of the car and leaned in to inspect the engine. Unconcerned about the delay or his passenger, the driver ambled into the office, put a coin in a drink machine and popped open a can.

Sullivan sat still for a moment, then jerked toward the frontseat. "Pull up a little closer, then go in there and tell the driver you saw him stop. Ask if you can help, one cabbie to another. Offer to take his passenger where he was going. If he agrees, you scratch your head, and I'll slip out and get lost before the passenger gets in your cab. Then you come back here and take me to the address where you let him off."

Sullivan's driver followed his instructions. Sullivan watched as he talked with the other cabbie. He didn't scratch his head or waste any movements but turned quickly on his heels and hurried back. He opened the front door, hauled himself in and whipped around to face Sullivan, black eyes intense. "There is no passenger in that taxi."

Sullivan lunged forward, grabbing the back of the seat. "What? Goddammit, that can't be."

The black man looked apologetic, as if it were somehow his fault. "The driver said the man who got in his cab at the airport gave him a hundred, told him to drive around for thirty minutes, because he was trying to lose someone who was following him, then slid out of the other door next to the traffic and went back in the terminal."

Sullivan braced himself, trying not to think that Christmas had slipped from his grasp, but he had. In that one moment at the airport when he'd taken his eyes off Christmas to look for a cab, the bastard had made his ultimate move. Now he had disappeared into the cover of a city, population more than a million.

Sullivan lit a cigarette, realizing his hand trembled. How did Charlie know he was following him? Had he seen him at the San Diego airport? If so, why did Charlie board the plane knowing he was on the flight? Unless . . . Sullivan crushed out his cigarette and sat upright. The son of a bitch wanted to lure him to Dallas, separate him from the others for a better shot at them.

Now, because of a clever move on Christmas's part and an amateurish one chalked to his column, Christmas had him exactly where he wanted him. Sullivan sat still, his thoughts jumbled. He crushed out his cigarette in the overflowing ashtray.

"What's next?" the cabbie asked.

"Wait." Sullivan got out of the taxi.

In the teeth of a hot wind that stiffened his face, Sullivan hurried to the service station. He grabbed the greasy phone book and looked up the airline's number. Pulling some coins from his trouser pocket, he jammed them in the slot and dialed. He was told, as he suspected, the last plane of the night to San Diego left fifteen minutes ago, with one stop in Phoenix. His only consolation was the stop, which would buy valuable time.

He put in a collect call to Castro's house but got no answer. He slammed down the receiver, clamping his teeth together so hard his jaws hurt. He had told them to go there and wait. Had they gone to eat somewhere? Maybe they had gone to get Carole. He didn't know the number where she was staying. On the off chance they'd gone to his house, Sullivan dialed his number, getting a busy signal. When he asked the operator to interrupt for an emergency call, she checked and informed him there was no conversation, but there was trouble on the line. He hung up, remembering his answering machine sometimes went haywire and caused problems. Providence or fate or whoever controlled things certainly wasn't giving him any breaks tonight, he thought irritably. Now he needed help from two people, neither of them pushovers, but Evelyn's survival depended on it.

Driving down Interstate 5, Lieutenant Adams turned on Laurel and headed for Lindbergh Field. His policeman's instincts resented Sullivan's demanding call. Citizens didn't have the right to direct law enforcement officers on their whims, and the shorthanded force wasn't at liberty to expend their time and energy on what someone thought might happen. Still, Hawk Sullivan's request had a frantic note about it, and the case had brewed to a boiling point. Castro and Sullivan were convinced a serial killer was on the loose. Their convictions and Captain Gordon's refusal to consider such a possibility had almost put his ass in a sling. Now he'd placed himself on a small limb again, but if something actually resulted from his actions, the rewards far surpassed the risks. He'd be filling shoes Gordon left vacant. "Captain Adams," he said out loud, liking the sound of it.

Adams stuck a cigarette in his mouth and fumbled for the lighter. The two-man stakeout, one at Castro's and one at

Sullivan's, he had ordered for the night wasn't the biggest waste of manpower he'd seen. Then, on his own time and for good measure, he'd decided to meet the plane arriving from Dallas. He had no idea what good that would do, armed only with Sally Bricker's description of the killer and what Sullivan had added. Still he felt there was a chance of spotting someone suspicious.

He pulled into the dimly-lit parking lot, careful not to abuse any privileges by leaving his car curbside. His footsteps echoed across the almost vacant area as he walked to the terminal. Flicking his cigarette on the concrete, he took a deep breath of fresh air, the ocean's breeze cool on his face.

Looking up the gate number, he proceeded through the terminal. Peering out the expanse of glass, his nose pressed close, he saw the plane pulling to a stop. Positioning himself for the best possible view, he stood against the wall opposite the opening where passengers would spill from the ramp into the mainstream of traffic.

Trying his best to appear casual, he scrutinized every single person who disembarked, especially those off first who had flown first class. Only one man was anywhere near the age of the person he was looking for, and he wasn't dressed as Sullivan had described. In old khakis and a pullover, the man walked with a distinct limp, bent forward from his waist as if he'd been in an accident. His mouth sagged on one side, suggesting a possible stroke. He was, however, over six feet and dark. For an instant, Adams thought the man's eyes had singled him out, recognizing who he was. But how could he? Surely his imagination was working overtime. Shuffling along, the man was in no hurry.

On the edge of a decision, Adams took a tentative step forward, then decided he was looking too hard for quirks. The man had no way of knowing who he was. Adams began to feel foolish. Sullivan could be off base, way off. And, as a law officer, Adams had learned the hard way that he couldn't be too careful about procedure. He couldn't, without reason, go barreling up to a tall, dark man and question him or ask for identification. This wasn't Russia. Citizens had rights.

Satisfied with his actions, Adams headed for his car. A pile of work waited at the station, while he wasted time chasing someone who might not even exist. He'd done more than he was asked. Not for Sullivan, but for Castro and the twinges of guilt he felt about his suspension.

Adams stopped at the airport newsstand and bought cigarettes. He fanned through several magazines, then proceeded to his car.

Adams picked up his radio from the dashboard and called the station. "Adams here. I'm just leaving the airport. If Hawk Sullivan should call back before I get there, tell him I checked out the passengers on the Dallas flight and didn't spot anyone from the descriptions he gave me. Have you gotten hold of Castro or Evelyn Casey yet?"

"No, sir. Tried Castro's, got no answer. Sullivan's line was out of whack."

"Well, it doesn't matter. Just for good measure, I'll leave the stakeout at Castro's and Sullivan's for the night."

Adams replaced the radio, thinking he should get the operator to patch him through to Castro and Evelyn Casey. If any of them should hear or see the plainclothesmen, it would scare the shit out of them. Just as he reached for the radio, a figure rose from the darkness of the backseat, knife poised.

The two photographers, heading for an assignment, had dropped Carole off at Castro's house. Evelyn, Carole, Olga, and Castro had spent the first couple of hours after Sullivan's departure in frenzied conversation, each talking at once, speculating nervously about the outcome of his Dallas trip. Castro checked on the Dallas-bound flight from John Wayne Airport and found it had been delayed over an hour. He predicted Sullivan would meet the flight and, when Christmas stepped off the plane, would follow and eventually corner him. It could take days to establish Charlie's patterns, Castro suggested. Carole thought Sullivan might nab Christmas in the Dallas airport rather than risk losing him. Evelyn felt Sullivan's approach would be more subtle than Carole's supposition, but she knew he'd take his chance if the opportunity presented itself. She wanted Sullivan safely back, even if it meant foregoing Christmas's capture. But Sullivan wouldn't forget Christmas. Not now. Sullivan wasn't invincible, as much as he'd like to think so. He could be in peril, she thought, trying not to see Charlie's face behind her closed lids.

Each was tense for their own reasons: Evelyn's close brush with Christmas, the uncertainty of the outcome of Sullivan's sudden flight, Olga's frantic dash against time to summon Castro and Sullivan, Castro's suspension from the force. Carole suggested they all needed food. Olga apologized for her unstocked shelves and bare refrigerator. Her mind had been on matters other than shopping.

"I know a great Italian take-out place. I don't think anybody operates very well on an empty stomach, especially me. We've got a long night ahead of us." Carole said. "We can spend it eating. And speaking of spending it . . I don't see but one bedroom here at your house, Castro."

Evelyn reminded them that Sullivan had warned there was safety in numbers. All four agreed Sullivan's house was the place for the night. His key was always under the front mat. When Sullivan called and got no answer at Castro's, he'd know to try his house.

Castro pulled into Sullivan's garage next to the old Peugeot Sullivan called a "chug" and waited for the girls to get out. Then he closed the solid wood door and followed them into the house. Hearing a clicking noise, Carole went to Sullivan's answering machine and reset it, as she often had to do with hers.

Over dinner and a pot of coffee, they talked until they were drowsy. Castro and Olga prepared to settle for the night in Hawk's bedroom, Carole and Evelyn occupying the guest room. Evelyn watched Castro kiss Olga reassuringly on top of her head, a gesture that brought a small stab of pain to her chest and the threat of tears to her eyes. Before they could form, Evelyn turned and quickly swiped at her face with the palm of her hand. Now was not the time to show her fear that Sullivan might not return.

Unbuttoning her blouse, Evelyn heard the phone in the den ringing. She raced to answer, Carole on her heels. Picking up the receiver, she listened.

"Lieutenant Adams here. Is this Evelyn Casey?"

"Yes." Puzzled, she looked at Carole, an odd premonition

settling over her. She couldn't decide if it was good or bad, but it was there.

"Mrs. Casey, I've got some good news for you. Hawk Sullivan just called me. Charlie Christmas has been apprehended at the Dallas Airport. Christmas is in police custody there."

"My God!" Evelyn gasped. "Is Sullivan all right?"

"Fine. Told me to tell you he'll be here tomorrow. He'll probably call later when he has a `chance. Lots of red tape there to clear up."

Evelyn turned to Carole. "Hawk's got Christmas! It's over!"

Carole doubled her fist and raised her hand over her head. "I'm going to tell Castro."

With a relief as great as she'd ever known, Evelyn returned to her conversation with Lieutenant Adams and asked for details.

"Matter of fact, I've had a couple of calls from Hawk Sullivan tonight from the Dallas Airport. At first, he was afraid Charlie Christmas was on his way back to San Diego. Couldn't reach you to warn you, so he called me to put a stakeout on his and Castro's house. I went to the airport to meet the plane Sullivan thought Christmas might be on. He wasn't, of course. Then Sullivan called back with the news. Who's there with you?"

"Carole Wheeler, a reporter; Castro and his wife." Evelyn drew in a quick breath, her heart skipping a beat. "About Sullivan . . . how did he get Christmas?"

"Mrs. Casey, this is still official police business, and I'd be out of line discussing it further with you until the case is completely tied up. Tell you what, I'm about to knock off here at the station. If Castro wants to meet me, I'll give him the scoop, and he can tell you."

Evelyn glanced around at the sound of Olga and Castro hurrying down the hall. "Meet you where?"

"Say . . . the Pelican Bar out by the pier. He'll know it. Not far from the station. I'll be there as soon as I can. Oh . . . I've already relieved my man at Castro's. We haven't been able to rouse the one at Sullivan's on the radio. He's probably out of the car. If he should come to the door to inform you he's there, he's a plainclothesman, tell him for me that he can come on back. He's not needed.''

Evelyn hung up and looked at Castro, no scale high enough to measure her degree of joy. "Lieutenant Adams says Hawk got Christmas at the Dallas Airport. He's in custody. At first Hawk thought Christmas was on his way back to San Diego. When he couldn't warn us, he called Adams for help. I guess he's about the only one left who was familiar with the case. Adams wants you to meet him at the Pelican Bar out near the pier. He'll give you all the details.''

Castro's moustache made his grin look even wider. His eyes, only hours ago narrowed by concern, sparkled with renewed vitality. "What news!" He chuckled. "So, old 'Ice Ass' Adams came through. The hearing must have shook him up.'' He let out a rush of air. "Got to hand it to Sullivan.'' He picked up his car keys. "Be back when I can.'' He pecked Olga on the cheek. "You girls hold down the fort.''

Carole picked up her tote bag. "I'm heading for the paper to get going on the story now. Lots of background work to do and tomorrow . . . I'll write the ending.'' She twirled around. "Castro, give me a lift? It's on your way.''

After they had gone, Evelyn went to Sullivan's bar and picked out a bottle of wine. She lifted it in the air. "Let's open this and celebrate, Olga. This is the best night of my life.''

"Why not? I could use a drink.'' Olga's lips shaped into a smile, but Evelyn saw the pinched expression and realized how thoughtless she'd been. Her problems were solved, but with Castro on suspension, Olga's were just beginning.

Evelyn pulled the cork screw out and poured two goblets of wine. She cocked her head to one side. "Is that the wind, you think?''

"What?'' Olga turned toward the window.

"Like a scratching noise . . . bushes brushing on the screen.''

Evelyn walked to the window and peered out at the darkness, the slice of moon giving off minimum light. "Maybe it was the man Lieutenant Adams sent. I can't really see anything.'' An unexplainable pall settled over her. She had no reason to feel uneasy, she told herself. Christmas was in custody. Sullivan would be there tomorrow. Everything she'd been through had jiggled her emotions slightly off center.

She walked down the long hall toward the double French doors leading to the balcony. Olga padded along behind her as if Evelyn were some sort of protective shield. Opening the doors they stepped out on the deck. Inky clouds roiled toward the coast, bringing strong winds. Waves crashed against the rocks below, then silence filled the air as the tide sucked back for another charge. The whole scene took on an eerie quality, as if the two had been suddenly transplanted alone to some alien place. Evelyn's imagination frightened her. They were in the middle of San Diego at Hawk Sullivan's house, she told herself.

"I wish Manny was here with us. I don't like it out here." Olga's voice sounded like a small child's. "Let's go back inside." She was shivering.

Evelyn closed the doors, and they went back into the den. Evelyn poured another glass of wine and checked her watch. Castro should be back in an hour or so. They could hang on alone that long. Nothing was going to happen in that small time space. Why was she so uneasy? Everything was under control.

Sitting in Hawk's chair, Olga flicked on the television to catch the news. Evelyn decided a hot bath would soak away all tension. She had simply been allowing her emotions to get the better of her. She had to cut it out. The nightmare of Charlie Christmas was over. She should be ecstatic, not uneasy.

The Cypress Oil Learjet sailed down the runway, tires screeching as it tried to slow. Sullivan checked his watch, knowing they were behind the airliner's scheduled arrival in San Diego even though the Cypress pilots had made up precious minutes. He thought of Quinn Stewart with new respect. When he'd called, explained the situation, and asked for the loan of company jet that Quinn Stewart said had just touched down from Houston, he'd expected a small lecture or at least an "I told you so." But a levelheaded business man like Stewart knew when quick actions, not wasted words, were required. Stewart immediately alerted the pilots that they had another flight to make.

Sullivan unbuckled his seat belt, ready to bolt from the door. Two bumpy flights in one evening pursuing Christmas through the skies were taking a toll. He knew he had to gear up for the climax that would come tonight. Christmas couldn't afford to waste time. He prayed Adams's assistance would take up the slack his absence left.

When the pilot opened the door, Sullivan saw the car Quinn Stewart had ordered waiting on the runway. He hurried across the tarmac to the open door. As he got in, he waved to the pilots, the blazing terminal lights reflecting off the Cypress emblem on the jet's tail. Being rich and able to command a jet on short notice was everything it was cracked up to be, he decided. The driver, already alerted, pulled away fast, listening to Sullivan's directions.

Traffic was light at that time of night, and they made Castro's neighborhood in what Sullivan considered a record. They slowed turning onto Castro's street and cruised down the deserted area. The house was dark, with no sign of Castro's car. Spotting a dark vehicle in the alley, Sullivan told the driver to go around back. The stakeout might have some information.

A rush of anger flooded through Sullivan when he spotted the plainclothesman obviously sleeping. One of San Diego's finest, alert on the job, he thought as he jerked open the car door. Didn't the bastard realize who he was dealing with? Charlie Christmas wouldn't be asleep at the wheel.

Sullivan took a step back, catching his breath. Anesthesized with cold shock, Sullivan stared at the bloody figure whose throat was cut. Evelyn, Castro, Olga, Carole . . . they had to be at his house, where else? He only hoped Charlie Christmas wasn't there also. If he wasn't, Sullivan knew he was on his way. He couldn't even entertain the idea that Christmas had already been there. He had to beat him. They were targets like the fourteen women Christmas had stabbed one-by-one. Castro was with the women, Sullivan's only consolation. With judo, Castro could lay anybody on his back faster than any six men using fists. He ran his fingers through his hair, turned, and got back in the car.

Telling the driver to get to a phone and call the police, Sullivan slipped out of the car a short way from his house, so he could reach the back without being seen. He figured the plainclothesman would be waiting there, if he was waiting at all. The back balcony would be Charlie's point of entry into the house.

Olga concentrated on the television. Curled in the chair, she nibbled at the last wedge of pizza, crumbs falling in her lap. Over the television's noise, Olga heard a faint knock at the front door. She got up, hurried over and opened it. Smiling, the tall men in khakis and a pullover, stood framed in the entry.

"I was sent by Lieutenant Adams." He stepped in, keeping one arm behind him.

Olga returned his smile. "The lieutenant said you might come to the door. He said to tell you that you can go back—" She stopped when she saw the knife raised high above her.

Sullivan made his way through overgrown yards and orchards toward his house. Bushes scratched his face and tore at his clothes, but he moved as quickly as he could, now and then slipping to his knees. Peeping around the corner, he saw what he was afraid he'd see: a dark figure lying on the ground.

Turning the man over, Sullivan's eyes held on his throat, where a slash looked like a second mouth opened to scream. Touching him, Sullivan found he was still warm, blood flowing freely. He had been dead only minutes, maybe seconds.

Sullivan looked up at the cantilevered deck stretching over the deep precipice, obviously Christmas's entry point. What kind of scene was he about to barge in on? He let out a wild snort, insulating himself against everything but raw will and the raging determination to kill Charlie Christmas. He lacked Christmas's athletic prowess, but he had no choice but to scale the posts stabbed securely into the cliffs. To make his way around to the front would not only alert Christmas, but also waste more valuable time.

Heaving himself up, Sullivan heard the distant sound of waves crashing against rocks, then noises he determined were muffled voices, maybe the television. He pushed harder, straining with every reach to hurry.

The goblet holding the last few swallows of wine sat on the tub's ledge. In the water's warmth, Evelyn finally relaxed, tensions melting away. She reached for the glass and thought nothing was quite so luxurious as sipping wine in a tub. Her earlier apprehensions had been baseless, an imagination in turmoil now laid to rest.

She could hardly wait for Castro's return and the scenario of Christmas's capture he'd relate. She tried to picture Hawk's confrontation with Christmas and how he'd played it. She smiled to herself, reveling in the fantasies dancing through her mind. She would have given anything to have been there, to see Christmas's expression, to hear his words and Hawk's. Excitement built in her as she anticipated how she'd relish Castro's every word.

Suddenly she bolted upright, spilling wine into the tub. Something Lieutenant Adams had said . . . official police business . . . he'd speak only to Castro. Castro had been suspended from the force . . . he was no longer official or entitled to police information . . . Adams knew that. Was that really Adams on the phone? She had never spoken to him before. A voice was easy to disguise. Who would want Castro out of the way? Adams said a plainclothesman was watching the house and to let him in if he came to the door. Could the caller have possibly been Charlie Christmas? How would he have known to say he was Adams? If Christmas had been following them all along, as they suspected, he would have seen Adams looking in Sullivan's widow the night Sullivan gave chase to the lieutenant, thinking he was the killer.

Her heart lurched as she heard footsteps. They were quiet, carefully placed, not Olga's. She strained to hear. The doorknob to Sullivan's room was softly turned, a quiet prevailed, apparently time for someone to survey the room. Another knob faintly clicked. The guest room. Then, the hall closet. Where was Olga? Who was out there? Evelyn glanced quickly round for some weapon. Nothing, not even a razor in the guest bath. The bathroom door had no lock. Her eyes held on the doorknob. She watched it turn slowly . . . watched the door ease open by inches.

Grabbing a towel from the rack, Evelyn spun around and gasped.

"I've come for you. We're all alone now."

Charlie Christmas stood in the doorway, his presence exuding a tightly coiled power. He advanced slowly toward her, his eyes narrowed and honed in on her, his mouth drawn down into a crescent. She moved back, the cold tiles bracing her back.

Her eyes widening; she looked just over Christmas's shoulder at Sullivan moving down the hall.

Christmas smirked. "You think I'd fall for that? Nobody's here but us, Evelyn Casey." He held up his bloodstained knife.

Sullivan didn't like the angle at which he'd have to fire. Evelyn was too close. He couldn't take the chance. He sprang forward, bashing into Christmas's back, his finger tight on the trigger of Castro's gun. Christmas caught himself in mid-stumble and whipped around. An instant of satisfaction flashed through Sullivan as he caught Christmas's startled expression.

With lightning reflexes, Charlie kicked forward, sending the gun skittering down the hall and out on the deck. In one quick move, he turned, drawing back his knife, and sprang at Sullivan.

Sullivan slapped his hand around Christmas's powerful wrist and twisted with all his strength. Christmas weakened, but only momentarily, then regained his stance and thrust himself at Sullivan. They fell to the floor, rolling out in the hall, Christmas still holding the knife. Locked together like lovers, they wrestled, pulling and rolling through the open, double French doors to the balcony. Christmas kicked Sullivan's gun off the side of the deck, sending it flying to the rocks below.

On his side, Sullivan used all his strength to fend off Charlie. He strained, grimaced and propelled his knee into Charlie's groin. Charlie let out a grunt and for a second relaxed his grip on the knife. Sullivan felt Charlie's breath hot on his face. He butted his head into Charlie's arm, and the knife bounced on the wood, sliding to the edge of the bal cony. Sullivan grabbed for Charlie's hair, clawed together a handful and jerked his head back.

Charlie snarled into Sullivan's face, his eyes turning into narrow slits. "To think . . . an old bastard like you and a stupid woman got on to me . . ."

Sullivan heard Evelyn's excited words falling over each other as she called the police, asking for help and an ambulance. He was relieved to hear Olga was only wounded, but help for him would be too late coming if he couldn't subdue Christmas.

Breathing hard, Sullivan slammed Charlie's head to the floor. As if infused with new energy, Charlie whipped over on top of Sullivan. He lunged, swept forward, and grabbed his knife.

Drawing back, then thrusting, Charlie aimed for Sullivan's heart. With lightning speed, Sullivan moved sideways on the floor. Christmas's knife rammed through his shoulder, pinning him to the deck. A hot flash of pain spread through him.

Christmas got to his feet, leaned down, and grabbed for the knife. Sullivan knew he was going to wrench it from his shoulder, then finish him with an accurate stab. Clasping his hands around the knife, Sullivan strained to keep Christmas from freeing it, each tug from Christmas sending him into agony.

Evelyn bolted through the French doors, took her stance, braced the .357 magnum in her hands and aimed at Christmas. Lying on the deck, Sullivan was out of the line of fire. The weapon, so different, so much heavier than the .38, felt like a cannon. She squeezed the trigger. The recoil from the powerful weapon almost knocked her flat; the report from the bullet that missed Christmas resounded through the canyons.

She knew she was telegraphing her discovery—only a trained marksman could accurately handle a weapon of such magnitude. Sirens suddenly screamed in the background. Christmas took his chance and sprang to escape over the balcony. Straddling the railing, Christmas turned back to Evelyn before jumping to safety. "You're not much of a shot. I'll be back for you one day, bitch, when you least expect it."

Impaled like a specimen butterfly, sweat pouring down his forehead, blurring his vision, Sullivan yelled at Evelyn in a tone that would etch steel. ''Both hands, low, barrel down and to the left.''

Just as Christmas leaped, Evelyn fired.

Christmas's chest exploded into confetti.

Evelyn peered over the balcony. The crash of Charlie Christmas's body against the concrete below pounded in her ears. It was a sound she knew she'd live with for a long time.

EPILOGUE

ON A WINDSWEPT HILL outside Dallas a week after his death, last rites were said over Charlie Christmas, his unclaimed body buried courtesy of the State of Texas. Evelyn Casey and Hawkins Sullivan, his arm in a sling, attended the burial. They weren't positive of their reasons. Perhaps it was to make sure he was really dead. Carole Wheeler was there for her exclusive. The three planned a celebration later with Castro and Olga.

As the preacher spoke, Sullivan caught only swatches of the service, his mind a kaleidoscope of images. "The *Lord* is my shepherd, I shall not want. *He* maketh me lie down in green pastures . . ." Sullivan's mind's eye saw Christmas's handsome face in repose. "*He* restoreth my soul. Yea, though I walk through the valley of the shadow of death, I shall fear no evil . . ." Sullivan glanced at Evelyn, who looked straight ahead. He pictured her, gun in hand, ready to fire at the smirking Christmas. "For *Thou* art with me. *Thy* rod and *Thy* staff shall comfort me . . ." Christmas's chest exploding into thousands of pieces. "And I shall dwell in the house of the *Lord* forever, and ever. Amen."

Sullivan watched the lone woman in a faded dress standing

a discreet distance away. If she was who he thought, she must have lived a tormented life, locked in despair for having spawned a monster. After the brief service, she walked over to the minister and in a deep Texas drawl was overheard saying, "You did the best you could under the circumstances. I only wish I had."